WICKED

"A charming and very romantic story with lots of laughs along the way. The ending puts a perfect cap on the story. I look forward to reading more books in this series to see what happens to some of my favorite supporting characters."

—Fresh Fiction

"Ah, l'amour. I adored this story and the wonderful hero and heroine, who shed all their inhibitions and fears in order to go on the most powerful journey they ever embarked on ... falling in love."

—Smexy Books

"An exciting and sweet historical love story. It has everything that I look for in a good fairy-tale retelling while also tying back to Bradley's earlier books. I am really excited to see more of this series, particularly because of the out-of-control but still entertaining Worthington family."

—Feminist Fairy Tale Reviews

"A laugh-out-loud-funny novel from Celeste Bradley, the third in the Wicked Worthingtons series. Lighthearted but with a few profound moments, it is filled with deception, misunderstanding, exaggeration, cross-dressing, and mistaken identity."

—Harlequin Junkie

On Bended Knee

The Wicked Worthingtons Series

New York Times Bestselling Author

CELESTE BRADLEY

*This book is dedicated to all those who struggle
with the lifelong aftereffects of trauma.
Please be strong.
You are more than just your shadows.*

Acknowledgments

I could not have written this book without the help of several marvelous people, some of whom are old friends and some I haven't met yet.

For her unfailing support and gentle prodding for 40 years, I thank Darbi Gill.

For her sharp eyes and literary mind, I thank my secret weapon, Robyn Holiday.

For his steadfast love, his unwavering belief in me and his highly overqualified tech support, I thank the Geek God, Charlie Fitch.

For their lifelong patience and attention while I talk endlessly about writing, I thank Thing One and Thing Two. I love my girls more than life.

For their loyalty and tireless effort, I thank the loveliest ladies ever, my Chatelaines.

For her delicious Instagram feed (@life_in_swaledale) that made me feel like I know Swaledale and Yorkshire far better than I actually do, I have to thank the real Jenni Gosling, whose images of her shepherdess life inspired so much within this book, including my favorite character, Topknot. Jenni, I wrote you a book for a wedding present!
I hope I meet you both someday.

Prologue

T HOSE DEPLORABLE WORTHINGTONS are not the sort of family a respectable person should associate with," the first lady whispered from behind the cover of her painted silk fan, "unless of course, one is terribly interesting or innovative—or perhaps inclined to align oneself to a family who have the mercurial Prince Regent's respect."

The lady's companion leaned forward to take on her conspiratorial whisper. "And they make such interesting party guests—as long as one has the resources to make a few minor repairs after the festivities. Wherever they go and whomever they associate with, fascinating things happen that keep London Society thrillingly agog—even though, mind you, we don't truly approve of such goings on."

"Agreed." Lady First smiled knowingly. "Just look at the oldest daughter, Calliope, who married that strange recluse in the Cotswolds! Rumor has it that there was a sword-fight—or was it a duel?—and that Sir Lawrence is a scarred and frightening fellow indeed. Then again, I've also heard that he is wealthy as a lord and keeps poisonous snakes in his wine cellar, so there is simply no trusting in rumor."

Lady Second whipped open her carved ivory fan with the dexterity of long practice to shield her half of the conversation from the rest of the ballroom. "It is those twin brothers, Castor and Pollux Worthington, who are the *real* scandal! Do you recall when they burned down that brothel fighting over a stunning widow, Miranda Something-or-other? I heard the battle was so fierce that one brother was driven right out of London by the other!"

A bit of happily scandalized head-shaking ensued.

Lady First looked smug. "Oh, yes. Of course, things calmed down a great deal once Elektra Worthington wed that nice Lord Aaron Arbogast. No one ever really believed those terrible things about him, not really. Those ten years he spent in the tropics were to learn estate management, not because of some silly public shunning. Such a fine fellow now! He is likely to become the Earl of Arbodean very soon. With all that wealth and power soon to be under his control, it isn't wise to repeat any of that deliciously wicked history, don't you agree?"

Lady Second, flustered at being caught criticizing a potential duke, grasped at another topic. "Oh, I remember that scientist brother, the one named Orion. The nonsense those Worthingtons named their children!"

The two indulged in a gleeful tsk-tsk before the second lady continued. "It was rumored that Orion Worthington was headed for greatness in the world of scholarly pursuits—that is, until he fell passionately in love with that bluestocking ward of Sir Geoffrey Blayne. I heard that Francesca girl was half-Italian, so who knows what madness she caused in that household? Sir Geoffrey is still locked away in Bedlam, is he not?"

Lady First nodded with a satisfied purr. "Quite so. Then there was that other young lady, a cousin, I believe. An uncommonly pretty girl, that Bliss Worthington. We all thought she was heading toward a very satisfying union with the young Duke of Camberton—until she ran away in the middle of the night and wed his bastard brother instead! Who in their right mind would choose an illegitimate ship captain over a duke? Who were her parents, did we ever learn? Well, no matter. It turns out she was just another mad Worthington after all!"

Lady Second shivered with delicious dismay. "And there is the silent brother, the darkest one, Lysander Worthington, the one who never truly came all the way back from the war. Goodness, I wonder what will become of *him*?"

Chapter 1

I F THE DEVIL kept sheep—and Lysander Worthington, of
the London Worthingtons, had no reason to suppose
that the devil *didn't* keep a fiendish herd in some fiery version of the Yorkshire Dales—then the devil would have had
Lysander's adversary as his personal pet ram. The creature
had surely come straight from hell.

*I was only riding through. Just through the blasted village and
out again.*

It wasn't simply the eerie narrow iris of the ram's eye.
All sheep had a similar gaze and Lysander had met a few
perfectly angelic woolly creatures in his thirty-one years. It
wasn't the ram's multicolored face, splotched with black
and white in a highwayman's larcenous mask. Lysander's
own mount, his brother's fine riding horse Icarus, had a
striking white blaze down his nose, and Icarus was as well
behaved as any slightly nervy thoroughbred could be.

Perhaps it was the creature's curling horns that twisted
a bit wrong, spiraling straight out from each side of its
hellish head like armored corkscrews. The cruel projections
had clearly been waxed to a fine shine by the ram's atten-
tive owner. Lysander had a light-headed vision of a scarlet-
skinned devil, cooing fondly at his straggle-woolen pet
whilst stropping the beast's horns with a polishing cloth.

No matter from where the truculent creature had come,
it clearly believed itself the rightful master of this otherwise
unremarkable village common. The beast stood stiff-legged
and twitchy, aggressively challenging Lysander and his

borrowed mount, Icarus. The maddened gaze heated. The hell-spawn ram scraped a cloven hoof on the scattered straw in warning. Apparently the fluffy fiend took offense to Icarus's elegant long-legged form, which surely looked quite strange to its tiny mind after a lifetime of thick, stolid draft horses and plow ponies.

Aristocratic Icarus, on the other hand, visibly trembled in terror before the snorting demonic creature bountifully festooned in multicolored festival day ribbons, which twisted and flapped in the afternoon breeze in ludicrous counterpoint to the lethal twisting horns.

Lysander had a single instant to wonder if Icarus, London creature that he was, had ever actually *seen* a sheep.

The previously amiable horse let out a shrill neigh of panic and performed a gyrating, rearing hop that not only faced the gelding away from the rage-maddened ram, but also aided in putting a nearly instant quarter mile between himself and the nightmarish creature.

Unfortunately, Lysander was not invited on this retreat. The world flipped on its axis and he found himself facedown in the mud with the wind knocked clean from his lungs. Shaken by the fall and his sudden change in stature, he madly scraped the mud from his face and eyes and drew his breath in with a strangled gasp.

Mud. *Mud* and *blood* and *pain. Thunder.*

In time, he would look back to comprehend that the pounding that shook the earth was merely the retreating hoof beats of the fleeing Icarus. Unhappily, in that moment Lysander instead heard the thunder of cannon and storm.

And any moment icy rain would pour from the war-blackened sky and the earth would run with blood.

His heartbeat sped until he could hear nothing but the hammer of his own pulse and the hoarse gasps of his own breath scraping its way out of his throat. There was no village festival, no shattered prize sheep's pen, no gaping crowd of astonished Swaledale farmers around him. There was only the rocky fist of memory, knocking him heedlessly backward in time, flinging him down on a mud-and-blood spattered field of war in Spain.

Thunder. Cannon. Enemy. *Battle.*

The ram lowered its head and gave a threatening snort, taking up the challenge with vicious glee. *Battle indeed*, it seemed to say.

To the death, if necessary.

Chapter 2

TWO DAYS EARLIER....

I N A ONCE elegant but now rather dilapidated neighbor-hood in London there stood a large rambling house composed of soot gray stone and ivy vines. The structure had passed "tattered gentility" several decades back and was well on its way to "ramshackle ruin." Yet like a grubby, much-loved toy, the crumbling structure had a heart and soul that made it almost a member of the family who lived within.

Inside Worthington House, Atalanta Worthington paced the long hallway upstairs. Back and forth, from one end of the worn runner to the other, very slowly. The figured paper on the walls was faded in odd places and there was a patch halfway down that she clearly remembered peeling away, although her brothers insisted she could not remember something she'd done when she was two years old.

If she took normal steps it was seventy-two paces. When she was smaller, it had been hundreds of paces but that was because she'd been climbing around and over and through, a brave adventurer beating her path through a dangerous forest, weaving her way through great teetering towers of books. Thousands of books that had only been a small portion salvaged from the fire that had consumed the once great library at Worthington Manor. If she closed her eyes, Attie could still smell the tinge of smoke that had lingered within the pages and filtered through the air until she had believed that all books smelled like a house afire.

There were no books in the hallway anymore. Attie's

sister-in-law Miranda had gently forced the family to clear the stacks away and sort them. At Miranda's tender but steely request, the Worthington brothers Daedalus, Castor and even Lysander, had built bookcases in every room from the floor to the ceiling to contain them all, since the London house had no real library of its own.

It made sense, Attie supposed grudgingly. After all, she'd been trapped beneath book avalanches a few times, and Philpot had taken a fall, at which point the stout housekeeper had declared herself retired from all upper-story chores.

The maze of random and often unsuitable knowledge had been a strange and wonderful playground but Attie reminded herself that she didn't need a playground any longer. She wasn't a child. And being fourteen years of age, she had responsibilities.

Furthermore, the long empty hallway was now a marvelous place in which to practice sequential high-velocity cartwheels.

She reached the end of the hallway and, spinning slowly but precisely, she began to smoothly walk back. She was so good at it now that she could probably balance a book on her head. This was something that Miranda had told her she'd been required to do as a girl. What a silly use for a book! Although Attie supposed if it was a stupid book, like a volume on etiquette, or hairdressing, or the history of puffed sleeves.

The bundle in her arms whimpered and Attie realized that she had stopped still for a moment as she contemplated the many stupid books in the world. Back to carrying! Six-month-old Aurora was so often passed hand-to-hand in the Worthington family that Attie doubted if Aurora's little pink feet would ever touch the floor.

But like the rest of the family, Aurora wasn't at her best today. Attie understood. The house was too hushed, with every sound causing an unearthly echo she would swear had never occurred before. Everyone moved slowly and wearily and far too carefully, strange in a house that had only known heedless, boisterous action for as long as Attie could recall.

Even the tiniest Worthington recognized the discordance. There were some things that only the warm arms of your family could fix, so Attie had swaddled her stout little niece in a cozy shawl and taken her for a long, long walk in the hall.

Aurora made a creaking noise, long and slow like a door with sticky hinges. Attie nodded. "Yes, Aurora. I comprehend."

Attie wouldn't be able to maintain this peace much longer. Aurora was hungry. Since she was still vociferously opposed to solid food, she would be needing her mother quite soon.

Attie eased her embrace to study her niece's blue-green eyes and furrowed, barely-there brows. "Matters certainly would be simpler if you would eat some porridge. Although, I do not blame you for your low opinion of porridge. I commiserate wholeheartedly." Worthingtons didn't use infant speech. That sort of thing was for Other People.

However, Attie's sister-in-law Miranda had been up all night with Attie's mother, Iris Worthington.

Sometimes sharp but mostly dreamy and abstracted, Iris was more beloved family pet than a true maternal figure. Too absentminded and artistic to handle the fundamentals of the real world, Iris was happily kept in abundant paints and long trailing scarves and never permitted to handle money or order cabbages from the grocer.

Of course, that was before.

Attie allowed her thoughts to veer away from the uneasy topic of her mother and return to contemplating the clock standing tall at the far end of the hall. Miranda had only been asleep for a few hours. Attie wanted to keep Aurora soothed a little while longer.

The creaky complaint began to rise in volume. Attie gently jiggled her niece and kissed her silky red-haired crown. "Don't wake everyone, Ginger-biscuit. It isn't as though anyone would actually let you starve."

Attie turned and began to walk toward her brother's suite of rooms. When Miranda had married Cas, instead of Poll, his twin whom she'd been fond of first, Cas and Miranda decided to remain in Worthington House.

Poll had been upset at the loss of Miranda, and in many ways the loss of Cas as well. He'd decided to remove himself from a situation too hurtful and confusing to bear. So Poll took off gallivanting.

At one time, Attie had liked the word "gallivanting." Now she despised it. People who had a family who missed them should never gallivant. It shouldn't be allowed.

Cas, on the other hand, had stoically accepted that Iris, who was already living half in a dream world, would not take it well if both her twin sons left her at the same time. Miranda, who had lacked for family her whole life, was quite happy to move into the bustling, shabby, outrageous Worthington House. Attie couldn't blame her. Anyone sensible could see what a wonderful place Worthington House was.

Attie tapped twice on the door, very lightly. In fact, she tapped so lightly that she made not a single sound. However, if asked, she could truthfully say she had knocked. In this particular instance, it made no difference to anyone if she knocked or not, but Attie made it a practice to leave her options open.

Attie walked through the sitting room. It was a comfortable, overstuffed sort of place done up in cream and peacock blues, and usually extremely tidy, although at the moment things were in a bit of disarray. There were teacups on the scrollwork side table and a few scattered news-sheets on the floor. There was also one very large brother sprawled across the sofa with one arm crooked over his eyes, fully dressed and dead to the world.

Attie continued through the sitting room without waking Cas. He'd had a very long night tending to Iris. Everyone took a turn. Right now, Attie's father Archimedes Worthington and their housekeeper, Mrs. Philpot, were teaming up to take care of Iris. That worked out well, for between the two of them they almost made up a competent adult.

Attie moved to the bedroom door of the suite and again tapped feather light.

When she entered, the room was very dim. The heavy draperies had been pulled tight against the midday light. Attie wasn't quite sure how to wake Miranda. While she was very fond of her sister-in-law, who was a perfectly nice person and very nearly a proper Worthington, there had always been a bit of distance between them. Miranda was a lady through and through. And while Attie's sisters Calliope and Elektra were also ladies—and Elektra was actually Lady Arbogast—the state of ladydom was more of a coat they buttoned on when necessary and took off as soon as they pleased. Miranda, on the other hand, was very likely a lady even when she was all alone.

Attie felt a little sorry for her sometimes. Miranda was so kind. Perhaps that was why Attie didn't truly understand her, because for all her gifts, Attie was perfectly aware that no one would ever describe her as kind.

There was no need to wake Miranda, after all. Aurora twisted her little round head to see that her mother was near and let out a bellow. "Maaaaaa!" The half-word rose to a shriek that could slice through an iron lamp post.

Miranda opened her eyes. "My tiny tyrant calls."

Attie stepped closer. "If you would go on and have more

children, she would have some healthy competition." The more Worthingtons in the world, the better.

Miranda smiled gently as she sat up and wearily pushed back her hair. "Auntie Attie, you have seven siblings and none of them have ever given you a single second of competition."

She held out her arms. Attie plunked Aurora into her mother's grasp and then plunked her own bottom onto the foot of the bed. Miranda pulled her feet up just in time. "That's true." It was.

Aurora stretched fat little fists toward her mother. Miranda glanced at Attie and hesitated as she reached for the neckline of her nightdress. Attie rolled her eyes. "Oh, all right. The privacy bit. I know."

She slid off the high bed and strolled to the bedchamber door as if she didn't care at all.

"Attie? How are things?"

Attie stopped but didn't turn around. "Cas is asleep on your sofa. Archie and Philpot are with Iris. Dade is driving that latest doctor back to wherever he came from. Useless man. Elektra and Aaron cannot travel from Shropshire at all. She's confined to her bed so she doesn't give birth too soon and he won't leave her. Bliss and Morgan are at sea, along with Orion and Francesca, so they won't get their letters until they make port. Bliss and Morgan are doing ship-captainy things and Orion and Francesca are researching on the hereditary family structure of porpoise pods. Still, I know they would all come running if they could. Callie and what's-his-name are due in a few days from the Cotswolds. There's a roast in the oven. I'm going down to go scrub the potatoes now." There. Had she forgotten anything? "Oh yes. Lysander hasn't spoken for three days. I think he's getting worse."

"He's worried about Iris, too. He doesn't seem to be taking it well, I agree." Miranda stroked her daughter's cap of shimmering red hair for a moment. "What about Poll?" Miranda's question was soft.

Attie shrugged uneasily. There was so much history between Poll and Cas and Miranda. Her brother Poll hadn't come home in over a year and his letters, never frequent, had begun to trail off. "I posted your letter two days ago just as you asked. No word yet. We don't even know if he's still in Edinburgh. He wrote from there months ago."

Miranda looked down at her tiny daughter and did not meet Attie's gaze. "It would be good if he could come. Soon."

Soon. Attie's belly turned to ice. Iris's "silly little cold", the one she'd caught wandering about the riotously overgrown and damp garden one moonlit night, the cold that hadn't gone away, that turned to a fever, and then to a terrible bubbling cough that sounded as if she were drowning, that the doctor called pneumonia—

There. That was the thing Attie had been trying not to think about. But the tone of sadness in Miranda's voice and the deathly quiet tension in the house and the way that everyone tried so hard, so very hard, not to say it—well, they might as well have screamed it.

Iris might die.

Attie was afraid as she had almost never been afraid, except for that time she accidentally shot Callie with a rifle—and when Attie was afraid she got angry. Very, very angry.

Someone had to do something! Something, preferably, that Attie wanted them to do. There was one person she could always count on, someone who would not argue with her, or tell her that she was being strange or unreasonable, for he himself was far stranger than she.

She went to find Lysander.

LYSANDER WORTHINGTON STOOD in the front parlor of Worthington House. His gaze was fixed on the window. He was not looking at the short patch of garden in front the house or the walkway up to the entry steps, or the bustling street beyond, where passed a few gleaming carriages among the more workaday vehicles. Nor had he a glance for the house across the street, built in the same era as Worthington House but rather better well-kept and somewhat charming.

The city life of busy London held no interest for Lysander. His gaze remained fixed upon a patch of dirty grayish sky visible through the top of the window. It was just a peek between two brick chimneys but it called to him like a doorway. He was only standing in the parlor because his brother Cas had exasperatedly requested him not to stand in the foyer pining at the front door like a wistful hound.

For some time now, it had been Lysander's habit to slip from the house whenever his beloved family became too much for him, which was rather often, or when they gazed at him with that perplexed mixture of fondness, confusion, and wistfulness that made him flinch. Their longing for man who no longer existed hit upon his raw nerves like ice on bad teeth.

But most of all, he could not bear the beaming vagueness of his mother's gaze.

When he was a boy, she'd always been dreamy and absent-minded while painting, yet also quick-witted and clever.

It had been his sister Elektra, in her direct way, who'd explained that it had been the news of Lysander's alleged death that had sent their madly creative mother into simple madness.

"She's never been the same since your name appeared on the lists. She improved, at least somewhat, when we received the letter that they had not properly identified you, and that you were in a hospital in Portugal. And when you actually came back, she grew better still." She gazed at him for a moment with fearless belief. "And she'll be entirely herself again when you come back to us properly, won't she?"

So the weight of his family's expectations increased a thousand-fold. It near to crumpled him flat.

The Worthingtons accomplished so much by sheer will. It was the pressure of that combined, focused, thrice-damned will that drove Lysander into the streets of London. There the burden attenuated with distance, even though the crowds and noise ate at his calm in other ways.

They were all counting on him.

Yet he could not heal himself. He could not heal Iris.

So he would escape and stride furiously, sometimes for many miles in a day. Occasionally he paced through the finer parts of town but most usually through the grittier bits, the areas where people didn't even attempt to make eye contact or to speak to him or even nod in his direction, where the constant pressure to hide the darkness within him eased, for dark spirits abounded in the narrow dirty streets he frequented.

Sometimes rough men jostled him, looking to vent their resentment against the gentry. Sometimes rough women called to him from dim alleyways where they plied their wares. Sometimes rough children followed him and begged for a coin or a sweet, all the while nimble fingers swept his pockets with a touch lighter than a fluttering breeze. Lysander ignored them all.

He wanted nothing from them, not the fight, nor the lust, nor even to grab a small skinny arm and teach a waist-high pickpocket better manners. He had nothing in his pockets to lose. When he'd come home from the war hospital—and when he finally left his room—he'd chosen only the darkest of his old clothing to don. The vibrant dan-

dified waistcoats, gleaming boots and glittering cravat pins
of old now rubbed him as raw as jagged gravel.

Now, he swept through London as a swift shadow of a
man, lost in a strange state that was both overly sensitized
as well as bleakly deadened.

But now Iris was truly ill and his family was frightened.
As much as Lysander longed to flee the agonizing tension
and eerie grim silence that permeated the house, he could
not abandon them. He knew he was of little help, but to
leave simply to ease his own twitching discomfort seemed
too base an act.

The sky eased a trifle bluer as he watched. There must
be a breeze from seaward shifting the ever-present soot
aside.

Stealthy feet slipped into the parlor. Lysander did not
turn. He knew it was his sister, Atalanta, come to count
heads, a restless guardian circling the house, somehow
feeling the weight of responsibility to know where every
member of the family was at all times. Round and round
her path took her, upstairs and down in a constant, edgy
circuit. Lysander understood this. He had no need to do it
himself, for he could feel the presence of his brother and
sister-in-law and little Aurora and his father and Philpot
and even the faint, semi-conscious light of Iris breathing
fitfully and shallowly in her bed. Some of them felt as cool
and soothing as a hand on a feverish brow, like Miranda, or
the rasping edge of Philpot's loyal fretfulness, while Cas
splashed hot and cold toward the world, saving his simmering warmth for his beloved wife and tiny child.

Fourteen-year-old Attie felt like knife-edged steel, like
the flat of the icy blade. It was not the dangerous edge, not
toward her family, although she could cut deeply when she
wished. Attie was clever, gleaming and strong, and was
uniformly both adored and treated cautiously by the
Worthington clan.

Attie felt like a good sword by Lysander's side as she came to stand with him at the window.

"The sky is clearing."

Of course she understood what he was gazing at. Attie cleaved through nonsense and took brusque offense to what she considered useless behavior, which invariably included needlework, housekeeping, hair brushing, and the wearing of flounces. Lysander tended to agree with her on the flounces.

They stood together in silence for a long moment, the tall, lean, darkly-clad, haunted-eyed brother and the skinny tatterdemalion with untamed red hair and sharp emerald gaze. They both contemplated the patch of blue. Lysander felt less like the hound that Cas had described him than a wild thing leashed by obligation, a creature by nature unfit to live within four walls, a rough beast that everyone mistakenly believed to be thoroughly domesticated.

"I want you to go to Scotland to find Pol."

Oh thank God. A task, a mission, a way out. A way to help—and a way to escape.

Attie handed Lysander a piece of paper with an Edinburg address floridly scrawled upon it. Attie went through phases with her handwriting, taking cues from the signatures of great persons of history. She did not seem to have a handwriting of her own quite yet, but appeared to be quite able to forge documents in the style of Henry VIII. Should one be required.

Lysander took the scrap of paper and closed his fist tightly around it. He didn't speak. Words tended to fly through his grasp like small, swift birds he was too clumsy to catch. Because of this, one of his wealthier relations, Elektra's husband Lord Aaron, had insisted that Lysander see this or that "finest physician in England".

"Constipated." They had all frowned at that diagnosis.

"Head trauma. Displaced humors." Lysander had not

suffered a head injury in the war. Various other painful things had happened, but not that. He couldn't speak to the humors diagnosis, but it sounded like balderdash.

"Commotional." That had actually been the best diagnosis so far. Many things made Lysander feel commotional. Physical violence, excessive noise, injustice. Once the screams of a woman from a filthy alleyway had made his heart and head pound and sick darkness rise within him. When the red and black had receded from his vision, he found himself standing over a cowering, bleeding man. The fellow's victim, a young, battered prostitute was crawling desperately away. The terror in her eyes when she stared over her shoulder at Lysander had sent him shaking and puking against the alley wall. She'd looked at him as if he were a monster, this poor abused creature who'd no doubt seen more than her share of horrors in these lawless streets—yet it was *he* whom she feared.

None of his family knew of that particular episode. Iris and Archie persisted in believing him to be, at heart, the young man he'd once been. Lysander's brothers were aware that his "commotional" explosions were out of control, but even they had never truly witnessed him in that terrible state.

Lysander knew that his family told themselves tales— that he was getting better, that he was calmer now. That his nightmares were less, that he was leaving the war farther behind him, that his darkness was lifting into light.

Lysander thought he was faking it all rather well.

But now he had a helpful mission, a search, a goal—a clear-cut direction in which to go. Far from this house of terrified, tragic love and illness.

Far away.

Chapter 3

LYSANDER WORTHINGTON had been in the saddle for two days—or was it three? Not that he cared terribly. On horseback, it was much less necessary to speak to anyone. There were a few people on the road and if he timed the pace of his mount correctly he could either fall back or pass ahead of any other rider or cart with no more than a quick jerk of his head and a tug on the brim of his hat. He tried to remember manners, although it was much easier for him when he didn't actually need to use them very often.

Beneath him, Icarus moved with contented grace and far more style than Lysander deserved. Then again, Icarus wasn't actually his horse. The fine mount belonged to Lysander's older brother, Dade. "Daedalus and Icarus" sounded much more imposing than "Dade and Icky", but that's what everyone in the family called them.

Lysander knew that Icarus was a very good horse. He'd loved horses once, been entirely mad for them, in fact. He remembered that feeling. To be more precise, he remembered that he'd once had such a feeling. Feelings themselves had become a bit distant to him now. He was a man groping in the dark when trying to reach for his emotions of the past.

With the ease of great practice he allowed his mind to slide sideways, away from consideration of the changes that the war had wrought in him. That was the best thing about riding alone for days. With no members of his raucous, beloved, unbearable family around him he could pretend for a few miles at a time that he was just a man on a horse riding down a road.

Occasionally, however, the road became too heavily traveled for Lysander's comfort. It must be market day, for he was beginning to pass more laden carts and wagons full of expectant families. One cart driver kept pace with Lysander for half a mile, telling Lysander more than anyone ever needed to know about his success growing early greens and the high price he planned to ask for them.

When a fork to the right came along, Lysander took it immediately. The instant relief was so great that he made it a practice whenever the road became too full of people and voices and questions and greetings. As long as he continued to travel north, he would arrive in Scotland eventually. Just to ensure he was not putting himself too far behind schedule, he took to running Icarus at a gallop on every long stretch of empty road. Icarus was all for it, for the great thoroughbred loved nothing better than to run as fast as possible.

This worked reasonably well for most of the morning until Icarus threw a shoe. Lysander dismounted immediately and checking the gleaming black hooves of his mount, discovered that Icarus was unharmed. Lysander pocketed the shoe, for surely there would be a blacksmith somewhere ahead.

There was no point in regret. After all, when one has made such vast and monumental mistakes as Lysander had in the past, running his mount out of a shoe seemed rather minor. Finding a proper smithy would be good, but with the undamaged horseshoe in his pocket Lysander thought he might be able to make do with a barn and some tools. It was his own fault, but speaking to people and possibly asking them for help would be a heavy penance.

He followed the road he was on, the peaceful country lane snaking its way through a verdant valley following the banks of a picturesque river. Looking about him, Lysander noticed for the first time that he had reached the Yorkshire Dales proper. He'd never been there before and he found the quiet walk next to the cheerfully burbling river to be extremely soothing. One never found silence like this in London.

It was almost a shock when Lysander turned a bend in the river and found an active village square before him. It seemed a hardworking but not terribly prosperous village for such a large population. Then Lysander realized that despite his best efforts, he'd walked right into some sort of local festival.

Several giggling children ran past him as they played a game of snatching streaming ribbons from each other's grip. Icarus startled violently at the shrill shrieking and the wildly fluttering ribbons, so Lysander thought it best to get back into the saddle. He could better keep control of Icarus and afford himself some relief from walking among the crowd. And it was a useful vantage, for Lysander spotted the smithy immediately. He and Icarus headed for a stone building with an open shed to one side where Lysander could clearly see an anvil. The cheerful crowd parted respectfully before them.

Nearly twitching with discomfort, Lysander looked anywhere, everywhere except down at the faces upturned to eye him curiously. Something caught his eye, a graceful movement on the edge of his perception. He found his attention snared by a slim form on the far edge of the crowd.

There was a sort of pavilion set up on the common. It was an unlovely structure that served the very practical purpose of protecting the festivalgoers from sun or weather. Lysander had a vague impression of a giant parasol cobbled together from old carts, the posts looking like wagon tongues, taken from between the horses and plunked upright. The thing was little more than a rickety freestanding roof with no walls. The patchy, hand-hewn shingles had lain in place long enough to acquire a green mossy growth on the northern slope.

He'd caught the woman in the act of brushing away a strand of dark hair from her face. It caught on her lower lip, the brunette lock pointing a perceptible arrow at the soft plump curve of her mouth. She stood on tiptoe, bracing one hand against the pavilion post to gaze out over a number of temporary livestock pens. Lysander wasn't sure what made him think that she was sad, for her lovely ivory features held a small smile and her gray eyes snapped with lively intelligence. Yet he had the instant conviction that she was all alone in the crowd, separate somehow, watching but not belonging.

What should he do?

Lysander's twin brothers, Castor and Pollux, would have sent her a flirtatious smile or swept a courtly bow. Yes, it could be done from the saddle. Archie had insisted that they all practice it until Iris approved the romantic gesture.

It would have been a strange education, if one was not a Worthington.

A part of Lysander's mind, a very quiet, small part, the part that remembered the way life had once been, applauded the notion. Lysander had no idea what he should do. Never once had a pretty woman snared his attention since his return from the battlefield.

That distraction turned out to be hazardous.

Without Lysander quite realizing it, well-trained Icarus had angled his walk in the direction of Lysander's focus. As they came near, Icarus snorted in spoiled equine offense at the heavy odor of lanolin and sheep dung. Lysander noticed distantly that they had come quite close to the livestock pens, but since he was still generally en route to the smithy he didn't bother to turn Icarus aside.

Their path had brought them closer to the fascinating

lady beneath the pavilion, although she still had eyes for something few yards farther on. Lysander managed to tear his locked gaze from the gray shadows in her eyes to follow the direction of her attention.

He saw that she was watching a farm family. There was a great strapping father, an astonishingly pregnant mother and four clean-as-a-whistle youngsters whose white-blonde heads formed a stair-step of their ages, right down to the smallest boy, who looked to be barely walking. They were all glowing proudly at the tallest child, a skinny girl of perhaps ten years, who wore a smile so wide it threatened to divide her face. Her straw-colored hair was done up in bows and her flowered muslin dress seemed quite at odds with the substantial black and white piglet squirming in her arms.

The family looked on with pleasure as another, even more massive fellow tied a bright blue ribbon around the piglet's neck and finished it with a delicate bow, which was astonishing considering the thickness of his fingers.

Lysander surmised that he'd spotted the blacksmith. It was obvious from the girth of his forearms and the ruddy features weathered by fire and steam. Lysander sent one last glance toward the pavilion. The lady was gone. Lysander's visceral awareness of the lady bloomed in the fog of his consciousness, strange and unlikely and not at all welcome. He'd fought so hard for some tiny fragment of equilibrium. Now she had disappeared and he fought a ridiculous sense of loss.

It would be a very good idea to leave this hamlet as soon as possible.

The smith, luckily, was still within reach. Having awarded the winner of the Fat Piglet Competition, the man had clapped the proud papa on the shoulder and begun to walk away.

In his haste to have the horseshoe replaced so he could

be gone from this hamlet and back on the road alone, Lysander nudged his heels into Icarus with more force than necessary. Obediently, Icarus shot forward. His great shoulder impacted the corner post of the woven willow livestock pen.

Apparently this had been a most important post in the scheme of things. Once that went down, the entire arrangement of posts and basket-weave fencing came apart like the unraveling of a poorly knit glove.

Startled by the crashing fence parts, the livestock within scurried and bolted in all directions. Squealing pigs ran beneath Icarus's legs. Ewes and lambs flowed around them like a white river around a black rock. It was all too much for the finely bred horse. He was a civilized creature, accustomed to cobblestones and rubbish bins and ladies with fluttering skirts and cursing cart drivers and newsboys waving gossip sheets. All of that was familiar and sane, while this scurrying, trampling, baaing horde was peculiar and alarming. Icarus reared on his back legs as if he couldn't bear to have the woolly bodies brush against his hocks anymore.

Lysander clung on as Icarus rose and remained high like a rook on a chessboard poised for his next move. The horde of smelly fleecy offenders trickled to the odd dashing lamb and Icarus let his hooves fall to the ground with a relieved thud.

Movement caught Lysander's eye as an enormous horned beast abruptly focused his upset on Icarus—and by default, upon Lysander.

Chapter 4

I T WERE MADNESS, I tell ye! The fight o' the century!
The Legend o' Goose-Gogs! That ram is the pride o'
Swaledale, he is!"

"To Goose-Gogs!"

"Aye!" The crowd of farmers bellowed in unison.

"To Swaledale!" cried one.

"To fightin'!" cried another.

"To beatin' down snooty Londoner toffs!"

"Aye!" The timbers shook.

In the last high-backed settle in the coaching inn taproom, as far from the fire and the crowd of locals that one
could get, Pollux Worthington, of the London Worthingtons, sank a bit lower in his seat.

Not that he was snooty in any way whatsoever, or an
actual Londoner, for that matter. He'd been born in the
pastoral county of Shropshire. He didn't consider himself a
toff at all, except that he occasionally enjoyed a hand of
cards with the Prince Regent—which hardly counted for he
always had to be careful to *just barely* lose. However, these
gargantuan louts in their rough boots, now slamming their
pints together in celebration of someone named Goose-
Gogs, didn't seem the sorts to make such fine distinctions
when they were in their cups. And Poll didn't need any
trouble when all he was trying to do was to get back to the
aforementioned London and his ailing mother, Iris.

*I'm only riding through. Just through the blasted village and
out again.*

"Oh aye, it were a fine battle!"
"Battle!"
"Tell it again, Orren!"
"Orren!"

God, it was like a bloody Greek chorus! Of course, Orren turned out to be the biggest and loutiest of them all. When the massive fellow stood and planted himself before the fire, he nearly eclipsed the great stone hearth. Poll deeply regretted adding that vain touch of lace to his shirt cuffs. He lowered his hands to his lap and tried surreptitiously to tuck the offending finery into the sleeve of his thankfully rather severe dark-green superfine surcoat. He was wearing one of his less vivid weskits, too, a dignified pale blue with hardly any gold thread embroidery.

Don't mind little old me, I'm just having a pint of ale to sustain me as I continue on my long ride home. He would have simply left, but the lout brigade had multiplied to form a full platoon of the loutishly inclined. The mob had now grown past the point of safe escape and the shifting mass of muscles and coarse linen remained firmly lodged between himself and the door. Still, when the giant Yorkshireman began his tale with a certain theatrical relish, Poll paid attention. Theater, after all, was his stock in trade.

The Battle of Goose-Gogs

"It were like a battle of old, it were! The invader riding into the village on his fine high horse, the valiant defender standing his ground. With one stamp of his mighty foot, Goose-Gogs sent that fancy black horse into fits of fright! It flew off up the dale with its shiny tail flying like the flag of a general in retreat!

"Goose-Gogs boldly charged that dandified intruder. The gent was fast though, like dark lightning. He dodged old Goose-Gogs in a blur. With a fearsome foul roar, the fellow flung himself on Goose-Gogs's back with one arm wrapped 'round a great twisting horn."

"What he want to do that for?" muttered from the back row.

"Yeah, don't he know nothin' about sheep?"

Orren pointed a thick finger at the man so rudely interrupting.

"Oh, but the stranger *did* know something about fighting. He wrestled Goose-Gogs straight down into the mud, and he'd have pinned him there were it not for brawling with a four-legged beast. That ram scrambled up out of the mud so fast, white-hot fury glowing in his eyes! No one had ever challenged Goose-Gogs before and come out on top! No one had ever made Goose-Gogs eat dirt!"

"I thought he said it were mud."

Orren ignored the heckler. "The great warrior Goose-Gogs, the finest Swaledale ram ever bred, the pride and joy of his village and the entire dale—"

"Oh, aye and the next dale over, too!"

"This mad invader would not defeat our Goose-Gogs!"

"What did they call him Goose-Gogs for? Ain't that just a gooseberry?"

"Aye. It's because when he was coming up he had the littlest tiny—"

Orren worked his jaw in irritation but went on. "Great Goose-Gogs stamped his cloven hooves in the mud, waving his magnificent twisting rack of horns, lowered his giant heavy head and—"

"—stones no bigger than a pair o' gooseberries, but they grew in just fine later on."

"The evildoer braced himself, the black fire of battle in his dark eyes, his fancy clothes smeared with mud, and prepared to face the great ram's charge."

Orren paused to down a rather unbelievably large tank-

ard of ale in three gulps, knowingly leaving his audience on
the edge of their benches. Then he wiped his mouth on his
sleeve and gave an appreciative belch before tossing the
tankard to the ale-wife, who caught it deftly, and resuming
his tale.

"Goose-Gogs charged! And as he neared the stranger he
gathered up his forelegs and launched himself up into the
air like a stag a'leapin'—"

*"It's a good thing they'd not et him when he were young,
then!"*

"WOULD YOU KINDLY SHUT YOUR YAPPER?"

Orren wasn't simply a large man. He was a very large
man. Yaps were shut.

"Right then." Satisfied, Orren continued. "The mali-
cious stranger ducked out of the way at the very last moment and that's when we all saw it, the terrible trick the
dastardly intruder played on an honorable beast! Goose-
Gogs slammed into the central post of the pavilion with all
the force of his mighty rage! The evildoer had hidden the
post in his own shadow and tricked our great Goose-Gogs
into knocking himself dead silly on that post!"

"Aw. I thought he said Goose-Gogs won this one."

Orren pointed at the disappointed audience member.
"Aye, and that's how we know how great our Goose-Gogs
is, being a true Ram of Destiny—because that's when the
miracle happens! That crazed stranger attacks the crowd in
the pavilion, y'see. He grabs up wee children and flings
them away, to be caught by their own desperate mothers!
He knocks three full grown men right over the railing of the
pavilion with one blow! He picked up a poor widow woman
and threw her into the air to land on the ground!

"That idiot even grabbed Goose-Gogs—well, he was up
and about by then, don't you know. Shaking his head and
looking a bit waggle-eyed, truth be told. And that muddy,
black-eyed stranger picked up biggest ram in Swaledale and

flung him into the air!"

A hush of wonder settled the boisterous crowd.

A whispered voice broke the silence.

"And then what happened?"

The giant Shepherd Orren stood in the dusty beam of the sunlight slanting through the grimy tavern windows with his thick arms raised high, and a transcendent gleam in his eyes.

"A righteous bit o' justice, I tell ye! The pavilion fell square down on top o' the bastard!"

The entire male population of three-and-one-half villages rose to their feet with a mighty roar, lifting their fists to the sky and chanting, "Goose-Gogs! Goose-Gogs!"

And there cometh my cue. Pollux Worthington stood and slipped quietly between the taproom wall and the thick backs of the entranced audience. Like a flickering shadow cast by the fire in the great hearth, one moment he was there and then he was gone.

It was a grand old tale. Memorable, he thought, as he bridled his rested and fed horse, a rickety but good-natured nag—Poll had dubbed him "Yorick" for the clear evidence of his skeletal structure—bought from the knacker by means of trading a couple of polished brass buttons.

Mounting Yorick, Poll continued plodding his way south toward London, home, and *her.*

He thought about the tale of Goose-Gogs. Orren was a rather good performer, in Poll's experienced estimation. The fellow had stood tall and disdainful as he played the invader, then braced and square as the defender. He'd even spooked and staggered backward as the fleeing horse. For added detail, he had waved his thick hand to demonstrate the retreating flag—er, tail.

If I were looking for a giant to add to the troupe, I'd recruit that fellow. Sadly, as matters stood the troupe was picking the lint from its pockets to buy oats for the wagon horses.

They certainly couldn't afford to lure another actor inside. Besides, how would they ever manage to feed such a monumental fellow?

It would make a jolly play, or at least an opening skit. The country folk would love it. He'd have to change the name. The Legend of Goose-Gogs. Who in their right mind would ever name a mighty ram something as silly as that?

Still, it had ended well. After battling the heroic ram and destroying the village festival, including the winning vegetables, the nefarious intruder had redeemed himself by saving the beautiful princess, flinging her free of the destruction before the tower—er, festival pavilion—had collapsed upon him, therefore earning his own justice in a most Shakespearean manner.

With a little work, it could be quite a hit. Poll only wondered where on earth the troupe could find a sheep costume.

Chapter 5

M RS. GEMMA OAKES picked herself up off the trampled grass of the common with the help of a few residents of the village of Farby.

"Thank you, gentlemen. No, no. I'll be fine." The act of dusting off her skirts belied that statement when a mere twist of her wrist sent a nauseating stab of pain through her.

Gemma, being Gemma, paused and immediately began running through the appropriate treatment of sprains in her mind. She had no cool water to soak in, nor salts, nor even strips to bind and support the joint. Resolving upon the one thing she could do, which was to raise her wrist above her heart to diminish swelling, she cradled her right hand high on her left shoulder and supported the entire arm with her other hand. She imagined she looked as though she were scratching her own back. Then she put all that consideration aside and moved forward to inspect the wreckage.

Someone had come riding into the village and in a matter of seconds had devastated the entire preparations for today's festival, including Gemma's special project, Farby's first country dance assembly. Despite that, Gemma's first concern was for the man who lay injured beneath the shattered remains of the village's old pavilion.

And the ram, of course. "Is Shepherd Orren's ram all right?" She looked to the nearest farmer. "He took no injury?"

"Oh aye, Missus. 'e's right as rain, no doubt. No thanks to that big off-comed 'un."

That meant "stranger." Just ahead of Gemma, two of the younger men struggled with a piece of shingled roofing, which they heaved away with timed grunting.

"There he is. That's him." The other men peered at the stranger.

"I never seen him afore. He donna be from any village in Swaledale."

The man on the ground was very long, which matched Gemma's brief impression of his height. He had lost his hat and his dark hair covered half his face as he lay upon his side. He wore a deep blue coat and buckskin breeches with tall black boots.

London. Gemma wasn't sure how she knew that. After all, there were many large towns and cities in England where men on a fine horse could come from. But he *looked* like London to her. She was certain she was correct. Perhaps it was his finely made but worn clothing, or the careful polish of his boots although she could see the soles were in need of refurbishment.

One long arm lay stretched out toward her, the large hand open palm upward as if in plea. Even his hand look like London. A gentleman's hand, with naught but a horseman's callouses, unscarred by hard labor.

All this she took in as she swept past the watching villagers. Keeping her right hand high on her shoulder as she knelt, she took the pulse of that exposed wrist with the fingers of her left hand.

"He's alive." Reaching with assurance, she swept back his hair before carefully raising one eyelid, then the other. "Hmm." Concussed, there was no doubt about that. Without jarring him in the slightest, she slid her hand around his head. Her fingers stroked through that thick, overly long hair to gently probe for any sign of—oh yes, there it was. A sizable knot was forming on the back of his skull. Lucky fellow, for that was the hardest part of what was quite certainly a hardheaded person in the first place.

And handsome. Heavens, had she ever seen a more beautiful man? Perhaps it was the mystery of his sudden arrival but she had the oddest sensation something important had just happened.

Who in their right mind would take on a fully grown ram? A man perhaps well-conditioned to ferocity, she mused. A soldier, one who still carried the battlefield in his soul.

"I believe he should be brought to the manor. I must keep an eye on him overnight." She stood and several hands reached to aid her rising. She retreated a few steps, and the villagers flowed into the space she had left like water when a river stone was removed.

"You hurt yourself, then?" The voice came from one side of her and Gemma smiled at the familiar brisk tone.

"It's only a sprain, Jennie. I landed wrong on my wrist. It could've been worse. It could be me they pulled from the wreckage."

"Aye, that was a good thing, him flingin' you out, though too roughly done."

From beyond Jennie, Gemma heard a giggle. Two of the village girls gazed rapturously at the unconscious newcomer. "Oh he's a fine one, ain't he?"

Gemma remained composed, although she had just been thinking the same thing. *I don't think I have ever seen such a magnificent man.*

Beside Gemma, Jennie sniffed. "Fine is as fine does." Jennie crossed her arms over her maternal torso. It was clear that Jennie would be delivering the fifth Gosling child in a matter of weeks—and tilted her head as she gazed narrowly at Gemma. "You'll be wanting to take care of him, I suppose. Like you take care of every crick and crack in this village, even down to the dogs and cats." Jennie shook her head. "I'll not try stoppin' you, because it won't do a bit of good. But you watch that one. We don't know him and we don't know his people."

Gemma glanced at the spot where she'd landed, which was really quite astonishingly far from the dangerously broken wreckage. *He is so strong.* "He saved me, Jennie."

Jennie spared another suspicious glance at the limp fellow now being lifted on a section of shattered planking. "You wouldna needed saving if he hadn't happened by in the first place."

Gemma smiled at Jennie, for she was greatly fond of the outspoken farm wife, though Jennie was a few years older than herself. "Not back'ard at comin' for'ard" Farby denizens said of Jennie Gosling, but Gemma understood her. Jennie saw the village and the entire dale as an extension of her own little cottage and her own hearth.

She wasn't far wrong. The people of the Dales had been wedding amongst themselves for very long time. Most families could call each other cousins of a sort from one end of Swale River to the other, down the long valley it cut through North Yorkshire.

To be frank, Gemma's favorite thing about Jennie was that Jennie spoke to her as an equal, woman to woman, not as a farm wife to a lady. It likely broke every rule of class distinction, but Gemma most assuredly didn't care. Alone of all the people of Farby—respect her as they might, even look after her as they sometimes did, as she looked after them—only Jennie spoke to her instead of deferred to her.

Gemma hadn't noticed her isolation so severely when her husband was alive, for Edmund and his medical practice had been company enough. Furthermore, Dr. Oakes had enjoyed a vigorous correspondence with other physicians and doctors in England and afar. Those respected colleagues had visited now and again, often bringing wives and children to fill the big house with guests and energetic discussions of medicine, hunting, whiskey, tobacco, mothering, sibling rivalry, and "Gemma, darling, when are you and the doctor going to start a family of your own?"

Never. It had never happened, and with the carriage accident that had taken Edmund from her, it never would.

She was a lady alone in the dale, surrounded by Yorkshire farmers and shepherds, roughly respectful but keeping their distance. The local women shifted away from her when she entered the shop, giving her first place in line when she stopped at the little desk run by the postmistress, ducking their heads and keeping their gaze on their shopping.

How she hated that wordless moving aside, the scuff of rough shoes on the floorboards, the rustle of heavy skirts and stiff aprons. Even the way her own shoes sounded different, as her outdated but still fine skirts swished more silkily and her voice came more softly and lightly. She did not truly wish to be a Swaledale farm wife, for that would deny all that she had learned and accomplished in her thirty-four years.

What she did wish for was acceptance. That would never come, for this community that she loved so dearly seemed as closed to her as a locked room.

"We've loaded him in the cart, Missus. Best be headin' back now so we can tend to your arm."

Gemma turned to find her manservant Mr. Bing at her elbow. He'd pulled off his cap and stood with one shirt-sleeve mopping his forehead, although she knew perfectly well he'd not lifted a finger to load the newcomer into the pony cart they had arrived in. Mr. Bing was never inclined to physical labor when there were younger, stronger folk available. He was very conscious of his prized position as the late doctor's majordomo and now as the primary—only—staff to Mrs. Oakes. He considered himself a cut above the dale folk, for he was from the fine town of Whitby, perched on the sea, which seemed to increase its sophisticate value, and therefore his own, at least in Mr. Bing's mind.

Of course, that did not stop him from joining the farmers and shepherds for a pint or three in the public house, which was really just a room off the sundries shop. There were very few businesses of that sort in Farby, population not yet one hundred souls. The postmistress, in addition to selling the sundries, was also the local alewife and brewer. Most people wore several hats in the small community. And being near them all, so did she. Arbiter of womanly disputes, primary purchaser of the aforementioned sundries, herbalist, healer, puller of bad molars and soon, by the size of Jennie Gosling's belly, midwife.

Over the past winter, the dale's midwife, old Mrs. Hirst had died at the age of eighty-two. Lofty and self-important Mrs. Hirst had archly allowed Gemma to attend several births in Swaledale, but she was only permitted to watch. Frustrated by the woman's medieval methods and superstitious practices, not to mention her abysmal lack of cleanliness, Gemma had been forced to hold her tongue in the face of the fearful worship the women of the dale had held Mrs. Hirst.

Now that Mrs. Hirst had gone to her reward, Gemma would have a chance to prove herself to the mothers of the dale. Jennie, knowing of Gemma's determination, had been the first to ask. When Jennie's child was safely delivered, Gemma knew that the other women would come around as well.

On the common, Gemma moved carefully through the scattered remains of many a farm wife's prized vegetables and flowers. Mr. Bing tut-tutted at the wholesale destruction.

"The smith ain't even 'anded out t' ribbons on them yet.

And there'll be no dancin' now. Poor Jem Toms has gone and polished up his fiddle for nowt. T' village lads'll not be fond of your new stray, not now. Whoever he is, you'd best patch him up and send him on his way, before one of t' lads decides to take out his woman's tears on that toff's posh hide!"

"I don't think it was his fault," Gemma said quietly, for Mr. Bing's ears only. "I think he's a soldier, like you. He went so strange and dark after he was thrown from his horse. The way you were sometimes, after the war."

Bing shot her a sharp look. "Aye, I saw that too. I think he's some worse than me, belike. Mayhap it ain't his fault, but these folk won't understand. Not a single one of theirs came back from t' war."

Gemma looked around at the hard-working people of Farby as they began to pick up the pieces of their festival, just as they had solemnly and stoutly picked up the pieces of their families after losing so many sons to Napoleon's troops.

"Then we shall just have to understand for them."

LYSANDER LAY VERY still. His head pounded with such breathtaking ferocity that he counted that fraction of a second between the spikes of pain and cradled it, waiting for that absence of agony as other men might wait for a moment of pleasure.

A cool cloth touched his face and it did soothe the ache. The rest of his body seemed to be very sore as well. His ribs protested with every breath, and any slight shifting seem to bring on hot twinges that made no sense in the muscles of his shoulders, back and legs.

Perhaps if he'd been able to maintain a thought for longer than a fraction of a second between the hammering in his head, he might have remembered how he came to be lying somewhere dark, on something soft, covered by something warm, being touched by something cool. Yet every time the dimmest impulse of curiosity struck him, that curiosity was slammed out of his thoughts by the re-verberation of his own pulse through his aching head.

There was a sound. He could almost hear it through the hammer blows. What was it? It was nice, low and soft and sweet.

He couldn't hear words. Just a soft singing.

Oh it hurt.

The pain reminded him of something bad, but honestly he could not even recall what it was, except that it was something he would probably rather *not* remember.

Focus on the sound. It made him feel better. Calmer. What was it?

A sweet lilting voice. It was a song. A moment of memory, and then a faded image of a woman rocking a tiny flame-haired infant.

Iris. His mother.

Sister. He had a sister.

Oh my head.

A sweet song. A soft comforting song in the dark. So soft. Warm. Like something from before the thunder and the mud, the blood and the rain.

A cool hand stroked back his hair. The cloth, refreshed with chill water, draped over his brow. The sweet, breathy voice sang on.

Warmth. Touch. Music.

He slept, a true healing sleep this time.

THE STRANGER SLEPT properly now. Gemma let her soft song fade away to nothing. It was an old trick, known by women through millennia most likely, anyone who would ever soothed a fussing child or wounded man or an ill elder knew the trick of distracting someone from their ills long enough for them to gain a bit of rest.

She set the folded cloth back into the pan by her side and took a moment to stretch in her chair. As she rolled her neck she winced at the soreness in her shoulder and the way her wrist ached.

She was certain that Mr. Bing thought her safely in her stillroom downstairs, far away from the outsider. Mr. Bing would not approve of her nursing the stranger by herself. He was protective of her, even fatherly in his gruff way. But her aches had kept her from her tasks and she admitted, at least to herself, to an abiding curiosity about the man she cared for.

It certainly hadn't been a romantic moment, being tossed from beneath the collapsing roof of the pavilion like a sack of flour. She understood that it was only a physical response, so she tried not to give credence to the way his effortless strength now made her catch her breath in memory. Yet to find herself lifted and held for that fraction of a second had been the first time she'd been touched by a man in years.

Her husband had been killed in a carriage accident more than four years ago, but Gemma felt he'd begun dying a long time before. He'd not reached out for her once in his last few years.

Seven years since she'd felt something like what the stranger aroused in her. Her gaze lost focus for a moment as she recalled it. Big hard hands grasping her waist, lifting her high.

Heavens, he is strong.

Furthermore, he smelled incredibly good. Not of cologne but of horse and leather and clean male skin.

Mr. Bing had stripped the fellow's clothes and dressed him in one of Dr. Oakes's old nightshirts. It was a pity that the voluminous linen did nothing to lessen the square solidity of his shoulders and the muscles rippling down his body.

He'd been beautiful and wild and strange, grappling with the ram, a medieval hero battling a dragon.

Now she was just being fanciful. Who would believe it? Anyone who would had ever met Gemma Oakes would never think to describe her as whimsical. But surely under her own roof, in the privacy of her own mind, she could have a moment of fancy?

It wasn't as though she had any attachment to this striking, otherworldly fellow. She suspected he was quite broken. A broken beautiful man. And she was quite sure she knew, more or less, what it was that had broken him.

When she had been young and foolish, and swept up in the deepest admiration for the man she had wed, she'd believed herself intrepid. Fearless Gemma, the doctor's right hand, his student, his assistant, his bride. Dr. Edmund Oakes had been a brilliant physician and a good, ethical man. He'd been much admired for his analytical mind and gift for difficult diagnosis.

Not a fiery lover, though. Perhaps his intellect prevented a certain warmth, or at least excused the lack of it. He'd been ardent in the beginning, at least often enough for her to believe herself admired and wanted. He was her world and all was right with that world.

And then they had gone to war.

Battlefield surgeon and his battlefield bride. She'd been mad, that was all. Mad for her husband, obsessed with proving herself to him, proving that she was good enough for him, willing to suppress all dread, all fear, all recoil as she'd waded through blood and mud and gore, stepping past bodies blackened by fire, broken by cannon and torn apart by shot. Dying, moaning, screaming men and boys, some so young she could not believe anyone had thought it wise to wrap them in woolen uniforms and give them firearms.

Although she'd never served outside the medical tents, sometimes the front line had come so close that she could hear the boom of cannon fire, and the cries of the wounded and dying carried by the wind, along with the smell of smoke and burning flesh. She still dreamed of the strange, heavy odor of blood so strong it became a taste in her mouth.

So yes, she'd seen the broken, the shattered and the stunned.

"Commotional," Edmund had called it. The strange state of a mind so battered by death and destruction that it could no longer carry the same soul and personality that it once had held. Over-reacting to the world, that broken soul, as sensitive as the newly born, as mindless, sometimes, as the truly mad.

Foolish, unwise, fearless Gemma. She had spent herself on those fields of blood, much the way that Edmund had. The pace, exhaustion and failure—more often than suc-cess—had broken him in a different way. When the war had ended, he'd wanted nothing more than to return to the house left to him by an aunt. He'd spent a few summers in Yorkshire as a child. "It is clean there," he told her.

It was clean, she'd thought when she'd arrived, because it was damned empty. In time, she had come to love the wide sky and spacious dales. The village worshiped her husband. Dr. Edmund Oakes could have had a prosperous city practice but he stayed in Farby. He had grimly devoted himself to the people of Swaledale, but the war had stolen his passion for healing.

And his passion for her as well.

That was the past, as cold and gone as Edmund himself. He left her with this house, a small income and just enough knowledge for her to help in some small way the people of her dale.

As well as newcomers to Swaledale. She looked down at her unconscious companion. Her days had been much the same for a very long time. She worked hard and it was rewarding work. She told herself that she was fortunate, reminded herself that many a widow had been left with nothing but sad memories and a sadder lack of prospects.

The magnificent newcomer, with his air of mystery and obvious urban sophistication, was like a change in the wind. She felt on edge, something long buried in her spirit stirring.

Jittery ... as if she felt a storm brewing.

Perhaps it was not the stranger himself that disturbed her, but simply the reminder of a world outside the Dales, a world where people like the ones that she used to know laughed and talked, drank tea together, sang and danced, made love in the dark of night, made children, made families.

She had once believed it was her duty to mourn Edmund eternally. Now she found herself less sure of that.

Perhaps I am not so terribly old. There might still be something like that for me somewhere.

Yet how could she leave here? How could she go beyond these dales to find companionship of the sort that she did not have here? Should she leave before Jennie birthed her child, with no one but Shepherd Gosling and his silver-haired mother to help her?

The spring storms were coming and the river would swell. It was a dangerous time for the children as well. Could she walk away from the broken bones and the childhood fevers and leave her people with nothing?

For they were her people. She'd not been born in the Dales, but far away in Cambridgeshire. She was no duchess, no lord's wife. She had not been born into a position of noblesse oblige. Her father had been the Head Librarian for Cambridge University. A learned gentleman indeed, but not one to concern himself with stature.

Yet here she was, the accidental Lady of the Dale, dispenser of medicines, binder of wounds, birther of babes. And here she must stay, or she could never again meet her own gaze in a looking-glass, knowing she had deserted a community that needed her so desperately.

The Lady of the Dale. Alone in her castle—well, rambling manor house, with a leaky roof and far more rooms than needed. Her acres were rented out for grazing and farming and she was not terribly forceful about receiving those rents, especially during the recent lean years. All those sons who had not come home had left their families so profoundly bereft of help and hope.

Gemma sighed and brushed her hair back from her forehead with the back of a damp hand. She might be a gentleman's daughter, but she was a bit over-qualified to be a lady of leisure, and at the same time felt terribly under-qualified for the rest of her role.

Look at this fellow before her. This man might be beyond any help she could give. How was she to heal those inner hurts? Should she even try? Should she bind up his head, put him back on his fine horse and send him on his way?

For the rest of her life she would wonder what became of him twenty miles farther down the road. Mr. Bing was quite correct about one thing. She was rather too liable to take in strays, although she had never taken in one quite as handsome as this.

She adjusted his covers, smoothing them across his shoulders. Fine, wide shoulders on a well built man. Too thin, that was for certain. She ran her hand down his arm lying above the covers. The sleeve of the loaned nightshirt was a little too short, revealing a beautifully muscled forearm. Absently she took his pulse, then let her fingertips wander upward over the warm fine-grained skin between his wrist and elbow. He seemed somehow as if he were being burned up from the inside. Worn to muscle and bone. Even in sleep, the small creases around his eyes and mouth did not entirely ease.

There had been that flash of dark eyes in the single moment when their gazes had met. Shadowed eyes. Tortured?

So many things had been done in war, so many terrible things asked of the boys and men and yes, the women too. Things no one should have to do. She shut her eyes against the memories of the medical tents.

Then she realized that she still had her hand on him, was still smoothing the covers over his chest and shoulders, then stroking her fingers down to that bit of warm skin of his arm. She pulled her hand away, alarmed by being so starved for touch. It was one thing to acknowledge her own loneliness. It was quite another to pet her unconscious patient.

She leaned back in the chair and wearily closed her eyes. There was a state of half sleep, something that all nurses and doctors knew. A watchful sleep, ready to awaken at the slightest sound. She could spend all night sitting in a chair in that state and had done so more than once in the past. Yet, as her thoughts slipped into that wakeful sleep she let her memories slip back to what it was like to have a husband. To sleep next to a man, to feel his touch, to lie with him and wake with him and dine with him and live with him. And to live without him.

Edmund had been nearly fifteen years her senior. As her thoughts faded away she wondered what it would be like to be touched again by a man her own age.

Chapter 6

MEANWHILE, BACK IN LONDON…

A TALANTA WORTHINGTON STOOD in a grim, dripping alleyway behind a row of posh shops. No one would notice she was gone from Worthington House and Attie wanted, just for a moment, to feel as though she wasn't slowly fading from human sight. Nor was she being neglectful of her duties. Some people perceived her as a child run wild, she knew, but she had her own ethical philosophy, built from reason and evidence and not simply habit or tradition.

She would do absolutely anything for any Worthington family member, born, wed or adopted.

The rest of the world could go hang.

So far this morning, she had kept company with Aurora, which helped Miranda and Cas rest. Benefiting three at once, which appealed to Attie's sense of efficiency. She'd peeled and chopped everything for Philpot to prepare a stew for dinner, which fed seven. She was supposed to be resting at this very moment actually, but Attie had never been much of a sleeper.

Iris used to tell stories about Archie walking the halls of Worthington House all night long reciting plays out loud to wakeful infant Attie. He'd run entirely through Shakespeare more than twice, he claimed.

A half hour of dozing curled up in the big chair in Miranda's sitting room had dealt with Attie's exhaustion and filled her with a restless desire to escape. She'd slipped out through a parlor window because using the front door bored her. In her boyish garb, it had been a simple matter to saunter unimpeded through the streets of London. No one glanced at her twice in the gray of the afternoon drizzle.

The very fine dressmaking shop of the famous Lementeur backed up to this alleyway. Attie had come to see her friend Button.

After all, Miranda had promised to keep certain people informed of Iris's condition. So Attie was simply here to keeping that promise. She'd come to apprise Button and his assistant Cabot of the situation (benefiting three, including herself, for there would be tea and biscuits).

Attie wasn't likely to admit it, but it just might be that right now she was the one in need of a bit of comforting. It wasn't as though she could ask such a thing of Miranda and Cas, or weary Philpot or exhausted, terrified Archie.

So here she was. She could knock, or she could keep walking. In some way it suited her to be cold and grim and gray. It was as if she didn't want to be comforted, as if being cheered up would somehow betray those in Worthington House who were so very worried.

Something cold trickled between her toes. She looked down at the scuffed and apparently leaking boy's boots that she wore, inherited from one of the twins probably. She had found them on one of her raids through the empty rooms in Worthington House, the ones on the upper story, the ones Miranda had not quite put in order yet.

The dusty chambers were filled with trunks and strange oddities, like theater props and outrageous masks and strange and lumpy things that looked as though they were meant to look like rocks or tree trunks but were actually seats. There were spangled lengths of cloth and exotic embroidered sashes and funny shoes that curled up with the toes and even bizarre wigs that had gone a bit discolored and didn't smell at all nice.

Among the flotsam and jetsam of her parents' former lives there were also trunks of old clothing, mostly that of growing boys saved for the next growing boy to wear. There were no more boys to come. Only Attie, who found trousers comfortable and vastly more durable than something silky and restricting that she had to be careful of and couldn't sit on the floor in, or climb in, or make her flinch away slightly in alarm when she caught a glance of herself reflected in a window or looking glass.

Attie had no interest in growing up and even less interest in becoming a "young lady" as Miranda put it.

Ever.

"I realize that my humble shop cannot offer the same comforts as this fine alleyway, but if you should feel so inclined, I believe Cabot has just made a nice hot pot of tea."

At the familiar, kindly voice, Attie didn't look up from her station leaning against the brick wall of the building opposite and standing with her arms folded across her thankfully still-flat chest as she watched the rain dripping from her hat brim. "What kind of tea?"

It was a marvelous brew of Chinese tea, actually, accompanied by a truly sumptuous plate of iced tea cakes, each crowned with a single perfect candied hazelnut. Elektra would have said it was too pretty to eat. Attie thought that was foolishness. After all, if she didn't eat it, it would eventually become a pile of rotted cake. And therefore no longer pretty, whether she ate it or not.

As she drank the hot tea and munched a sizable dent into the bounty heaped on the plate, she felt her spirits rise in the cozy, familiar environment of Button's workroom.

When Attie had been small she was wont to spend her time playing beneath her mother's easel. This habit had nearly driven her elder sister Callie mad with frustration, for it had been Callie who felt the need to comb and sometimes cut the spatters of oil paint from Attie's hair.

To Attie, that spot had been a lovely place to sit and read or draw or just have a think, until she had grown regretfully too tall and her head began to bump into the crossbars of the easel. Iris had borne it far longer than she should have, but she was disturbing her mother's concentration as she dabbed at another marvelous portrait of Shakespeare, With Rooster, or Piglet, or sometimes With Pigeons.

Iris never breathed a word about the bump-induced flaws, the pigeon that had three legs or Shakespeare cross-eyed or how there would be no fixing the lopsidedness of the great man's mustache. But Attie respected her mother's innovative talent too much, so she'd bid goodbye to her favorite place.

Button's workroom felt like that place. It was terribly messy and outrageously cluttered, a constantly expanding explosion of talent. Sketches and watercolors and swatches of fabric and lengths of ribbon and patches of lace were pinned up on every wall and scattered across every surface. They were layered, year upon year, season upon season, lady after lady. The life's work of the foremost dressmaker in all of England.

"S' good!"

Attie slid her gaze toward her companion, who had his cheeks stuffed like a chipmunk with teacakes. The slightly bushy eyebrows over his bright blue eyes wriggled up and down as he chewed with delight.

Of course, the cakes were good. Cabot had made them. Cabot did everything perfectly. Tall and soulfully beautiful, Button's screamingly glamorous assistant was the exact opposite of short, balding, puckish Button. Some people believed they were artist and model. Others believed they were genius and protégé.

Even Attie, who knew them as well as anyone except perhaps Iris, found their relationship intriguing and mysterious. She was fairly certain that Cabot would never wish to be parted from Button. She was also fairly certain that Button would quietly expire without Cabot.

Yet for a time in the past year they had separated while Cabot took on the important and prestigious honor of fashion consultant to the Prince Regent. Prinny was old and very chubby and probably ought to be thinking about more important things than the shape of his shoe buckles, but far be it from Attie to judge another free spirit.

Besides, Iris liked him. She smiled whenever he came up in conversation, and referred to him as "dear Georgie", although Attie didn't know why.

It annoyed Attie that some things were barred from her knowledge until she reached her full height, developed a bosom, and somehow obtained the key that opened the magical door of adulthood. Well, if no one would tell her, she would simply interfere and investigate and pry until she learned it for herself, the way she did everything.

She swallowed the last bite of cake and washed it down with the dregs of her tea, enjoying a noisy slurp. Button joined her in the sip and the slurp and when the cups were set down upon the tea table, Button leaned back in his tattered, overstuffed velvet chair.

"It's finished."

With relief, Attie realized that Button wasn't going to endlessly hash over Iris's condition and the tense situation at Worthington house. Unfortunately, he'd chosen another one of her least favorite topics.

She scowled down into her empty teacup. "I don't want it."

Button smiled and went on as if she hadn't spoken. "It's perfect. It will fit you exquisitely, bring out the vivid red of your hair while simultaneously making your green eyes shine. You'll be as slim as a willow and as graceful as a deer. There isn't a young lady in London who wouldn't want this gown."

The dreaded, fabled "Young Lady". Attie was well on her way to hating her.

"She can have it," Attie lashed back. "Fetch me a pair of shears, and I'll cut her a piece."

Cabot, who had entered on stealthy feet to retrieve the tea tray, ruined his usual discreet invisibility by narrowing his eyes at Attie and then flicking her on the ear with the snap of his finger.

Attie clapped a finger over her ear and glared at Cabot. Most people in Attie's acquaintance avoided that glare. It usually presaged some sort of entirely unique and creative revenge, something that would occur when Attie was nowhere about to blame.

Cabot wasn't most people. He simply gazed at her without any expression whatsoever, his perfect features an absolute mask of neutrality.

Attie wilted. "Sorry. No shears."

Cabot made no response whatsoever other than to release Attie from the brutal lance of his even gaze. He swept the tea tray from the room without the merest clink of silverware.

Attie looked back to Button. "But I really don't need a new dress. I still have the one you gave me last year. The yellow one."

"Ah, yes. Isn't that the yellow dress that you wore whilst climbing a tree and leaping upon the back of a murderer? In the woods? During a duel?"

"That's the one." Attie idly toyed with a length of ribbon she'd found beneath her chair. "It still fits fine."

"It's mended. And stained. And too short. You've grown a mile."

Attie rolled her eyes and slumped back into her seat in disgust. She thought of a thousand cutting things she could say about the dress but Cabot might be listening. Her ear still stung. "I like trousers," she grumbled. "Trousers have pockets."

"It's a beautiful dress and it's already finished. You may as well take it as not, for I doubt there are very many willowy young ladies who could carry it off." Button leaned back in his own chair and steepled his fingers. "Or who could afford it," he said with some satisfaction.

Everyone knew that Lementeur gowns cost the moon and a half. Every fashionable lady of London recklessly bankrupted her family coffers for one or two of the exquisite works that were guaranteed to make the most of her assets and render her flaws negligible—or even miraculously turn them into assets as well!

However, Worthingtons didn't pay. Attie didn't know why and she really didn't care, but although their house was comfortably shabby and their carriage rickety and their horses old—but beloved!—they all still wore the most brilliant fashions of the great and elite Lementeur.

Attie had decided some time ago that Button must've lost a bet. Probably with one of the twins.

It didn't really matter to her, for she had no intention of dressing in other than her own preferred wardrobe of baggy gowns swiped from her elder sisters storage trunks accessorized with trousers and boots swiped from her brothers. In the alley, she'd worn a shepherd's cap and an old seaman's coat. Her cousin Bliss had married a ship captain. Attie had scrounged in their storage trunks as well, on a boring rainy day much like today. Secretly, of course.

Abruptly she wearied of Button's insistence. Time for a counterattack. "I want to know the truth about Cabot."

Button's cordially piercing gaze dropped at once. If he had been anyone else, Attie would've felt a twinge of triumph. But scoring points off Button—sweet, generous, loving, uncomplicated Button—well, it was simply cheap. She was ashamed of herself. Wild horses and bamboo splinters under her nails would never convince her to admit such a thing out loud, but she did have a fledgling, awkward sort of conscience. It was creaky from disuse, and she preferred to keep it locked in a cage and fed rarely, but she had one nonetheless.

She couldn't take it back without making it worse so she looked away too and said nothing more, giving him the opportunity to ignore her.

To her astonishment, Button actually answered her.

"Cabot is working with me again, having tendered his resignation with the Prince Regent. It's wonderful to have things go back to normal, of course. I'm terribly happy about it."

Attie knew she wasn't the most sensitive person in the world, but even she could see that Button was not quite happy about it. She very seriously doubted there was anything normal about it either. If the two of them were any more stilted or awkward with each other, she'd have imagined them to be strangers.

She thought for a long moment and then carefully ventured a neutral comment. "He seems satisfied to be back."

Button's pensive expression lightened somewhat. "Do you really think so? Such a prestigious position to walk away from! Of course, it must've been a terrible sacrifice."

From the stories that her family told of 'dear Georgie', Attie thought perhaps working closely with the Prince Regent might be a mixed bag of gifts, rather. Some delightfully intriguing, and some rather like smelly cheeses that were terribly expensive but no one wanted to eat.

"But things are quite usual again, now. Better even!" Since Button's happiness looked a bit like grim determination and wistful confusion, it must mean that he found Cabot as inscrutable as everyone else did.

Attie narrowed her eyes in frustration. "But *why* did he come back?" And why had he left in the first place?

"Well, I suppose. I mean, clearly—" Button's fingers folded around each other and he stared down at his whitened knuckles. "I—"

"Miss Atalanta."

Attie swiveled her head on her neck without sitting up, to look over her shoulder at Cabot standing in the doorway with a dancer's—or an assassin's—poise. "Yes?"

"I have retained the services of a hack to return you to Worthington House. You mustn't walk home in the rain." His gaze sharpened on her somewhat. "It would not do for you to become sick as well."

Home. Quiet, tense, disaster-tinged home.

Attie stood and, without consciously doing so, matched Cabot's dignified stance. "Very well. Thank you, Cabot."

Dear Button was like an uncle to her. Or a playmate. Attie dropped a kiss on his thinning hair. Although she was rarely affectionate, when he touched her cheek in farewell, she pressed his palm to her face with her hand. Even lost in thought, Button was the most comforting person she knew.

Aside from Iris.

She followed Cabot out in silence, assuming that he was still irritated with her for her obnoxious behavior. Attie was well aware that she'd been obnoxious. She usually didn't care.

However, as Cabot helped her on with her boiled wool pea coat and her still damp cap, he lifted her chin with one finger and gazed into her eyes. "If you'll wear the dress he made for you, *I* will tell you 'the truth about Cabot'."

Attie gazed at him for a long moment and for the first time got an inkling why most women became instantly scatterbrained when encountering Cabot. He really was incredibly handsome. As perfect as a prince in a painting—and just as unattainable. Poor Button.

"Will it have pockets?"

Chapter 7

LYSANDER KEPT HIS eyes shut tight and waited for the next hammer blow to his brain. Much better. The pace of the blows was flagging, and the force was mercifully less.

Now that he could think past that attack from within, Lysander took a moment to ponder the fact that he clearly lay in a bed, a proper bed, and not some pallet in a barn, for example.

He listened for a moment but heard no sound. Not Worthington House then. Though large and rambling, Worthington house was full of people, full of sound, full of music and poetry and the never-ending chatter of people who lived loudly and large.

All tinged throughout with just a hint of Iris's turpentine. It was everywhere.

Iris painted as the spirit moved her, in whichever room of the house took her fancy, although Miranda had finally managed to convince her not to perch on the front steps in a paint-spattered nightdress even though the light was "marvelously luminous" out front.

Thinking of Iris, Lysander was reminded of the true state of affairs at home. Iris was ill. There was no laughter at home, just a tense and worried silence. He'd previously thought the raucous household sometimes more than he could bear, but that had been nothing in comparison to the weight and pressure of his family's worry for their mother.

Pol. He was on his way to find Pollux. A useless mission,

following the trail of a months-old missive, but one that Lysander had welcomed for the excuse to leave that twisting tension behind.

He had been riding. Yorkshire. A turn down a side road. It would take longer but Icarus could surely make up the miles.

Icarus. Where was Icarus? He could not remember. Daedalus would not be happy with him, not at all.

Perhaps it was the urge to find out what had become of his brother's fine horse that finally pried open his eyes against the thumping in his skull.

He saw nothing. He blinked, again and again, trying to clear his vision. Then he felt something cold drip onto his ear. He reached a hand to his face. The movement hurt a bit. He ached everywhere, as if covered in bruises from a beating. His hand touched damp cloth.

His eyes were covered but not bandaged. He moved to remove the cloth from the upper half of his face. A gravelly voice halted him.

"Leave it, lad. Let me pull t' curtains first. It's still a bit bright out."

Lysander heard the thumping of boots on a wooden floor and the thick rustle of curtains moving. He sensed the room became dimmer even though masked by the cool cloth.

"Aye then. Go ahead."

Carefully, Lysander lifted the wet fabric from his face and blinked, frowning painfully.

"Can you see, then? Can you see clear?"

Lysander rolled his head to one side, focused on the source of the voice. He blinked and brought into view a man, a wiry older fellow, although not as old as Archie Worthington.

The fellow was smaller than Lysander's father, bent and dressed in rough country clothing. His waistcoat was a lumpy knitted affair and he wore the boots of a farmer. Despite his balding head, there was nothing vague about the man's quick blue eyes beneath his bushy salt-and-pepper brows.

"I see." Lysander cleared his throat. "Horse?"

The fellow's upswept brows lifted and he gave a grunt. "It's nice to see a young lad with his priorities in order." The man stood. "Your silly horse be takin' a lap about the dale. There's nowt can catch him, long-legged racer that he is. Some of the village lads are keeping an eye on him. Got a pocket full of carrots ready for when he calms down."

Lysander swallowed and began to push against the bed, trying to sit up. "I can—" Except, clearly he could not.

He did manage to sit up a bit, leaning against his pillows on the headboard. There didn't seem to be anything wrong with his body other than its bruised condition. Lysander ran a careful hand over his head and discovered the lump on the back of it.

Oh yes, that hurt. It even hurt to touch his hair. The pounding in his head increased for a moment but after he remained still, it eased off somewhat. He returned his gaze to the man. "Icarus. Icky. Call him."

"Icarus." The fellow shook his head in disgust. "The things you posh sorts name your beasts."

You should meet my siblings.

The man moved to the door of the room. "I'll tell the missus you're awake. I expect you be wantin' me to walk all the way into the village, just to tell someone to trudge about the dale, yelling 'Icky' at the top of his lungs. And me with t' war wound!" With a faint noise of derision, the man limped from the room.

Lysander took that moment to absorb his surroundings. It was a large room, albeit quite plain and functional. He could see from the arched casement of the window and the fine marble mantle on the fireplace that this was a larger house and not a simple shepherd's dwelling.

Yet the room was bare of anything but the bed, the small table at his side that held the basin, and the chair the man had been sitting in. Even a servant's room would have more furnishings than this, although it was clearly a spacious bedchamber.

His curiosity lived at some distance and did not inspire any deep interest. He thought it odd, a puzzle, yet it was a puzzle he felt no urge to solve. It was simply information which he had no idea what to do with. Even the country man's obvious scorn had no effect on him. In fact, it was very nearly soothing to know precisely what someone was thinking and not be put to the strenuous effort of solving yet another human riddle.

Icarus wasn't a stupid horse, nor was he exceptionally flighty, but horses were notional creatures sometimes. If Icky had taken a scare, he would simply have to run himself out. He was well trained but he was also something of a family pet, and Lysander had no doubt that when the horse's belly began to rumble he would find his way to those oats.

The missing shoe was a problem. Lysander hoped the thoroughbred didn't crack a hoof.

The dale itself was nothing but a great grassy swath, with the river that had cut it running cheerfully in the deepest crease. Even the stone walls that Lysander had seen would not pose a danger to a high-jumping thoroughbred like Icarus. If the sheep were safe in the pastures, so then should a somewhat foolish horse be.

Lysander stayed very still and with the ease of great practice, emptied his mind. This was a very quiet house, in a simple, unoccupied way. He let that silence seep into him, breathing it in like cool, clean air. It was beautiful, that barrenness. Unpolluted and uncomplicated, like this room.

The thin line of brightness shining between the drawn

curtains began to fade. Evening came early in the North. He did a bit of math and realized he'd been out for more than half the day. That certainly explained the pounding in his head. He closed his eyes again, not resisting the pain, not really caring about it either.

He remained that way until he detected sounds outside his door, footsteps on wooden stairs and down the hall, growing louder as they approached. He recognized the stomp of the man's rough boots but there was another lighter step as well, barely audible over the first.

He heard a whispered consultation outside the door. Lysander didn't bother to interpret it. He simply didn't care. He was clearly in the hands of people who had cared for him and meant him no harm. That was all he needed to know.

He opened his eyes at the turn of the latch and looked toward the door, resigned that now there would be conversation and questions and answers and that people would expect things. He only hoped that the ordeal would be quick and they would leave him alone again in the quiet of this room.

He blinked at the glare of a candle and realized how dark the room had become.

Then *she* stepped through the door, the pretty woman he'd seen in the pavilion. She was even more entrancing at close examination. A cool, quiet beauty dressed sedately in a somber gown that didn't quite manage to hide her lithe figure. Lysander found himself unable to look away from her.

As she walked toward the bed, Lysander realized that his first impression of her youth had been incorrect. She looked to be close to his own age. There was just a faint suggestion of lines in the corners of her eyes, but it was more than that. She did not have the gaze of innocence or the eager, seeking look of youthful questions.

She was all the more intriguing for it. Lysander felt a strange sense of surprise at himself to be supporting such a thought. In his life, he was surrounded by fine-looking women. His sisters were considered beauties all. Even Iris still wore the gently fading blush of her own tremendous appeal. His brother's wife, Miranda, was known to be a stunner, as well. Loveliness was no novelty to him. He would've thought it beyond his notice.

Perhaps it was not the symmetry of her cheekbones or the smoothness of her brow or the way that her hair, twisted sensibly up on her head, caught the gleam of the candle to show all the colors from russet brown to black. As he remembered, her eyes were gray, with startlingly dark lashes. Her skin was not the protected porcelain of a lady of Society, but something rather more lively, kissed by sun and wind.

As she set the pewter candleholder down upon the small side table, she moved with refined grace, the sort taught from infancy to ladies. When she sat in the vacated chair she posed herself upright with her hands on her lap. Lysander had the oddest impression of formality. *She's come to tea*, he thought.

For that was the way she gazed at him. There was nothing but cool inquiry in her eyes. They held no particular welcome nor any particular aversion. There was no sign at all of avid curiosity.

With the feeling that she expected very little of him, Lysander felt a wash of relief. He waited in silence. She would surely ask questions. Hopefully not too many.

Yet she said nothing. She tilted her head once and her gaze became distant and clinical as she looked him over keenly. It reminded him of the impersonal examination of a physician. Then, apparently satisfied with what she saw, she returned to her cool and expectant poise.

Lysander didn't want to speak first. He never spoke

first. He spoke as little and as shortly and as rarely as absolutely necessary. Gathering words exhausted him. Yet he found himself taking a breath and parting his lips.

"Thank you," he said flatly.

The woman nodded. "You are welcome."

No questions. Not even a remark to express hospitality, to ask him from whence he came, or to inquire into his purpose there.

Now he was the one seized by curiosity about her. She was clearly a lady, but not well-off. Her gown was plain and serviceable, a darker gray than her eyes.

The country fellow remained standing by the door and Lysander was caught by the hint of a man on military guard duty. The man was a former soldier.

Lysander's mind fled that notion and fixed his attention once more upon the lady facing him. It occurred to Lysander—and things rarely occurred to Lysander—that he must look very strange to her. He lay in a bed in what was likely her house, wearing a fine linen nightshirt that ran a bit tight across the shoulders. He was fairly certain that the country man was not the source of the nightwear. The fellow was quite slight and this nightshirt was very nearly Lysander's size. Did it belong to a brother? A husband? Her dark dress could be considered the color of mourning, or perhaps it was only a practical color in this rural life.

He found himself looking at her hands. However, they gave no clue, settled neatly in her lap, half covered by the cuffs of her long sleeves.

Something bubbled up from deep within him. If he was not mistaken, it was the urge to speak more to her. He considered that for a moment. Then, choosing his question and calculating the least number of necessary words, he spoke. "What happened?"

"You rode your horse into our village and destroyed our festival. You broke the pavilion and it fell on you. You have been in and out of consciousness for several hours."

How beautifully succinct. How soothing. Not a shred of extraneous information, no expression of emotion, even though she clearly considered that he was responsible for his own state. He remembered riding into some sort of spring fair. He'd seen ranks of trestle benches bowing with the weight of vegetable and flower displays. There had been dogs and children underfoot and temporary pens put up in the square containing piglets and lambs.

Sheep. "A ram."

The man beside the door shuffled his feet and gave a grunt. "A prize ram. He's Shepherd Orren's champion stud, the pride of Swaledale. Ruined the festival, you did. The whole village has a bone to pick with you, lad. The women in partic'lar. Every lass in the dale was intent on dancin'."

The lady did not turn to regard her companion but kept her gaze fixed upon Lysander. "Yes, there was a ram."

Lysander held one palm hard to his temple, counterpressure against the thumping in his head. "Icky. Took offense."

"The offense appeared to be mutual. And then you made the entire matter worse." The woman regarded him evenly. "I have never seen a man wrestle a ram before. Is this something they do where you are from?"

Finally a question. "No." He could not recall encountering many sheep in London.

"Well, lad, in the kerfuffle ye broke all the prize flower displays, set loose the pigs, and took down the pavilion what Dr. Oakes himself paid to put up." The country man shot Lysander a glare full of indignation. "You could'na made more havoc if you tried. You broke everything."

The man nodded his head toward the woman with accusation in his eyes targeting Lysander. Everything?

Lysander looked again at the woman in the chair. Beneath her polished calm, he finally noted the slight shadows beneath her eyes and a small scrape high on one cheekbone. His eyes traveled down, looking for more damage. Then he realized that her hands were not actually folded in her lap, but that her left hand cradled her right wrist and that the wrist itself was thickened by bandages beneath her long sleeve. Lysander's belly flipped queasily. What had he done to her?

Although his battlefield experiences had left him unsure of many things, of right and wrong, of socially suitable reactions, the one thing that never faltered has been his protective instinct toward his mother and sisters, toward all women.

Clearly he had done a great deal of damage in his extreme response.

You broke everything.

"I'm ... sorry." He wished for better words. He wasn't quite certain what had happened, but there was that dark empty place in his memory. That was never a good sign. Eventually, the memory might come back to him. Or it might not.

That shadowed blot was the stain of war, of that frenzied state that left him outside himself as if all other parts of him were evicted for a time so that the house that was Lysander could be taken over by a fiend made of pure battle instinct.

"I hurt you." It was not a question. It was clear in the expression of the man that Lysander alone was responsible for the lady's injuries.

"You threw me. It was the landing that did the injury, in fact. I find I much prefer landing a bit wrong on soft grass than to have the pavilion crush me as it did you."

Lysander studied her, ignoring his throbbing head to focus on her expression and her words. He desperately needed to know. "I helped?"

"You truly have no memory of it? Well, when the pavilion began to fall—"

"When you made the pavilion fall!"

The lady ignored the man by the door. "You dashed into the pavilion, picked me up and tossed me aside, among others. Rather incredibly far, if truth be told. You are very strong for being so thin."

"And the roof fell right on your thick head." The man clearly felt that this was no more than Lysander deserved.

Lysander felt such intense relief that his head began to spin a bit. He had not ever intentionally injured anyone in his life—except in the time of war—but in the past few years the dark battle instinct had taken him over on rare occasions.

As if echoing that thought the woman spoke again. "I suppose you were in the war? You are clearly not entirely recovered from your harrowing experience. Are your relations aware you ride through England on your own?"

Lysander's heart sank. He had thought he'd been doing well enough. He had even dared hope, once in a while, that he was getting better, for the nightmares came much less often now and he recovered from them more quickly when they did.

He now walked about London on without incident, for the most part. If this woman, a total stranger, took one look at him and knew that he was broken, he was clearly far from well.

"My sister asked. Find our brother."

She blinked her storm-sky eyes slowly at him for a long moment. "You have siblings."

"Seven."

Something crossed her expression. Longing? He was watching her very carefully, he realized. Watching her every reaction, when for so long he had avoided even meeting the gaze of anyone not immediately related to him. She riveted his attention to a degree he had not experienced in a very long time.

A fresh spike of pain startled him, driving into his skull like a red-hot nails. He flinched and squeezed his head between his hands, clenching his eyes shut. The spikes of light behind his lids flashed like sparked gunpowder.

"Hmm. I suppose that is enough talk for now. A bit of laudanum, I think, Mr. Bing. He is now out of danger of losing consciousness too deeply. I shouldn't think it will do him any harm."

The gravely voice, full of concern. "I'll not leave this room with you in it."

"Very well." The woman let out a sigh, and Lysander heard the scuff of her slipper and the rustle of her skirts as she stood.

"Don't—want it." He'd been kept under the fog of it in the military hospital, subduing his agitation so deeply that they'd not even been able to learn his name for weeks. His family had thought him dead while he languished there in a spiraling opiate dream.

"Well," she said with a hint of asperity, "I don't want a sprained wrist but we must endure, must we not? Just a very little, for the ache in your head. I do insist upon it."

Lysander tried to sit up. *I must go.* The words couldn't hack their way past the searing ache in his head.

"If you rest, you may get up in the morning," she told him briskly. "Until then, you will stay right where you are."

Lysander swallowed his protest against that tone of command. Even the man Bing shifted to when so ordered. After escorting the lady out, he was back with a tiny vial in mere moments and watched carefully while Lysander tipped it back with no more protest. The man clearly meant to make his lady's will happen no matter what Lysander's opinion of it might be.

"Listen to the missus, lad. You can't go anywhere until someone manages to catch that nervy horse of yours, anyway."

Lysander lay back upon the pillows, somewhat reassured by the fact that it had indeed been a very small dose. As the throbbing in his brain began to distance itself and his drowsiness grew, he realized he had not been offered the lady's name.

And he really, really wanted to know.

MR. BING FOUND Gemma in her stillroom, putting away the bottle of laudanum she kept in a locked cabinet. The room smelled of flowers, or perhaps cooking spices, and the sometimes stronger smells of camphor and linseed oil. Bing tended to stay out of that room. He was much too modern a fellow, he assured himself, to believe in talk of witches and such—but when his employer lost herself in her work for days at a time, and he would wander in to find her looking pale and peculiar with her gaze distant and her thoughts elsewhere, he had to wonder.

Well, there was no such thing as witches, and that was that.

Tonight the stillroom was dim with the light of a single candle and there were no mysterious potions boiling away on the small stove in the corner using the pots that she wouldn't let him use for food—not saying that she made poisons exactly, or perhaps she did. He would have no way of knowing.

"It ain't goin' t' work, you know that, Missus."

She didn't look at him as she carefully reattached her small ring of keys to its elegant chatelaine on the hook at her waist.

"You can't bring home every stray and hope to fix 'em all," he insisted.

She ignored him. Instead, she picked up a broom and began to sweep a floor that didn't need sweeping. She was a stubborn one, his Mrs. Oakes. As strong as any Daleswoman, for all her refined Southern ways.

He wasn't going to change her mind, and there was no reason why he should, for he'd never been able to before. Bing gave a heavy, obvious sigh.

"This is the bloody House of Last Resort," he grumbled to himself as he left his mistress to her work.

GEMMA CONTINUED TO put on a show of puttering about amongst her herbs until she was certain Mr. Bing had gone to his room.

Then she slipped from the stillroom with her candle and made her way down the hall to her chamber. As she passed the base of the staircase, she cast a glance upward, but all was silent.

Her visitor was asleep.

All in all, Gemma was rather proud of her dignified exit from the stranger's sickroom earlier. She was fairly certain that Mr. Bing had not detected her profound attraction to the man.

Well, it was certainly understandable. Heavens, what a mouthwatering fellow! If he'd been very handsome when unconscious, he was absolutely devastating while awake!

Those eyes. Gemma walked slowly down the hall, trailing her fingertips lightly on the wall in the dimness. Had she ever seen brown eyes so dark they seemed black? And his fine, well-cut features held Gemma's interest even as they turned her thoughts to wandering. He looked fierce and dark, the very opposite of Edmund, who had been fair and blue-eyed and ruddy from the weather.

Fallen angel.

What a silly notion! Why had that thought popped into her mind?

In her bedchamber, Gemma did without the candle,

nipping out the flame with quick fingers. She preferred the privacy of darkness for some very unusual thoughts. As she struggled one-handed with her gown and her underthings, she let her mind drift to the way the stranger's muscles moved under the borrowed nightshirt.

Gemma had never been immune to noticing a handsome man, for all that the people of Farby thought her aloof. It was only that taking a lover from the dale meant taking a husband or son, brother or cousin of at least a dozen other people who looked to her for help. People who took pride in their decorous and dignified Lady of the Dale.

In the dark privacy of her little room, however, Gemma allowed herself to imagine having a lover. Someone from far away. Someone who would stay and be only hers.

Someone dark and tall, with a shadowed gaze, who would not prattle of gambling or gossip. Someone who had seen the world, who had seen what Gemma had seen.

Her uninjured hand stroked down her neck and skimmed over her breasts and belly. She was too thin, she knew. Hard times had eaten away her curves and left behind some rather unbecoming muscle. She thought she was looking downright boyish these days.

But her breasts were still high and she had good teeth, so she supposed she hadn't entirely lost her looks.

Her hand trailed lower still and she was astonished to find herself damp and ready.

I blame his voice. Although his speech was brief, his voice was so deep that it seemed to rumble right through to her bones, vibrating in places that she'd long ago put away as useless to her.

Heavens, what a stunner.

She realized then that she had not gotten his name. And she really, really wanted to know.

Chapter 8

MEANWHILE, BACK IN LONDON...

I N WORTHINGTON HOUSE, Iris's room was only dimly lit by a small candle in a glass chimney on the side table. The draperies were shut tight, leaving nothing but shadows. It turned the sickroom mysterious and far, far too peaceful.

Iris was never peaceful. Attie stepped stealthily into the sickroom. Her father snored in the chair by the bed with his head tipped back. Archie hadn't bothered with a cravat and Attie looked away from the wrinkled vulnerability of his throat.

The ache that pounded inside her was deafening in the silence. Why couldn't the whole world hear it? Attie wanted to scream, to run, to break things and hit people until they understood the writhing snakes of terror and worry inside her.

For the first time in her life she wished she was older. Either that, or younger, as young as Aurora. It would be heaven not to know, not to worry, not to care.

Attie always thought of her mother as being rather tall and—as Archie put it so fondly—statuesque. But Iris barely made a hillock under the covers and Attie thought there was too much empty bed surrounding her.

Attie had never been the sort of child to tumble into her parents' bed, frightened by a nightmare or thunderstorm. Orion had explained that nightmares were simply her imagination and that thunderstorms were what happened when warm air collided with cold.

Still, she had seen her parents snuggled together with Archie snoring away, Iris's head tucked under his chin. Iris's hair should be streaming glinting silver over the pillow and she should carry a slight smile of delight on her lips as she slept. If dreams were imagination, then Iris must have the most astonishing dreams, for she lived every day in a world of her imagination.

Attie crept onto the large mattress stealthily as might a disobedient family pet.

But Archie was asleep and there was no one to shoo Attie from the sickroom or remind her that she was not a comforting sort of presence. It wasn't true, Attie thought rebelliously. Otherwise why was she the only one—well, almost the only one—who could keep Aurora soothed to let Miranda rest?

Attie crawled closer until her head shared her mother's pillow and she lay staring unblinking at Iris's profile. Iris smelled of lavender soap combined with the revolting laudanum-tinged cough concoction left by the physician who had seen her the day before. Attie rather thought she would throw the bottle across the room before she would take a drop of it, but the first time in her life she didn't have the answers. She had no way to help Iris get well.

It was just a cough. A silly little cough from being caught out in the rain. Of course Iris, being Iris, had stayed out of doors to enjoy the scents of the garden. She said she liked to feel the rain running down her cheeks, and the vibration of the thunder rumbling through her bones.

When she'd come inside, Miranda had rushed to fetch a blanket, calling for Philpot to brew a fresh pot of tea. And Archie had rubbed Iris's cold hands and teased her, calling her his goddess of the spring storms. And Iris had shooed them all away and dreamily rambled on to them how she had seen the mother bird sitting on her nest with her wings spread over hatchlings with her own head tucked down to avoid the downpour.

"*When yellow leaves, or none, or few, do hang,*" Iris had quoted, her voice fragmented by her shivers. "*Upon those boughs which shake against the cold, Bare ruin'd choirs, where late the sweet birds sang.*" She'd turned a vague half-smile on Archie.

The next day Iris had been flushed and a bit tired. By that night she'd had a terrible ache in her head and the lung congestion had begun. "Just a silly cough."

Now Attie closed her eyes and whispered, "Sonnet 73." Iris cared about proper attribution and what the words were about, not just what they said. Attie clenched her eyelids shut tight and thought hard about how she loved her mad, dreamy mother, who was nothing like anyone else in the world, as she listened to the breath moving in and out of her mother's body. A thin sound, strained and tight, with a terrible liquid gurgle at the end.

It was just a silly cough.

LYSANDER STOOD IN a field of smoking rain and thunder—both cannon fire and real thunder, for the barrage had not halted to wait for fair weather. He was wet to the bone, both hot and chilled at once. Rage and terror, in a sick roiling stew deep in his belly. He gripped a musket in his hands but his powder was wet, and he was out of shot. The bayonet was his only defense. Yet as he watched, it disintegrated before his eyes. The crimson blood upon it turned to brown, then to iron flakes that bubbled up and washed away in the rain. The downpour obscured everything, washing the world away, washing the blade right out of existence.

His hands empty now, he was defenseless against the enemy. He wasn't quite sure who the enemy was—was it the French, or the weather, or the muddy pit of Death itself that strove to suck him under?

Again and again, the collapsing siege tunnels closed in. Each time men died choking to death on mud. Lysander clawed his way out against the consuming maw of the blood-tinged mud, slipped, clawed, slipped again, until the dream allowed him to slither out upon solid ground. He was free.

That freedom didn't matter, for he didn't know where to go. He couldn't flee to the medical tents behind the line. Nothing but death awaited anyone who crossed into that canvas wrapped hell. He could not turn toward the enemy and scale the castle walls to attack them where they sat safe and shielded, and watched Death take their side in the conflict. It was some comfort that at least they were as wet as he.

He wanted to call lightning down upon those heights, strike after strike, his fury brought to life in jagged streaks of fire and destruction, but he was powerless.

Powerless. Useless. Helpless.

The thunder boomed louder and louder, and the cannon and the musket fire and the screams of the struck and the dying.

Lysander jerked awake to find himself kneeling on the floor in a darkened room, his mouth stretched open in a silent rictus of dread. He remained quite still at first, freezing himself in place. He knew if he didn't, the dream would carry him on, and things would be broken and people might be hurt. He held himself immobile by force of will, trying to catch the breath which burst from him in great gasping sobs and that he could not seem to get back.

He must stop. He could hear that he sounded insane. He mustn't allow himself to sound mad. He must breathe.

He couldn't tell himself the nightmare wasn't real because it was. He *could* tell himself, however, that it was past. That it was over. That it had ended and he had left it far behind him, even if that assurance felt like a lie.

Why must he carry it? Must he carry it forever?

He knew the answer to that. Of course he did. He knew why he deserved this burden, and why it must follow him.

No. Don't think about Theo. No.

Instead, he thought about his hands. His dry, if somewhat clammy, clean hands. No mud. No blood. They were fisted so tightly he was losing sensation in his fingers. With his full and total concentration, he willed his fists to slowly relax and for his fingers to open one by one.

He had no need of fists to defend himself here. His hands need hold no knife, no firearm, not even a bludgeon. He flattened his open hands downward and rested them on something cool and smooth.

He made himself focus on discovering what that was. It warmed beneath his touch more quickly than stone. Wood, yes. If he slid his fingertips a bit he could feel the grain and the seams between the boards. It was very clean, for no more than a speck of grit presented itself to his touch. Cool and clean, and solid and real.

The wood was a floor. Where was this floor?

Not Worthington house. Too uncluttered and bare. Nor some barracks tent. Not a battlefield pitch. Not a worn marble floor like the hospital. He spread his hands apart, stroking them along the floor seeking clues. His breath was slowing, his lungs laboring much less. When his hands shook slightly he pressed them firmly to floor until they stopped.

Now he remembered. He reached his hand to one side and yes, there was the bed. The clean sheets still smelled of spring line drying. The lumpy featherbed. The thick soft blanket that carried a faint scent of lanolin in its undyed wool.

He was in the clean, quiet room. In the lady doctor's house.

Had his nightmare woken her? He listened but no one

seemed to be rushing to his aid. Perhaps he had not made as much noise as his dream suggested. A chill ran up his back and he realized his nightshirt was sticking to him, soaked with perspiration. Unable to bear the tacky chill, he pulled it from his body and left it in a pile on the floor as he stood. There was a very faint seam of light coming from a window. He made his way toward it, feeling carefully, but no furniture blocked his path in this empty, clean room.

He reached the window and parted the curtains. Yes, there was a bit of light, surprisingly. He thought it would be darker in the country, but although there were a few clouds in the night sky they did allow the gleam from a half-moon to stretch into the room. He waited for a long moment for his eyes to adjust.

He saw the outline of the bed and the bulk of the chair beyond it. There was a table there, he knew, but it was tucked in the shadow to one side of the window.

He remembered seeing his clothing hanging on pegs near the door. Turning, he looked long in that direction. Once his eyes adjusted, he walked to them easily, reaching for the mingled dark and light of his trousers and shirt.

His coat was not there but his feet kicked something on the floor. He reached down and found his boots. That was enough.

In trousers, boots, and his shirt untucked and open, for there were no studs to be found, he stood for a long moment in the empty room. He would not sleep again. There was no point in trying. The dream was too close, hovered too near, whispering to him in the back of his mind. He needed to think of something else. He needed to do something else.

He needed to walk. The view from the window drew him. The bucolic dale outside was only lightly brightened by the shy half-moon, but it would do. Outside would be better, where he could smell the grass and feel the breeze and know that it was not raining and there was no fire and no blood and no screaming.

To leave by making his way through a house he did not know seemed insurmountable, while just outside this window began the slanted roof of what looked like a portico of some kind. It would do. He climbed out, his mission giving him surety of hand and foot. His desperation to leave the dream behind gave him incentive to clamber down to the ground. He had to drop the last bit but he landed softly in the grass.

The scent hit him first.

Lysander had long repressed his sense of smell, for it seemed that everything in the world was tinged with the metallic stink of blood, from the coal soot and carthorse droppings of the London streets to the dusty bookshops he'd used to love to visit.

Now, with the drop from the roof pushing the breath from his lungs, he inhaled the full and heady scent of rose. He drew back from the power of it, but there was no escape. It was all around him. He'd dropped into a small grassy patch in the middle of a rose infestation the likes of which he'd never seen.

No tame city garden this! The canes towered and tangled in a wall that began in a fall down the side of the house and wound all about him. He blinked and hesitated. How to escape the entwined vigor of it? He could not climb them, for even a brief touch informed him that the arching staves that absolutely dripped with blooms also carried thorns with intent to bodily harm.

Helplessly, he peered up at the moon only to see the leafy canes silhouetted black against the light. The richness of the air was as heady as wine, and he felt near to drowning in it. It was mad. It was ridiculous. It was an aggressive wealth of overgrowth and extravagance, especially after the monastic cleanliness of his room.

Iris would adore this.

Lysander, however, did not appreciate the confinement, no matter how potently scented. The high walls nearly formed a tunnel, and the very thought made him break into a sweat once more. Thorns or no, he was leaving this floral prison and he was leaving it straightaway.

His eyes began to make some sense of the shadows—it was *not* a tunnel, he reminded himself grimly—and he saw a slightly grayer distinction in the darkness off to one side, heading away from the house. Careful exploration led him to a curve in the wall and a paler grassy path leading onward. The passage through the riotous blooms didn't appear to go anywhere at all, until he found another turn, and then another. A few more yards and he'd freed himself from the mad profusion to see nothing before him but the moonlight on a grassy hillside stretching onward into the night.

Away. He didn't care which direction. Away from the dream and the room that had held it, away from the bed where he'd dreamt it, away from anyone who might come running with candles and sympathy and tea and questions.

He simply walked straight until something made him turn. A brook, a stone wall, a slope too slick and steep. He stopped once, breathing hard, realizing that he had very nearly been running.

Slow down. Slow breaths. Be aware of where you are. Nothing is chasing you, you have nothing to fear.

He heard a slight sound behind him. Whirling, he lurched backward, his hands out as if to fend off an attack, his body crouched ready for a fight.

There was no one there. No one, except a dog, a shaggy multicolored thing. Lysander could see a gleam of its white teeth as its mouth hung open. It panted happily at him, and Lysander wondered how long it had been trailing in the wake of his mad rush. The animal seemed entirely pleased with him, as if Lysander had asked it along on a companionable ramble in the middle of the night.

There was no farm nearby but the house he just left. Did it belong to the lady doctor? Or the man?

In the dim moonlight, Lysander couldn't tell the dog's color but he could see gleaming dark eyes peering out from under shaggy brows and large feathery ears that looked very nearly bat-like in the dark.

Lysander supposed that people ought to speak to dogs, as he was certain that he used to do. However, the dog seem perfectly content to simply sit on its haunches with the end of its tail flipping methodically on the scruffy grass of the hill. The creature tilted its head at him curiously, but when he did not move toward it, the dog jumped up and scuttled awkwardly off a few feet away. Then it stopped and looked back at him intently.

It was exhausting enough trying to puzzle out the humans around him. Lysander had nothing left to give a dog tonight. He turned his back on it and continued on his way, albeit at a more leisurely pace than before. Perhaps it was the distraction of the animal, or the cool crisp night, or perhaps he'd merely worn the dream out in his furiously paced walk, but he felt much calmer now.

He tried to think seriously about what he ought to do next. Surely that was what sensible people did. They put some thought into what they ought to do next.

Lysander usually waited for someone in his family to indicate his direction. It was easier that way, for they became disturbed when he went off on his own, or reacted strangely. Since he woke in the hospital with his shoulder bandaged and his mind full of waking nightmares, Lysander had realized that there was something rather permanently wrong with him.

Even his own family were like strangers. When first he'd been brought home, he very nearly feared them, for they seem to know so much about him and he seemed to know nothing about them. He remembered them, of course. It wasn't as though he had his memories cleaned from his mind as some of the soldiers had. It was more as though his emotions had been wrested from his heart instead. There stood before him his mother and his father and his sisters and his brothers.

And he felt nothing.

That had passed finally, for one could not remain in the midst of all that generous outpouring of love and not absorb such a tutoring of the heart. His love was different now, however, fierce and mute and protective instead of gentle and laughing. Sometimes he almost thought it ran deeper than before. He'd been careless with that love at one time. He'd been careless with his friends, his brothers, his sisters, and most especially his parents. Someone named Lysander had grown up in that house so immersed in love that he breathed it in and considered it as little as he did the very air around him.

He'd sauntered fecklessly away from that love, donning a uniform as if it were yet another costume, a bit of family playacting, a merry bit of theater. He remembered that the other Lysander had done that but now he could not imagine he had ever felt that way himself. Careless, stupid man—to have no fear of what was to come.

"Hero" wasn't a word that Lysander believed in anymore. Neither was "Coward." He'd learned through harsh experience that there could come a dark place of fear so deep that one really had no choice about how one reacted to it.

A scuffling sound came from in front of him and Lysander look down, pausing in mid-step. The dog was in front of him, facing him with its head lowered. The bushy tail no longer whacked happily. Eyeing it warily, Lysander moved to step around it. The dog moved to match him and continue to block his way.

It is herding me.

Was he a sheep, to be so directed by this shaggy beast?

Lysander took a moment to seriously ponder the question. Now that he thought about it, it did seem sheep-foolish to be stalking around an unfamiliar landscape in the dark. The moon was dimming behind a thin sheen of clouds. The bit of light he had might soon be gone.

He lifted his head and looked about him. He could still see the vague line of the path he was on cutting through the grass but very little else was visible. Even if there were farmsteads within sight, likely they would have no lanterns lighted at this hour.

Lysander looked back down at the dog.

How is it that you are allowed to ride through England on your own?

Perhaps the lady doctor had a valid point, if this madly tufted shepherd dog had more sense than he did to be strolling about in the dark of night.

He turned around in place to face the opposite way. The dog came to his side and panted up at him happily. Apparently, this was the correct direction. His hand was hanging at his side and the dog shoved its cold damp nose into his palm. He let his fingers linger in the shaggy, silky fur and toyed with the ridiculously large ears for a moment.

Then he began to walk, with his new friend at his side. He had faith that the dog would take him where he needed to be.

Chapter 9

G EMMA AROSE AN hour after dawn. Her room was a small chamber on the first floor, not far from her stillroom. It was probably meant to be a housekeeper's room or lady's morning room but she managed to fit her bed into it after the mistress's chamber had developed a leak in the eaves. She had asked some of the village men to help patch it up and they had begun the work cheerfully enough, but had not been done before winter, and then lambing season had kept everyone so busy, and then there was planting to do.

Well, their livelihoods were certainly more important than fixing the damp and musty bedroom.

She'd liked her old room for the windows. She'd always risen effortlessly when that beautiful early light poured through the glass. Her current bedchamber remained dark far later and when she awoke, she tended to feel cross until she'd downed her first cup of tea.

Dressing herself was exasperating. She did up most of her buttons before she donned her gown. She'd never had a lady's maid, not being an actual lady, even when Edmund yet lived. The only full-time man had been Mr. Bing then, as now, but Edmund had provided cash employment for many other day workers.

Gemma grimaced at the memory of considering herself busy when her sole responsibility was supervising others and cooking only when she was in the mood.

Of course, she'd sometimes accompanied Edmund on

his rounds but her role had been that of an assistant when he thought he might need an extra pair of hands.

Her wrist and shoulder twinged sharply as she slid her arm into the long sleeve of her gown. Heavens, if dressing was this onerous, how was she to manage all the work she had to do?

For a moment she allowed a spike of hopeless exhaustion to have its way with her. She could scarcely manage Yew Manor when she was well. She and Mr. Bing worked themselves to exhaustion every day and still the manor deteriorated around them!

When she became a widow, she'd considered herself fortunate when she learned that she might stay in her own house and that Edmund had put some investments in her name to maintain herself in comfort, if not style. It was not a large enough fortune for Edmund's relations to quibble over. None of them had any interest in residing in Yorkshire and the much more important entailed wealth and properties had moved seamlessly into the hands of Edmund's cousin, Galen Oakes. Gemma knew that Edmund's family bore her no ill will, with the possible exception of Galen, but neither did they hold her in esteem. They had cared nothing for Edmund and as Gemma had done them the great favor of remaining childless, they had likely already forgotten her existence.

This suited Gemma perfectly well. And when the populace of the Dale had continued to look to Yew Manor for medical assistance, she had set herself to learning everything she could to help them. The mission had occupied her lonely days as she adjusted to being the lady of her own house.

Then the investments had begun to fail. First one, then another, until all that came to Gemma was a fraction of her former income.

Gemma sat on the edge of her imperfectly made bed

and sadly held her aching wrist in her lap. It was going to be difficult day, she feared.

Then she stood up, dabbed at her incipient tears with a handkerchief and looked her reflection in the eye. "There is only ever one task," she reminded herself. "Whatever you are doing at any given moment."

She let out a breath, bound her wrist with a wide length of stiff canvas and left her dark room. Just like every day, she would not see it again until very late.

In the kitchen she found that Mr. Bing had started the fire in the stove as always. There was a kettle full of heated water set to the back of it. What would she do without him?

Don't even think it!

Kneading dough was out of the question. Fortunately she'd expected to stay late at the fete and had baked a few extra loaves for this morning. She set the day-old bread to warm near the stove while she gathered eggs. Taking a large basket, she awkwardly threw on her oldest woolen shawl and made for the extensive coops behind the stables.

On her way she saw Mr. Bing limping toward the stables leading an extremely fine horse that looked rather familiar.

"So the mighty Icarus has finally come down from his flight?"

Mr. Bing rolled his eyes. "The things folks name their beasts." Yet he rubbed the horse's questing nose when it bumped into his shoulder. "But he's a fine, friendly creature. Spoilt as a baby, no doubt. He'll be wantin' me to fetch him carrots and the like, and be about lording it over t' goat and t' pony."

Gemma felt a tremor of unease. "Do you think he'll get on well with Bad Pony?" Her cart pony was a stubborn animal, and could be most ill-mannered at times. She felt sorry for the creature. It was a strange short-legged beast, heavy-bodied and strong, but it had never taken to her and barely tolerated Mr. Bing. Their fine carriage horse had perished along with the carriage, and Edmund himself on that night he'd been summoned to deliver twins in a storm. Bad Pony was all that remained. The creature had taken Edmund's fancy while they served on the Peninsula and for some unfounded reason he'd brought it home with him, although Gemma was certain Edmund had never meant to put it in the traces.

But Mr. Bing didn't seem to be too worried about that pony's churlish temperament. He thumped the tall, gleaming thoroughbred on the shoulder with rough affection. "Aye then, Icky's a fine boy, a proper horse. He likes everyone, don't you Icky?"

Encouraged, Gemma stepped forward and held her own hand out flat. She wished she had known to keep a carrot in her pocket. She would from now on. Still, the friendly horse nuzzled her palm and gave a hopeful waffle through his nose. Gemma smiled. "Do you think it says something about our visitor that he rides such a lovely horse?"

Mr. Bing shook his head. "Couldn't speak to that. I've known some real bastards who could pick out good horseflesh. But to that lad's credit, there's nowt sign that spurs have ever touched them glossy sides."

From Mr. Bing, that was practically a stamp of approval. Then he slid his gaze in her direction. "You know yon fellow went walkin' last night."

Gemma raised a brow. "Did he? I was quite certain I heard him shouting out in his sleep. I didn't want to go in to him unless it seemed he could not calm down, but then everything became very quiet after that."

"Aye, because he went straight out t' window and climbed down t' porch."

"Really?" Gemma considered that for a moment. "I cannot decide if that is alarming or considerate. It could be that he simply didn't want to wake anyone."

"It could be he thought he needed to run for his life. It

could be he's as mad as a hatter, and there ain't a thing you can do for him."

Gemma waved that away with a slight swing of her basket. "Well, he's back in his room now. I looked in on him. He's in a sound sleep, fully dressed on top of the covers."

Mr. Bing bristled. "You are not to be alone with him, you hear me?"

Gemma sighed. Mr. Bing was only being protective. She was tempted to point out to him that should the very much larger and younger gentlemen in the upstairs room decide to do battle, it was not likely that Mr. Bing could do much about it. Then again, she'd seen Mr. Bing's wiry strength in managing Bad Pony and she had no doubt he would fight in a ferociously dirty gutter style that would do considerable damage, should it be necessary. She herself had kept a kitchen knife by her bedside last night, although she would never admit it to Mr. Bing.

"Mr. Bing, I shall remind you again that the gentleman didn't even hurt the *ram*."

Mr. Bing screwed his face into a frown that drew his bushy brows into a single spiky line. "Well, that's true enough. I still don't want you alone with him. It ain't proper. What would the doctor say?"

The same doctor who'd dragged his nineteen-year-old bride into battle? Gemma rather thought that Edmund would've handed her a fireplace poker and told her to watch his back, but she didn't bother trying to convince Mr. Bing any differently. She changed the subject. "I'm making eggs for breakfast," she said brightly, simply for the fun of teasing him.

Mr. Bing only scowled and stalked away, leading the horse to the stables and muttering under his breath. Gemma was quite sure the words were unfit for a lady's ears. She did not bother holding back her snicker as she continued around the barn to the coops.

She would make a fine plateful of eggs for the visitor, served with the toasted bread. In her experience, men always seemed to find large amounts of hot food to be quite mollifying.

"Food in belly," she growled in a primitive fashion. "Rowr."

THE BREAD WAS toasty and hot by the time their guest managed made his way down to the kitchen. Gemma heard his step in the hallway. She smiled to herself when she also heard Bing's boots thumping up the walk from the stables. The siren song of warm bread had struck once more.

"Won't you join us in the kitchen, sir?" she called out. "We don't stand on ceremony here, for there's no one to serve us but ourselves."

The shadowy form of her guest appeared just outside the door from the hall. He paused before he made his way into the kitchen.

Gemma had steeled herself against his fine looks. Yet she still found herself looking away when her troublesome responsiveness sent a tug through her lower belly.

Setting herself to industry as a means to fending off her inappropriate attraction, she set out a full dozen eggs to go into the bowl, then after a moment's thought, set out a half dozen more. Eggs were plentiful and her guest had not eaten in at least a day. She was able to smile calmly at him in welcome. "You may sit at the kitchen table with us, unless you'd rather eat in your room?"

He didn't quite flinch when she spoke to him but it was a near thing. Nevertheless, she could hear his stomach growling from where she was. She reached down her whisk from its hook on the wall and awkwardly carried over her big earthenware bowl. Oh dear. Whisking left-handed was going to be difficult. "Your horse has arrived safely," she went on. "He seems in good spirits."

The gentleman's gaze shot up to the back door. Goodness, he was eager to be on his way! Unfortunately, she could not allow that. He was strung as tightly as a wire and just as close to snapping. By taking him in, she'd made herself responsible for him. If she turned him loose on the world, she was quite certain that someone would come to harm, most probably him.

"You can't ride him out directly. He's exhausted and he's thrown a shoe. That hoof has gone a bit lame, I fear. Mr. Bing is giving him a rubdown and a hot porridge breakfast. Icarus is young and strong but he's had a very tiring few days." She gave him a stern glance and he relaxed his fixation on the back door. Gemma nodded toward the table again. "Sit down and keep me company while I cook."

She turned to her task and promptly fumbled the first egg onto the floor attempting to crack it with her left hand. Oh drat.

Suddenly, the dark form of her guest loomed at her side. He took the damp cloth from next to her pump and swiped the mess from the floor. Gemma bit back an objection to abusing one of her good tea towels for a job more suited to a rag. She was too fascinated to see what he would do next.

He took the bowl and whisk from her and began breaking the eggs with decent ease.

He was not solely accustomed to life in the upper classes, then. Of course, not every gentleman lived his life in fear of visiting the kitchen, especially those who'd had to fend for themselves in wartime. Edmund had been good with a knife and would sometimes chop the vegetables for her. Gemma thought twice about offering the same chore to her guest. Perhaps no knives, not quite yet.

Into the fray, then. "Did you enjoy your walk last night?"

He gave her a startled glance then looked away. She

pressed on. "The dale is lovely by moonlight, is it not?"

He nodded shortly. She waited as he attacked the eggs with the whisk, holding it oddly, like a sword. She let herself examine him fully, forcing herself to look past the stunning exterior to see him as a healer would. He looked a little tired, but not as badly as she would have expected, especially regarding his night wanderings.

He had not responded to her words yet. She kept her eyes on him in friendly expectation. *You will answer me.*

He swallowed. Then nodded again. "The air is … clean."

Her smile became a bit fixed. Edmund had said that about the Dales. She understood that notion perfectly well, but the cleanliness and barrenness of the dales also meant loneliness and solitude. She found them beautiful, of course, but there ought to be more to life than seeking emptiness in lieu of tranquility.

She began again. "You walk a great deal in London, I imagine. Walking is very helpful. Calming, I would say. "

He neither agreed nor disagreed with her assumption of his origin. He looked down at the bowl and released it, the enemy eggs well and truly trounced by his lethal whisk. His fingers traced the wood grain of her table. He slowly spread his flat palms down on the well-sanded surface.

He did not seem agitated, however, so Gemma decided to push him a little. "Don't you think?"

The glance he gave her was positively hunted. But he lifted his chin and met her eyes. "Helps."

"What does it help with?"

"Sleep." He said it with finality and she knew she would get nothing more from him on that topic. Still, she felt the glow of triumph for luring him to admit that much. Onward.

"I am Mrs. Gemma Oaks. I'm a widow. My husband was Dr. Edmund Oakes, who served as physician for Swaledale and beyond."

He stared at her for a long moment. She tilted her head. "How long has it been since you've met someone new and had to tell them your name?"

His jaw dropped open a bit and he seemed about to speak. Just then Mr. Bing bustled into the room with the dog close behind.

Mr. Bing tried to shut her out. "Aye then, dog! Missus Oakes don't need you trackin' up her kitchen!"

"Oh, her feet aren't any dirtier than your boots, Mr. Bing." Gemma set down her bowl. "Good morning, Topknot! I have something for you." Gemma turned and fetched a beef bone from this week's broth from the marble shelf of the larder. She knelt and held it out. "Here you go, pretty girl," she coaxed sweetly.

Topknot came closer but reached out only as far as absolutely necessary. She primly took the bone between her teeth, as far from Gemma's hand as she could get. Once Gemma had pulled her hand back, Topknot whirled back to the door. She pressed her forehead to the wood and waited.

Gemma gave a sigh of disappointment. "Oh, go on and let her out, Mr. Bing." She'd worked so hard to gain Topknot's trust and she had come a long way, but deep down she wondered if the dog would ever forgive her.

She stood and wiped her hands on the cloth at her waist before going back to her preparations. When she glanced toward the table, she saw her guest gazing at her with real curiosity. Well, that was new. Perhaps his detachment was not so complete after all.

Then he spoke spontaneously. "Shy."

He truly had mastered brevity, hadn't he? Gemma sighed and pulled the heavy iron pan onto the hottest corner of the stove. "She's better than she was. She will take food from my hand now, but she will not yet let me touch her."

"I did."

Gemma turned to stare at the man and then shot an astonished glance at Mr. Bing. Mr. Bing looked just as surprised as she did. All the animals trusted Mr. Bing, for was he not the bringer of fodder? Even the chickens thought he hung the moon. But Topknot, though she followed him everywhere, would not stand for petting even from him. Gemma fought to hide her surprise. "Well, if she takes to you, I would appreciate it if you would use a brush on her." She kept her tone off-hand and light. "She runs loose about the pastures and gets terribly tangled."

She glanced back toward the table to see that the man had returned to his perusal of the wood grain. Deciding that it wouldn't hurt to show a bit of impatience, Gemma slapped the scoop of lard down on the pan, hitting the spoon on the side with rather more force than necessary. "Now, although I thank you for your kind assistance, I really do think I deserve to know the name of the man I am about to feed."

"Lysander. Worthington."

Lysander Worthington? What a mouthful. She glanced over her shoulder at him in amusement. "That's rather a lot of syllables, for Yorkshire. No, I can't think of anyone that will actually call you by that name."

Mr. Bing shook his head with a whistle. "No, too right they won't. My grandfather's name was Bingington. But everyone called him Bing, and my father Bing, and me Bing, so now it's Bing, even on the census rolls."

Gemma nearly laughed at the puzzled look her visitor gave her. "My name?"

"We are teasing you, Mr. Worthington. It's all right. Your name is just fine."

He looked quite taken aback. She must be gentler with him. Had he always been so literal-minded or was this a symptom of some kind? She had no books on the topic of war trauma. She wasn't sure there were any. The understanding of emotions did not seem to be included in any of Edmund's medical texts. Not even *Childbirth and the Practices of Midwifery*, which really ought to have some grasp of female emotional concerns if anything did.

She was going to have to make this up as she made her way, with Mr. Bing's help. She had little to go on but her own experiences with men in the medical tents, and Mr. Bing, and sadly, Edmund.

However, Mr. Worthington was ready to be done with them. "Cannot ride?"

Gemma exchanged a glance with Mr. Bing, who shook his head firmly. "Not if you don't want yon beastie to come up lame, permanent-like. That lad needs a long rest on a pile of straw. You're lucky he didn't split a hoof on the limestone. It's everywhere in the dale, sometimes only just under the sod. You think it's just a wee bit o' stone, when it's really the breadth of a barn."

"Iceberg."

Gemma and Bing glanced at each other and looked back to their visitor. "Iceberg?" Gemma said curiously.

"Sea ice," he said slowly. "Hiding ... under the surface. Large as castles." He looked up at them rather defensively. "My youngest sister—likes to know things."

Gemma understood immediately that here was a man who not only loved his sister but listened patiently to her when she nattered on about the secret life of sea ice.

I like him. She shouldn't, for he was a patient. Still, perhaps it was better to like a patient than to dislike one. Not that it mattered to her duty of care.

"And it is in London that you reside? What part of town?" She asked with airy familiarity, although she'd never been to the city herself. She had a good reason for asking, although she wasn't planning to tell him why.

"Worthington House." He looked discomfited. "Worthington Square."

His family had a city square named after them? How very grand. Yet his clothing was well-worn, even his boots. Very mysterious, this Mr. Lysander Worthington.

She began to lift the bowl without thinking and winced as her wrist reminded her. Before she could set it down, it was lifted from her hands. Mr. Worthington stood so close she could feel the warmth of his body on her skin. Suddenly rather dry of mouth, she could only gesture toward the pan. He carefully poured the giant bowl of beaten egg into the sizzling pan. Then he stepped back.

She was grateful for that. Unfortunately the room seemed suddenly much more chilly.

Standing about dream-weaving? There's work to be done, Gemma.

Stirring the cooking eggs left-handed proved simple enough. She concentrated on her task until her pulse slowed. "After you've eaten, Mr. Worthington, I wonder if you might help Mr. Bing with a few jobs about the manor. We could certainly use a bit of help, if you're feeling up to it. Since your horse needs time to heal."

He'd returned to his seat at the table. When he saw her waiting for some sign of agreement, Mr. Worthington nodded carefully.

All part of her nefarious plot. Mr. Bing nodded as well, in a conspiratorial fashion. "I'll keep me eye on him, Missus. Won't let him go at it too hard. It might feel good to work them gone, lad, the bangs and bruises."

Gemma turned away and smiled to herself as she dished out the steaming pile of scrambled eggs on a platter. She managed nicely enough left-handed, only dropping a bit on the floor.

He would stay and he seemed willing enough to engage with both herself and Mr. Bing. She could consider the first step of her plan completed.

Chapter 10

L YSANDER FOLLOWED BING outside, after he had downed the largest breakfast he had managed in years. Mrs. Oakes made excellent eggs.

As directed by Bing, he'd left his surcoat on a peg in the hall, donning a rough, oilcloth coat against the spring morning's chill.

It was the first opportunity he'd had to see the exterior of Yew Manor in fully daylight. Without the mystery and shadows of moonlight, it was clear that the main house and stables, once gracious in a classical Palladian style, were now becoming rundown and decayed. Still, the gardens were neatly kept and the working yard of the stable was extraordinarily clean.

There didn't seem to be anyone else on the house grounds at all but Mrs. Oakes and Bing.

Bing saw Lysander glancing warily about and snorted. "Not to worry, lad. The boys from Farby'll be too busy working two day's labor to come after you here. Not that they'd pester the Lady of the Dale, no matter how much ruin you caused the village yesterday."

"No workers?"

"And what would I be needin' with a bunch of layabouts to muddle up my ways of doin' things? We've got the jobs down, me and the Missus."

Lysander must have looked as dumbfounded as he felt, for Bing turned on him to shake a finger in Lysander's face. "Don't you be thinkin' she's some useless flibbertigibbet, like your London lassies!"

Lysander didn't bother trying to explain his astonishingly not-useless sisters and sisters-in-law, because in all honesty, there were many ladies in Society who did very little that was useful. He couldn't even begin to capture the right words to do so. In addition, Bing didn't give him the chance.

"Our Missus went to war, you know! She were right there, by the doctor's side for four years, knee-deep in blood and filth in those damned tents!"

Lysander stopped in his tracks. *She was there.*

There had been a few women close to the battlefields, he knew. Officer's wives, not many, and camp followers, who provided a service for a farthing, or so Lysander had been informed.

But to work in the medical tents—God, he couldn't even imagine what she'd gone through, what she'd had to do every day. More men had been lost than healed, he knew that from experience, lost to internal damage, gangrene and the things that cannonballs and musket balls and bayonets did to fragile human flesh.

The tents were a benefit, to be sure, and Lysander didn't want to contemplate fighting a war without them. Yet he, like all the others, enlisted and officers both, had skirted those tents as if they'd held plague.

In a way, they had. Those canvas walls had contained the very mortality that no man wanted to acknowledge. It was very nearly a superstition among them all, as if to walk into the tents, one might look upon a dying man and see one's own face.

Cultured, comely Gemma Oakes had entered them day after day. She had touched the death and rot and fever, and the next day she had willingly done it again. And again.

Four years.

Bing scowled at him still, clearly waiting for a response.

Lysander looked down at the shorter man, made shorter still by a bent back and a stiffened leg. "You?"

Bing rolled his eyes. "Nay, lad. I fought. Foot soldier, me. I ain't as old as I look. Eight months in, I were run right over by French horse with a sword in its belly. Silly nag bled to death and dropped right on top of me." He narrowed his eyes at Lysander. "But don't you be thinkin' I'm easy takings. The doctor patched me up and set me to work as his batman. Me, from t' whale oil docks of Whitby, orderly and aide to a Regimental Surgeon!" He puffed his chest with pride. "Took care of them both, I did, when they come back from those tents as white as ghosts, shaky in t' knees from working day and night and another day, too sickened to eat."

Bing turned away, shaking his head. "It broke him, it did. He weren't never the same after t' war. But not her. She's got a backbone of steel, that one, for all her gentle raising."

Bing stumped ahead, his head bowed, still grumbling. Lysander turned to look back at the beautiful, crumbling manor. He experienced a deep stirring in his long-benumbed curiosity. Mrs. Gemma Oakes was an anomaly, a lady misplaced. When was she widowed and how? Why had the doctor left her so reduced in circumstances?

She must have loved him a great deal to follow him to war. Did she love him still?

"Aye then, lad, didn't you wish to see your Icky horse?"

Icarus. Yes, it was time to head home, if he could. He meant to give up this useless search for Poll, who either lived in Edinburgh and therefore had received Miranda's letter, or did not, which meant that Lysander would not find him soon enough to matter. He felt an uneasy twist of shame in his gut at the way he'd leapt to leave Worthington House. He didn't truly want to go back, but he knew that he should do so. People did that. They did what they should do.

He walked after Bing, as the man pitched and reeled on his damaged leg across the cobbled stableyard.

That was when Lysander noticed the dog, Topknot, had a strange gait as well. She was so shaggy he not realized it before, but when she ran ahead of him, lurching after Bing, he could see only one rear leg. There seemed to be nothing below her right haunch. When she ran, she twirled her tail like a squirrel, using it to counterbalance.

Bing saw him looking and nodded as he came abreast at the wide stable door. "Aye, that's another one of Missus's strays. Always taking in t' frail and t' fallen, she is. Topknot was Shepherd Gosling's best sheepdog until she fell athwart a wagon wheel. Gosling tried to bind it up and save her, because t' children were so fond. But t' leg got t' gangrene and he decided it was time to call it a bad 'un. The eldest Gosling lass came running for the Missus, begging her to save the dog. The Missus did her best but it was hard and it was ugly and t' poor thing took a long time to heal. By the time she was up again, she wouldn't leave. I took her back to Gosling's three times, and every time she wobbled her way back over all those miles and ended up sleeping in t' stable next to Mrs. Apples. Come on, I'll introduce you."

First, they visited Icarus in the stable. Lysander could see that Icky was extremely content, although the leg was indeed hot and swollen. Bing had done an expert job of wrapping it in cloth strips soaked in something herbal. Furthermore, the gelding had been brushed to a mirror finish, covered in a cozy if somewhat threadbare horse-blanket and was currently eyes-deep in a battered pail making sure he had consumed every last particle of his warm porridge breakfast.

There would be no riding Icarus today, nor tomorrow either. Lysander let his goal of immediate departure go with a vague sense of mingled guilt and relief. He would have another day away from the stifling fear and overwrought silence that permeated Worthington House.

The gentle thoroughbred seemed entirely unconcerned about sharing his large box stall with a small round-bellied goat.

"That there be Mrs. Apples," Bing said by way of introduction. He seemed to expect some response to that, so Lysander gave the goat a gentlemanly nod of greeting, although she lost interest in him immediately upon discovery that he carried nothing edible in his hands.

"Blind as a bat, she is, but she does all right for herself. She'll be having that kid soon. I'm hopin' for a doe, and then we'll have t' start of a little herd. It'll be nice having proper livestock about, instead of nothin' but those dratted chickens."

Lysander looked across the stable at the only other occupied stall, which was as far away from Icarus and the goat as could be managed. A short-legged, heavy-bodied pony stood there in the most shadowed corner of the stall. Lysander could only see one bitterly dark eye peering through its overgrown forelock.

Bing grunted. "That there be Bad Pony."

Lysander gave Bing a dubious glance.

Bing shot a loathing glance toward the stall. "I like a good pony, me. Nothin' better than a nice, friendly Dales pony. *That's* some foreign thing the doctor brought back after the war. He's a spiteful, bloody-minded beastie and fond o' bitin', so I'd be keeping your distance unless you care to lose a chunk out of your arse."

From the specific tinge of anger in Bing's voice, Lysander surmised that he was not speaking figuratively of the pony's temperament. It was a curious creature, to be sure, and brought a faint recollection to mind. Lysander let the hint of memory go without pursuing it. After all, his memories spent far too much time pursuing him.

He set to work mucking stalls after Bing moved the

strange pony with the lure of grain and the added defense
of a sturdy broom. He spread straw, scrubbed pails and
filled several of them with cracked grains for the chickens.
The amount of feed seemed excessive, but then, Lysander
didn't know much about chickens. When Bing led him
around the back of the stable and Lysander saw the vast
array of coops lined up neatly as a field of regimental tents
over nearly a full acre, he thought perhaps he should've
tried to find another pail to fill.

Some of his astonishment must have shown his face,
for Bing uttered a very ungentlemanly word. "Blasted
chickens. I canna stand 'em. Me mum kept chickens and I
never minded 'em one bit, but we've come on three years
now that folk hereabouts have been paying t' Missus in
nowt but chickens. She's too kindly to insist on hard coin,
so it's chickens. And do you know what chickens do all
day?"

Lysander had no idea but Bing stared at him expectantly. "Eggs?" he ventured hesitantly.

Bing threw out both hands. "They lay bloody eggs! And
those eggs turn into chicks, and those chicks turn into
chickens, and those chickens lay *more* bloody eggs! I be so
blasted sick of eatin' eggs and chicken that I would sell you
and that damned dog both for a single bite of bacon!"

His outburst done, Bing let his arms fall to his sides and
gave a great gusting sigh. "Aye then, lad," he said with
resignation. "Time to feed t' chickens."

After depositing the grain in flat pans and scattering a
bit around the coops, Bing gave each of the pails an extra
thwack on the bottom to make sure they were empty.
"We've got a well up to t' house, but it's a good time to fill
the water barrels in the stable. Since I've got your young
arms to do the haulin', we'll head down to t' river." Bing
gave him a fierce look from beneath his bushy brows.
"Mind you say so if you start feelin' poorly. Missus will be

that upset with me if I work you too hard."

Lysander replied by taking up several pails in each hand and started off toward the river.

Bing followed him, spry on the path despite his rather rollicking limp.

They reached the river and after removing his coat and boots, Lysander waded in a bit deeper to access the clearest water. The current ran faster in the center, dark and swift. The farther Lysander stepped in, the more he could feel the tug of the current trying to pull the buckets from his hands as he filled them. Methodically, he filled every single bucket and set it neatly in a row on the bank while Bing perched on a tree stump and Topknot lurched back and forth along the bank as if worried that Lysander would cross the river without her.

"I can see you like to finish a task once ye've started it." Bing nodded approvingly, although Lysander took the compliment with a grain of salt, considering that Bing seemed quite happy not to wet his own boots.

Lysander heard a splash and glanced over his shoulder but he saw nothing untoward. Then he realized he could not see Topknot anywhere. He dropped the last bucket without caring that it sloshed his dry boots and took off at a run along the downstream bank. Dogs could swim perfectly well, he knew that. Four-legged dogs could swim perfectly well. He kept his eye on the rippling surface as he ran. Surely there would be some sign?

He saw a black nose break the surface accompanied by the merest flash of white-tipped paw. Lysander made a leap from the bank that landed him just ahead of that spot. He dove under the water. It was clear and green when he opened his eyes, casting this way and that as he let the current carry him.

There. He saw the dog struggling for the surface. Her tricolor coat waved and swirled with deathly beauty while her three legs tried to climb the watery ladder with all their might. But it wasn't enough. The current rolled her over and pulled her down once more.

Lysander kicked off hard and shot through the water. Reaching his long arms for the dog, he wrapped them about her ribs and held her tightly. They began to sink together as the current pushed them along. Lysander used the opportunity to push off from the rocky Swale River bottom and thrust them both toward the surface.

Topknot struggled wildly. She was already so far gone in panic that she could not recognize that she was being rescued. She twisted violently, then gagged and vomited water in his ear. Lysander was quite grateful that she didn't seemed inclined to bite for their faces were entirely too close.

As he worked his way to the bank and his feet found the bottom, her struggles caused him to fall again and again, her wild snaking motion knocking him off balance and causing his feet to slip on the slimy mud. No matter what, he kept his hold on her until made it to his feet once more and fell the last time on to the damp earthen bank. He eased his grip and Topknot sprang from his arms. She scuttled away into the grass, taking a moment to vomit more copiously.

Breathing hard, Lysander lay on his back on the grass and gazed up at the perfect blue and white Yorkshire sky.

APPARENTLY, FARM WORK didn't pause for congratulations of daring three-legged dog rescues. When Lysander returned to where the pails were, he found Bing relaxing on a fallen log and cleaning his nails with a penknife. At the sight of him, Bing raised his bushy brows. "The Missus just laundered them clothes. You do get yourself dirty, for a toff."

Topknot had followed Lysander along the bank, although she skirted both men warily. Nevertheless, she did wait at the top of the path for them.

It was only then that Lysander detected that Bing thought his actions a bit extreme. "She can't swim," he offered awkwardly by way of explanation.

"Neither can I." Bing hove to his feet. "Blasted dog. Neither use nor ornament, that one. Still, t' Missus would be that sorry to lose her." Bing sent Lysander a shadowed glance. "It's a hard life in t' North, lad. Harder still for t' broken, I'd wager."

Bing bundled the abandoned boots and coat under his arm. He clapped Lysander on the shoulder in an affable fashion and hobbled back up the path. "Come along, you daft Londoner. T' water won't fetch itself!"

Lysander was not used to casual friendliness from, well, *anyone*. He stood, still dripping, and stared after Bing for a moment before he hefted a double load of pails and followed man and dog back to work.

Chapter 11

GEMMA'S WRIST THROBBED, but it was her own fault. She wasn't accustomed to sitting about and resting. Surely it wouldn't do her any harm to take an inventory of her stillroom, she had told herself. A bit of lightweight occupation was just the thing.

Of course, she should've realized that when one did an inventory, one discovered that things were lacking. Then one set about correcting that lack, and then one ended up awkwardly grinding herbs for tinctures with one's left hand while using the right—injudiciously removed from its sling—to brace the mortar from shifting.

Then of course, one might decide to rearrange the awkward position of her stored vials and corked bottles.

Then once she had pulled all of that off the shelves and turned her stillroom upside down, her wrist was too painful for her to put it all back.

Perhaps she should've selected *Childbirth and the Practices of Midwifery* and taken a seat by the stove as Mr. Bing had recommended.

Physician, heal thyself. Wasn't that always the way? Healers put themselves last, at least the good ones did.

Yet what choice did she have? If she wasn't a healer then she was nothing. Nothing but a weary widow alone on her hillside farm—except for the ridiculous population explosion of chickens, of course.

Perhaps she should title her memoir thus. *In the Company of Chickens. Surrounded by Squawks. One Hundred Ways to*

Cook an Egg.

How would she sign it? Mrs. Oakes? Mrs. Gemma Oakes? The Widow Oakes?

Heavens no. That made her sound as if she were eighty-eight years old. And despite the ache in her wrist, she was not quite ready for a life of sitting by the fire.

The pain in her wrist depressed her and her inability to work depressed her and the thought of living alone on this farm until she was eighty-eight years old depressed her, which explained why she took the opportunity of any distraction.

"You'd best not track all that mud into the house, lad," she heard Mr. Bing say out in the yard. "You can wash the worst off here at the rain barrel."

At the sound of Mr. Bing's voice so close by Gemma spared a glance through the stillroom window. The rain barrel lay directly outside the stillroom window, offering her a marvelously unspoiled view of Mr. Worthington stripping off his shirt.

Oh goodness, goodness me.

He is stunning.

Mr. Worthington had been magnificent, in a mad foolish way, when fending off the ram. He'd been mysterious and achingly handsome unconscious in her late husband's bed. This morning at breakfast he'd been very attractive in his tongue-tied way.

Yet nothing could have prepared Gemma for seeing Mr. Worthington half-naked and entirely soaking wet. Her body pulsed in response.

The cold water from the pail that he dumped over his head made him toss his head back, his long wet hair flying, his mouth open in an unselfconscious gasp. Gemma realized then that she would never be able to forget that moment, especially after it made her wonder what Mr. Worthington looked like when he orgasmed.

His face damp with sweat, over hers, pleasure thundering through his body, him swelling inside her....

Yes, it would definitely stay with her always.

His shoulders were broad and although he was a bit thin, his muscles lay strapped tightly to his frame. His thinness only revealed the rippling strength all the more when he hauled another bucket of water high to sluice it over his upturned face.

He took the icy blast more stoically this time, merely giving a quick animal shudder like a fine horse. Then he used his hands to sweep the rest of the mud stains from his skin, leaving him clean and gleaming in the afternoon light.

Oh Mr. Worthington, you are beautiful. Those wide shoulders tapered to narrow hips. Soaked trousers clung to the firm buttocks and thighs of a horseman. He lifted a hand to sweep his wet hair from his face and she was treated to the intimate awareness of his paler ribs and dark tufted underarm. She felt like a spy. A deliciously wicked voyeur. *Show me more.*

The ache, the one she refused to acknowledge, the one that woke her up some nights with feverish dreams, the empty, cold feeling of stretching her hand to meet nothing but chilled linens on the other side of the bed—yes, that ache—roared to life from some hidden place inside her, taking her breath away with the sudden relentless force of her hunger. *I want him.*

She leaned forward closer to the window, her uninjured hand pressed to the glass as she watched the muscles of his back ripple when he put both hands up to squeeze the water from his hair. She bit her lip as it ran in rivulets down his spine, all the way down, to where his soggy trousers hung low on his hips and she could just barely see where his buttocks began. She went up on tiptoe, striving to be taller, hoping to see more.

He turned her way then and her jaw dropped. If she

thought the rear was handsome, she was in no way prepared for the frontal view. The hair on his chest and belly was dark and curling, beaded with water. The damp hair made a tempting inky arrow pointing down, down across his flat muscled abdomen down to his naval and beyond. Was it an invitation? *Come this way.*

The wet trousers clung. Mr. Worthington was—well, one might say that his large frame and long hands and feet did not disappoint.

Gemma swallowed hard. Oh, so *hungry.*

She wanted it to be her hands stroking down his body. She wanted to feel the slickness of his wet skin. She longed to run her fingers down the long hard muscles that wrapped his broad shoulders and twined down his arms. She wanted to stroke a fingertip down the raised veins of his forearms, down over the inside of his wrist to feel his speeding pulse, to spread her hands in his, palm to palm, and let their fingers interlace.

She wanted it to be her fingers thrusting into the thick black hair to push it away from his face, her fists tangling in the unshorn length, pulling his head down and his mouth down to hers. The front of her gown would soak up the water on his chest and it would dissolve against her until he would feel her hard nipples jutting into his rippling chest.

She wanted to kiss him and to be kissed by him. Oh, how she wanted to be kissed! She wanted him to wrap his long arms around her and pull her hair down free and press one large palm against the small of her back to pull her as close as he could.

I miss kissing. I miss wanting and being wanted. I miss the hardness in my secret softness. I miss gasping and sighing. I miss the Chinese rockets of orgasms.

I really, truly miss orgasms.

Until this man had arrived in her dale, she'd not

touched herself since before she became a bride. She was tempted to do it now. Instead she squeezed her thighs together beneath her gown and leaned so far across the table to the window that her breath began to fog the glass.

He stood there, magnificent, tall and lean, rippling with muscle, just like his fine thoroughbred horse. The light gleamed across his wet collarbone and the cords of his neck as he turned his head.

And gazed directly into her eyes.

LYSANDER FROZE.

From the first moment he'd spotted her in the village, Mrs. Oakes had snared his attention. Now, the sight of her gazing at him with open, aching hunger—with her palm pressed to the window as if reaching for him—now he was absolutely riveted by her.

No one had looked at him that way for very long time. Possibly never, not with that particular lonely, aching longing. She had seemed so cool, so distant and controlled. Now, there was darkness in those eyes, sweet and wild and primal. Mrs. Oakes would not be prim in the bedchamber, he understood that well enough. Unleashed from her ladylike bindings of practical hair and drab gowns, she would be hot and writhing and eager.

Lysander became aware that his cock had begun to swell even in the icy clamminess of his soaked trousers. He could not break his gaze away from her stormy eyes. He continued to harden. He decided not to quail but to let her see him, the way that she had let him see her.

When her gaze dropped and she noted her effect on him, her eyes widened and she flinched back from the window, and then her pale face disappeared into the shadows of the room.

Released from the spell of her devouring gaze, Lysander

staggered back a step. He drew a deep gasping breath into his panting lungs and then, closing his eyes tight, he plunged his entire head into the icy water of the rain barrel.

It didn't help. The hunger in her gaze was imprinted on the inside of his own eyelids. He would never forget the way she looked at him. He never *wanted* to forget it.

ONCE LYSANDER HAD changed into the only other shirt he had tucked into Icky's saddlebags, he discovered that his boots could be salvaged by a night by the stove. He stuffed them with clean straw and left them tucked neatly to the side. Outside, Bing mercilessly handed him a pair of rough work boots and a hammer.

It had been a long time since Lysander had worked with his hands. Worthington House had a marvelous workshop in the old stables off the back garden, but it had been years since he had tinkered out there on his brothers' inventions.

Now, he couldn't seem to hammer a nail without slamming his thumb. The nail seemed to slip and wiggle in his fingers and the hammer swung erratically. He hoped Bing couldn't see how his hands tended to tremble.

"Take your time, lad. That plank isn't walking off anywhere." Bing's raspy voice sounded very nearly sympathetic as Lysander tried to repair the ancient stable door.

Lysander flinched from such expressions of pity. He had no right to it. He had his strength, he had both arms and both legs, and had come away from the battlefields with only a few scars. Others had seen so much worse.

Then Bing rolled his eyes and scoffed. "Hold on to t' blasted nail, lad! Pretend that if it gets away, it's going to bite you!"

Lysander relaxed somewhat, secure once more in Bing's refreshingly blunt disdain. He grasped the nail as if it were a viper as instructed, and swung the hammer down.

He smashed his thumb but good. The wild bolt of pain brought those frightening black edges to his vision. His shaking hands curled into fists. *No, not now. Please not now.*

Topknot came to press herself against his leg and shoved her cold nose into the curl of his fist. He looked down at the dog and managed to uncurl his fingers a little. She shoved her narrow snout deep into that half-open fist and licked his palm. Then she pulled back and gazed up at him with a toothy doggy grin and whacked her tail upon the ground.

She ought to be afraid of him. Everyone else seemed to be constantly watching him to see if he would lose control. Even his own brothers and sisters tread warily around him, except for Atalanta. The last time he'd felt on the edge of control around Attie, she had wrapped her skinny arms forcefully around him and whispered, "You're my favorite. Don't tell."

That was how Topknot was looking at him now. If ever a dog had said, "You're my favorite," shaggy Topknot was saying it now.

"Aye then, lad. It do come upon a fellow now and again."

Lysander shot a glance at the wiry older man, but Bing had his crossed arms resting on the top of the stone wall and simply gazed down the dale with a sleepy expression.

Lysander realized perhaps he did not mind Bing's erratic and distant sympathy. Bing had been to war. Bing knew what Lysander knew. Yet here he was, working in the peaceful dales and looking after the lady doctor. Bing didn't seem a bit like a primed pistol about to fire.

Lysander had to know. "What do you do?" He struggled for the words. "When it comes?"

Bing scratched his head for a moment, knocking his cap askew. "Well, I like to find me something to hammer on, usually. Slow and easy, y'know, like ticking on the clock or t' Sunday chapel bells in t' village."

Slow. After a moment of thought, Lysander found another nail, positioned it on the gate planks and lifted his
hammer. *Bang.* He took a breath. *Bang.*

He didn't hit his thumb. The nail went in straight and
true. Instead of a violent and furious noise, the hammer
and nail met with a clear pure sound that rang out across
the grassy fields. Like a heartbeat, slow and steady, and
strangely calming.

Without thinking Lysander set three more nails, forming a neat square where the planks overlapped.

Bing tucked his wayward cap straight and peered closer.
"Well now. You be right handy for a toff."

As the afternoon waned, Lysander applied the same
logical and soothing process to repairing a section of fallen
dry-stone wall.

"Let the stone do what it wants, now. Stone'll be stone,
be no makin' it clay." Lysander held the field stones in his
hands, and examined each one closely and carefully, com-
paring it to the space it was meant to fill. He found his
mind both sharpened and soothed by the methodical spatial
problem.

"'Tis a shame you'll be ridin' off soon. With this bum
leg, there's only so much I can do about the place. I don't
like to let the Missus down, although she'll never so much
as hint at it, no she won't. Still, I know she worries."

Lysander wanted to ask about Mrs. Gemma Oakes. He
wanted to know everything about her. His piqued interest
had flared into burning curiosity since that moment by the
window. The slender, lovely Mrs. Oakes was an enigma.
Until their heated moment through the window, he'd
thought her cool and distant, even solitary. Now her hidden
passionate side had been revealed to him. What else was
there to learn?

He'd seen a small library full of well-loved volumes on

his way down to find the kitchen, but the room had the air of a place long undisturbed. Had she no interest in reading or was she too busy healing dale folk and dogs? And strangers?

Bing went on. "She's a good woman. Rock solid, as they say. She's stronger than she looks, but it's a hard life in t' North."

Harder still for them what's broken.

Was Mrs. Oakes broken? This morning that thought would not have crossed his mind. She'd seemed entirely collected and in control of her rustic corner of the world. But the dark, lost, lonely gaze of the woman in the window belied that impression. She may not be broken, but neither was Gemma Oakes entirely whole. He knew that now.

"I'd take it as a kindness if you'd linger a day or two. 'Tis a big job to get t' place into shape after such a harsh winter. The local lads will help when they can, but it'd be a right blessin' to get a head start on t' job."

Stay?

Lysander felt torn. He was supposed to be helping his family by looking for his brother, Poll. However, he'd suspected from the start that it was a hopeless chase, trying to track down the nomadic theatrical troupe that Poll traveled with, based on nothing but a six-month-old postal address. It been Attie's restless inability to help and his own inability to bear up that had sent him on this road.

He should go home straightaway. He should go back to Worthington House and wait with the others—wait to see if Iris healed or worsened, to watch as she bloomed or faded like the flower for which she was named.

Perhaps he did believe in cowardice, for he felt like a craven at the very thought of going back to that hushed, intense household that filled him with dread. It made him want to run as fast as he could in the opposite direction.

Even considering returning made that terrible, itchy agitation tighten every muscle in his body.

He let his gaze rest on the vast and lovely view down the dale. It was better here. He liked working with Bing and the animals. Here, no one gazed at him with wistful curiosity, wondering when he would go back to the way he used to be. He couldn't go back to that man. He couldn't even *find* that man. He would never be that boyish Worthington prankster again, that laughing flirt who ran off to play soldier as much out of boredom as out of patriotism.

But perhaps in a place like this—this windswept, silent place—he could simply be as he was. A silent man. A man without some other self, some past self, to live up to.

Iris had most of the Worthingtons to help her, and more would have arrived by now. Gemma had a lame soldier and a three-legged dog.

And him. A commotional toff with a lame horse and tendency to tilt at windmills—or at least, joust with goats.

Chapter 12

T HE LONG DAY of work ended, leaving Lysander feeling a sense of satisfaction that his endless frenzied walks about London had never given him. His injured head pounded but he ignored it in favor of having dinner with Mrs. Oakes. On Bing's advice, this time he cleaned up in his room using the bowl and pitcher of water and donned his good coat.

Dressed as well as could be expected of him, Lysander hesitated in the doorway to the kitchen to watch Gemma.

He liked her name. It was sensible and yet rather poetic. She was a gem, gleaming softly yet without ostentation. A pearl perhaps. No, an opal, simple on first impression, yet when one looked more closely, full of secrets of light and color.

She managed quite competently despite her sling as he watched her. Then came a memory, out of nowhere. Iris, younger and slimmer and with a quick bright clarity in her gaze. She stood in the front sitting room of Worthington house, with the draperies pulled back, and the sunlight streaming in. He could not have been more than eleven years old, for Iris was painting with one hand and the other kept tiny Elektra balanced on her hip. Iris's eyes had been bright with fascination as she brushed brilliant colors on canvas. Elektra's hair was a halo of pale, flaxen curls and Iris's was more warm maple than the silver it was now. It was just a flash, a moment out of time. A moment when his mother spotted him and flashed him a smile and called him

Zander.

Iris wasn't like that anymore. She had taken too many emotional blows. She'd barely survived Attie's birth and her recovery had been long and difficult. Then Worthington Manor on their Shropshire estate had burned nearly to the ground, and they had all moved to their current home, bringing only what they could rescue from the manor. The books, some furnishings, yes, but the home of their combined memories was lost. Iris had regained her health but in Lysander's recollection, she'd remained fragile.

And then he himself had died. That's what his family had been told. The name Lysander Worthington appeared on the list of the deceased. A simple wartime mistake. Only Lysander was aware of the hidden irony of that cosmic error.

That younger man was gone. He'd never come home from the Peninsular War. The things he had seen, the things that he felt, the things that he had done.

His mind slid away from that thorny thought, that knowledge that existed within him like a fistful of bramble, unable to be held by any fashion without experiencing piercing pain.

Gemma was humming. The sun had set outside and she was cooking by the light of the lantern. Some women were their most attractive by daylight. Some women seemed more beautiful by candlelight.

Lysander held very still as she glanced in his direction and caught his intent gaze. Her clear gray eyes widened and her soft lips parted slightly. His headache and the soreness in his body disappeared at the shimmer of awareness in her guileless eyes.

Gemma Oakes was lovely in every light.

She looked away quickly, but Lysander saw the blush creeping up her neck and heating her cheeks.

He felt rather overheated as well. And it wasn't just because he come in from the crisp, invigorating evening to the warmth and golden light of the kitchen. It was the memory of her achingly hungry gaze this afternoon. It was the sight of her now. She made his heart beat faster. She made him conscious of the blood rushing through his veins. It was startling and alarming. He had felt nothing for so long. His body had seemed like a mechanism that he had little interest in operating. He'd sometimes felt as if his soul floated just outside of his body, bound by only the most tenuous tie to his physical form.

Now he felt fully dressed in his own skin. His pulse pounded. His skin prickled. His throat felt tight and his palms tingled. His hands wanted to reach for her and slide his fingers up her soft bare neck, over her soft cheek, and to tip her chin up and slide his tip of his thumb across her lower lip.

I am awake.

It came as a startling notion.

Whirling back to her bubbling pot, Gemma banged the wooden spoon against the side of the pot so hard she knocked it out of her own grip.

In instant, Lysander was there, picking up the spoon from the floor and handing it to her.

"So clumsy. Heavens." She gingerly accepted the spoon from him, clearly taking care that their hands did not touch in any way. She carried the spoon to the sink and wiped it with a damp cloth before returning to the stove.

"I'm glad you're here." She didn't look at him, not quite.

Lysander realized that he probably ought not to allow his heart to lighten at the notion she was glad to see him.

"You're tall enough to reach the soup tureen on top of the cupboard. If you wouldn't mind?"

It might be rather pathetic, but he wasn't even disappointed. He was more than happy to be of use to her, in any capacity. He reached the tureen down to the worktop. Gemma clucked in dismay and wiped at the gleaming porcelain with the cloth, although Zander thought it looked quite pristine.

"Would you mind dishing the stew into this?" She stepped back. "I fear I shall only make a bigger mess with only my left hand."

Lysander nodded silently. He took up the full, steaming pot quite comfortably and transferred the creamy stew into the tureen.

"Thank you." She still didn't look at him, not quite. Her gaze tended to rise to his cravat and no higher. Lysander didn't care. He was standing close to her and she smelled like herbs and good cooking.

The man he'd been had always favored good cooking. Now, not only was Lysander feeling interested in eating the supper she'd prepared, he thought he might be becoming rather fond of herbs as well.

"Are you hungry? You must be, for Mr. Bing has worked you like a stable hand all day. I hope you were careful not to overdo."

Lysander simply shook his head. Then he felt the unusual pressure of words wanting to bubble up. He wished to tell her the things he learned today, about working slowly and breathing through the overwhelming moments, and that he'd discovered that the silence of the dale helped him. He hadn't known that before. In Worthington house—and verily, in London itself!—there was never true silence. Not like this, not the bone-deep peace of the dales.

Soon they had all seated themselves at the table, Gemma without her apron, Lysander and a freshly scrubbed Bing, who wilted somewhat at the sight of the creamy chicken stew. Thanks had been offered. The silent dining tradition observed by the hungry and hardworking lent a peace to the room. Lysander savored his first spoonful of the hearty stew and discovered that his long-lost appetite had somehow returned to him.

No one spoke for quite a while, for they had all had a very long day. Lysander could not help his gaze fixing across the table upon his hostess. She managed to find anywhere else to look at while they supped.

She looked to be very tired. Lysander saw her wince in pain for a moment and her left hand came up to cradle her right wrist in the sling. As soon as she noticed his gaze, she dropped her hand. She didn't seem to blame him at all, and he rather thought he deserved blame. He was willing to share responsibility with the demonic ram, or rather the sheep-herder who had not tied it tightly enough, but that did not detract from the solid fact that had Lysander never ridden into the village, Gemma would not now be pale from the ache in her wrist.

He should say something. He should offer well-meant words, fluid expressions of regret, or something solicitous, shouldn't he? Didn't people like to hear those things?

Or did they? He could not quite pin it down. He had already apologized. She had accepted his apology. To ask her to accept another one seemed rather self-serving. As if he expected *her* to make *him* feel better for what had happened.

However, since no one spoke, Lysander had no idea how to break the silence. Then he remembered how the clouds had begun to come in low and heavy and there been a sharp scent in the air.

"Will it rain?" There! That had come out in a very nearly civilized fashion.

He waited for Mrs. Oakes to respond, but it was Bing who spoke around a mouthful of stew. "Aye, it may, a bit. I shouldn't think it'll amount to much." His tone of vast experience with the local weather seemed to put a halt to the topic.

Silence fell once more. Lysander began to worry about Gemma. She seemed to be fading, too weary or too sore to finish her bowl of stew. She had not touched her bread and Lysander realized that she not been able to tear it the way he and Bing had.

He solved that issue by simply reaching across the table and doing it himself. Gemma blinked at the sudden action and then smiled at him in thanks.

Lysander spent the rest of the meal dazed by that smile.

AFTER MR. BING had scraped his bowl most thoroughly with his spoon, he bobbed a gruff "Thank ye, Missus," in Gemma's direction and stomped out the kitchen door "t'see to the beasties."

When Mr. Worthington started to push back his chair to follow Mr. Bing, Gemma waved him back to his seat. "There's no need. 'Seeing to the beasties' is merely a euphemism for sitting in the stable with Mrs. Apples and having himself a pipe. He knows that I do not approve of smoking tobacco."

Then she gazed at Mr. Worthington in dismay. "Unless you care to join him? I didn't think to ask if you like tobacco as well."

Mr. Worthington gave his head a quick shake, and then, wonder of all wonders, began to clear the table. Gemma uttered a feminine noise of protest and moved to stand, but it was Mr. Worthington's turn to wave her back to her seat.

She remained in an entirely enjoyable state of bemusement while a tall, handsome gentleman did her washing up.

Of course, he failed to heat the water in the kettle hot enough to properly scald the dishes, and he made such a lather with the lye soap that she suspected it would not entirely rinse away, but her wrist ached too much to spur her to action on behalf of perfection. Besides, from her current position at the table, she had the most marvelous view of his broad shoulders and backside. Gemma sat back and looked her fill.

He removed his coat and rolled up the sleeves of his shirt as naturally as if he were in his own house. She did love nice forearms on a man. *Hmm, with rippling tendons and wide, capable hands.*

The throbbing in her arm eventually bid her to rise in order to fetch herself a bit of willow bark from her still-room. A cup of the hot bitter brew sweetened with a touch of last summer's honey would be a wonderful accompaniment to her voyeurism.

She had taken no more than three steps when he was at her side, drying his hands on a towel. He followed her to the stillroom and reached down the glass jar of willow bark shavings for her. He followed her directions closely, wrapping the brittle bark in a piece of linen and pounding it small, then measuring it into the teapot and filling it with steaming water from the kettle on the stove.

She found herself seated on her throne once more with her cup. He put the small pot of honey before her as well. Imagine it, a pot of tea without ever lifting a finger herself!

Briefly, she wondered if this in any way resembled having a wife. Or perhaps a really, really helpful husband.

Dr. Oakes had been patient and kind, and hardworking—really, so devoted to the dale folk—but if Edmund had ever made a pot of tea on his own, Gemma would likely have dropped dead on the spot in surprise.

The willow bark dulled the ache in her wrist and imparted a pleasant humming state of relaxation and the honey cheered her, but what was she to do with the sudden visceral awareness that she was alone in the house with a handsome, arousing man she barely knew? Last night, Mr. Bing had taken his repose in the small chamber off the stillroom, which he only used in the bitterest weeks of winter when his quarters off the stable became impossible to heat. Like a crusty, muttering duenna, he seemed most intent on protecting her virtue. She had supposed he would come back to the house after his pipe, yet the hour grew late and her chaperone remained distinctly absent. She was surprised at his neglect, for he was usually highly protective of her.

Then she recalled Mr. Bing's strange obliviousness to the young, handsome, half-naked guest washing in the rain barrel outside her stillroom window. Surely Mr. Bing had realized that Mr. Worthington ought to have cleaned up in the stable watering trough instead of dirtying her pure rainwater?

What was Mr. Bing thinking? It could not be what she suspected. Could Mr. Bing be encouraging this companionship?

When Mr. Worthington had thoroughly toweled off the dishes and stacked them neatly by the sink he meticulously dried his hands, fastened his cuffs, and put his slightly shabby, beautifully-fitted coat back on.

He meant to depart to his bedchamber, she could tell. Without quite meaning to, she stalled him. "Do you read much, Mr. Worthington?"

He gazed at her for a moment. "Did ... once."

Amused, she regarded him with her head slightly tilted. "Does that mean you *once* read a great deal in the past, or that you *once* read a book?" She could not keep a smile from her lips although she tried. This must be an additional effect of the willow bark. She'd quite forgotten to be self-conscious about their intimate moment through the window glass.

His eyes widened slightly. "My family. All of us." His brows drew together. "So ... many books." He spread his hands as if helpless to describe his meaning properly.

All of us. Seven siblings, he'd informed her earlier.

Gemma allowed herself a wistful pang. She'd always longed for brothers and sisters.

She smiled at him once again. She had noticed that it tended to make him go rather still, like a wild animal caught in the flash of a lantern. His fascination made her feel as though she still had her looks, despite her lack of time for primping.

"I fear that my injury is bothering me greatly this evening." *Oh, I am entirely without scruples.* "I could do with a bit of distraction. Do you think you might fetch a book from the study for me?"

He glanced toward the passage and then turned back to her with a question in his eyes. She supposed she could pretend she didn't know what he was asking. She could force him to say it out loud, which would surely be good for him, but she took pity on him. He had been most willing and generous with his assistance thus far.

"Anything will do," she said gently. "Anything at all, except for that one book on blood diseases and the use of leeches. That one is, I fear, *not* ideal after-dinner entertainment."

He did not smile at her joke, but only nodded and strode toward the study. She'd barely taken a single sip of her tea when he returned with a volume in his hand. Had he indeed plucked "anything" off the shelf, or had he seen a favorite immediately? Everything he did begged a question, or six. He was a mystery, a puzzle, a present to be unwrapped. Oh, to see what lay underneath!

Which was a most improper thought for a practitioner to have of her patient! *Really, Gemma!*

Remained focused. He is a patient. And this is meant to be a remedy.

"Shakespeare!" She said with surprise when he handed her the volume. At the implied question in her astonishment, he reached to take it back, presumably to fetch her something else, but she quickly pulled it out of range.

"No, this is lovely. The Sonnets are particular favorite of mine." Well, she remembered them fondly anyway, the single time she had read them, in another place, another life before the dales. Yorkshire shepherds and farmers did not often partake in poetry reading. They preferred the Christmas tableau and "Punch and Judy" and who didn't love a genuinely accomplished juggler?

Now for the somewhat underhanded part of her plan. She pressed her fingertips to her temple and squinted her eyes. "Oh dear. I fear I have taken the headache. Perhaps reading was not such a fortunate notion after all."

Mr. Worthington gazed at her for a very long moment. She wondered what sort of battle carried on behind those shadowed eyes. Was even the smallest thing so difficult in the dark and isolated world in which he lived?

She smiled at him kindly and reassured him with a direct request. "Would you read to me for little while, until the tea works upon my pains?"

Once set upon a task, Mr. Worthington was a most thoughtful and helpful person. This she had noticed today while watching him work with Mr. Bing. She was not surprised when he obediently opened the book to a random page and clearing his throat, began to read aloud.

> *"Shall I compare thee to a summer's day?*
> *Thou art more lovely and more temperate.*
> *Rough winds do shake the darling buds of May."*

Gemma nearly gaped at the beauty of his warm, deep voice as he spoke smoothly and easily. It was as if having the words supplied to him by the book solved all the usual hesitancy and reticence within him.

Concealing her surprise, she closed her eyes and leaned her head back on the chair to allow the sound of his voice flow over her. It was not the poetry that she lost herself in. It was the mystery of a man so tangled in his mind that he had mislaid his own words. And yet when supplied with a rich and detailed soliloquy, he spoke so beautifully, with such emotion and intention! His slightly roughened baritone voice slid over her senses, stirring up thoughts and images best kept to herself.

She opened her eyes. It was her turn for revelation and a strange sort of dismay when she realized that although he missed not a single one of Shakespeare's words, his eyes were not upon the book at all, but fixed enigmatically upon her. Their gazes locked as he continued.

> *"O let my books be then the eloquence*
> *And dumb presagers of my speaking breast,*
> *Who plead for love and look for recompense*
> *More than that tongue that more hath more expressed."*

Gemma swallowed hard as his gaze darkened upon her, but she could not look away.

> *"O learn to read what silent love hath writ!*
> *To hear with eyes belongs to love's fine wit."*

What sort of man was he, a man of such education and talented oration? How had the war stolen that much from him as to render him very nearly mute? Were his thoughts so scrambled, was his mind so far from this world, that he could not cross that void with his own communication?

He had been robbed by battle, locked away from himself. The world had been robbed, much worse off with the loss of the man he must've been.

How much was left inside him? Was he whole within, merely struggling to return to this world? Or was he hollow, a soul drilled clean through by battle and trauma?

So beautiful. So gifted. So broken. The monumental task she taken upon herself suddenly terrified her. Who was she to think she could reach inside to take his hand, to lead him back across the shattered bridge to join the rest of the world?

He spoke on. He recited beautifully and probably flaw-lessly, every line cadenced just enough to let her know it was poetry, yet not so on the beat that she felt hammered by rhyme.

He moved smoothly from the twenty-third Sonnet to the twenty-fourth.

> *"Now see what good turns eyes for eyes have done:*
> *Mine eyes have drawn thy shape, and thine for me*
> *Are windows to my breast, wherethrough the sun*
> *Delights to peep, to gaze therein on thee."*

Oh heavens. She'd forgotten the passionate nature of the Sonnets. *Mine eyes have drawn thy shape.* Gemma felt her cheeks flush and she tore her gaze from his to stare blindly at the tabletop.

Mr. Worthington half-naked and soaking wet in the sunlight. The shimmering water running down his muscled body, over his flat, rippled stomach, down to the arrow of fine dark hair, just where his trousers sagged low on his lean hips.

Delights to peep, to gaze therein on thee, by gum and no mistake!

Her face burned and her thighs clenched. She could bear it no longer. She held up her hand to halt him. When he stopped short and carefully closed the book, she drew a deep breath and lifted her head to give him a rather tremu-lous smile. "That was lovely." Could he tell how breathless he'd left her? "You spoke beautifully—but you did not read. You know the Sonnets by heart?"

The fingertips of one hand traced across the gold-lettered spine. "Archie. My father. A ... favorite."

He had a father and he called him by a familiar first name. Gemma leaned forward, fascinated. "And your mother?"

"Iris." He looked down at the book in his hands and slid his touch from it as something came over his still features. He glanced aside, over her shoulder, as if at something far away. "I must—"

Bang! Bang! Bang!

Chapter 13

LYSANDER STOOD ABRUPTLY at the noise, his pulse jolting. He felt better standing, more ready, although he could not have said what he was preparing himself for.

Gemma answered the knock. The man at the door stood with his hat in his hands, nodding respectfully to Gemma even as he cast a wary glare at Lysander. Bing appeared behind the man with a scowl on his weathered features, but relaxed when he clearly recognized the newcomer. "Aye then, Orren."

"Mrs. Oakes, I'd be obliged if you'd come to the farm. My youngest boy fell in the barn and hurt his leg. It's a bad break and I fear it's needin' a proper set."

"Oh, of course!" Gemma clearly wanted to leap into action but her arm made it difficult. Lysander was there to help her before he even thought of it. She accepted his assistance but then stepped away from his touch on her elbow. "I'll fetch my medical kit at once." She looked at Bing. "Please put Bad Pony to the cart, Mr. Bing."

Then she stopped and turned her horrified gaze at the man. "But I cannot drive the cart. Did you come in your wagon, Shepherd Orren?"

The fellow's mouth made a perfect "o" of regret. "No, Mrs. Oakes. I didn't think on it. I rode me old horse." He twisted his hat. "I'd let you ride him back, Missus, really I would, but I didn't saddle him first."

Gemma paused, clearly considering it.

Lysander straightened. That would not do.

"I'll drive you."

Everyone turned to look at Lysander with astonishment, as if a potted palm had spoken. He stood very straight and tried to seem not at all leafy. "I'm good with horses." He slid a glance at Bing. "And ponies."

Bing shifted, clearly willing but just as clearly weary to the bone. He grumbled. "It ain't like he's a real pony," but he subsided quickly when Gemma nodded briskly.

"Yes, thank you, Mr. Worthington. That will do very nicely." She turned to the sheepherder. "I shall follow along directly with my kit. Mr. Worthington will assist me, won't you, Mr. Worthington?"

Lysander nodded. He had no idea what he would be doing, but he vowed to himself to do it as well as he was able.

The man nodded gratefully and backed out of the doorway that he had never entirely entered. Lysander felt a passing oddness in that. The way the man had addressed Gemma was the way that common folk in London addressed the nobility. Did she hold herself so very high to the local folk?

He followed Gemma into her stillroom. He found her opening a strange folding box and checking its contents. It looked like something his brother Orion would use to run chemistry experiments, for it was full of small bottles. Some were filled with liquids of different colors and some small jars held dried plants or powders. He recognized the milky contents of one bottle. Laudanum.

After plucking a few things from her shelves and inserting them into the case in an exacting manner, Gemma tried to refold the sides. She struggled, and Lysander stepped silently to her side and took the job over. The case closed to a neat square box of a size that could ride behind a saddle or on the seat of the cart. Gemma murmured thanks and quickly snapped a set of latches tight. However, when she tried to lift it by the handle, Lysander simply hefted it from her grasp.

Once they were outside in the crisp evening air, Gemma in a woolen coat and Lysander in an ample knitted scarf that she had insisted he add to his own outerwear, Bing had led Bad Pony into the kitchen yard with the elderly cart rattling behind. Two lanterns were affixed to the front corners, for the clouds obstructed the moon. Shepherd Orren had ridden on ahead.

Bad Pony gave a belligerent snort and stepped restlessly sideways, knocking his haunches into the traces and jostling the cart. He even took a forward swing at Bing with his front hoof. Undeterred by the failure, he snaked his head out with teeth bared. Bing stood well back from the animal's reach.

"Hvatit!"

Bad Pony jerked his head about and tilted his shaggy ears in Lysander's direction, clearly at full alert.

Gemma took advantage of the pony's distraction and allowed Bing to help her up into the seat of the cart. Lysander stepped forward until he was very close indeed to Bad Pony.

"Watch yourself, lad!" Bing called out. "He's a fast 'un."

Lysander nodded. Indeed, Bad Pony would be fast. Swift and powerful, running low to the ground with his rider perched with stirrups high, practically kneeling on his back. *"Hello, Brave One,"* Lysander murmured in Russian.

At least he was fairly certain that was what he said. His Russian rested uneasily somewhere between a boyhood craze for the comedy of Fonvizin and a collection of battlefield curses assimilated from the Cossacks who drove the forward line of battle.

The pony gave a deep, resounding moan and pressed his flat forehead hard against Lysander's breastbone. With a great shudder, the pony submitted to Lysander's fingers scratching deeply behind his ears and down his neck along the base of his stiff mane.

Poor soldier, far from home. In his terrible mixture of Russian, Lysander explained the situation to the pony and asked him the great favor of pulling the cart gently and steadily, for there was a lady on a mission aboard. They were all counting on the pony to pull them through.

The pony breathed out a much calmer waffling snort and stood sedately while Lysander unclipped the lead and swept up the rains as he climbed into the cart next to Gemma.

He became aware that both Gemma and Bing stared at him in a sort of wide-eyed wary awe.

GEMMA BARELY KEPT her astonishment to herself. First Topknot and now Bad Pony. Even taciturn Mr. Bing. "All the silent ones," she murmured.

Mr. Worthington did not ask her what she meant by that. He left the reins easy and simply uttered what sounded like a command in Russian. The pony pulled away at a brisk trot and circled toward the gate to the lane. Mr. Bing ran jerkily ahead to open it wide, and then stood upon the lowest rung, watching them roll on.

Following Gemma's whispered directions, Mr. Worthington did little more than twitch the rein to the left or the right to have the pony make a turn.

He glanced warily at Gemma, who realized she stared at him still. She didn't speak, or ask any questions, despite her simmering curiosity. Mr. Worthington shied from questions. She realized now that he flinched from people's expectations.

They reached the farm in good order and Mr. Worthington jumped down to help Gemma from her seat. There was no step set into the cart that would accommodate a lady's skirts, so in the end Lysander simply took her by the waist and lifted her down, reasoning correctly that she didn't care to waste time. Gemma swallowed a squeak of surprise and accepted the help with a gracious thanks. She sounded a little breathless even to herself as he set her feet on the ground. He reached into the cart and lifted out the case, clearly preparing to follow her into the farmhouse.

She halted and leaned close. "We need to tie Bad Pony, or he'll simply run off," she whispered, a little afraid of upsetting the pony's newfound good nature.

Mr. Worthington took a look back at the pony. "No. He won't."

Gemma glanced uncertainly at Bad Pony, but then she cast Mr. Worthington an admittedly awed glance and accepted him at his word.

THE FARMHOUSE WAS little more than stone hut with three rooms. While the tearfully grateful farm wife bustled about getting the "Missus" some tea over Gemma's protestations, the man climbed a stair that was little more than a ladder up into the cottage loft. In a moment he reappeared and carefully descended the ladder with a bundled up child in his arms.

"Yes, thank you Shepherd Orren," Gemma said crisply. "I'll take a look at him here by the fire where it's warm."

With only one chair to offer Gemma, the man simply sat upon the floor with his child in his arms while Gemma unwrapped the blanket to reveal the boy's bare and spindly legs.

One was normal and healthy, if thin. The other was quite definitely injured, purple with bruising. Lysander felt a sickening chill swirl in his gut at the sight of the broken shinbone pressing up against the boy's skin from within.

"Oh well, that's nothing at all!" Gemma's voice was cheerful and assured. "We'll have to do a bit of this and that, and you will need a sturdy crutch that I'm sure your papa can make for you. Of course, you'll be bored silly with all the sitting about, but you'll be better soon, you'll see."

Lysander had four brothers. Between the five of them they'd broken more than a few bones in childhood. None had been as severe as this damaged child. The boy's injury looked more like something he had seen on the battlefield, where men's bones were crushed by bouncing cannonballs and dying horses.

The icy chill began to spread outward from his belly and climbed his spine. His mouth went dry and his hands began to turn numb. *Not now.*

Then Gemma turned her head and caught his gaze, pinning him in place with her clever gray eyes. "Mr. Worthington, if you would be so kind?"

MR. WORTHINGTON FOLLOWED her orders with only the barest hesitation. While Shepherd Orren held his son tightly on his lap, Mr. Worthington wrapped two large hands around the boy's skinny ankle.

"Don't jerk your hold," Gemma warned them both. "Slow and steady but once we begin, we cannot ease up. I've given him enough laudanum to relax his muscles, but I fear I cannot give him more. He is too small." She placed her hands on the boy's damaged shin, carefully wrapping her fingers around the healthy bone on either side of the fracture.

"You will pull until I say stop. I'm going to guide the ends of the bones into place. You will pull." She gazed evenly into Mr. Worthington's dark eyes, and then captured the gaze of Shepherd Orren as well. "And you will not slack until I say the word 'stop'. Understood?"

She had expected at least a smidgen of argument from Shepherd Orren but the man simply nodded and set his jaw grimly against his own child's oncoming pain.

"Now begin. Slow and steady."

Both men did as she asked. Gemma ignored the father's low grunt and the child's wail that quickly climbed to a shattering shriek. She ignored the dark, silent presence of Mr. Worthington at her side. She ignored the pain in her wrist and the gasps of Mrs. Orren and the concerned murmurs and rustlings of the other Orren children. There was nothing in the world except the bone in her hands and the two broken ends. She watched, and listened, and tried to sense through her fingertips as the bone shifted beneath the boy's skin. Almost there.

Then she had it. She felt and saw and heard the leg bone straighten and the two ends realign. "Hold there! Do not move! Keep the tension but do not pull further." One part of her brain hoped they understood what she meant but the other larger part of her tried to sense the way the bone was fitting beneath the skin and bruised flesh of the child. "Mr. Worthington, please rotate the lower leg ever so slightly clockwise." It was important that the bone heal straight, not twisted. She wanted to see this little boy run fast and wild over the slopes, not hobble.

Mr. Worthington did as he was asked, and he did it with a sort of perfect slowness, as if he had done it before. Gemma tucked that thought away for later and bent over the child's leg, trying to see beneath the swelling. "Light!"

The eldest Orren son scuttled forward with the candle from the table. Gemma tilted her head and stroked her thumb over the boy's lumpy shin. Then Mr. Worthington's careful rotation caused something to change and the two of the ends of the bone almost seemed to snap together as if magnetized. "Stop!"

After that, the rest was just bustle and weeping as Gemma took the four slats that Shepherd Orren happily broke from his best chair and bound them lengthwise around the boy's battered little leg. As she neatly tied off the last strip of binding, she looked up to see that the child had fallen into an exhausted sleep in his father's arms.

Shepherd Orren regarded her worriedly. "He went out like a snuffed candle. Will he be right?"

Gemma felt the boy's skinny wrist for his pulse and then smiled at the child's father. "He's fine. It's the laudanum, that's all." She turned to smile up at the worried Mrs. Orren. "He's to stay abed until I see him again. He's not to walk at all, not even a step. I'll be back in a few days to check on him. You must watch his foot. It will swell a bit, but mind it doesn't turn dark and that he can still wiggle his toes and feel a pinprick. Understood?"

"Raise it up."

Everyone turned to look at Mr. Worthington, who had spoken for the first time since entering the house. He stiffened a bit and no wonder, for it was as if a piece of furniture had spoken. He swallowed. "Hurt less, raised up."

Gemma couldn't help it. She grinned at him, a wide smile she rarely used, but there was something about his wary reticence that brought to mind a glorious stag halting in alarm in the forest before leaping magnificently away. "Mr. Worthington is entirely correct. Keeping his leg raised on a pile of quilts or pillows should ease the throbbing quite a bit."

Mr. Worthington had stopped looking at the sheep herder's family with alarm. His attention was now entirely fixed on her. Her grin faded at the darkening intensity in his gaze. She withdrew slightly from the contact, turning to her open case beside her on the floor and rummaging for a moment. She took out a small vial and tipped a measured amount of laudanum into it. She corked it and handed it to Mrs. Orren. "He may have three drops in a glass of milk after a meal. Give him stews and things that are easy to eat. We don't want him moving any more than necessary. And the milk is important. Have you a cow?"

"No Missus Oakes, but we've a fine milk goat for t' children. Will that do?"

Gemma nodded. "As good or better. Watch for fever. A little bit is to be expected and cool cloths can be applied. If it gets too high, you must fetch me." Not that there was a great deal she could do if the boy took infection. Nonetheless, she would try. She also reached into her case and handed the good wife a folded paper packet. "Willow bark tea will help for fever and even a little bit with the pain. Start weak and only get stronger if need be."

Mrs. Orren held the medicines to her bosom and nodded most seriously. "Yes Missus. Thank you so, Missus. It's good of you to take the trouble. Look at him sleeping now, like it never happened."

Gemma nodded, although when the laudanum wore off the little boy would most definitely be making his unhappiness heard once more, but Mrs. Orren was an experienced mother. Gemma felt ill-equipped to offer any advice other than medicinal.

Mr. Worthington felt no such restraint. "Strap him down."

Mrs. Orren looked appalled, but Shepherd Orren nodded sagely. "Aye. Nothing less would hold me down as a lad. I'll get a bit of soft rope from the barn."

On one hand, Gemma was relieved to have had the notion so easily accepted by the man. On the other hand, she had to wonder if the radical advice would've taken root when uttered by a woman.

She latched her medicine case closed. It was only then that she once more became aware of the throbbing pain lancing up her arm from her injured wrist. She was sure she had not made a sound, but in an instant Mr. Worthington was at her side, helping her to stand. He hefted the heavy medicine case with one hand and kept the other firmly under her elbow as they left the cottage.

Shepherd Orren relighted their lanterns. Mrs. Orren and the rest of the Orren children assembled on the steps to wave them away.

Gemma slumped on the seat of the cart with her good hand cradling her arm to absorb the jostling of the cart. She knew that they would be watched until the group in the door could no longer hear the clopping of Bad Pony's hooves on the lane.

Chapter 14

T HE WAR PONY gave Lysander no trouble at all on the drive back to the manor. The lanterns showed them the paler strip of road clear before them. The dale rang with silence. Even the birds had long gone to bed. There was no noise at all but the clop of Bad Pony's hooves on the packed soil and the creak and jostle of the cart. Lysander felt passable. Adequate. Something unfortunate had happened and he had been called upon, and instead of losing control, he had done well. Gemma had smiled at him in that wonderful way she had.

Mrs. Oakes. She was Mrs. Oakes and her smile had been naught but her own relief and pleasure at a job well done. Not for him.

Still, it was a notable occurrence. People, especially ladies, did not often look upon him and smile. He was well aware that his demeanor distressed people. He wasn't precisely sure what he was doing that was so alarming, although once Elektra had told him that he seemed to exist a mere instant away from darkness and destruction.

He hadn't been able to explain to her that the destruction she spoke of was still close behind him, breathing down his neck. It had followed him home from the Peninsula like a starving wolf followed a man in a winter forest.

It isn't me, he'd wanted to tell his sister. *It isn't I they should fear*, except that he had come to understand that somehow he had absorbed the beast and that he now took it with him everywhere. He rather suspected that the wolf must shine through him like the glowing coals of predator eyes in the darkness.

And yet this woman beside him had smiled at him, and patted his arm, and said, "Oh, that was well done, Mr. Worthington!"

And the Yorkshire man and his wife had smiled at him and thanked him and when they had driven away, the entire family except the injured boy had piled out onto their steps and waved them away. "Good night, Mrs. Oakes! Good night, Mr. Worthington!"

Just as if he were an actual person. It had been the strangest evening.

As if she was thinking the same thing at the same moment, Mrs. Oakes turned to him. "Your quiet manner serves you well here. Yorkshire folk work hard and have little patience for idle chatter. I know many a quiet man who is respected here."

Lysander turned to look at her. The bit of light from the lanterns shimmered on her porcelain skin. Even bundled up as she was with her scarf nearly covering her chin and her practical man's knitted hat pulled down over her ears, she glowed. She reminded him of a luminous alabaster angel in a midnight garden. She caught his intense gaze with her own and wrinkled her nose at him.

"I know I look a mess. You must be used to a much more fashionable sort of lady. New gowns every Season and a different bonnet for every outfit."

Lysander considered that for a moment. "Sisters. A lot of gowns. Mostly." He was thinking of Attie, who had grown into a gangling adolescent while he'd been at war and her inquisitive mischievousness had turned sulky and intense. He had never seen Attie in a dress without trousers beneath it nor had he ever seen her hair pinned up in a shining mass or even anything ornamental on her person whatsoever. "Not all of them."

Mrs. Oakes leaned forward and squinted at him as if trying to read the printed word on the page of his face. "How many sisters do you have?"

Lysander felt the intensity of her focus, but there was something reassuring about her that made him trust her. Her intense regard did not alarm him the same way as that of most strangers, or even the silent longing of his family's wistful gazes. "Three."

"How wonderful." She sighed wistfully. "I had no siblings. One should share. It does seem rather greedy of you to take all the siblings. Do you suppose you got mine?"

The accusation was so ludicrous that Lysander made a rather shocked noise in his throat. He was being teased? Him?

"You laughed." She narrowed her eyes at him. "That was a laugh. Yes, I've taken stock of the situation and I had decided to declare that a laugh."

Teasing. He knew it when he heard it. He did have all those siblings after all. But no one had teased him for years. They spoke so gently, so carefully, so earnestly, their words kind and their voices filled with compassion—and pain and need and loss until the weight of it closed his throat and silenced his voice.

Tonight he had not been a disappointment. He had not let anyone down. He had driven Mrs. Oakes and had helped set a little boy's leg so that the child would heal strong and active and fast on his feet. He had seen gratitude in the eyes of people around him and approval in Mrs. Oakes's peaceful cloudy sky eyes.

"You were—" *I need a word. Think. What is the right word for Gemma Oakes?* "Splendid."

He felt her jolt of surprise and he was aware that she'd turned her head to look at him again. This time he kept his gaze on Bad Pony's fuzzy flanks and the road ahead. When she let out a soft sigh, he felt it cross his cheek like a benediction.

"Thank you. That was a very nice thing to say to me, Mr. Worthington."

He wanted to say more. He wanted to tell her about the way that they had all looked at her. She hadn't seemed to notice it or to understand what she had done. A broken child would now grow straight and strong. She had changed lives tonight.

"You take care ... of your people."

He looked at her shyly. She shook her head slightly and looked down at her hands. "I am not a lady. I'm merely the daughter of a librarian. The doctor married a bit below his station, I fear. I never quite understood why. But I try my best."

"You are *their* lady."

"I am no better than anyone in this dale."

Lysander's thoughts tripped on their own feet and tangled themselves on the ground. He wanted to tell her that she was wrong. And he wanted to tell her that she was right. Concepts of class and responsibility and labels and preconceptions, those were complicated things that required complicated words.

His uncooperative tongue frustrated him. For the first time he found himself longing to speak to someone. He wanted to tell her things.

When he'd read the sonnets tonight, he had given himself over to recitation of words he had heard all his life. The words had flowed from his tongue as if it had belonged to a different man.

He had not tried to read aloud since he returned. He had tried to read, for he had once enjoyed it greatly, but as much as he wished to concentrate, his memories would steal their way into his thoughts. Even the driest volume of Greek philosophy would trigger recollections of blood.

Reading aloud to Gemma Oakes had been as effortless

as breathing. The words had come from behind his memories of battle, from so far back that they carried with them hints of the carefree joy of his youth.

He hadn't thought of his childhood in so long. When he turned to look behind him, he only saw the catastrophic defeat at Burgos Castle. He saw the muddy medical tents that leaked the rain until the floor ran with rivulets tinted red by dying men.

Bad Pony nodded his head and the reins jerked in Lysander's loosened fingers. He tightened his hands quickly and the pony settled once more into his plodding walk. The stalking wolf of memory tried to howl again, even here in this peaceful quiet, with the golden lantern-light shimmering upon the sweetly weary features of the woman beside him.

She was silent now. He saw that her eyes were closed and her head nodded in exhaustion. Her left hand cradled her bandaged wrist to her bosom. She was injured at his hand. She was astonishing. She was important. She was needed.

How could he make it right? How could he stay to help until Gemma healed, when his mother lay ill and his family remained spread far and wide?

AT YEW MANOR, Mr. Worthington took on the task of bedding down Bad Pony while Mr. Bing helped Gemma carry her medical case back into the house. While he was setting it carefully on her worktable in the stillroom, Gemma positioned herself to barricade the only exit. She had something she wanted to discuss with dear Mr. Bing.

"Mr. Bing, I noticed that Mr. Worthington became rather muddy in the river."

Mr. Bing grunted and answered without turning his head. "Aye, t' fool lad went in after that useless dog of yours. Silly creature got herself into deep water."

"Yes, he mentioned that. What he didn't mention was the precise reason why he did not clean up in the nice warm privacy of the stable." She saw Mr. Bing's shoulder twitch slightly.

Mr. Bing lifted his chin and dusted his hands as if he had done something far more laborious than carry a medical case that she'd been toting by herself for years. Then he turned to look her straight in the eye. "Saw that, did you?"

Gemma became rather painfully aware that she was blushing. Drat. Here she was trying to take Mr. Bing to task when suddenly she was breathless with the memory of water running down Mr. Worthington's flat muscled abdomen. There was nothing she could do about the redness of her cheeks, so she narrowed her eyes at her sometimes-employee, sometimes-father figure, occasional pain-in-the-arse dear Mr. Bing. "I did see that. As I'm sure that you intended me to. May I ask why you felt it was necessary?"

Bing gave up gruff bark of laughter. "Missus, I know you want t' world to think you're made of steel and porcelain, but you forget how long I've known you. If you spend another year alone in this great, crumbling house, you're like to go battlefield mad yourself."

Gemma's jaw dropped. She would have protested, but Mr. Bing was not yet done.

"That fellow's a bit odd, I'll grant it. But he's all right underneath. He saved that worthless dog, didn't he? He gives more than he gets, just like you." Mr. Bing scratched his balding head. "You know I'm as loyal as could be to Dr. Oakes. But he's dead, ain't he? And you're not! I hate to see you wasting that big heart on medicine alone when you orta have a family of your own!"

Gemma had no words to challenge Mr. Bing's sudden outburst. The nerve! The unmitigated gall!

The truth.

Oh, it was a truth she did not want to acknowledge. Especially not before Mr. Bing, who was nearly old enough to be her father! And yet here he was, in his strange way, the closest thing she had to a friend.

He had purposely arranged that bit of theater at the rain barrel! As what, *temptation*?

Even so, when the hot flush of memory swept her she could do nothing but clench her eyes tight and turn half away from the pity and understanding in his eyes.

He brushed by her on his way out of the room and she stayed right where she was until she could no longer hear the clump of his boots in her house.

Drat the truth.

AS SHE MADE her weary way to bed, Gemma spotted the book of sonnets on the kitchen table and took it with her.

The manor was incredibly silent this late at night and for the most part, Gemma enjoyed the peacefulness. She had always been a quiet person.

Perhaps that stemmed from being raised in a library. When she'd been very young, her mother had fallen sickly. Gemma's nurse had been enlisted to care for her mother and her absent-minded father had apparently forgot to ever secure another.

Her well-meaning but undemonstrative Papa had simply taken tiny Gemma to work with him. In the vast chambers of the Cambridge University Library, Gemma lived her earliest memories in a forest of bookshelves, as tall as giants and as impenetrable as walls.

She learned to play quietly beneath her papa's desk, for it was a serious breach of trust for the head librarian of the main library to allow his tiny daughter free rein in those hallowed halls, and she learned to love books.

When she turned fourteen her mother had been gone

for seven years. Gemma scarcely remembered anything but a sweet, pale face upon a pillow and the touch of a thin, weak hand upon her cheek.

Gemma had begun assisting her father at the library in the off hours, replacing books and cataloguing. A young student found her in the section on poetry and self-righteously reported her presence to the university.

Gemma knew perfectly well that had been nothing but a nasty piece of revenge, for the young man in question had tried to force a kiss from her. Gemma had slapped him with all the power of her innocent shock and fear—and also the dense volume she'd forgotten she held in her hand.

Her father had nearly lost his position and Gemma had been banished from the place that meant more to her than her actual domicile. She'd been torn from the hushed luxury of the library to go home and keep an empty house for her father.

However, she brought home the book that saved her virtue. A volume of Shakespeare's sonnets.

Not long after that, a man came to visit the librarian and his daughter. He was a student unlike any they had seen before. For one thing, he was older than the other young men. At eight and twenty, Mr. Edmund Oakes had found his calling and decided to study medicine. His social standing did not require a career and he had no need of income, but he had a fine mind and a stalwart code of ethics. He had come to apologize to Gemma and her father for the poor behavior of his younger cousin, Galen, or as Gemma thought of him, "the student in the stacks."

Gemma liked him and her papa admired him very much. Edmund Oakes became a frequent guest and family friend. One day after her nineteenth birthday, Edmund noticed that Gemma wasn't a child anymore and Gemma noticed him noticing her.

He was Dr. Oakes by then and a marriage seemed like a

fine idea to all concerned. It was not until Gemma went to Edmund's family home to meet her new in-laws that she realized how far beneath himself Edmund had wed. The Oakes were not so much cruel as unapologetically appalled and mystified by Edmund's choice. They seemed so certain of Gemma's inferiority that for the first time in her life, she began to doubt her worth.

When Edmund told his new bride that he planned to apply his knowledge of medicine to help the war effort, Gemma had leapt at the opportunity to go with him as his nurse and assistant—and leave the imperious Oakes family far behind them.

Gemma, alone in her claustrophobic little bedchamber in Yew Manor, set her candle on her nightstand and sat on the edge of her bed. She smoothed the rich, red leather cover of the volume of sonnets with tingling fingertips.

Who was Mr. Lysander Worthington really? What did she know of this stranger she wanted so badly to help?

And why did she feel compelled to?

Who better than you? You were there.

Yes, I was there.

By the time Gemma and Edmund had returned from the war, Edmund frail and recovering far too slowly from a fever, Gemma's father had died quietly in his sleep. The newly appointed head librarian had taken up residence in her father's house, which was owned by the University. Gemma was saddened by the loss but after so much horrible death all around her, she was grateful that her papa's end had been so painless.

And she wasn't really alone, for she'd had Edmund. Except, as she discovered in the following years, only a portion of her husband had returned from the war.

Gemma decided to select a random page, deciding with a rather depressed whimsy that it would hold the answers. The volume fell open to Sonnet 25.

> *"The painful warrior famousèd for worth,*
> *After a thousand victories once foiled,*
> *Is from the book of honor razèd quite,*
> *And all the rest forgot for which he toiled."*

Well, goodness. How fitting. A valiant soldier had returned from a terrible war, only to be considered mad and dangerous. *How do you know he is valiant? Perhaps he is a coward. Perhaps that is what he flees from.*

Recalling the ridiculous battle with the ram, and his reckless disregard for his own safety as he flung her far from danger, Gemma found it hard to imagine Mr. Worthington bolting from a mere human adversary. She would wager her entire stillroom that he'd fought bravely and well against the enemy.

Gemma thought of Mr. Worthington's dark eyes. She remembered his sculpted chest gleaming in the sun. She closed her eyes and replayed his deep erudite voice speaking verses of passionate love to her. She allowed the image of him half-naked the sunlight to roll across her inner vision. The muscles that laced tightly around his narrow waist. The way his trousers clung to his athletic buttocks. His large hands sweeping the water from his skin. She imagined them on her skin instead and a deep ache pulsed within her.

She didn't realize that her hands trembled as they lightly rested upon the book in her lap.

> *"Then happy I am that I love and am beloved*
> *Where I may not remove nor be removed."*

Chapter 15

LONDON STILL SMELLED like London. With the familiar scents of coal soot, carriage horse urine on the cobbled street and something gone bad at the butcher down the road, came so many memories.

Pollux Worthington stood at the base of the once-grand marble steps leading to the doorway of Worthington House. He'd been gone a long time. Despite that, the house seemed unchanged, though the façade appeared cleaner and more well-tended. Poll saw that removing the London soot and dirt had actually revealed the shabbiness all the more clearly.

It wasn't just a house. It was Worthington House, containing both haven and heartache for every Worthington—himself most especially.

It had been rather diabolical to have it be Miranda who summoned him from his sojourn with the traveling theatrical troupe. He likely would not have responded for anyone else, not even Iris herself. He suspected the machinations of his youngest sister, Attie. All things diabolical usually boiled down to fourteen-year-old Atalanta Worthington. Attie would stop at nothing to get her way, for she was the most Worthington of all the Worthingtons.

But Miranda never lied, or exaggerated, nor even embellished. Therefore, the situation must be every bit as dire as the letter had described.

Miranda. Beautiful, unattainable Miranda. *I found her first.* That fact always flashed across his consciousness whenever he thought of Miranda married to his twin brother Castor. He had found Miranda first.

Then Cas had come along and swept her away from him. In that moment, Poll had not only lost the finest woman he'd ever known but he'd lost his twin, his closest friend, his brother.

Before then, he'd scarcely spent a day of his life without his brother at his side. Now he was returning after months away from his family. Had it really been over a year?

Poll took a deep breath and hefted his rucksack over one shoulder to mount the steps to the door of Worthington House. There was no such thing as a butler, nor even a footman here. One either knocked and was let in by member of the family, or one simply walked right in. The door was never locked, for the Worthingtons were always at home.

The door swung open at his touch and Poll noticed that the hinges hardly creaked at all. Yes, someone had been very busy. The foyer was still cluttered but vastly less jumbled and he noticed that there were actually a couple of places one could sit down. However, it was clear from the rectangular impressions of piles of books on the tatty velvet upholstery that the two spindly gilt chairs would never recover.

The house was so quiet that Poll actually felt a chill of foreboding. This house was never quiet.

"Hello?" His voice rang oddly through the empty downstairs. Poll walked through the foyer and down the hall. He moved quickly, only pausing to cast an uneasy glance into each open darkened room. Part of his mind noticed the fact that there was now a rather posh jumble of comfort rather than the chaotic spill of years past. The rest of him became more alarmed the farther he searched while finding no one.

The parlor that Iris used as a painting studio lay still and cold. A half-finished painting on the easel looked to be a depiction of Shakespeare with something spiny atop his head like a lumpy cap. A hedgehog?

But the paints on the pallet beside it had hardened and the stinging scent of turpentine had faded to nearly nothing. Poll ran one finger across the paintbrush lying along the lip of the easel. The pigment had hardened, the bristles ruined now beyond a soaking. His fingertip came away dusty.

How long had Iris been ill? Miranda had not specified in the note. Fear clutched Poll deep in his throat. Was he too late?

Mrs. Philpot was always in the kitchen. Poll strode quickly to the backstairs and clattered down them at speed. The kitchen was dim, lighted only by late afternoon light seeping in through the high cellar windows, but it was enough to see stout Mrs. Philpot sleeping in her chair before the fire. Something was bubbling away on the stove and there were chopped vegetables on the worktable, so Philpot was clearly cooking for the family.

Where were they? Leaving Philpot to her rest, for at best Mrs. Philpot was a forgetful sort of person, though hardworking. She was not, however, the person one should turn to for coherent answers to urgent questions.

Abandoning thoughtful progress for speed, Poll dashed back up the back stairs and then continued up the main stairs to the bedchamber floor. It was so quiet. Too damned quiet.

"Hello?" He heard his voice crack slightly. God, if he was too late in coming home...

"Hush. If you wake Aurora after all the work I had putting her down, I shall put bees in your chamber pot."

With a rush of relief, Poll turned to see his sister Attie glaring at him from a darkened doorway. "Attie!" He quickly modulated his tone to almost a whisper. "Thank heaven! The place is damned grim."

Attie crossed her arms and glared at him. Attie was a glaring sort of person, but this was a glare with intent. "Hello, Poll. Welcome home."

She was taller than when he'd last seen her, and angrier. Her tone was flat, almost bored, but her arms were crossed tightly over her torso and he could see her jaw clench.

Good God, Attie was worried sick. Diabolical she might be, his little sister was clearly exhausted and terrified.

Poll held out his arms. "Come here, you monstrous brat."

Attie thudded into him so hard he staggered. Her wiry arms wound around his waist as she pressed her hot face into his cravat. She wasn't one to weep but he could feel her quivering with tension in his embrace. He ran his hand over her thick unkempt braids and gave one an affectionate little tug. "Come on, buck up. Tell me what's going on with Iris. Where's Archie? Where's—" He cleared his throat. "Where is Cas?"

Attie sniffled and rubbed her face against him. Poll suspected she had wiped her nose on his cravat. But he didn't care.

"Cas is in the sickroom. Callie and the scarred man she insisted on marrying came in just this morning and they're resting." Attie claimed not to like Callie's husband, Sir Ren Porter, although everyone knew that Ren was one of the few people Attie actually respected. "Archie's exhausted, as is Miranda. They won't let me in, so I look after Aurora mostly. Why won't they let me look after Iris? I can be very restful company."

"Of course you could, pet." Poll highly doubted the fact. Even on her good days, Attie was a complicated and splendid being but restful company she was not. "Come on then. Let's go look in on Iris."

Attie drew back and nodded. Her eyes were reddened

but they were dry and her pointed little chin was firm. "Mrs. Philpot said I should call her mummy, since she is sick. I think that is a rotten idea."

"Oh, Philpot. No one listens to Philpot. Iris is Iris, and that's all. Nothing will change that."

Attie drew a deep breath. "I knew you'd know what I meant."

As they turned to walk side-by-side to the mistress's bedchamber, Poll felt Attie's bony little fingers clinch his. Good Lord, if Atalanta Worthington wanted cuddles, things were dire indeed.

POLL ENTERED HIS mother's bedchamber and stepped quietly across the carpet to the heavily curtained bed. The room was dim though it was midafternoon. A large wing-back chair was pulled close to the side of the bed and Poll saw a male hand draped over the arm of it that looked very much like his own hand.

"Hello, Castor."

The hand twitched and a lean face looked around the high-back chair at him. A face very much like his own.

"It's about bloody time." Cas's tone was more weary than angry. He sounded husky with exhaustion but when he stood and turned to greet Poll, there was a slight smile on his face.

Poll considered his brother for a long moment. In the past many months he had thought about Cas with emotions ranging from betrayed hatred to boyish longing for his brother at his side. Perhaps it would never be simple between them again. Every feeling was barbed, ready to catch and hold another emotion until it was no better than a tangle of fishhooks.

"So, you are a father now. I got letters."

"Letters which you rarely answered," Cas said as he

rubbed a hand over his weary face. "But you're here now. It's good that you're here now."

Poll's throat tightened and he finally dared a glance at the still figure in the great bed. Iris lay bundled in quilts until only her pale face was visible amidst a cloud of wavy silver hair. She looked like a wax figurine of the real Iris, the creation by some not so talented sculptor with little gift for capturing his subject's spirit.

"May I?"

Cas stepped away from the chair and waved Poll into his place.

"I need tea. And Philpot was supposed to bring soup. Poor old thing is spent. I'd better go down."

Poll felt his brother's presence leave the room and his shoulders relaxed a fraction in relief. That was a skirmish for another time.

He bent forward with his elbows on his knees and took his mother's limp hand into his own. Iris's hands.

Poll couldn't think of a time when Iris's hands had not been in motion. Fluttering scarves, dabbling paintbrushes, gesturing theatrically to emphasize her poetic ramblings. Poll felt the lack of her greeting him home most severely. She should come sailing down the stairs, cooing and trailing diaphanous clothing, speaking fine nonsense and touching his cheeks with her warm hands.

Poll opened his mother's hand and pressed her palm against his cheek. He closed his eyes and imagined what she might've said.

My beautiful boy. Oh what wondrous fortune has bestowed upon us your dearest presence!

Iris always sounded as if she were reciting a play, whether she was teasing the Prince Regent or telling a joke to a potted palm. She treated everyone with fond endearments and forced them to brutal independence with her complete lack of maternal supervision.

She was Iris to every single one of them. She always had been, even before she had slipped so far away from reality. He could recall tiny Attie screaming for Iris "Iris! I fell down, Iris! I need a kiss, Iris!"

An unconventional mother she might be, yet she was his mother still. He could not bear the thought of the world with an Iris-shaped hole in it. He curled her fingers in his and kissed them. "If you please, my darling Iris, I would very much like it if you would sit up and speak to me. Better yet, I'd like to see you back at your easel. You must finish that painting of Shakespeare and the hedgehog."

"Thistle."

The word was faint. Poll doubted his own hearing for a moment. He opened his eyes and peered at his mother's still face. "What? Did you say something? Iris?"

She lay still as ever, only the slight rise and fall of her chest telling him that she was still with him, still with all of them in Worthington house.

Poll heard a step. He would recognize his brother's tread anywhere and anytime. He laid Iris's hand back down on the coverlet and smoothed her limp fingers straight before he stood and turned to face his brother.

"Did you say something?"

Cas looked up from the tray he was maneuvering through the doorway. "What? No. I made tea and Philpot scrounged up a tea cake for you from somewhere. I haven't seen a tea cake for a week. You always were her favorite." Cas shot the jest out in a careless tone, seemingly from pure force of habit.

Poll was in no mood for the old game of vying for the primary spot in Philpot's pastry-filled affections. They weren't boys anymore. Cas was someone's husband—*Miranda's husband*—and someone's father, as well. Their lives no longer ran in tandem. They were no longer partners in crime, no longer a pair, no longer the two of them against the world.

Poll took the tea and drank it down black and strong, ignoring the cream and the tea cake on the tray. "What has the physician said about Iris's condition? Someone has seen her, haven't they?"

Cas set the tray down. "No, we thought we'd let her ride it out, catch-as-catch-can." He rounded on Poll with black fury in his eyes, spitting out the words in a fierce whisper. "Of course, someone has seen her! The Prince Regent has sent his own physician thrice a week but there's nothing that can be done! If she is strong enough she will survive it. If she is not—"

Cas's rage choked off. He swallowed hard and bleak loss replaced the anger in his eyes. The eyes that were just like Poll's eyes.

Poll pulled his dejected brother into his arms. Sometimes he hated Cas. This was not one of those times. Cas pushed at him for a moment and then relaxed into Poll's hard clasp.

"God, Poll. I don't know how to fix this. There's no sneak-around! There's no secret passageway or bad invention or great escape! She simply gets sicker and sicker and there's not a damn thing I can do about it!"

Poll shook his head. "You don't have to do anything. You don't have to fix it. Take care of her. Pour Philpot's soup down her throat. Sing silly songs and remind her that she loves us and that we want her to stay. And then she will! She will stay, Cas. For God's sake, she has a grandchild now! Can you picture Iris Worthington missing out on that?"

Cas let out a hoarse sound, part sob and part laugh. "She dotes on Aurora."

"Why is this all on you? Where is Dade?"

Cas straightened and shoved a hand through his hair. "He's been called up before the Prince Regent for something or another. He tried to tell Prinny to bugger off because of Iris, but she talks about Prinny as if he's a friend of hers. Perhaps it's true. He'll be back soon, but just like the rest of us, he's worn flat. Before this, Dade was up in Shropshire, helping Aaron rebuild Worthington Manor. Elektra is terribly sickened, apparently."

"Elektra? She's ill as well?"

Cas stared for a long moment. "Damn. You have been gone a long time. Elektra is expecting. As big as a house, according to Dade. Miranda was only ill the first few months. She tells me that it's not uncommon for some women to unpack their baskets every single day of their condition."

His family had moved on without him. Poll took a breath. "Damn. I can't imagine Elektra is taking that well at all. She hates admitting to weakness."

Cas let out a long sigh. "Don't we all?"

"What about Lysander? Isn't he helping out?"

Cas turned to stare at Poll. "I thought Lysander was with you. He was sent to bring you back."

Poll blinked. "I had a letter from Miranda and rode hard home, night and day. I have no idea where Lysander is."

The two stared at each other in consternation for a long moment. The silence was broken by a thready whisper from the curtained bed.

"Then I daresay … someone ought to go find him … at once."

ATTIE LEFT CAS and Poll to their reunion and wandered down the front stairs, too edgy to even consider riding down the banister. This would have been alarming if her worried thoughts could have settled on the notion for more than a split second.

Poll had come home without Lysander.

This was not acceptable. Attie had made a plan. Lysander would ride out and do Attie's bidding, both freeing himself from his quietly desperate state of agitation and serving the doubly useful purpose of bringing home the unbearably absent Poll. It was a perfectly efficient notion.

Had she made a mistake? Attie wasn't much into self-examination, so she dismissed the notion out of hand. Someone, somewhere, had undoubtedly committed a grave error, but she was quite certain it had not been she.

After all, Castor and Pollux Worthington were at that moment having a civil conversation, right at Iris's sickbed yet! If anything could revive Iris's will to survive, it would be the reunion of her beloved twin sons.

In the front hall, Miranda had risen and dressed and was bouncing Aurora on her hip as she turned away from the front door.

Attie wasn't terribly concerned with clothing and hair and the presentation thereof, but she was not blind to the fact that Miranda looked a bit more well turned out than had been her custom these last worrisome weeks.

Attie sat down on the bottom step and plunked her elbows on her knees and her chin on her fists. "Did you change your dress when you knew that Poll had come home?" It was always best to begin with the real question. It saved a great deal of time and had the added benefit of making people want to be rid of her, which distracted certain ladylike persons from urging Attie to put a ribbon in her hair or change out of her brother's old clothes.

Miranda pretended to care about the handful of letters she'd just paid the post-boy for. Lately, the post had been ruthlessly tossed into a brass spittoon kept by the front door, for Worthington House had larger issues to attend to at the moment. No one in the family give a single damn about invitations.

Miranda glanced up, clearly realized that her avoidance

technique wasn't working. As if Attie could ever be distracted from her intentions! Miranda let out a sigh.

"I know it must seem silly. It isn't that I want Poll to be
attracted to me. He is my brother now and I'm quite content with that. I hope he can be as well."

Attie didn't comment. Waiting silently whilst staring
was far more eerie, she'd discovered.

Miranda kissed Aurora on the top of her silky curls. "I
suppose I wanted to look nice because I want Poll to see
that I'm well and happy, not exhausted and ill-kempt.
Which, when I say it out loud is even more—"

Miranda trailed off as she peered at one of the letters in
her hand.

Attie twitched with curiosity. She been bored already
anyway, for Miranda was far too sensible to be entertaining
when provoked. "What? What is that letter?"

Miranda looked up at Attie with puzzlement etched on
her fine features.

"Do we know anyone in Yorkshire?"

Chapter 16

T O THE FAMILY of Mr. Lysander Worthington,
I write to you regarding the well-being of your relation,
Lysander Worthington.

Mr. Worthington is currently lodging near Farby in Yorkshire
due to the minor injury of his mount. There was a contretemps in
the village square involving Mr. Worthington and a prize ram.
Although no one was seriously injured, the situation made it clear
to me that Mr. Worthington might best be served by remaining
out of the public for some time.

He has convinced me of your loving regard, so I have made so
bold as to write without introduction so that I may reassure you of
the safety and wellness of your brother and son.

Should you feel distress that his visit is an imposition, please
rest easy on my account. He has proved to be of immeasurable
help to me even as I strive to assist him.

Signed,

(with heartfelt apology for the appalling script, inescapable I
fear, due to an injury)

Mrs. Oakes
Yew Manor
Swaledale, North Yorkshire

In the largest and most elaborately ornamented bedchamber in Worthington House, a family meeting had been
called amidst the festoons of lace, bouquets of dried roses
and randomly stacked paintings bearing vivid images of a

recognizable William Shakespeare, usually accompanied by a bizarre interchangeable menagerie. Iris and Archie's room, of course.

Dade looked up from the letter he had just read aloud to his family and frowned. "Prize ram? What the hell?"

Poll clapped a hand over his mouth and snorted laughter into it. Dade cast a sour glance his way.

"Is there something you would like to share with the class, Poll?"

They all turned to stare at Poll.

The entire family (at least those not at sea or imprisoned by bed rest) had wedged themselves into Iris's bedchamber, crowding around her sickbed the same way they used to gather round the large table in the kitchen when a family meeting was called.

Grumbling, Philpot had hauled her old bones to her bed, for she'd taken a turn at nursing Iris the night before and "—need my rest, not like you youngsters, it's about bloomin' time you children showed up to visit your poor mother, and her on her last breath until just this afternoon—"

They'd all hung themselves upon her in gratitude, smothering her with hugs and kisses and "dear old thing" and "darling Pottie" until her grousing was reduced to the low, background simmer it had ever been.

Now, Calliope, the eldest next to Daedalus, sat upon her husband Ren Porter's lap on a shabby armchair, dandling little Aurora on her knee and entertaining her with a yarn doll. Beside them, Miranda and Cas snuggled close in another mismatched and mended chair. Dade and Archie stood on opposite sides of the headboard of Iris's bed much as the Royal Guard stood beside the throne.

For her part, Iris, her fever broken at long last, presided over them like royalty. She sat back upon plumped pillows, her silver hair combed and braided, her eyes bright in her pale face and her hands alight with motion, albeit slower and more wearily than usual. Attie sprawled on the bed at Iris's feet, one hand curled gently over her mother's ankle as if she feared to release her.

Poll waved a hand limply at them all, laughing too hard to continue. "Goo—Goose—Gogs!"

Dade narrowed his gaze at his younger brother, but there was no quashing a Worthington on a laughing binge. "When you've finished cackling over gooseberries, Poll, you may explain the joke to the rest of us."

He turned back to the rest of the clan. "So Lysander has stranded himself in Yorkshire, of all places. With my horse!" He cast an exasperated glance at Attie. "I don't suppose you thought to consult me before sending him out? I'd already decided to hire a Bow Street Runner to fetch Poll home if he didn't arrive shortly. Which, I might point out, he did."

Attie regarded Dade without alarm. "So you agree it was a good idea."

Dade opened his mouth to contradict her, then closed it again. "Never mind. Lysander is soundly stuck and from the tone of this letter, he won't be on his way home soon."

Attie sent a foul glare at the letter and, by association, the letter-writer. "She can't keep him. He's ours."

"Attie!" Callie frowned at her sister. "She has hardly kidnapped him! She is clearly concerned for his well-being. She was under no obligation to take him in, nor even to write to us of his troubles. She sounds kind and concerned."

"It's so romantic," Iris whispered to Archie, her sweet voice worn away by her terrible cough. "Do you remember Yorkshire, darling? *A Midsummer Night's Dream*?"

Archie bowed to his queen and kissed her pale cheek. "I do, indeed. You wore Titania like a second skin, my dearest."

"And you made a delectable Oberon!"

"And we danced in the rain, refusing to close the show

even though the audience had fled the storm." Archie slid his knuckles down her cheek as she sighed happily up at him.

The Worthington siblings went still, their deep gladness for their mother's recovery joining them despite their wrangling. Callie reached out for Miranda's hand and clasped it tightly.

"Thank you for caring for her," she whispered to her second-newest sister, her lashes darkened with unshed tears.

Miranda, former widow and orphan, now as much a Worthington as anyone, simply shook her head and squeezed Callie's hand in turn.

Cas leaned his cheek on the top her head. "You," he murmured, "never cease to astonish me."

Miranda closed her eyes and breathed in her husband's admiration with a serene smile. Then, recalling their audience, she cast a wary glance in Poll's direction.

Poll sat alone in a chair. His amusement had faded and he now gazed down at the carpet. Then he looked up, sending a single tortured glance directly into Miranda's eyes.

At her small gasp of dismay, Callie leaned close. "Don't you dare have regrets, Mira. In time, Poll will be all right." She gave a tiny snort. "I love him to bits, but he's always had a tendency to wallow. This is a prime opportunity for a bit of romantic heartbreak. He'll fall passionately in love again before you know it."

Miranda nodded and looked away. She fervently wished she and Poll could be as close as they had once been, back when he'd been her charming, witty friend and kindly sharer of interesting books. Before he'd declared his feelings. Before she'd met his twin brother and developed feelings of her own.

She hoped Poll would fall in love soon and end this terrible tension between them. Of course, the future love interest would have to be just the right sort of person. Someone who could embrace the uncommon, peculiar, occasionally terrifying, devoted, accepting Worthingtons. Miranda would fight to the death to keep anyone from ruining her bizarre, beloved adopted family.

She looked at Attie in bemusement. Attie had always been prone to meddle with her siblings' promising relationships. Occasionally, this interference had involved poison and firearms. *I think I understand you even better now.*

Attie looked back at Miranda, and then at Poll.

Attie knew Poll still thought he was in love with Miranda, which was idiotic but very Poll. He was the most powerfully loyal of them all. It made sense that he would cling to his original feelings long past the point of logic or reason.

She had known that Poll would not learn to live with Miranda's choice of Castor unless he came home to confront their absurdly close relationship and see it for what it was—true love. Having accomplished her aim of bringing Poll home, she must now resolve Lysander's absence before that highly suspicious Yorkshire person managed to set her hooks into Lysander's breakable soul.

Mr. Worthington might best be served by remaining out of the public for some time.

Hmph! As if being away from Worthington House could possibly be good for him! Who did she think she was, claiming their brother should remain "out of the public" as if he were fearsome or dangerous? There was nothing wrong with Lysander that time with his family couldn't fix!

Attie considered the problem as she looked over at Poll. "You should go fetch Lysander home," she said bluntly. "After all, this is your fault."

Poll stared at her. "How is this my fault? If it's anyone's fault, it's yours! You told him to come after me, when you didn't even know if he could find me! You should go!"

Callie rolled her eyes at her younger brother. "That's ridiculous, Poll. She's fourteen. She can't go alone."

"She's more dangerous than any bandit," Poll growled. "They should be afraid of her!"

Attie didn't smile, although matters were proceeding precisely to plan. People smiled too much and then it stopped meaning anything at all. "I'll go alone."

That flat, determined statement made them all go a bit wide-eyed and alarmed, except for Iris and Archie, of course, who were still mooning at each other—which made Attie's heart hurt a little in a glad way.

She ignored the flying protests and reasons and urgent convincing arguments regarding the importance of blah-blah-blah and simply waited.

"It's settled then," Callie said finally. She glanced at Dade, who nodded, for Iris was beginning to fade. "Attie and Poll will go."

"You'll need dear Button, darlings."

They all turned to look at Iris, whose eyes sparkled knowingly at them in one of those random sharp moments that lanced through her usual dreaminess from time to time.

"What does Button have to do with any of this?" Dade frowned. "It isn't as though anyone will be needing a fashion authority on a rescue mission."

"Oh my dear boy." Iris waved a graceful hand. "One never knows, does one?"

"YORKSHIRE?" Button blinked in bemusement. "As in the Shire of York? All swooping valleys and looming hills?"

"I wouldn't know. I've never been north of the Cotswolds. But yes, Yorkshire." Cabot nodded. "I've just received a message from Worthington House. Apparently Mr. Worthington has got himself into a bit of a pickle in a place called Farby in Swaledale. Perhaps I am not reading Miss

Atalanta's decidedly florid handwriting properly but it appears to have something to do with a giant sheep."

"Lysander Worthington wrote a letter to his family?"

Cabot held out the note he'd received from Miss Atalanta. "No, the letter from Yorkshire was written by a Mrs. Oakes. Miss Atalanta comments upon her excellent spelling but sadly deficient penmanship."

"An educated lady? Rusticating away in the Shire of York? I shall always call it that now, I have decided, for I much prefer it. It always did seem a place out of pace with time." Button steepled his fingers thoughtfully and narrowed his eyes. "A mystery lady keeping poor Lysander away from his family? I must know more."

Cabot watched the gleam rise in Button's pale blue eyes. Oh, no. Marrying off the Worthington clan, one by one, seemed to be Button's *raison d'etre.*

It was just as he feared.

"The Shire of York should be lovely this time of year," Button mused as if to himself.

Cabot made no response. Looking up, Button smiled at him sweetly.

It was the puckish tilt of his head that did Cabot in every time. He hid the ache behind his usual severe demeanor and said nothing.

"I'm well aware that you prefer the city," Button said in response to Cabot's silence. "You need not accompany me. I shall merely tag along with those Worthingtons whom are set to travel the Great North Road."

Cabot gazed evenly back at Button. As if he would stay behind. "Someone should come along to keep you out of trouble. Worthingtons aren't, as a rule, equipped with a great deal of common sense."

Button nodded agreeably enough. "If you insist."

Cabot turned away, his elegant fingers creasing the note closed with great exactitude. "I insist."

As if he would ever allow Button to leave his sight again.

One night. One random act of thievery in his desperate nineteenth year. One breaking of a lock to search for something, anything to sell for food or shelter.

He'd been so hungry, so clumsy. He had knocked over a small cabinet in the dark. It had crashed to the floor, its myriad tiny drawers casting a spray of buttons out onto the floor.

He'd tried to make a run for it, slipping and falling again on the button-covered floor, when a gentle voice had spoken from the darkness in the back of the shop.

"You look cold. Would you like a hot cup of tea? There's a room in the attic. You don't have to pick up the buttons until tomorrow."

A young man who'd known little kindness and no love at all, whose heart was as shattered and lost as the delicate cabinet, had his tentative life of crime cut short by a heap of buttons. And a very singular man.

Button was a genius. A national treasure. A jewel in the crown of fashion and style. A dream giver, a wish grantor, the beneficent uncle to any lady doubting her own beauty or worth.

All of that aside, Cabot needed Button to remain safe the way that he needed air to breathe.

Yes, I bloody well insist.

THE NEXT MORNING, Gemma awoke later than usual. It was not surprising due to her late-night doctoring. She stretched luxuriously and blinked with pleasantly guilty satisfaction at the light streaming through her bedroom window. She was rarely allowed to enjoy the sight, for she customarily rose much earlier.

She sniffed. What was that tantalizing scent? Something savory from the kitchen? Someone was cooking? Someone who wasn't her?

She sat up, tossing all nascent thoughts of laziness aside, for her curiosity would not allow it. She swiftly washed and dressed. She was fortunate to have another gown that buttoned in front. From now on she would own nothing else. After all, she had no maid, nor did she want one. From the perspective of her hard-working life in York-shire, she now found it quite astonishing that some women required anyone else to help her dress. Moreover, they sometimes changed clothes up to ten times in one day! An outfit for every activity, even eating breakfast. Goodness, how wasteful!

As she awkwardly set her hair to rights, she reconsid-ered the perhaps somewhat necessary extravagance of maids. Still, she managed something acceptable by jam-ming in an inordinate number of pins to keep it in place.

Her belly rumbled, for she had missed breakfast. And if someone else felt like cooking, she certainly felt like eating.

She felt lighthearted this morning. The breeze blew through her half open window, smelling sweetly of green grass and roses. The late morning light struck the cut glass bowl on her bedside table and she smiled at the glorious beauty of the prisms created within the crystal. Peaceful. She felt peaceful.

Even happy.

Well, it had been a very successful bone-setting last night. She was justified in taking pride in that. And a good night's sleep was never to be scorned. Yet her heart danced a little as she trotted lightly down the stairs.

She was a woman, scrambling down the stairs to catch a glimpse of a handsome young man, like a girl with her first crush.

Well, he was handsome. And kindhearted. And so unas-suming, if that was the right word for his calm acceptance of her directions. Perhaps it was only that she had met with so much opposition to her role as healer that the sheer novelty of encountering a man who accepted her expertise and trusted her enough to allow her to take the lead without argument—well, she rather felt as if she had found a unicorn in her stable!

Her mouth watered. Something smelled good!

Nibbling at her lower lip with curiosity, she hesitated outside the kitchen and peeked around the doorjamb. There she saw two men, one small and bent, the other tall and dark. One loud and one quiet. One old and one young.

Mr. Bing was wearing her apron as he lifted a pan out of the baking oven set into the wood-burning range. Mr. Worthington stepped aside to make room for Mr. Bing with one hand holding a dripping whisk in the air.

Mr. Bing cursed and dropped the pan on the worktop yanking one hand away and promptly sticking his thumb in his mouth. Mr. Worthington glanced at him, then once he saw that Mr. Bing was more irritated than injured, he turned back to his brisk whisking of something on the stove.

How charming! Men wearing aprons in her kitchen? Gemma felt a slow, wide smile spread across her face. This was a most agreeable development indeed!

She straightened, cleared her throat rather obviously, she thought, and sauntered into the kitchen. At the sight of the two fine fellows there, she pasted on a ridiculous expression of astonishment and clapped her hands like a child.

It did not do to be too subtle with menfolk.

"Oh my heavens! What an absolutely marvelous smell! What are you two up to?"

It was adorable how they both eagerly presented their offerings. Mr. Bing had puffy Yorkshire pudding in his pan, though dropping it had flattened it somewhat. Mr. Worthington mutely held out a pot full of lumpy gravy.

Despite the odd choice of dinner-for-breakfast, Gemma admired it all tremendously, lathering the praise on thickly. Another woman would've looked askance at her exuberance, but the men simply looked very pleased with themselves. Even Mr. Worthington wore an expression of unsmiling pride.

Gemma allowed them to see her to the table and serve her. The pudding was over-baked and leathery, and the gravy had curdled and suffered an excess of salt but she chewed valiantly and took small sips of water. She managed to clean her plate of the very generous serving which she had been bestowed.

She pushed her plate away and dabbed at her lips with her napkin. "How wonderful! And so thoughtful. And not at all under-baked, Mr. Bing! Mr. Worthington, the gravy was highly savory!"

There. They were well praised and not a bit of it had been a lie.

She sat back and allowed them to pour her a cup of overly steeped tea and add in rather too many lumps of sugar before she took it gratefully and smiled after her first sip. "Mmm."

The two of them sat down and devoured the rest of the pudding and gravy with the single-mindedness of ravenous beasts. Then Mr. Worthington diligently washed up while Mr. Bing gave Gemma an adventure-filled account of the morning's events. Gemma supposed that when one cooked so rarely, one found novelty in the cracking of every egg.

Then Mr. Bing rose from the table and fetched a basket. He turned to Gemma with a glint in his eye. "Young Farmer Hamme sent word that he would like for you to stop in today."

Gemma frowned. "Farmer Hamme? Is someone ill?" Hamme's smallholding was a long ride away. She would be gone most of the day there and back.

Mr. Bing shrugged and glanced away. "All I was told was that he wants you to come. Best you get on if you want to make it there and back before supper. Worthington has got Bad Pony under his spell good and proper so it orta be a peaceful ride. Why don't you take t' young fella up to the Nine Standards? It'll be a pretty prospect from the top of that fell on a fine day like today."

Gemma looked down at her tea and slid a glance down the table at Mr. Worthington. "It is a very fine view, Mr. Worthington, if one is fond of high vistas."

Mr. Worthington gazed at the tablecloth and gave a short nod. Did that mean he liked views of the landscape or that he was agreeing to the drive? Perversely, Gemma decided she didn't care which one it was. If the fellow had a strong opinion either way, it was up to him to express it.

Suddenly eager to be out of doors on a gorgeous morning, Gemma rose from the table. Mr. Worthington stood at once and Mr. Bing stood a few beats later.

They were terribly sweet. She hoped to never eat their cooking again. She smiled at them and slipped off to her stillroom to make sure her case was well stocked for any eventuality. There was no telling what might be going on at the Hamme farmstead. There were three generations under one roof and rather a large number of young children. She should pack a few hard candies as well. Children were ever so much easier to convince when one had an arsenal of sweets.

She was lashing the case closed when Mr. Worthington entered the stillroom. He came close to her and she found her pulse increasing even as she found herself breathless. He reached out for her and her breath stopped entirely. Then his hand closed over the handle of her case and lifted it easily from the table. He nodded to her and silently left the room, clearly intending to carry her medicine case to the cart.

Ninny. Going all weak-kneed just because a man walks past you in a small room?

A truly handsome man? Oh yes.

Gemma smoothed her suddenly damp palms on her skirt and licked her lips. Suddenly the distance possible between two people on the seat of a small cart seemed very narrow indeed.

Mr. Worthington carried her case to the harnessed cart. As Gemma slowly buttoned her jacket and tightened her bonnet against the breeze, Topknot came lalloping up to them. Without a word, Mr. Worthington reached along the running board and let down a rough wooden step hinged beneath it. Topknot wagged her feathery banner of a tail and used the step to scramble awkwardly onto the driver's seat of the cart. Gemma stared. That had not been there before.

"Aye then, Topknot," Mr. Bing said with approval. "That works a treat, lad," he said to Mr. Worthington.

Gemma looked from Topknot's proud doggie grin to Mr. Worthington's casual indifference to the generosity of his invention. What sort of man took the time to do such a kindness for a dog?

Gemma remained very quiet as they drove the winding road up the dale. She remained astonished at Mr. Worthington's effortless command of the heretofore barely controllable Bad Pony. She watched as his hand occasionally reached to rub behind Topknot's feathery ears.

The dog made an excellent chaperone. Her fluffy rear took up the precise distance on the bench between Gemma and her companion. Gemma did not know whether to be pleased or disappointed.

When they arrived at the Hamme farmhold where Mr. Bing had sent them, the family at the farmhouse was confused but welcoming.

"Ain't no one sick right now," Farmer Hamme said,

having taken off his cap to scratch at his head. "Still, as long as you've taken the trouble, my gran has t' bone-ache somethin' bad."

With a silent accusation sent winging down the dale toward Mr. Bing, Gemma nodded with a smile. "Of course. I'd be happy to help."

She did a bit of simple doctoring, grinding her willow-bark for the elderly woman's arthritis and giving her a warming salve as well. Then the list grew. The children had insect bites and "Da has the corns somethin' awful."

Gemma rather thought she might start dropping in on more of the dale's populace, for it seemed people weren't coming to her as often as they ought. She could bring them chickens, which would guarantee her welcome. She smiled to herself. Mr. Bing would be so pleased.

While she was busy, she saw Farmer Hamme walk out to the barn with Mr. Worthington.

LYSANDER PUT HIS new calming skills to work to help Hamme mend a gate. Hamme was a silent fellow who never seemed to pass by his plump dark-haired wife without a touch to her shoulder or hand. Lysander put a good effort into fixing the gate, which was definitely a two-man job.

Mrs. Hamme banged a spoon on a cookpot to call the children inside and Lysander watched the black-haired horde pop up from all around him and stream into the house.

Life in the dale seemed very challenging to him, with the harsh winters and the hard work. Hamme's place wasn't a hovel, but neither was it prosperous. The house was a ramshackle mix of wood and stone and the barn a three-sided shed dug into the hillside with an earthen rear wall.

Yet the children were sturdy and well-tended and they had laughed and tussled as they obediently ran indoors.

Hamme laughed heartily when Lysander's riding boots slid on the damp slope, landing him on his arse, but there was no meanness in it. People in the dale had a hard go, that was certain, but they also seemed to know how to have a bit of fun.

That made Lysander wonder. Why did Gemma Oakes never seem to have any fun?

Chapter 17

A FTER LEAVING THE Hamme farmstead, Gemma decided to take Mr. Bing's none-too-subtle advice. "If you follow the fork in the lane to the right, the path will take us up to the Nine Standards." She smiled at Mr. Worthington. "It's quite an astonishing view of the dale."

Oh dear. She'd forgotten how smiling at him quite turned him to a statue. She reached a hand over his to tug gently on the reins he held. Bad Pony veered smartly onto the path and continued his astonishingly well-behaved trot.

After leaving the lane, which had never been any wider than the cart wheels, the path began to narrow and turn bumpy with exposed rock and twisting turns that wound ever higher. To Gemma's surprise, Bad Pony took it all in stride. Mr. Worthington slowed him to a more careful walk but the pony nimbly picked his way through the chunks of half buried limestone. His short, sturdy legs pulled the cart with great ease despite the incline.

Gemma shook her head in wonder. "He's like another creature altogether."

To her surprise, Mr. Worthington shook his head to refute her. "He's the same. We've changed. We understand now."

Was he speaking of the war pony, or of himself? Either way it was the most spontaneous conversation she'd ever had from him. There had been no prying questions required.

Was that perhaps the secret? To make mild statements

of general curiosity instead of direct questions? It made excellent sense, now that she'd thought of it. After all, she wasn't terribly fond of direct questions herself, especially when those questions intruded on very personal matters. Encouraged, she tried something else. "I don't think that I have ever stood upon a point so high as this." She waited.

"No."

Just when Gemma had decided she would get nothing more from him, he went on.

"St. Paul's. Bell tower." He slid his gaze from the road to meet her surprised one. "Prank. Four brothers." As if that explained everything. Then, "Ale."

Perhaps it explained a great deal. Heavens, five sons! It sounded wonderful—and somewhat terrifying. Gemma had always imagined herself with a houseful of children, but as time went on she'd resigned herself to two, or perhaps one. Then Edmund had been lost and that one child had never come.

Still, five sons. "Your mother must be exhausted."

Mr. Worthington did not answer. When she looked at him again his expression had gone quite set and his jaw tensed. Oh dear, the four brothers were not a touchy topic, but apparently his mother, Iris, was too tender a subject to touch upon.

"I'll stay to drive for you." He glanced down at her well-wrapped wrist. "Until you're better."

Oh, yes. It would not do to forget that this man had been on his way from somewhere to somewhere else when they had met during the ill-fated festival. Was he headed home to his mother then? She had gathered that his family was in London, although perhaps that assumption wasn't correct. Some thought was required to come up with the appropriate indirect statement.

"I think the Dales are lovely. The winters are severe, but so worth it when spring comes. Do you know Yorkshire well?"

He shook his head quickly, not looking at her.

Unconcerned, she continued. "It is very different here from where I was reared. I was born in Cambridge. It is a fair-sized city, although nothing compared to London."

"Born in Shropshire." This time he did meet her gaze. "Sheep there too."

She had to grin, for although he remained very nearly expressionless, there had been something in his eyes, a flash of awareness of such an absurd link in common. He was teasing her. Weakly, and not well, but it was a sign to Gemma that there was a man inside, perhaps not whole, perhaps not entire, perhaps not yet. But Mr. Worthington was no drilled-out shell of a person. He was ever so much more than that.

Gemma leaned back on the bench seat and braced her heels against the footrest so that she would not need to hold on with her sore arm. She savored her delight quietly as she tilted her head back and looked through the tunnel of her bonnet brim at the blue sky above. She was not quite sure why she felt deeply affected by this new knowledge. Perhaps it did not matter. Perhaps it was simply gladness that at least one person had not been entirely eradicated by war.

LYSANDER HAD NEVER experienced such stillness. The war seemed so far away in the dales. Of course, no patch of England had escaped her losses entirely, for Lysander had seen sons of every county go down in the muddy fields outside Burgos Castle. If he asked, he knew that he would learn of many families who were one, or two, or three sons lesser than they had been.

Yet however grieving, the dale folk carried on through their seasons of loss and plenty. Sorrow might fill their insides with broken shards but the rhythm of the days went on. Lambs needed birthing, sheep needed shearing, wood needed stacking for the winter, gardens needed tending.

Now spring had come, with life renewing all around them. It seemed that everyone had a role to play. Perhaps they had learned some secret, a lesson Lysander not found in the clamoring, rattling, never-ending round of London life.

He looked down at his hands that held the reins so gently upon the war pony's mouth. Even this tragically misunderstood creature still moved forward, still fought for life and understanding. Although the battlefields were evident in the scars on its flanks, the tough little soldier kept on fighting forward.

Lysander let his gaze rise from the pony to the winding cart path ahead and then upward still more. He realized that they had climbed a great distance on this meandering back and forth trail. Already he could see far down the dale, so far that the sloped, emerald pastures cut by grey-brown dry-stone walls began to haze in the distance. A patchwork quilt tumbled upon an unmade bed.

The pony stopped and Lysander's gaze dropped back to the path before them. It had narrowed even more so and there was simply no managing the cart from this point.

"Will anyone come?"

Gemma blinked at him. "Oh, I shouldn't think so. In fact I would think that this is the first cart to make it this high. I'd expected we would walk the last mile or so." She waved a hand up the slope.

When Lysander stepped down from the cart he absent-mindedly flipped down the step he'd created for Topknot. The dog scrambled joyfully down and followed at his heels as he walked around the cart to help Gemma down. Then he began to unhitch the war pony.

"You're setting him loose?"

Lysander nodded and continued to efficiently unbuckle the rigging of the harness. "Have to. Can't turn it by himself."

She walked up to regard him across the pony's rough mane.

"The cart! Oh dear, I hadn't thought of that. I'm glad you did. I suppose you think he'll stay nearby."

This time Lysander noticed that she did not phrase it as a question. How long had she been doing that? It was true that he felt much less tension when not trying to answer a specific question. She was very clever to realize that, when he had never clearly understood it himself. Clever and understanding and generous.

He saw her eyes widen and her lips part slightly as if she had seen something startling. Except she was only looking at him. He raised a hand to his face in curiosity and found the remains of a smile disappearing.

IT WAS GEMMA'S turn to be frozen in place by a smile. It might have been described as a poor effort by anyone else's standards but on Mr. Worthington it was miraculous. It entirely shattered her perception of him as a broken soul. How astonishingly handsome he was!

For a moment, she mused upon the probable character flaws such a powerfully attractive smile would bestow upon a young man. He'd been a charmer, she decided. Wickedly and carelessly unleashing devastating smiles on unwary female hearts. She decided quite firmly that she would not have liked him at all, that young wastrel. Except possibly if he had made her laugh. She had little defense against a genuinely attractive sense of the absurd.

Edmund had had an acerbic sort of humor, a rare but truly witty view of the world and humanity upon it. She'd seen little of it after his years as a battlefield physician, but she remembered it well. It was what had made the difference in their ages and their station disappear, that meeting of humor and wry understanding of the way of the world.

She laughed out loud now, for Mr. Worthington's expression was priceless. He actually looked down at his own hand as if it had somehow betrayed him by detecting a smile upon his somber features. She tried to cover her gust of laughter with her gloved hand but it only made matters worse, for now she was decidedly snickering. She clasped her hands before her, swallowed hard and pressed her lips together. One ought not to laugh at one's patients.

Except he was smiling again, the same rusty half smile that lit his face with a charming flash of white teeth and brightened his eyes. There was a wonder in those eyes as he gazed at her. Wonder and an awakening awe.

At her? Himself? At being able to smile again after everything he'd been through? Perhaps all three.

UNHARNESSED, BAD PONY happily stumped over to the grassy verge and plunged his oversize jaws into the greenery.

"I hope he will be all right. I shouldn't like him to harm himself." Gemma herself was puffing somewhat as they continued up the grassy path cut through the low mounds of vegetation around them.

"He's a steppe pony. Independent. Cossacks expect them to do for themselves."

Gemma eyed her personal war pony with a new feeling of satisfaction. "Edmund never explained that. I have no idea where he obtained him. I thought perhaps he took pity on his abnormality."

"He is a soldier," Mr. Worthington said with finality.

Gemma nodded agreeably and looked ahead on the path. "See? We're coming up on the first two cairns."

Two oddly shaped stacks of stone reaching several feet high lay on either side of the path at the crest of the hill they now climbed. Gemma turned her head to see Mr. Worthington looking supremely unimpressed. She supposed that to an outsider the cairns looked rather like a fallen jumble of children's stacking blocks. But to the people of the dales the cairns were an ancient treasure.

"When we walk a little higher you'll see the rest of them."

As she had predicted, a few more steps brought the next hilltop into view and the seven remaining cairns marched like soldiers along the crest.

Now Mr. Worthington was looking at the cairns with more curiosity. "How old?"

Gemma laughed and shrugged. "I haven't the foggiest idea. I've heard some people claim they are thousands of years old. I've heard others say that they date from before the days of Robin Hood. Did you know he was rumored to originate from Yorkshire?"

Mr. Worthington was not to be deterred. "What for?"

Gemma inhaled deeply of the sweet spring air. "I don't believe anyone really knows. The story I've heard most often is that these stones mark the exact boundary between Swaledale and Westmorland. Apparently, it boils down to a matter of cheese."

"Cheese."

She nodded happily, enjoying the small absurdity of it. "A defined boundary would be necessary, you see, so that cheese made on the east side of the cairns cannot be labeled with the same origin of the west side of the cairns. There is a long and fervent history of competition."

"Which cheese is better?"

"Why, Swaledale, of course!" Her loyalty was staunch, although she was laughing by then. "To be sure, cheese is a very important local industry."

"They stacked rocks?"

Gemma smirked at him. "Just wait until we get closer. It's a bit more significant than simply stacked rocks."

LYSANDER ENJOYED THE walk. The steepness of the slope kept his usual furious pace to a more normal stride and he found that he had the time to look about him. High grass and low growing vegetation surrounded them rolling over the undulating landscape. They must be getting higher now. The wind had an insistence not found on lower ground, with trees and structures to block its force. The sky was a deep and clamoring blue. One never saw such as sky in London.

The perfect air filled Lysander's lungs with every inhalation, and when he exhaled it was as if the purity of the air was cleansing him. Of what? Grief? Anger? Helplessness?

There was something about this place. He felt drawn to it, to being still for a while, to allow his endless battle vigilance to ease, to take the peace where he could.

He slid his glance to the woman who walked sturdily beside him. Her head was bent slightly to watch her footing and her good hand gripped fistfuls of her skirts so that he could see her practical boots stomping upward with energy. With her bonnet on she could not tell he was staring at her. Lysander looked his fill. As she walked, concealed by her blue coat and practical straw bonnet, he was shielded from her breathtaking beauty. That helped a bit. Freed from that distraction, he looked at her not as a stunning woman but as a person.

She was an astonishing woman by any account, beauty or not. Lysander had never been a victim to the lure of beauty alone. Even in his younger days he had been immunized by close association with his own lovely sisters and even Iris, who wore her own slightly faded glory with an effortless serenity, confident in her husband Archie's adoration.

It was not merely the arrangement of lips and cheek-bone, nor fortuitous distribution of ample and lithe feminine parts. Mrs. Oakes was beautiful because she what she did was beautiful. She *lived* beautifully.

She took instant and selfless action on behalf of others. He'd never heard her speak ill, not even of the frustrating war pony she had been burdened with. Her eyes saw truly and easily into his own swirling inner turmoil. She *saw* beautifully.

Perhaps of all the women he knew she was most like his sister Calliope. Callie had once carried that hint of sadness in her eyes, although Lysander had not noticed it until it was gone, a shadow of isolation most effectively brightened by the flaming love she'd found with Sir Lawrence Porter.

Gemma is lonely.

Lysander took that thought and turned it in all directions, examining it for accuracy. This was a woman who was rarely left alone. She was constantly called out to serve her community. She had the sturdy devotion of Bing and although she did not realize it, Bad Pony and Topknot as well. That shepherd's wife, Mrs. Gosling, also seemed a stout and stalwart friend.

Yet Mrs. Oakes had evidenced, through the merest of comments and expressions, a wistfulness whenever Lysander mentioned the massive pile of Worthingtons he was usually surrounded by. His family felt like a securely tied burden upon his back, or rather an encompassing swath of suffocating blankets. Or perhaps a tiny closet with nails protruding from every wall so that no matter which way he stepped their need pierced him with his inability to be who they wanted him to be.

But Mrs. Oakes had not known him before. She had no expectation that he ought to return to some former cheerful and easy-going state. Mrs. Oakes didn't want him, Lysander, to be anything other than calm and at ease with himself. He thought he was managing that fairly well—aside from that earlier contretemps with old Goose-Gogs. That hardly been his sole fault.

Yet the silence on the fell was much more than simply lack of expectation. There was a generosity to it, a bounty of stillness that flowed down from the vast sky and up from the ancient earth. Even the noise within his own thoughts faded away.

> *"Shall I compare thee to a summer's day?*
> *Thou art more lovely and more temperate."*

He'd always liked that line of Shakespeare's Sonnet 18. He'd found it charming and flirtatious.

Yet this clear, bright day in the high country was not a charming view. The slopes were steep and the living arduous. He knew the winter would be a struggle. It was a hard, demanding place, Yorkshire—and yet he felt his soul lift its wary head and look about in wonder.

It was no garden, no park. It was not beautiful because someone had made it so. It had always been beautiful, long before the first man set foot upon its rolling slopes.

Beautiful just as it was.

Just like her.

GEMMA FOUND HERSELF talking more than she usually did. Perhaps it was Mr. Worthington's silence that drew her out. A man so uncommunicative as he must have secrets of his own and would not judge her for hers. Nor would he be inclined to tell anyone.

Or perhaps it was simply that his reticent manner made him an excessively wonderful listener. There was no "that reminds me of something that I experienced" or "do you know what you should do?"

If she felt the need to pause in order to think of just the right words, he simply waited. There was no rush to fill the silence, no hastening to tidy up the space left by her careful selection of phrase. Because of this, her words began to come more quickly and less studied—as if the trickling tap had been opened wide and she felt free to express any and every thought that crossed her mind.

She rattled on, telling him about the folk in the village and how she had come to love this wide open sky and changeable yet eternal landscape. How she rejoiced in the lambs each spring and reveled in the patchwork gold and orange that took over the Dales in the autumn. She spoke of the harsh winters and how they had become a welcome time to close shutters and stack wood and conserve one's resources. Winter gave her time for thought and the patience to prepare the painstaking tinctures and ointments for the coming spring, when the folk of the dale would burst from their doors and go about their springtime tasks with such energy that her help would be much needed again. She read Dr. Oakes's medical books again and again, she told Mr. Worthington, and longed for the opportunity to gather more such knowledge. She watched what the sheep and cows and horses ate out of instinct and took note of which wildflowers the bees most rode attendance upon. In the fall, she collected those seeds and planted patches in the garden behind the coops.

"My little physic garden, full of weeds and nonsense" she called it in a self-deprecating way. She was proud of the knowledge she had gained and longed for someone to share it with, someone who would not brush her off as a silly woman or scold her for stepping into a physician's shoes. "It is not that I would not wish a true doctor for the dale," she assured him. "If someone should come to take up residence and practice here I would welcome them, and do everything I could to assist them and learn from them."

She was silent for a long moment. "But there is no one but me. I know they call me the Lady of the Dale, but it isn't so. I have all the responsibility of a lady with none of the power."

Or the pleasures. "I've never even been to a ball." She was embarrassed to hear the wistful tone in her voice. "Nor has any woman in Farby, and they deserve a fine evening, if anyone does." She politely forbear to mention that a certain recent event had been canceled due to excessive wreckage.

"Of course, Edmund had no thought of such frivolity. He was such a fine man, with a truly fine mind. It wasn't his fault that—" She felt a sudden urge to confess Edmund's distance and her own loneliness, even while her husband still lived. Horrified, she snuffed out that impulse. She looked down as she folded her hands in her lap. "Really, such a gifted doctor."

Mr. Worthington simply waited through the silence of the next few moments. Gemma forced herself to take a deep breath and smile at him. "Matters long passed do not belong in such a lovely afternoon."

"How long?"

She knew what he meant of course. "My husband passed four years ago." It seemed like a decade to her, for the years alone passed ever so much more slowly.

At some point Mr. Worthington had turned to the basket provided by Mr. Bing and had begun to unload a most copious, if somewhat rustic, luncheon. On the yards of canvas included within, Mr. Worthington arranged a spread of more of the crusty bread, a crock of butter, a jar of pickles that Gemma had put up the previous summer, a generous shank of ham, a wedge of crumbling Swaledale cheese delicately traced with blue, capped bottles of sweet spring water that still held the morning's chill, and the most extravagant prize of all, a tin of biscuits that showed its age in its dented sides and scraped edges.

Gemma bit her lip as she gazed upon it and glanced at Mr. Worthington. "The seal is still pasted down. It has never been opened."

He studied it with most serious consideration. "Years." Then, "Decades."

"Ginger biscuits." Gemma chewed on her lip. "He knows they are my favorites. It's terribly sweet of him."

Mr. Worthington peered at the box as if striving to see through the tin to estimate the condition of the biscuits within. "Dry. Not a spot of rust."

Gemma could bear it no longer. "Oh, do simply crack it open. If they are a bit past their prime, I shouldn't mind that very much. If they are completely inedible, perhaps Topknot would like one."

"Poor Topknot."

Gemma laughed again as he bent to the task of prying open the elderly tin to reveal the paper-wrapped package within. The edges of the paper had curled and gone brown and dotted with age. "Ah." Gemma made a face. "This is not looking well."

"Don't give up." Mr. Worthington gave the package a poke. When it withstood the intrusion, he gave it a more solid prod. "Biscuits. Or rocks."

Gemma bravely dove her hand into the twisted paper and pulled out a perfectly acceptable-looking ginger biscuit. It even had an attractive dusting of sugar crystals across the top. She sniffed it. "It smells of ginger and treacle." That she thrust it at Mr. Worthington. "Go on. Give the nice biscuit a try."

He stared at the biscuit in her fingers in his brows creased slightly. "Another test." It was not a question. Gemma realized that an intelligent fellow like Mr. Worthington had, of course, understood her gentle series of investigations into his emotional state and her attempts to draw him out. Unashamed, she simply smiled widely at him. "Absolutely. Eat the biscuit."

He tried. He really did. But he could not manage to bite even the tiniest crumble from the edge of the rock-hard confection. After three attempts, he lifted his head and clicked his fingers.

Topknot, who had never come to Gemma's call, not once, not ever, bounded out of a nearby bramble thicket and galloped to Mr. Worthington's side, her awkward hop only discernible when she slowed down. Mr. Worthington simply glanced at her and gave no command, but Topknot planted her bottom and sat at attention immediately. Her ears perked and her head turned slightly as her bright eyes focused on the biscuit in his hand. *"For me?"* rang as clear as a bell.

He held it out for the herd dog to sniff. She did so delicately, and hesitated a moment, as if weighing the unusual bouquet of ginger and sugar. With her sensitive nose, she could likely smell the butter and flour as well. She opened her jaw and daintily accepted the offering. Mr. Worthington waved his hand and Topknot took off with her prize.

"Do you think she will eat it?"

He considered the question with utmost seriousness. "No. Bury it, perhaps."

"A well-deserved entombment, if so."

Topknot did neither. After lying down in the grass with the biscuit between her front paws, the dog gave it several tentative nibbles. Then she licked all the crystalline sugar off the top, picked it up in her teeth, and trotted over to where Bad Pony grazed with grumpy industry.

Bad Pony, who'd never missed a meal in his life, simply grazed the cookie along with the tough grasses and crunched the ancient treat in his powerful jaws.

"Oh dear. Don't tell Mr. Bing."

Mr. Worthington merely slanted his gaze in her direction, causing Gemma to laugh once more. "Yes. Well, I suppose that was an unnecessary request."

It has been so long since she'd been on a picnic, even longer since she'd heard a concert or seen a play. She confessed her feeling of isolation even among the people who respected and needed her. She felt very much at ease. Mr. Worthington was neither more nor less than her. They were equals in age and experience. They had both gone out into a war-torn world and seen things that the people they came home to could never understand.

Goodness, she was talking his ear off! Gemma soothed her self-consciousness by reminding herself that any woman would spill her thoughts to a man who actually held still and *listened*!

Chapter 18

AFTER PACKING UP the picnic they strolled leisurely along the crest of the fell, making closer examination of the ancient stone structures. Some were higher than others, at times taller than Lysander could reach, and sometimes truncated by time and damage. The cairns were by no means of uniform shape. He imagined a crew of indignant cheese makers storming the fell in the dark of night to erect the boundary stones by lantern light. That is how he would've done it, to startle the enemy—well, in this case perhaps the competition—with the sun breaking over the boundary stones as if they had erupted overnight from the earth.

Filigree lichen tickled his fingertips. He inhaled the dry mineral scent of sun-warmed stone. The scents of Yorkshire surrounded him, their subtleties allowed to come forth in this world free of coal-soot, carriage horse droppings and midden carts slopping down the street before dawn.

Lysander closed his eyes and drew in the scent of grass and flowers and even the distant whiff of sheep wool. The air washed into Lysander's lungs and out again, carrying with it the dark skies and acrid pain of the past. He breathed in again, and again, until the skin of his face tingled with the sufficiency of it. The silence, the sweet, blessed silence! It bowled him over, flattened him, forced him open and wrested down the stones he had built around his senses. He contained walls that kept out the noise, the people, the sounds and sights and smells and glances from his loved ones and the careful way they stepped around him.

Those inner walls shifted, their foundations shaken by the beautiful stillness.

He opened his eyes. And then there was Gemma Oakes, the Lady of the Dale. She'd undermined his walls from the first moment he'd lain eyes upon her. She had swept beneath his walls like a freshwater spring seeping up from the earth itself, pure and clean, gentle and yet ruthlessly determined.

She walked ahead of him now. Her bonnet hung from her fingers as she lifted her face into that pure breeze that teased her hair from its pins to flutter like a banner behind her.

Gemma. Healer, indeed.

She glanced back at him over her shoulder. The shy smile upon her face made him ache.

London? A thousand miles away. The muddy, bloody killing fields of Spain even farther. As Lysander passed between one cairn and the next, he felt as though he crossed a border of an altogether different kind.

Gemma walked the other way, and together their paths traced a twining meeting and parting, like the laces of a corset. When the cairns stood between them, Lysander felt a loss, as if stepping into shade on a bright chilly day.

She smiled at him in the crossing, as measured as a formal steps of a dance, and dipped a playful curtsey and swirled her skirts as she passed.

The next crossing, he bowed slightly, one hand on his heart, one hand behind his back. The flash of grin upon her lovely face was reward aplenty.

When he spied her at the next crossing, she was flapping her open hand like a fan, pretending to gaze aloofly past him. He lifted his chin and looked scornfully down upon her—a rift in the courtship, another step in the dance, another stone in the crossing.

Then he rounded the final cairn and she was not there. Lysander blinked, startled, and stepped forward.

She lurked yet upon her side, her back pressed against the stones. When he rounded the cairn and spotted her, she stepped forward with a smile and rewarded him with a peck on the cheek. The estranged courtship reunited at last.

Without thought, he turned his face to meet her lips with his. When her soft mouth pressed to his, he felt her lips part in a gasp of surprise.

He'd gone too far. He was always mucking things up, always getting things wrong.

She reached a hand to grasp his head and pulled his mouth harder to hers. His hat tumbled to the grass. Then he had her pressed against the cairn, his tall form curving over hers, his spread hand behind her head to soften it, the other cupping her jaw, lifting her to meet him even as she pressed upward on her toes. All the trapped intensity of his soul poured from him, into her.

The warmth of her open mouth transformed him. He stepped from the long and terrible night. The light shone warm upon his skin. He hesitated, startled, suddenly unsure of this path he was on.

She wrapped her other hand around the back of his neck, her fingers tight in his hair and slid her soft tongue between his lips.

Then he knew. This was the way home.

THEY LAY UPON the picnic blanket and watched harmless white clouds roam the sky.

They had parted breathlessly after the kiss. Gemma had been overcome by an unbearable shyness, her mind suddenly full of doubting thoughts. What did he mean by kissing her? What did he think of her kissing him back so enthusiastically?

Mr. Worthington had seemed rather stunned and had not met her gaze as he busied himself spreading out the old blanket from their picnic.

It was less an uncomfortable silence than a considering one. What had it meant? What came next? Gemma enjoyed feeling him close to her, but she was not yet ready to get closer.

Mostly, they kept their thoughts to themselves, as if unwilling to speak of what had transpired for fear that naming it would turn the mystery into something mundane. Only once did Gemma remark upon a cloud shape, pointing out a tall ship sailing the endless blue.

Mr. Worthington peered at it. "Sheep," he responded. "All sheep. Underfoot and overhead."

Gemma giggled and then the curlews' cries were the only conversation needed.

They remained on the crest of the fell until the afternoon sun made long shadows fall eastward from each cairn. If anything, those dark fingers stretching across the grass were more unnerving than the ancient stones themselves. Gemma shivered, just once, yet Mr. Worthington became immediately solicitous. After the cart was turned properly about, Bad Pony was cajoled into his traces by a few more rocklike ginger biscuits. Both animals were happy to finish off the water from the clay bottles, Bad Pony drinking from Gemma's cupped hands, Topknot shying past her to lick from Mr. Worthington's dripping fingers.

Mr. Worthington aided Gemma up the step and into the cart. Their hands clung for a sweet moment.

He had not tried to kiss her again, but that single reckless moment had stirred such a heat inside her that she feared she glowed with it.

She was no timid virgin. She's been married for nearly a

decade. The early years had been, if not passionate, at least genuinely satisfying.

I like the feeling of a man's touch. I miss it. I miss the warm shiver when a man's palm slid down the curve of my hip. I miss the taste of a man's skin on my lips.

The memories were only fuel on the glowing ember within her. It flared anew when Mr. Worthington settled next to her on the bench seat of the cart.

She laughed when the cart jerked into motion, feeling giddy and careless, as if she truly was simply a lady on a drive with a handsome fellow—along with one happily panting dog and a pony too tired to be grumpy, eagerly heading home.

We make an odd little family.

Which was a disconcerting thought, but Gemma was so immensely cheered by her lazy day out that she chose to find it amusing instead.

When the cart lurched on the poorly graded lane, Gemma shamelessly clutched at Mr. Worthington's arm and took great pleasure in the feel of his solid muscle beneath her touch.

They rode home this way in lack of words tinged with wonder, glowing with golden evening light slanting over the dale, scented by the vibrant freshness of the cooling air and yes, the ginger-scented dog breath over their shoulders.

When they descended to the level of the river and began to follow the winding road home, night fell as suddenly as a stone. Bad Pony slowed a bit, picking his way, yet still plodded on unceasingly, for he was well aware that at the end of it, he would find his cozy stable, a steaming pail of oat mash and the comforting presence of Mrs. Apples.

Topknot, weary from her day of lurching happily up and down the slopes of the fell, curled into a satisfied dog circle next to the picnic hamper behind the seat.

The stars came out above and the mist rose below to curl hazy fingers around the cart wheels and the pony's fetlocks. Gemma had the uncanny notion that they rode through a dream world, a private and secret country of their very own.

She let her head drop to Mr. Worthington's solid shoulder and half closed her eyes. She felt carefree as she once had, full of plans and potential, daring and careless and immortal.

At that moment, she could have driven forever at his side, discovering this new and magical world together. Her most secret self felt open, as if all her cares had lightened, being shared.

Had she ever felt so free?

LYSANDER, IN HIS turn, felt everything. His skin prickled with awareness, his vision seemed sharper. The intensity of his long-benumbed senses dizzied him.

Had he never before experienced the silken air of a spring evening? Had he never before heard the creak of wood and iron and the rolling of cart wheels on a rocky road? The worn leather of the reins between his fingers became warm and supple in his hands and he *felt* it.

The wall that Gemma had slowly and patiently undermined had lost all integrity, crumbling faster throughout the day, the mortar flaked away by the purity of the air, the foundation shattered by the peaceful vistas, and then—

The entire barrier incinerated to windswept dust by the kiss.

He'd kissed a woman before, but it was only a means to an end, the first step of many.

Gemma's kiss had been a single unmatched moment in time. He had begun his life when her lips touched his. He had flown when he'd dared to kiss her back. He had floated down to stand with his feet firmly, finally, planted on the ground when she'd drawn back with the stroke of her fingertips on his cheek as she'd slipped her hand from his hair.

Oh, here I am.
I am here.
With her.

THE NEXT MORNING Gemma, stood in the kitchen looking down at the brown-glazed pottery bowl that sat on the table, heaped full of eggs. A downy feather stuck to one of the shells and she watched it flutter as she breathed.

She had fallen asleep last night still enfolded in a sweet haze, swept away by a beautiful day and a marvelous kiss. This morning before she'd even opened her eyes, the voice in her head spoke, the one that always reminded her that she wasn't an actual doctor.

You kissed your patient.

Shock and shame engulfed her at once. *Patient.* Lysander Worthington was a deeply troubled man, a damaged soul! And she had flirted as irresponsibly as a reckless girl. How could she have done such an foolish thing?

And what on earth was she to do now?

There was only one thing to be done. She must be very clear with him. She'd been unprofessional and they must return their relationship to a much less familiar level.

It made excellent sense. Very rational.

You're afraid. After all, Edmund died and abandoned you. He left you twice. You couldn't help him, though you knew him so well. What if this beautiful, damaged man abandons you too?

Gemma *was* afraid. She feared for them both. What would happen to him if she became too involved to be of use to him?

She flinched slightly and closed her eyes when she

heard Mr. Worthington's footfalls in the hall. She must nip this mysterious, tempting bloom in the bud immediately. Furthermore, she should do it before Mr. Worthington could become any more attached to her.

When he entered the kitchen, she turned with a crisp smile. "Good morning, Mr. Worthington. I thought I'd see about making breakfast myself today." She held up her wrist to show him. "I'm ever so much better now."

She saw him stop short and despite her resolve, she ached inside to see the wary shadows settle over his dark gaze. He said nothing. Of course not. She knew that no matter what she said to him, he would take the blow as though it were no more than he deserved. God, how could she have made such a dreadful error? This unfortunate, battle-shocked man had trusted her and she had played coy little games—and that kiss!

No, it was really best not to think about that kiss.

"Yesterday was a charming holiday but there is much work to be done," she told him. Her voice sounded hideously false. She was only trying to move matters back to a more formal status, but how? What could she possibly say?

What in the world would not simply make this worse?

In his sensitive way, he saw that she was horribly uncomfortable and of course, he tried to ease her way.

"You wish to take it back. I understand."

"I—" Did she wish to take it back? Of course! Yes, definitely. Or possibly not.

She nodded. "If only that were possible." She looked down to realize that her hands were wringing tightly within her apron, causing her wrist to ache. "It was not fair of me. I indulged a silly whimsy and I fear I gave you—" false hopes? Why did that feel like a lie? In panic, she cleared her throat twice. Anything to buy time. Her mind raced ahead. "I fear I overstepped the boundaries of our relationship." Yes, that felt true. Achingly unfortunate, but true.

Mr. Worthington held completely still. "I know that I am not ... not what I was. But I would never hurt you." Then his gaze dropped to her hands and the way she rubbed her wrist. "You don't believe that. I understand."

Gemma swallowed against the twisting feelings at odds inside her. No. She had taken responsibility for healing this man! It was impossible that he would be ready for any such emotional entanglement.

And he is not the only one, is he?

She shoved that thought aside, packing it away swiftly. "I'm very sorry." Not good enough, blast it. She raised her gaze to meet his and looked into those shadowy eyes. "I have failed you. I wanted to help you and I thought I had—"

"I am better, but not yet real and whole." He stepped back once and then again. She felt something tear inside her as the light in his eyes began to go out.

She wanted to run to him, to tell them that she believed he could do it, that he could come back from where he had been.

To come to where she was.

She would never be that unfair to him. She could not promise that she would be waiting for him once he healed. If he healed.

LYSANDER WATCHED GEMMA Oakes give up on him.

It hurt. Pain found places that he'd forgotten existed inside him. All hope dimmed. Stiffly, he waited for the ice and distance. He waited for the barrier to rise again. It wasn't there. He remained as raw and open as a recent wound.

There was only Gemma, looking at him with shame and regret brimming in her solemn gaze.

He should leave her presence. Lysander turned on his heel and walked from the room. He hesitated in the hall, unsure of where to go.

The outdoors called to him. That wide, wild sky. Those stunning, unoccupied hills. The colors of stone and grass and blue eternity above. The light. The sweet, cleansing air.

He mechanically took off his frock coat and hung it on a hook, changing it for the sturdy canvas work coat that Gemma had loaned him. As he thrust his arms into the sleeves, he realized for the first time it had been her husband's coat. Dr. Oakes had been a tall man, close to Lysander's size. A handsome man? A man she had loved?

Did he look like her husband? Did he remind her of him? Had yesterday been a fantasy of some sort, a play upon her past, of a man she had cared for and lost?

I don't suppose it matters now.

He tugged the coat snug and stepped out into the morning. There were chores to be done and Bing needed the help, but most importantly Lysander needed to check on Icarus. If the swelling in the thoroughbred's foreleg had subsided entirely, he could take Icarus to the smithy and replace the shoe today.

He could be on his way by nightfall. It was past time, for there were urgent matters at home to tend to. He felt another different shaft of pain, this one older, something worn into his very bones.

He needed to get back to Worthington House. To his family and to Iris. This was not his home.

Clearly, it never would be.

He should go.

You should stay.

He shoved his cold hands into the pockets of the farm coat and stood there, paralyzed between the house and the stable. Leave or stay? London or the Dales?

What would Dade do? Lysander's eldest brother took care of them all, a fatherly role that Archie Worthington was constitutionally unsuited to perform. Yet Dade had a rather medieval code of nobility. He might well feel honor-bound to stay and rescue the damsel he had endangered.

It was no good trying to predict what his brother would do. This time Lysander could not allow his family to direct his course. He must decide for himself.

The past, or a shining possible future?

Gemma.

Lysander cursed his own wooden tongue. He remembered that there had been a time where he'd swiftly dismantled a woman's resistance with glib charm and easy familiarity. He simply hadn't a clue how he done it.

Furthermore, Gemma was no Society widow looking for a dalliance with a handsome young ne'er-do-well. Gemma was ....

She was Gemma. She was so much more than any woman he'd ever known. He understood now how his twin brothers Castor and Pollux had come to blows over the delicate Miranda. He would pummel Daedalus himself for Gemma if he must. Yet how could he battle her own common sense? She was so right about him—and yet she'd got it all wrong.

She thought his soul was in hiding from what had been done to him. She thought him sunken, besieged.

Broken. Well, there was no denying something had snapped inside him. But Lysander did not live in fear, unless it was of what lurked within him. He was not fragile. He was pent, trapped, stuck behind the wall of his own halting speech, dragged down by the shackles of the darkness inside him. There was a thing in a locked room, that scratched on the door, patiently and pitilessly. A wolf who had eternity on its hands.

Gemma thought him inappropriately attached, that he'd imprinted upon her. As if he was one of the chicks in the pen, swirling in a yellow flood around her ankles as she cast the morning seed.

A dependent. A tragic, leechlike well of need.

He stopped and closed his eyes, his fists clenched tightly in his pockets, and asked himself that question.

What is she to me? Was Gemma merely a line thrown to save a drowning man? Was she shelter from the storm? Benevolent mother to a broken child?

No. No it wasn't so, it wasn't! Gemma was fine and beautiful, kind, brave and clever. She astonished him. Her strength and independence impressed him. But he had changed. For her.

Gemma did not make him feel dependent or needful.

She made him want to grow, to expand, to build a new man with a new character and a whole mind—a man who deserved her. A man she could depend upon, trust and lean upon, a man who believed in her mission to help the dale and stood by her side as she achieved it.

There had been a time in his life where people had said of Lysander Worthington that "You'd best not stand in his way, for once he has his eye on something, he'll climb the bell tower of St. Paul's itself to get it!"

He remembered that man now. He felt him. For the first time in so long, there was something in life that Lysander wanted.

He wanted to be the right man for Gemma Oakes.

Best not stand in his way.

Chapter 19

O N THE GREAT ROAD that ran like an artery between Edinburgh and London, two luxurious carriages moved at a fast pace, northern-bound.

Poll woke from a slight doze at a sharp pain to his shin. "Attie!" He growled in warning as he rubbed at his shin-bone through his boot. He'd been very comfortable riding in the splendid carriage loaned by his good friend, the Duke of Camberton. Very unlike the suffering he'd endured over the past year or so, traveling the roads of England with his the-atrical troupe. The troupe's carts and wagons were stripped of their minimal comforts—which had been discarded or sold whenever financial matters grew ever more grim—and broke down more or less daily in turn.

Attie sat across from him now, an unrepentant scowl on her bony, freckled features. "I'm bored."

"Recite pi."

She rolled her eyes. "I've already done that. Forward. Backward. Set to the tune of 'God Save the King.'"

"You can't recite pi backward. There is no end with which to begin."

She shrugged. "Maybe *you* can't."

Poll didn't push the point. He was sharp as a tack him-self, but there was really no comparison. "Hamlet?"

Attie didn't even bother to glower at that entirely worthless suggestion. They'd all been dead sick of Hamlet by the time they grew old enough to open the front door unassisted and make a run for freedom.

"I know!" she exclaimed with deceptive sweetness. "We can debate the pros and cons of my joining your troupe!"

Poll swallowed nervously. Good heavens, he might as well set fire to his wagons himself! At least that way, he could be sure everyone would make it out alive.

"You can't." She really couldn't, he realized with great relief. "Because I will not take you. And you'll never find them without me."

Her eyes narrowed in eerie challenge. "I think I could."

Poll leaned forward. "No, you really couldn't." He had to keep her from trying it. "And you're not wanted."

They glared at each other for a long moment. Then Poll felt his stomach drop at the site of a single tear trembling on the lower lashes of her eye.

Attie? Crying? The world but fair to turned itself inside out. What was next? Green sky and blue grass? Rain falling upward?

Miranda declaring that she'd made a terrible mistake and flinging herself into Poll's arms instead?

And then he recalled Elektra at that age. The tears, the tempests. Perhaps Attie had more in common with ordinary girls than any of them had realized.

"Oh, you wretched little beast," he whispered tenderly. "What's wrong?"

She stayed very still, only weaving slightly in her seat with the swaying of the carriage. Her green eyes burned like foxfire in the shadow of her seat.

Her lips parted and for a moment Poll almost expected his little sister to spill out all her thoughts, to open up her soul and let go of her tightfisted grip on years of rage and precociousness and the pain caused by knowing far more than a child should ever have to understand about the world.

Silly Poll. He been gone too long, it seemed. He'd forgotten.

Attie leaped to stand on Poll's seat and bang her skinny fist on the driver's trapdoor. "Stop! I want out of this carriage now!"

IN THE SMALLER but vastly more pretentious carriage rolling behind the first, Button and Cabot rode in an awkward silence. Unlike the shop, the carriage was too small, to intimate for them to operate with the same unruffled distance.

There had been a desultory commentary on the changing landscape, but that was sparse conversational fare after so many miles. Button had delivered every scrap of cheerful gossip he could dredge from his memory, even though he suspected that Cabot already knew it all. Cabot always knew what everyone was up to. He had many friends, some high, some low, some very unusual indeed.

Button meticulously arranged every fold of lace dripping from the frankly ridiculous cuffs of his favorite shirt. They were too much. Everything about him was buoyantly, flagrantly too much—which was just the way he liked to present himself. "Part of my mystique," he would remind himself. "We must sell the mystery, mustn't we?"

Yet there was no one to play to on this journey. There was no one to entertain, to confabulate, to misdirect and astound. There was only the man riding opposite him.

Beautiful, astonishing Cabot.

Button had always managed to convince himself that his feelings for Cabot were purely the pride of the mentor for an exceptional protégé. The master to an excellent student.

His age made him immune to Cabot's devastating good looks, of course. Cabot was an incredible help. Cabot smoothed the tedious road of business, leaving Button free to invest his time and joy into the creation of beautiful gowns. Cabot impressed the clientele. It was an excellent business partnership. Button had even convinced himself of it.

And then Cabot had left.

An remarkable opportunity had come Cabot's way—to be the personal arbiter of style to the Prince Regent himself! Button had fixed a proud smile upon his face and blithely urged Cabot to accept.

The pain that had followed Cabot's departure hardly bore thinking about. As much as Button tried, he could not excuse it as the inconvenience of losing a capable assistant. He could not reconcile the aching loneliness as simply missing Cabot's unerringly tasteful input.

He missed Cabot. Not simply the companionship. Not the effortless creative flow unfettered by receipts and billing.

He missed the sound of Cabot's voice, the beauty of his lean, athletic body as he went about the business of his day, and the sharp communication of his breathtaking eyes.

The shop smelled empty without the subtle woodsy scent of Cabot's cologne. Button's soul felt hollow without Cabot nearby.

Then an adventure involving the Worthingtons had brought them together again, a team in stylish action once more. Afterward, with no discussion whatsoever, Cabot had simply relocated back to the apartment above Lementeur and showed up in Button's work room with a tray of tea and cakes as if he had never left.

Button, although perishing to know how the Prince Regent had reacted to this desertion, had never asked. At first tentative and self-conscious, the working relationship had gradually returned to its former satisfying ease.

Yet Button could no longer ignore the fact that his façade of avuncular pride in a fine assistant had been lastingly revealed to him as a self-delusion.

"You are not an age. You simply are, as I simply am, and age is what we make of it." Cabot had said it once, just once, before he had left. Button had tried to dismiss it, tried to forget it. He had told himself it was a meaningless moment in a singularly difficult time.

The fact was that when Button sat alone in his perfect little house before his perfect fire, he would take those words out of the past and turn them over and over in his thoughts until they were polished as smooth as river stones.

That was why he—the great meddler, the matchmaker, the schemer—had never even asked Cabot why he had left. And more importantly, why he had come back.

Quite frankly, Button did not dare.

Now, he sat in the dim luxury of his borrowed carriage and tried very hard not to look at Cabot.

He could ask now. It was a simple enough question, was it not?

Abruptly, the carriage slowed and rolled to a stop. Before either Button or Cabot could signal the driver to inquire the circumstances, the door to their carriage opened and Miss Atalanta Worthington scrambled inside.

"Poll is boring." She looked sharply back and forth between them. "What are you two doing?"

AT SOME POINT after feeding the seemingly thousands of chickens and tending the ever-popular Mrs. Apples, who now had Icarus mooning over her fluttering eyelashes, Lysander found himself with nothing to do. He curried Bad Pony, to the wonderment of Bing, Mrs. Apples and Bad Pony himself. Bing promptly handed Lysander a crate of shears, sharpened and stuck deep into oiled sand for storage to be taken up to the shearing shed. As it turned out, the shed stood far up the slope from the house and stable.

"Can't miss it," Bing told him. "See that little square box away up there? Get on with it then."

Lysander hefted the crate to his shoulder and stretched his stride to make the uphill trek. He didn't mind the chore. He liked to walk and he needed to think.

Icarus still had a bit of swelling in that right forefoot. The horse would soon recover, but not if Lysander rode him three days straight back to London.

Lysander would only get stuck again on the way and possibly injure Icarus permanently.

Torn between his responsibility to his family and his desire to stay and prove to Gemma that he was worth—what? Worth waiting for? That he was a suitable fiancé who, one day, would manage to spit out his wedding vows in a sensible manner?

Was he even sure he could become that man?

AFTER DELIVERING THE crate of shears to the strange lean-to cobbled onto the back of the exposed stone shed. Lysander stood in the open front of the shearing shed and gazed out at the dale. It seemed that no matter where he stood every view of the valley was uniquely and perfectly beautiful. A brisk breeze herded white puffy clouds across the sky while their shadows scurried over the grassy slopes below. Lysander braced one hand against the center post and breathed deep of the day.

The scent of green grass and wildflowers helped to wash away the lingering smell of sheep within the shed. When he opened his eyes, Lysander's gaze rested on the stone post beneath his hand.

It was a great pity that the pavilion had not been built so well.

Lysander tilted his head, staring at the post.

The fresh air must be good for his mind, for he had an

idea—something he had avoided with great diligence whilst tucked into the bosom of his family. They had far too many ideas as it was.

Yes. He turned around and faced away from the valley, gazing into the shady confines of the shearing shed. Oh, yes.

It took a few hours, but eventually Bing came looking for him. The old man huffed and puffed as he limped up the slope.

"What's all this, then? I didn't tell you to muck out the shed!"

Lysander glanced up and nodded at Bing respectfully, but continued with his task. He had cobbled together a fairly decent rake using a the lid of the crate and a splintery shepherd's crook, banded together with a strap of cracked leather, all contents of the lean-to toolshed.

The earthen floor within the building had been strewn with filthy straw, which Lysander realized was nothing but grass hewn from the hillside, tossed down to protect the shorn wool from being soiled. Lysander had been raking it out and heaping it onto an empty sack that was longer than he was tall, and then dragging the old smelly straw a good distance away.

Bing was waiting for him when he strode back into the now well raked shed.

Bing shook his head. "This is right kind of you, lad, but I've a few more compellin' tasks for you in the stable. If you're done here, that is."

Lysander looked at Bing. "I've just begun." He looked around and this time his gaze went to the stone walls on three sides. Clearly this shearing shed had been in use for a very long time, for there was a wainscoting of mud and felted wool running hip high around all the walls. Lysander contemplated it for a long moment. He should ask Bing. Bing would no doubt have some excellent advice on how to clean those stones.

Questions came hard. Then Lysander remembered Gemma's oblique method of questioning him. Lysander folded his arms and kept his gaze on the problem walls. "Mrs. Philpot cleans with vinegar. She says vinegar will cut through anything."

Then he glanced at Bing. Bing's face, always craggy and weathered, now wrinkled into an expression of appalled confusion. "You don't scrub the shearing' shed, lad. It'll just get manky again next shearin'. Is no point to it, is what I'm saying."

Lysander leaned his shoulder against the comfortable solidity of the central post. "I have to. Otherwise their dresses will get dirty."

"Dresses? Sheep dresses?" Bing looked as if he was seriously beginning to doubt Lysander's sanity. Doubt even more, that is. "Sheep don't mind a bit of dirt."

Lysander just nodded. "Ladies do. They'll wear their best. Manky walls simply won't do."

Bing opened his mouth, no doubt to say something scornful, and then slowly closed it again. His eyes began to twinkle. "Oh my lad. You're a smart one." But he began to look doubtful again almost immediately. "It's a massive job, lad. I'll help you as I can but—"

"It must be nice to stand about all day, whilst real men get to workin'."

Lysander and Bing turned. The comment had come from a burly man who leaned across the stone wall abutting the nearest pasture. Shepherd Orren nodded easily at Lysander. "London man." Then he looked to Bing. "Now then, Bing. How's tha been?"

Bing nodded sourly. "Orren. Nobbut middlin', to me vast regret."

The flock Shepherd Orren was moving milled behind him while his working dog went up on back legs to dangle

white-tipped paws over the top of the wall while his nose
identified the two men in the shed. The dog yipped. An an-
swering yip came from the tall grass beyond the shed. Topknot lurched out of hiding to tear across the path to greet
the other dog.

Lysander straightened, concerned. Bing clucked at him,
the same noise he used to bring Topknot down from high
alert. "Don't worry so. And why shouldn't she run to greet
her own cousin, then?"

Lysander was beginning to understand the complex in-
terrelated family structures of the dale, and it seemed that
the pedigrees of the best working dogs were as much common knowledge as the boundary lines themselves.

Bing stepped forward to address their visitor. "You'll be
glad enough when this young fellow is done with his task,
Orren! I happen to know that there is a lady in your house
who is still spittin' mad about getting all fitted up in her
finery for nothing." Bing rocked on his heels, enjoying
Shepherd Orren's confused expression, although Lysander
would've preferred not to remind the gigantic fellow of the
loss of a certain pavilion and therefore the sacrifice of a
cheerful country dance event.

Bing went on. "We was just deliberatin' the best method
of scrubbing down these walls. Unless you think your missus be wantin' sheep shit smeared on her best skirts?"

Orren's jaw dropped as he stared at them. "It's a shearing shed! It's nowt but a filthy—" The man's gaze focused
on the shadowy space beyond Lysander and Bing. Lysander
could almost hear the heavy tumblers dropping into place
in the fellow's mind.

"Oh, aye! I've got a few worn-out scrub brushes from
the dairy that'll do the job, right and proper." Orren
straightened and whistled a complex melody to his dog. His
dog took off to run a lightning circle around the flock,
hemming it in as thoroughly as any fence. "I'll send one of

the lads up with the brushes."

"Vinegar!" Lysander hadn't meant to bark it as an order. It'd been a very long time since he had commanded anyone. However, Orren only nodded. "Aye and a bucket of good clean sand from the riverbank for scrubbing."

Orren not only sent up the brushes, river sand and vinegar, but two of his older sons and a farmhand as well.

Bing was tartly elated at the prospect of others to do all the work. "Sam up, lads! The lasses will be a'kissin' the lot of you when we turn this place about!"

Orren's lanky, half-grown sons were hard workers once convinced that the shearing shed could be turned into a proper assembly hall.

"We'll be needing lanterns," one of them offered.

"Aye, and benches as well."

They sent the farmhand down to the village proper to beg spare lanterns. "Tell all the wives and daughters," Bing snickered. "That'll light a fire under the lads."

Something did indeed light a fire under the lads, for over the next hours more than a dozen men stomped up the path to the shearing shed. They brought lanterns and roughhewn benches and a brusque, eager energy for the task.

Lysander couldn't imagine why, but to a man they all looked to him for direction. At first, he nodded and gestured. Soon however, he was forced to give proper orders in actual sentences. It wasn't as hard as he thought it would be. After all, giving orders was nothing like carrying on conversation. With that realization, the tightness in his throat eased and he found himself using six or seven words in a row. That had to be some sort of new personal best.

Bing had no problem giving orders. The moment the first bench was set just outside the roof line. Bing enthroned himself upon it, puffing his ever present pipe, and sniped constantly on the speed and quality of work being performed. "When I was your age I'd've had this done already!"

It seemed astonishingly quick to Lysander. In very little time the walls were a respectable limestone gray from floor to ceiling and clean sand had been spread to level the gouged earthen floors. Someone had been out in the pasture scything giant armloads of fresh summer grass to carpet the newly leveled floor.

Bing sat upon his bench throne and passed judgment. "Aye, it's clean. It ain't so much pretty as it orta be."

Lysander realized Bing was quite correct. The village pavilion had been bedecked in colorful bunting and flower garlands woven into willow boughs.

Lysander turned on his heel and stalked away from the shearing shed.   "Where is he off to, then?" Orren's eldest son protested.

"He's off to t' river to get thee some willow, ain't he?" Bing announced scornfully.

"Me mam still has a bit of bunting left from doin' up the pavilion. I'll fetch it."

The voices faded behind Lysander until he could hear his own stride crunching on the path, Topknot panting at his heels and the clean Yorkshire breeze calling in his ears.

Willow branches would do all right but he needed something else. Something better. Something worthy.

He reached far back into his memory and found a grand entrance, the doorway to a ballroom, where each couple's arrival would be announced by an impeccably clad butler. All around the ballroom, the dresses would swirl like flowers opening and closing while above them glittered chandeliers of crystal.

He should make the entrance more beautiful. What would Iris do? His mother always made things beautiful, daubing paint on things, strewing lace and roses about.

Roses.

Lysander picked up his pace, thinking of the long arching canes of Gemma's overgrown roses, of the mad profusion of white and pink—and his willow doorway wound round with sweet smelling blooms.

A bower of roses.

Iris would swoon at the very notion.

Chapter 20

I N THE STILLROOM of Yew Manor, Gemma unwrapped
the stiff linen binding she'd used to stabilize her wrist.
Examining the joint critically, she tested her range of motion.

Really, it was better than she expected. She still felt a
twinge, but she'd been fortunate to have Mr. Worthington's
assistance over the past several days or she would surely
have over-exerted it.

She settled on a simpler wrapping, more of a cuff
around the smallest part of her wrist than an actual bandage. This would free her fingers up for all the work that
needed doing in the stillroom and yet serve as a reminder to
take care.

A brisk tap came on the back door. Even as Gemma left
the stillroom she heard the door open.

"Hello?"

Gemma quickened her step. "Jennie!"

Jennie Gosling was already inside and seated at the rustic table, fanning her flushed face with the copy of Shakespeare's sonnets.

"It's that warm out, I couldn't bear it. Don't be telling
Shepherd Gosling about this, mind. The man worries over
much as it is." With her other hand, Jennie patted her vast
belly. "Fifth one and all, you would think he'd trust me to
know what I'm about by now!"

Gemma nodded. It was likely that Jennie knew more
about childbearing than Gemma did, for all her books.

"Tea? Or a cool glass of spring water? I've had a pitcher chilling in the cellar all morning."

Jennie gave a wave of assent as she dabbed at her puffy cheeks and brow with a man-sized handkerchief. "Cool water, dear. That'll do me just right, thank you."

Gemma fetched a cooling glass for Jennie. For herself, not being advanced in pregnancy and prone to hot flushes, she put the kettle on.

"How are you feeling otherwise, Jennie?"

"Oh pish. Don't you lay into me as well. I'm as big as a barn and feeling every lump in my old mattress, that's all. Aye then, this one's a kicker!" She pressed her palm high on her right side. Nowt to do but see it through. Not that I wouldn't make Shepherd Gosling take his turn about it, it being his doing and all!"

Gemma giggled. She enjoyed Jennie's easy familiarity immensely. Her friend was outspoken and full of strong Yorkshire opinions—and endlessly kind and generous to all she knew.

It was then that she looked past Jennie's flushed features and ballooning belly to notice that Jennie wore her best dress and her grandmother's coral brooch. Gemma knew perfectly well that treasure was kept back for significant occasions such as weddings, christenings, and funerals. "My, don't you look fine today!"

Jennie set down her half-empty glass and smiled at Gemma with a twinkle of friendly mischief in her eyes. "Well, you're dressed to muck out that evil pony's stall. Best be changin' or we'll both be late!"

Gemma drew back. "I was working. Wait, what shall we be late for?"

Jennie waved a hand. "That's no matter now. All you need to do is change that gown and do up your hair and you'll be the prettiest lass there."

"Where?" Gemma narrowed her gaze at her friend.

"Jennie, you can order me about all afternoon and it will get you nowhere if you do not disclose the facts of the matter."

"Don't be a stick in the mud. For once, won't you let folks give you a surprise?" Jennie gulped from her glass, and pointed up the stairs with one finger.

Gemma pursed her lips. "Fine. I will be but a moment."

Upstairs, she wasn't sure whether to don her black silk (funerals), or the less fine but more cheerful ocher dotted-Swiss muslin (weddings and christenings).

Since she was certain she would've heard if there was a passing in the village, she quickly stripped and put on the muslin, which had the added advantage of being easier to clean.

A yellow ribbon pinned around the severe bun she created would do. Thinking of Jennie's proudly worn coral, Gemma fished in her meager jewelry collection for her mother's pearls. They were small but very fine, and she doubled the strand about her throat instead of letting it dangle.

A quick glance in the tall mirror declared her fit enough for any Yorkshire occasion, no matter that everyone in the village had seen her ocher muslin a hundred times and again. It was hardly mended at all, just the hem turned a few times.

As she ran lightly down the stairs, she could not deny the eagerness bubbling up inside her. She'd once loved surprises, a fact she'd forgotten in a life where unexpected events were invariably tragic ones.

ON THE ROAD NORTH…

OVER THE COURSE of the two day journey—which would've been longer but they'd kept both carriages light with two occupants each and minimal luggage (even But-ton!)—the very excellent borrowed horses had made supe-rior time. Attie had abruptly and for no apparent reason decided to speak to Poll as if nothing had happened.

Now she rode half outside the carriage, with her knees on the seat and her elbows on the window ledge, lifting her face to the breeze like a pet.

Poll had gauged the slimness of his sister against the narrow window and decided that since he had a high possi-bility of catching her sash if she tumbled out, there was no point in starting another argument over it.

Besides, if the past was anything to go by, Atalanta Worthington was well-nigh indestructible. Fearlessly acro-batic and agile as a cat underfoot in a stable, Attie had al-ready wriggled out of more dangerous situations than any-one in the Worthington household really wanted to think about.

Poll made sure not to nap in any case.

"She's old." Attie declared suddenly. She slithered backwards through the window opening and sprawled across her seat on her back. With her long skinny arms and legs, she looked as artlessly natural as a fawn.

Poll waited.

"Old and kindly and ... maternal." She chewed the end of one long braid meditatively. "She's a widow, in black, with gray hair all twisted up tight on her head." She looked at Poll. "She likes cats."

"I like cats." Anyone who knew his youngest sister had better like cats, in all their capricious moods and elegant disregard for opinion. If they weren't game enough for cats, they wouldn't last an hour in Attie's wildly unpredictable company.

Poll felt a pang. He'd missed her so. The world would be a terribly unexciting place without Atalanta Worthington in it.

Just to goad her, he shook his head. "She's young and lovely. I'll wager her nice words about Lysander weren't maternal at all."

Attie cut her green eyes at him. "Bite your tongue."

All the Worthingtons together had concluded the mysterious, letter-writing Mrs. Gemma Oakes had to be a widow.

"He has proved to be of immeasurable help to me."

"Me", not *"us."*

"Her penmanship is awful," Attie pointed out. "Shaky, like Mrs. Philpot's. Old, I tell you."

"Injured," Poll countered. "She said so in the letter."

"If she's young and beautiful, she wouldn't be alone out in the middle of—" Attie swept an arm grandly, trying desperately to scorn the heavenly Yorkshire countryside, but Poll wasn't fooled. Attie was dizzy with joy at the wild, open beauty of the place. She was even fascinated by the mines.

"I could be a miner," she'd declared. "I don't care about getting dirty."

Poll had rolled his eyes at that, for it had been a rather recent development for Attie to go willingly to her bath. As if fully aware of her own future devastating beauty and entirely alarmed by it, Attie practiced ignoring all things to do with vanity or glamour.

Poll wasn't looking forward to her debut either. They were going to have to dig a bloody moat around Worthington House to cut down on the suitors.

A moat with a crocodile or three.

With a certain satisfaction Poll concluded that their eldest brother Daedalus would be in charge of fending off the flower-bearing multitudes. Hmm. Perhaps he ought to invest in a flower business?

The carriages halted before a grand and charming manor—or rather, the remains of one. Its tumbledown stateliness graced an arching swath of flat land along the river road.

Neither Attie nor Poll cared to notice the peeling wash on the window frames, or the moss on the slate roof shingles, or that the roof in one corner of the house slumped badly.

Worthingtons never judged a book by its cover.

The door opened and a woman stepped out with one hand up to shade her eyes from the bright day.

Attie would never admit to the depth of relief she felt at the sight of the stout country woman—oh, even better!—the hugely expectant woman who stared out at them. She turned to Poll in triumph "I win. Mrs. Oakes is—"

"Gorgeous," Poll breathed.

"What?" Attie spun back to the window. Attie scowled at the lady who had stepped from behind the motherly woman. "What a horrible trick!"

Poll ignored her, still blinking at the creature that Attie was dismally certain was the true Mrs. Oakes.

Attie, to whom cold calculation fit like a favorite pair of boots, said nothing more. So what if Mrs. Oakes was attractive?

Actually, very pretty in a completely not vain, not trying-too-hard sort of way. She reminded Attie of an illustration she'd seen of Aphrodite.

Well, her beauty did not matter. Attie wasn't about to lose another sibling, especially not Lysander.

Mrs. Oakes would never see her coming.

WHEN SHE SAW the dusty grandeur of the two carriages, Gemma's first thought was that someone would shortly be sacked for getting their employers so exceedingly lost.

Then she recalled the letter—the one she'd neglected to mention to Mr. Worthington—and wondered desperately if it was too late to hide.

The footman aboard the first carriage leapt to the ground with alacrity to let down the steps and open the door.

A man disembarked. All Gemma saw first was a lean build and the top of his sleek hat. Then he straightened and Gemma felt her insides go as cold as a snow melt river.

The man was clearly a Worthington. His hair was a lighter brown, verging on reddish, but the nose, the jaw-line, even the way he stood was very much like Mr. Lysander Worthington.

Four brothers, he'd told her. Three sisters. With alarm, Gemma wondered if all the Worthington siblings meant to pile out of the conveyance onto her poorly maintained drive!

The other Mr. Worthington turned back to offer his hand to someone inside. A girl emerged, not much more than a child. She was flame-haired and freckled, caught in the grasp of that awkward gap between childhood charm and adult assurance—and she was still one of the most beautiful girls Gemma had ever seen.

The glare that the woman-child fixed on Gemma nearly took her back a few steps. Just in time she recalled that she was mistress of her own house. She stepped forward instead.

Then, bewilderingly, two men descended from the second, smaller, rather more gaudy conveyance—one tall and one, well, not.

The shorter one beamed at Gemma with open delight. The tall one—

"Sweet sheep on a hill," Jennie breathed beside her. "Look at that 'un! I'm mighty glad I've got my good frock on!"

Gemma was thankful that she'd changed from her old, stained smock, but not for the same reason.

All of them, from the beautiful man to the beautiful girl,

had every ounce of their attention fixed upon her, Gemma, as if she held the secret answer to a sacred question.

"Where is my brother?" the girl demanded.

Oh. Well, it seemed that she did.

ONCE THEY HAD all been ushered politely into the manor, Button found himself alternately charmed and appalled by the shabby gentility of both the lady and her house. If he was not mistaken, the crumbling edges of the Palladian-style manor had driven its inhabitants to occupy only the center rooms!

It seemed that poor Lysander was actually in residence at Yew Manor. Furthermore, the stunning woman in the truly unfortunate gown was, in fact, some sort of local nurse. Button twitched with curiosity. Pollux, in Button's considered opinion, wasn't asking any of the *interesting* questions! Button assumed Lysander had a perfectly good reason to battle a sheep. He wanted to know if Lysander won! Also, how did Mrs. Oakes impart that luminous tint to her skin? Did Yorkshire have a good theater?

Were she and Lysander lovers?

In the cool shadowy parlor of the manor, he struggled to remain appropriately uninvolved in the conversation between Pollux and the charming widow. At a tug on his impeccable sleeve, Button blinked at the rather abundant woman who had pulled on his arm.

"My stars, a shearing shed?" He thought he must be mistaken, but as the woman explained in a hissing mono-logue in his ear, Button began to smile. Apparently, a sur-prise was in store for the Lady of the Dale and it was past time to set out. "Well, of course!"

Then his gaze slid to fix upon the charmingly appealing Mrs. Oakes. And the dress she was wearing. "But not just yet, I fear."

Then he turned to his little friend Miss Atalanta Worthington. "My dear, did you by chance pack the gown you were meant to wear tonight?"

Attie did not cease the deadly glare she'd been pummeling poor Mrs. Oakes with for the last several minutes, yet still managed to cast her reply back over one shoulder. "Of course. I keep my promises." Masterfully, she managed to expand the lance of her disgruntlement to include Pollux, who remained in quietly intense conversation with the delicious widow.

Button smiled angelically at Attie. "Excellent, my dear." He turned that same expression on Cabot, who—knowing him so well!—gazed back a bit warily.

"Cabot, please go fetch Miss Atalanta's bag. And mine. Oh yes, I shall need that as well."

Cabot glanced at Mrs. Oakes who, despite her many sterling attributes, did not perhaps look her best in such a dull shade. Then he shook his head at Button in an exasperated fashion even as he turned to fulfill Button's request. Good old Cabot.

Attie, who had finally allowed a thought to penetrate her vengeful fixation, stomped over to confront Button.

"It won't fit her. She's too fat."

"Tut-tut." Button smiled gently at Attie. "Accuracy, please."

Attie folded her arms indignantly over her still nearly flat bosom. "She'll never fit the bodice."

Button gave his darling, slightly homicidal young friend a comforting pat on the shoulder. These days he had to reach up to do so. "No need to worry, my dear Attie. I always build in a bit of letting-out for my young ladies." The bodice would be tight, however, marvelously so. Button smile broadened. He couldn't have planned it better if he tried.

Cabot reappeared with the requested luggage. Button

clapped his hands together in glee.

"Oh, Mrs. Oakes?"

THE CARRIAGE HIT a pothole on the route that the dismayed driver had declared "not a road." Gemma lost her balance and lurched into Mr. Cabot's side.

The implausibly handsome dressmaker gently assisted Gemma upright on the seat again. Gemma knew nothing about the current fashions in London, but she would have bet her pony cart that no one in the great city was more stylish that her seat companion.

Except perhaps for the man seated across from her. Mr. Cabot's friend Mr. Button smiled at her warmly. He'd insisted on using the fine carriages, even though Gemma had offered up her pony cart.

He'd been cheerfully scandalized. "Oh, that would never do. When one wears Lementeur, one must make an *entrance!*"

Was that what she was wearing? It sounded a bit French and incredibly costly.

It wasn't her fault. The dapper fellow himself had stuffed her into it without regard to a word of her demure protest. If Gemma had any blushes left, she would redden at the memory of being at Mr. Button's mercy for the past half hour.

Miss Worthington had lounged on Gemma's bed during the ordeal, sprawled on her belly with her slipper-clad feet waving idly in the air. Her sharp eyes had missed nothing, Gemma was sure, but at some point the girl's lethal glare had eased into a mere curiosity.

On one hand, Gemma had been glad for the feminine company. On the other, the girl's adversarial attitude has left Gemma feeling somewhat besieged.

Mr. Button, however, was a dear man. A fashion tyrant

and a persistent style bully, but a darling sort of bully. He had shoehorned her into a shimmering silk gown in a refreshing pale green, which she had to admit looked very fine against her sun-warmed complexion. The fact that Mr. Button had personally arranged her bosom inside the bodice had been shocking, yet somehow all right. A dressmaker was rather like a doctor, she thought. They did not carry tales about the people they helped.

Astonishingly, the fine gown possessed two very deep pockets hidden cleverly in the side seams. Gemma approved wholeheartedly.

Then Mr. Cabot had made free with her hair, curling it with an iron produced from somewhere and heated on her stove. He'd tumbled it all into a perfectly casual pile on top of her head that looked abundantly natural and simultaneously as if it had taken two hours and three maidservants to arrange.

Her mother's pearls were declared "dainty perfection" and replaced about her throat.

She'd not even had a moment to see herself in the tall mirror before Miss Worthington scrambled off the bed, grabbed Gemma's hand and dragged her out to the largest carriage.

Apparently, Jennie and Mr. Pollux Worthington had gone ahead in order to take the road slowly for Jennie's sake.

And after all that, Gemma still hadn't the faintest idea where they were going.

There was nothing up this hill. It was all rock-walled pastures and sheep, sheep, and more sheep. The only time she had ventured up here was during the shearing, where she spent the days making meals and toting water to the tireless men with the shears.

She couldn't even peek through the carriage windows, for Mr. Cabot and Mr. Button had pulled down all the shades. It was frustrating—and yet she could not deny the little thrill of suspense.

At last the carriage halted. Mr. Cabot disembarked and held out one hand to Gemma. Eagerly she followed him, only to find herself standing between the two carriages. Pollux Worthington was only just then helping an awkward Jennie Gosling down the steps.

Gemma ran to take her friend's elbow. Jennie looked more than a little green.

"Aye, and I'll be walking back down on me own feet, thank you!" Jennie turned to Gemma and examined her narrowly, then nodded in satisfaction. "Well! Those London laddies know what they're about, I'll say they do!"

Gemma shook her head with a small smile. "I feel silly in this dress."

Jennie patted Gemma's hand. "You look like t' lady you are."

Jennie's face was flushed yet her hands felt a little clammy. Gemma frowned. Then her attention was distracted when both carriages began to move. As they rattled rapidly away, Gemma's thoughts froze in shock.

"Zander!" It was Miss Atalanta, stepping forward from their group with a glad cry. Pollux Worthington put a hand on her arm to hold her back.

Lysander Worthington stood in front of a doorway made of blossoms. Even in his somewhat well-traveled coat and riding breeches, he looked like a lord welcoming guests to his manor—his rustic stone and rose-bedecked shearing shed manor.

It should've been ludicrous. It was not.

Lysander's somber face was alight with expectation and his intense gaze was fixed only upon her. As his eyes roamed over her, his jaw dropped and his lips parted slightly. Gemma felt his indrawn breath as if it was her own.

I feel beautiful in this dress.

They each stepped forward, unable to deny the magnetic pull between them.

Chapter 21

L YSANDER STARED AT the elegant woman before him.
*It's a sheep-shearing shed, not a ballroom. Dolt. This woman
deserves a ballroom.*
As they neared each other, Lysander reached out. He wasn't
entirely conscious of the movement. All he knew was that if
he did not touch her right now, this moment, he might as
well not bother breathing anymore.

His bare fingers enveloped her cool slender hands,
which were encased past the elbow in the finest of silk
gloves. He didn't question the luxury of the gloves, or the
lavishness of her gown. It seemed only right that she be
clad in riches.

Beautiful Gemma, lovely, strong, smart, valiant and
giving.

She held his hands. She smiled at him. He didn't deserve such regard but it warmed the old, cold places within
him as nothing else ever had.

Then a ferocious red-haired projectile struck him from
one side. The impact staggered him and pulled him away
from Gemma. His heart raced with the shock of it but he
kept his reason. Red hair. Skinny arms wrapped tight
around him.

"Attie?" Lysander blinked down at his little sister in
astonishment. "Where did you—?" His gaze rose to take in
the carriages and the three men standing beside them.

Button? Why was he here? Cabot? Well, where Button
went of course, but—

"Poll?"

Oh God. Oh no. Iris. They'd come for him because Iris was gone.

Pain swelled, starting at the center of him, tearing through his heart and burning red-hot and ice-cold through his entire body. He'd stayed too long. He had abandoned his family and now he would never see his mad, sweet loving mother again.

He stared his brother. He was barely aware that Gemma had gripped his hand tightly. He felt nothing but the loss exploding from within him, threatening to shatter him from the inside out.

"When did it happen?" Gemma asked Poll quietly

Poll blinked. "What?" Then, realization clearly dawned. "No, Zander. Iris is alive. Better yet, she is growing stronger every day." Poll grinned. "She sent us!"

The pain bled out of Lysander abruptly, sinking away into the purifying Yorkshire earth. The crushing sense of loss disappeared, but it left an awareness behind that Lysander was not yet ready to examine too closely.

"And we knew where you were, of course, from the letter."

Lysander blinked. Letter? Then he turned his gaze on Gemma, who met his gaze with no apology whatsoever.

"Well, but really," she murmured closely. "You did battle with a sheep! Hardly a sensible thing to do. I thought someone should know you were here."

Then they were surrounded. Exclamations were exclaimed. He was tentatively pummeled by a brotherly fist. Attie remained clasped to him like a limpet on a sea-washed rock. Then he looked for Gemma, who was smiling a little through anxious eyes. She began to step away, excusing herself from the reunion, polite and well-bred as always. Lysander kept one arm around Attie and made a long reach with the other to catch at Gemma's fingertips.

I need not choose.

He drew Gemma, smiling more broadly now, into the circle of flying questions that answered themselves and each other before Lysander ever spoke.

Of course. They would not expect words from him.

Gemma, however, did.

"Mr. Worthington, I have absolutely no notion of why we are all dressed up and standing on a hillside."

Lysander gazed at her warmly. The clever not-question. Poll and Button went quite still and stared at Gemma with a sort of embarrassed confusion. Cabot, who had been trying to peel Attie away from Lysander, swiveled his head around to peer at Gemma as well.

Gemma merely continued to gaze expectantly at him.

Attie lifted her head from where she'd tucked it into Lysander's cravat. "Zander made—"

Lysander calmly placed one hand over Attie's mouth. "Thank you, Attie. I can manage." He gazed back at Gemma. "We made a ball for you."

It was a simple version of events, true, but he managed to say all the words together in a sensible manner, even in the shock of visitors swarming around him.

Her beautiful eyes crinkled corners at the corners. *Well done*, the look said. "That sounds—"

"You're *talking?*" Attie interrupted, clawing his palm off her face and gaping up at him.

"Well, what else would he do, Miss Atalanta?" Cabot caught Attie by surprise and unwrapped her arms from around Lysander. "Bark?"

"Indeed, Cabot," Button said with pure delight rising in his eyes. "Indeed!"

Then the questions began to fly once more, but Lysander found himself the recipient this time. Part of him, the part that had expanded in the peace and clarity of the dales, began to shrink away again.

Gemma took his arm with a country woman's grip of her daintily gloved hands and steered him swiftly away.

"My apologies," she called back over her shoulder in a gaily unrepentant tone, "but Mr. Worthington owes me a ball and I intend to collect."

ONCE GEMMA AND Lysander had made their escape from the Worthington's clamor, Gemma slowed her determined pace and stared ahead in wonder. "My shearing shed looks as if a unicorn might emerge at any moment."

Lysander looked at his handiwork and Gemma saw a corner of his lips work into a wry curl. "Perhaps a better notion than a reality."

She took at his arm. "Don't you dare disparage my first ball! Show me everything."

He stopped her at the wildly fantastic rose archway. It looked like a thorny blooming portal had grown up overnight, constructed by the little folk from a lover's wish.

My wish. I didn't know I wished it until I saw it.

"For me?"

"Aye," said Jennie, who had come alongside them. "And for me, and all the daughters of the dale. I'll be dancing all night, just you watch me!"

"Come along, my flower!" Shepherd Gosling, in his best waistcoat with his bushy hair slicked down, grabbed Jennie's hand and led her beneath the archway. There, he laid a resounding smack on his wife's lips that brought a cheer from the growing crowd.

Everywhere Gemma looked, she saw dale folk arriving up the hillside clad in their best, with cakes and pies, herding their children before them. All her people, the broken bones and the summer colds and the aching joints walked forward with smiles and happy greetings on their careworn faces.

"For you," Lysander told her firmly.

Gemma smiled sideways at him. "Those are my roses."

He nodded unrepentantly. "Every last bloom. Roses like cutting."

A man who knew his roses. *Oh my.* Gemma shook her head with a trembling little laugh. "This is astonishing, Mr. Worthington."

"My family calls me Zander. I like it when you say Lysander."

Gemma blushed, feeling like a giddy girl with her first beau. "Lysander," she repeated shyly.

I am ridiculous.

I am ridiculously happy too.

And why shouldn't she be? She wore a beautiful gown, had a handsome man on her arm, and all her friends and neighbors were here to celebrate with her.

She was well aware that she was disregarding her duty to remain uninvolved. Yet, in some indefinable way, Lysander seemed to have stepped through an invisible wall. He seemed less lost and more direct. She had the oddest sense that he'd come to some sort of decision.

She wondered what it could have been. Whatever it was, it had clearly helped him turn some sort of corner. Look at this assembly he'd created.

For me.

For all the women of the dale.

Are you sure you aren't simply rationalizing your wish to involve yourself with him?

She wasn't at all confident of her own motivations, but with all the folk of the dale approaching, what could she do but participate wholeheartedly? All would be well, she was sure.

For how long?

Gemma squashed the little warning voice. She refused to think about tomorrow, or next week, or next year.

Tonight she intended to dance with Lysander.

STEPPING THROUGH THE rose arch on Lysander's arm was one of the single most romantic moments of Gemma's life.

I truly believed I was beyond all this.

Yet her heart sped when she moved closer to him in order to pass through it together. His big body was warm and solid against her side and the heat from him seeped into her very blood, a tingling warmth running through her veins.

The heady, splendid scent of the massed roses sent some long-buried girlish part of her spinning sideways in fanciful thoughts.

A silly, adolescent game to play, to rank a long lifetime by a few striking moments. A vanity, to think that the real world could pivot around tiny stretches of time, no matter how thrillingly tender.

Real life was work, not waltzes, a voice within her reminded her sharply. Day-to-day struggle, while one's house decayed about one and one's face developed a disappointed little crinkle between the brows.

The scent of the roses was so intense, it overwhelmed that troublesome voice most satisfactorily.

Gemma had never loved easily nor lightly, as some girls had. She'd not had her wedding day planned from prepubescence, nor—she was quite certain of this!—had she ever pretended to stumble just to let a man catch her in his arms. Until now.

She did it even as the thought crossed her mind. Such a transparently coquettish move!

I blame the roses.

She wasn't at all regretful when Lysander's arm tightened about her. She soaked in every move of his powerful body as he clasped her safely to him until she righted herself.

Then he released her and stepped away, one outspread hand indicating the rest of the shed with shy expectation.

Gemma lost her breath at the vision of a charming, if rustic, ballroom. She felt a sense of wonder as she noted the scoured walls, the floor strewn with fresh, fragrant grass, the benches lining the room and the already groaning refreshments table where a freshly scrubbed Mr. Bing stood by a half-barrel punch bowl, his carved wooden ladle at the ready.

A low musical note hushed the growing crowd. Gemma saw Jem Toms in the corner, tuning his fiddle.

"Ah then, hold your horses, Jem. I've not yet lit up the candle-ear with the spill!" Shepherd Orren stepped forward, holding a long twist of burning paper above his head.

Gemma's eyes widened at the giant wagon wheel, minus a few spokes, hanging horizontally from the central beam. Dozens of candles, fat and thin, tall and short, had been crammed atop it. It was monstrous and frankly Gemma hoped she had enough burn ointment made up for when the candles heated and began to drip hot wax onto the occupants beneath!

Lysander must've felt her go up on her toes with anxiety, for he stepped bravely beneath the now glowing "candle-ear" and spread his arms wide to demonstrate its safety.

"Don't fuss yourself, Missus," Shepherd Orren boomed at her. "Yon lad built deep wells into them candle holders."

Gemma bit her lip and eyed the thing mistrustfully, but then nodded at the looming Yorkshireman. "Thank you, Mr. Orren. I'm entirely reassured."

At that point, the chamber seemed to burst into open activity, as if everyone had been waiting for Gemma's approval.

Jem Toms lifted his bow to his fiddle and the music began, a rousing country dance tune. Gemma stepped back and waited for someone to lead their lady onto the floor.

Then tall, handsome, somehow-suddenly-dashing Mr. Lysander Worthington moved toward her with his hand outstretched.

"May I have the honor?"

Gemma's breath caught in her throat and suddenly her hand was wrapped in his. So large. So warm.

And then she was dancing.

Someone was laughing, a delighted breathless sound. It was her, giggling and grinning like a giddy schoolgirl.

I don't care. I'm dancing!

The dance was a romping pattern with four couples, and soon the floor was filled with sets of dancers. Gemma caught glimpses of Shepherd Gosling doing the steps and carefully guiding Jennie, who moved like a ship under sail. Gosling's fair complexion had turned ruddy with the intensity of his concentration. He needn't have worried, for the crowd parted for Jennie and eased her way with a few affectionate pats to her ripe belly. Jennie looked serene and saintly, her cheeks pink and proud.

Gemma even caught a glimpse of Miss Atalanta Worthington dancing with Mr. Button. For all her gangling height, the girl moved with breathtaking grace. That and Mr. Button's vivid glee put well paid to their height difference and they were the most accomplished partners on the floor. Miss Worthington performed the reel with a bored sort of graceful style, theatrically weighed down with jaded *ennui.*

Really, what an odd girl.

The dance ended. Gemma fanned her face and accepted Lysander's offer to fetch her a cool drink. While she waited, she spotted handsome Mr. Pollux Worthington chatting up the two very pretty, if rather vapid, nieces of the village postmistress. The two young ladies gazed up at Lysander's brother with shining eyes while he told some tale requiring the use of both hands fanned out from his head like a set of horns.

"Oh dear," she murmured to herself.

The postmistress's nieces were renowned for their heartfelt, but swiftly forgotten passions. They always became enamored of the same fellow at the same time and the competition often shook the entire village.

"My dear Mrs. Oakes, do not fear for the ladies. Pollux is a rogue reformed. He's had his heart quite unavoidably broken, you see. He would never inflict that pain on another now."

Gemma turned to Mr. Button with a bemused shake of her head. "It is for Mr. Worthington—Lysander—that I fear. The village has only just forgiven him for his disastrous arrival. If the Lamb sisters take on a battle over Pollux, I fear the entire dale will resent Lysander for it."

Mr. Button's eyes widened. "Heavens, it's as fascinating as summer court at the palace! What fun!" Then, with a wink at Gemma, he stepped away to speak to Mr. Cabot.

Mr. Cabot gazed down at his friend with absolutely no change of demeanor, yet Gemma had the impression of a severe lack of enthusiasm for whatever Mr. Button suggested.

Mr. Button returned to Gemma's side as they watched Mr. Cabot move smoothly to the trio, gain an introduction by way of Pollux, and sweep the taller of the Lamb sisters away for a dance. Pollux, perforce, did the same. The two young ladies had to settle for glaring at each other over their partner's shoulders, each jealous of the other's conquest.

Gemma snickered. The Lambs were fine people, but the entire community would be relieved when those two were settled in homes of their own.

"Poor Cabot."

Gemma blinked. The Lamb sisters were exceedingly silly, but they were both considered to be quite beautiful. Yet Mr. Cabot, unlike Pollux, seemed entirely unaffected. In fact, Mr. Cabot appeared oblivious to everyone except for one silver-eyed glance at Mr. Button.

"Ah." She hadn't realized. "Swans."

Mr. Button turned to her politely. "I apologize. I didn't catch that."

Gemma smiled at him gently. "Swans. They pair up for life, don't they? Not always male and female, either. Cambridge University is absolutely puffy with swans."

Mr. Button sputtered and lost his composure for the merest fraction of a second. Gemma bent to kiss his cheek quickly. "Thank you for helping me dress. I do feel quite fearless in this gown."

Lysander returned with an earthen cup of something for Gemma. Mr. Button made a quick bow and stepped away. Lysander moved into his friend's place next to Gemma.

"Lemonade." He peered into his own cup. "Or possibly not."

Gemma raised her brows at the very purple liquid in her vessel, then she gave it a sniff. "Bilberry juice," she announced. "Perfectly safe." With a glance around the room at the many thirsty partakers, she added, "Nor shall I see a case of gallstones for the next year. Still, you should take care. It can impart the most vivid purple—"

She looked at Lysander, who even then had his head tilted back to drain his cup. "Mouth stain."

Oh dear. Gemma bit her lip but the impending giggle won out. Mr. Worthington looked down at her, bemusement etched on his handsome, manly, bilberry-stained features.

For a moment, a mischievous part of Gemma toyed with the notion of not telling him. After all, nearly everyone else in the improvised ballroom drank the "muckle-mouth" juice with relish. However, there was a trick to it, sipping small and swallowing fast. Mr. Worthington had guzzled his. Not very gentlemanly, that.

Still, Gemma believed in kindly impulses more than mischief. Some villagers were glancing his way, and Gemma began to suspect that the choice of the problematic bilberry juice had not been random. She grabbed Lysander by the hand and dragged him from the noisy shed.

"Come with me. And don't lick your lips, whatever you do."

Chapter 22

T HE AIR WAS cooler outside and the dew had begun to fall. Gemma had never considered how passionately romantic the dale looked by moonlight.

Until tonight.

Lost in her spinning thoughts, she stumbled on the slick grass. The matching elegant slippers she had borrowed from Miss Worthington were not meant for Yorkshire pastures. Instantly Lysander came to her rescue, just as he had on her previous coquettish stumble. *How carefully he watches over me.*

His warm hand cupped her bare elbow and his other slipped about her waist. Her back fell into his chest and the heat of him rose up to infuse her senses. Desire broke powerfully over her, crashing into her like a wave on a rocky shore. She was drenched, tumbled and breathless and deliciously confused.

She stayed, leaning into him, not stepping away as she very likely ought to have. He stayed as well, neither moving away, nor forward into some caress. He simply held her, allowing the moment to last just as it was.

I could love a man who understood such moments.

She tipped her head back to rest it on his shoulder. The sky above them was a riot of stars, the moon a brilliant disk that still could not outshine the shimmering swath of forever.

"We are so small," she whispered. "Insignificant."

"No."

Gemma felt the single word rumble through her body. Her knees weakened and her desire spiked. "No?" She murmured, just to feel his deep voice vibrated through her again.

"You are not small, Gemma. You are ... essential."

His words echoed inside her, provoking emotions and needs she had hidden away years ago. She realized she was shaking her head, denying his words, denying her response. "I'm not. I'm—" *Not a lady. Not a doctor. Not even a true Yorkshire woman.*

However, her usual litany of inadequacy no longer rang true in her mind. She abruptly realized how careful she'd become. So careful. So formal and awkward in her position of weighty responsibility.

She felt altered tonight, as if the gown and the attention had granted permission to some other Gemma to take her place.

Her pulse pounded. The rush of blood through her veins combined with the moonlight to brew a fizzy sort of indestructibility within her. The rules of propriety seemed suddenly pointless and limiting. She felt them slipping away, as if perhaps they had fit badly all along. Perhaps they had.

After all, she'd lived her first fourteen years in quiet rebellion against the rules, passing untold days drifting through the forbidden library. She'd gone to war when most women in Society could barely speak of it. Defiance had always been part of her. Now it stirred, awakening and stretching in the heat that suffused her blood with arousal.

For the first time in a very long time, she *wanted*. And what she wanted, she meant to have.

She turned to look over her shoulder at him. A snort of laughter caught her without warning.

Lysander still had a raging case of muckle-mouth. No matter. Gemma had the cure. She grabbed his hand and towed him onward.

LYSANDER, WITH GEMMA'S small strong hand in his, would have walked with her to the equator and back again as long as she didn't let go.

Sadly, their excursion ran somewhat shorter. She led him behind the shed and up the slope where a dry-stone sheepfold stood empty.

It was little more than a pen. As they entered it, stepping through the high grass within, Lysander saw that it had been built to encompass the meanderings of a small spring, surely meant to sustain the sheep being held at shearing time.

At Gemma's direction, Lysander crouched beside the spring to rinse his mouth of the deliciously messy bilberry juice. He stood and reached in his pocket for his handkerchief. It wasn't there. It was wrapped and tied about the wobbly leg of the refreshment table.

He glanced at Gemma, his face dripping. Wipe it on his sleeve?

She shook her head, smiling ruefully. "Mr. Button won't like me doing this." She took Lysander's chin in her cupped palm and used a silly wisp of handkerchief to dab at Lysander's face.

Enough. He lifted his hands to capture hers and tucked the sodden little ball of ruined lace into his pocket. "Gemma Oakes, I'm going to waltz with you."

As if by a secret signal, just at that moment Jem Toms began to play a lilting, mournful waltz on his fiddle. The tune floated out over the hillside, refined and sweetened by the fragrant breeze and the otherworldly moonlight.

Lysander saw Gemma's blink of surprise. Before she could recover, he swept her into the waltz.

She let out a sigh when he pulled her in close, just a soft breath that he felt on the skin of his cheek. That, and the way she melted into him, told him something he'd never realized.

Gemma Oakes was plenty tired of always having to be in charge.

Lysander would do anything for Gemma, unconditionally. If she asked him to dance like a monkey before the assembled folk of Farby, he would assume she had good reason for the request and comply. Yet realizing that something she lacked was someone to ease her burdens firmed Lysander's resolve, sparking a burst of clarity inside him.

What Gemma Oakes required in her life was someone strong, someone quick of mind and thoroughgoing. It occurred to him that she would not, in fact, prefer the old Zander to the new one. He had been light-minded, despite his intensive if outlandish education. Not weak, but yes, lazy and careless. He'd laughed at his sisters when he'd frustrated them to fury, he gambled when he knew perfectly well that old Philpot was struggling to stretch the meals to feed nine bellies. He'd not been cruel, nor corrupt. Simply, tragically convinced of his own immortality, never understanding that there were many kinds of death.

Foolish youth.

He was much wiser now. Wise enough to see into the widow's clear gray eyes and glimpse a future worth fighting for.

That was the man he would be for Gemma Oakes.

All that depth of understanding occurred in a matter of seconds as Lysander slid his hand down Gemma's back to rest there, palm inward. He could feel every ripple of movement through the diaphanous gown as they swayed into the steps of the dance.

GEMMA HAD BEEN wrong. When she'd stepped through the rose arch, she'd thought it the most romantic moment of her life. What a drab existence she'd had to think so highly of strolling under a charming arch with a handsome man. It did not compare with dancing high on a grassy hillside under a full moon, with the strains of a distant fiddle guiding their steps.

This is definitely the most romantic thing that has ever happened to me.

Abruptly, Gemma decided to stop thinking so much. In fact, she vowed to stop thinking at all. If this waltz was such a rare and random occurrence, perhaps now was the time to shut it and dance.

This man, this unusual man, gave her leave to be bold. But no one wanted to be bold all the time. She closed her eyes and sank into his large, muscled body as if she were falling and he was her only hope of survival.

Catch me, she thought, and danced.

The cool air on her skin competed with the heat of him against her. Gemma remembered the kiss on top of the fell. Had it truly been so remarkable? Or was it gilded by a lovely day and her feeling of skipping out on her responsibilities? Shouldn't she explore that more thoroughly?

Oh yes. I think I will.

She went up on tiptoe, drove her fingers into his silky dark hair and pulled his mouth down to hers. The spark of surprise at her own impulsiveness disappeared in the detonation that occurred when Lysander pulled her hard into his arms and kissed her back.

Oh my heavens.

THE BREEZE PICKED up slightly and the tall grass on the hillside turned to rippling pewter waves in the moonlight. Lysander breathed deep of the clear air and sweet grass—with just a hint of roses—and her.

The scent of Gemma was wholesome and reviving, like

the air of the dale, spiced with a hint of green, growing things and warm, wonderful woman.

She shivered slightly in her impractical gown and he pulled her closer. Their gazes held and he marveled at gray eyes gone silver by the light of the moon.

She kissed him.

He was surprised, and yet more ready for the touch of her soft mouth than he'd ever been for anything in his life.

Gemma's mouth. Gemma's lips.

Gemma.

His hands slid up her slim waist, lifting her closer still. She had her hands in his hair, tugging urgently. The sting only aroused him more fully. He wanted so badly to tumble her down into that tall grass, to kiss her throat, to tug her bodice down to taste her breasts, to slide those gossamer skirts up to find her hot and wet and ready to his seeking hand.

She moaned into his mouth and he nearly gave into his aching need.

The music changed to a sprightly reel and Lysander remembered why he could not drive himself into her warm and ready body in the concealment of high grass.

He would not embarrass her before her people. He would not walk her back into that gathering with grass stains on the back of her dress and on his knees, with her hair tumbled and the rash of his evening beard growth on her cheeks.

When he took Gemma Oakes, it would be in the privacy of the bedchamber, the light of a warm fire, and he would take his time, by God, to bring her as much pleasure as he knew how to give.

And he would know himself to be the most fortunate man alive—alive with the beating heart she had created in him again.

WHEN LYSANDER LIFTED his mouth from hers, Gemma tugged at his lapels, going up on the very tips of her slippers to follow those hot, tantalizing lips.

"No."

She stared at him. The word took a moment to penetrate her lust-fogged thoughts. "No?"

He stroked a breeze-blown strand of her hair behind her ear. "No. Your people wait. We should go back."

At that moment, Gemma didn't give a damn about the village or the assembly. He'd awakened the sleeping lover inside her, kissed it awake and driven it mad with that teasing tongue and that hot mouth. And then he said "no" and expected it to sleep again?

Abruptly, she was hotly, irrationally furious with him. Didn't he realize that she'd already given up so much? That she'd worked so hard and had never taken for herself?

She wanted this, this selfish thing. She wanted to feel like a woman again, to feel touch, to not be alone anymore!

She went to on tiptoe again and stared this unpredictable stranger in the eye.

"Kiss me now, Lysander Worthington. Or never kiss me again!"

He looked right back at her with those damned black eyes unflinching from her frustration. "You deserve better."

She swallowed hard and forced herself to step back, to move away from his big, warm body and his hot, caressing hands and that mouth that made her dream of things she'd never known.

"You're right, of course, Mr. Worthington. We really must get back to the party." She folded her arms over her chest, suddenly chilled.

He moved to offer her his coat. She turned her back on him and strode down the slope to the shearing shed, already working on the pleasantly noncommittal smile she would wear as she returned to the people who knew her better than anyone—and yet not all. This time she passed through the rose arch all alone.

LYSANDER WATCHED GEMMA go until she turned the corner of the building and disappeared from his view.

He did not follow her. He was fairly certain that she would rather fall on her face than have him there at her elbow, escorting her safely down.

Once she was gone, he turned his gaze upon the dale by moonlight. From this vantage, he could see the manor, its windows dark, and its decrepitude gilded over.

Lysander knew it could be saved, but work should begin soon or the structural integrity would be compromised. Surprisingly, the prospect did not alarm him. It had only been a short time since he'd had to leave Worthington Manor, the old family home in Shropshire, because he been too disturbed by the noise and bustle of the reconstruction to remain.

Now, the thought of a crowd of builders descending upon Yew Manor seemed very satisfying indeed, provided that "crowd" meant no more than a dozen.

What he could build for Gemma with the aid of a dozen men! Especially if a couple of them were Worthingtons.

He hadn't the right to hammer a single nail, and never would if Gemma didn't forgive him. He could be sure of that. Gemma wasn't one of his sisters, who had to relent eventually. He might've done terrible damage to Gemma's opinion of him by kissing her and then refusing her.

Women like Gemma—well, there were no women like her, not in all the world. None so generous, so hardworking, so selfless, so delicate and yet so strong. And, although she concealed it well, so vulnerable. She thought he didn't know her and perhaps he didn't, but he understood her.

He knew that when he rejected her advances on the hillside, she might never forgive him. However, if he'd embarrassed her before her people, she would have never forgiven herself.

BY THE TIME Lysander reentered the shearing-shed ballroom, Gemma had joined in a rousing *contredanse*, skipping down the tunnel of dancers hand-in-hand with Button.

Lysander claimed a bit of wall space and leaned one shoulder against the stone where he could watch Gemma. She seemed to be enjoying herself immensely and quite indifferent to the events of ten minutes past.

If he'd just met her for the first time, he would've been utterly convinced of it. But even on that first encounter she had set herself apart, held back, observing the enjoyments of others. Now she laughed aloud as she and Button went up on their toes in their part as a segment of the dance tunnel, the two of them hilariously trying to remain joined by the hands over the head of the massive Smith who was paired with his tall, voluptuous wife.

All the room laughed and teased the pair, telling Button to "Eat your mutton so you'll grow big and strong!" And the ladies calling out to Gemma that they could teach her to make a man "grow big and strong." It was all good-natured country fun, in a society where the breeding of young creatures of all sorts was considered perfectly appropriate conversational fodder.

Gemma laughed and blushed and shot Lysander a single glance full of defiance that clearly intended to instruct him that his refusal had no effect on her whatsoever.

Lysander was not disturbed. He knew for certain that he'd had a tremendous effect upon Gemma. No longer was she the reserved Lady of the Dale, outside looking in, held in wary deference by the folk of Farby. The village truly seem to embrace and enjoy this new Gemma, although Lysander noticed the that the teasing remained respectful and affectionate.

After pondering the change in her for another moment, Lysander stopped thinking. He simply watched his beautiful Gemma laugh and dance like a carefree country maiden. His gaze caught on the curve of her lips and the flash of white teeth as she giggled at Button's wickedly funny riposte to the worst of his hecklers. The room broke out in a roar of laughter. Lysander missed the point of the joke because he was focused on the graceful way Gemma's dainty, hardworking hand moved through the air, drifting on the music like a leaf floating on a breeze.

Poll joined him on the wall and handed Lysander a tankard. When Lysander drew back his hand in suspicion, Poll laughed.

"No muckle-mouth juice here. Just a very young ale. Watch out, it has a kick."

Lysander took a sip, grateful when the bitter nutty flavor further distanced him from the bilberry incident—although it'd had its moments.

He took his focus from Gemma long enough to become aware that Poll watched him over the rim of his own tankard. Lysander raised an eyebrow in question.

Poll nearly snorted ale up his nose. "Stop that! You look like Orion! One is enough for any family."

Lysander was as fond of Orion as any of his siblings, except for Attie, whom everyone favored and no one resented. He had been closer to Orion in childhood than to Cas and Poll, who had always paired up naturally.

He considered Poll for a moment. His brother looked strained. For the first time in a long time, Lysander had enough silence and space in his own mind to contemplate Pol's unenviable position.

"Do you love Miranda?"

Poll flinched. "God, you don't come back by halves, do you? Six words out of you in six years and now you go for the crippling blow right off the bell?"

Lysander waited. One thing silence had taught him was that people tended to fill it for you if you didn't. Poll looked away, took another swig, hiding behind the protection of his tankard. After a moment he gave a sigh and shrugged. "No. Yes. Sometimes."

Sometimes?

Lysander nodded, not because he agreed but because he understood something new about Poll and about himself. If he had to answer the same question about Gemma, the reply would be a short, definitive "yes."

Poll had had a confusing near-miss encounter with love. It was enough to awaken his formerly feckless heart to the promise of an entirely different rhythm of beating, yet not enough for him to rip it out, cage it, and pass it willingly, eagerly into the hands of another.

Gemma now danced with Cabot. They made a stunning pair and the room grew quieter as the village gaped at a level of grace and sophistication that Lysander would wager they had not seen for a long while, if ever.

Had not Edmund danced with his beautiful wife? Had he made her laugh until she gasped for air, or smile like a beacon when her dancing was greeted with stomping boots and whistling applause at the end?

But Lysander had no evidence of Edmund's treatment of Gemma either way, except for his cognizance of Gemma's painful dedication to her own dignity when he'd met her. She wore that dignified manner carefully, like a fragile crown she must not let fall. It had made her stiff and unapproachable. Lysander would bet Dade's very fine horse that it had been Edmund who had set that ill fitting crown on Gemma's young, girlish head.

Poll shifted to face out upon the crowd, no longer looking at Lysander. Neither said anything for a long few moments, but the lack of conversation felt comfortable enough. It occurred to Lysander that he felt no need to flinch from his brother or to run away from any questions and expectations Poll might have of him. He might be able to answer them if asked, or he might not, but it didn't seem as imperative to avoid them as it had in the past.

Lysander choose to think of that as a sign of improvement.

"So," Poll began, very obviously not looking at Lysander, "you seem better."

Lysander nodded. "I seem better."

"The northern air agrees with you. It seems a robust place, Yorkshire. Very, um, pastoral. Healthy."

Lysander nodded. "Pastoral and healthy."

"Hmm. So, Goose-gogs, eh?"

Lysander didn't look at his brother, because he knew perfectly well the smirk Poll would be wearing. He'd seen it often enough in his life. "We will not be discussing Goose-gogs."

"Really? I'm fairly certain it's a popular area of conversation in this village." Poll sounded very smug. That wouldn't do at all.

"Only because no one knows about the time you swam in the altogether and then found a leech on your—"

"That's not fair! I was but twelve years!"

Lysander remained relaxed and waited. Poll grumbled, then snickered a little in memory. Then Lysander felt a brotherly swat on his bicep. He glanced at Poll, but his brother had turned his attention to one of the pretty Lamb sisters as she danced past. Still, Lysander could tell that Poll felt comforted by the familiar ground of their prickly exchange.

Lysander felt as though he'd passed some sort of test.

I gave him what he needed from me and it wasn't even difficult.

Out on the dance floor, Attie had abandoned her veneer of theatrical sophistication and was chasing the Gosling children in a figure-eight game of tag between the dancing couples.

Childish games and a flawless waltz. Both were performances for Attie, who had never been a child and who would no doubt become a very unusual woman. She was amusing herself but not actually participating in any substantial manner.

Lysander was beginning to suspect that he ought to be very careful with Attie. She seemed brittle, somehow. Not fragile, precisely. More in the nature of a change in weather causing a prickle of unease at the back of one's neck.

Rough weather ahead.

Lysander saw Button watching Attie as well, with a smile on his rounded features but also a tiny crease of concern between his brows.

A storm is coming.

Poll remained focused on Lysander. "It seems that you'll be back to your old self soon."

"Never," Lysander stated matter-of-factly.

"What you mean?" Poll slid his gaze toward him. "Why not? You're better, you said so."

Lysander looked down at the new calluses on his palms. Not riding calluses or rowing calluses, but pail-carrying, chicken-feeding, goat-tending, wall-repairing calluses. And much more work left to do.

"He's dead." Lysander looked up at Pol. "He died at Burgos Castle. Stop looking for him in me."

Poll blinked at Lysander's rough tone. He opened his mouth to debate that statement, then stopped. He nodded crisply "Understood."

Lysander thought that of all of his family, Poll probably

did understand, at least somewhat. Poll's old life could no longer accommodate him either.

His gaze sought out Gemma in the crowd. He found her taking a tin cup from Bing at the refreshment table. It was likely spring water, for the bilberry juice had run out long ago and even the mountain of cakes had been reduced to a scattering of crumbs.

Gemma had gone to war, as had Bing. The survivors of battle had found each other, even down to Bad Pony. Was that the reason he felt he could truly understand Gemma, when most people seemed rather incomprehensible to him? Even among Worthingtons he was a wolf amongst the lambs, trying his damnedest to look fluffy and white instead of dangerous and dark.

Gemma wasn't afraid of his dark. She might be a bit leery of her own, however. The blackness of war had changed her, stretched her, challenged and frightened and expanded her.

No wonder her crown didn't quite fit.

Chapter 23

CABOT HANDED BUTTON a cool tankard of spring water. Button thanked him with an absent-minded smile. Cabot turned to see what held Button's attention.

Atalanta Worthington dashed by them, a boy of about six years chasing close behind. The child hadn't a hope of catching long-legged Attie. Yet Attie allowed herself to be tagged, and when the little boy sprinted off giggling with glee, Attie chased him in a leisurely manner. It was a kind way to play with a small child. That was why Button was staring.

Attie wasn't kind. She had her own somewhat irregular code of ethics, but falsifying herself in any way did not apply.

"Ah." Cabot turned back to Button. "How very worrisome."

Button blinked sadly at him. "Could she be developing some latent sense of decorum?"

"God, I hope not. How dull." Cabot was not alarmed. Atalanta Worthington had decided to don some local feathers. She was very likely studying the Yorkshire species, the way her sister-in-law Francesca Worthington studied the inherited traits of animals.

Button smiled sympathetically at him. "I'm sure you are finding this evening terribly mundane, after the entertainments of Town."

Cabot turned away to set his own tankard down on a nearby bench. Button often mentioned Cabot's exciting existence in London, imagining him off having steamy affairs with all his "friends." Button tried to accommodate this allegedly racy lifestyle by giving Cabot many of his evenings free.

Never. Not once since he encountered Button had Cabot had a "friend." There'd been a few casual encounters before that night, sometimes for fun, sometimes for security, but after the first cup of tea, after the first quarter-hour of Button's lively chatter flowing down over his own silence, after mere minutes of Button's generosity and kindly charm, Cabot had known.

It was Button. Always. Only. *Forever.*

Since then, his "scandalous" nightlife consisted of long evenings of reading. He been an ignorant street sneak and petty criminal. For years after his life had changed, he'd stuffed his brain full of knowledge in hopes of measuring up to Button's cultured ideals. Then Cabot had begun to find joy in the education itself and taught himself an eclectic blend of philosophy, ideas, history and reason.

Everything that Cabot read and everything that he observed in his new life only confirmed in Cabot's soul that Button was more than simply a kindly fellow, more than a loyal friend to many.

Button, diminutive, witty and ever-smiling, was nigh unto inhumanly good-hearted. An eternal optimist who managed to gently and persistently erode Cabot's streetwise mistrust. At first, Cabot assumed that his own gratitude had possessed him to place Button on a pedestal. He began to look for the hidden flaws, the secret cracks in such a pure, crystalline soul. No one was perfect. No one could be.

Yet Button was truly as kind and clever and generous as he had appeared to be in that first fatal quarter-hour.

Cabot only fell more firmly in love with him.

And Button had never noticed.

Attie suddenly popped up at Cabot's elbow. "Now," she

said to Cabot meaningfully. "I brought the dress and I would've worn it as well, if Button hadn't given it to the bosomy one." She crooked her thumb over her shoulder to indicate Mrs. Oakes, who did look exceptionally well-endowed in the snug bodice of the very lovely gown.

Cabot debated whether he ought to argue the point, to claim that not having actually worn the dress negated their bargain, but he decided to stand by the spirit of the law, rather than the letter.

He slid his eyes toward Button meaningfully. Attie promptly stopped breathing. Cabot waited, amused to see her intention.

When Attie's complexion had turned from pale and freckled to an alarming shade of fuchsia (and still freckled), Cabot nodded. Attie allowed her breathing to resume, and stepped around Cabot to Button's side.

"I'm hot," she stated.

Button regarded his youngest friend with alarm. "My dear, you're terribly flushed! Sit down at once!" Button all but pushed Attie down on the bench. "I'll fetch you something cool to drink!" Button disappeared into the crowd of taller shepherds and farmers.

Cabot sat down next to Attie. "Here is what happened. A little over a year ago, I told him I loved him. He flinched from me. Blathered something panicky about our age difference and feeling paternal. He believes I'm only grateful that he rescued me from a short, painful life. It hurt very much. I thought leaving would help. It didn't, so I came back. He would like to go on as if nothing happened."

Attie gazed at him flatly. "That's incredibly stupid."

No, there was no danger of Miss Atalanta Worthington developing a latent sense of decorum. "I couldn't agree more. But if it is the only way I can be with him, then it will have to be enough."

"No, I mean about the age difference. You are a thousand years old," she informed him archly. "It's in your eyes. You are like the melancholy angels painted on the cathedral walls. Button, on the other hand, is five minutes younger than I am. Why else do you think we are such great friends?"

Melancholy angel? Monk, perhaps. Cabot nodded grimly. "Tell him that. He is the one who needs to hear it."

Attie shrugged. "No. You are both being very boring and I don't want to play."

"Don't want to play at what?" Button emerged from the crush and handed Attie an earthen cup and watched her drink down the cool water held therein.

Cabot gazed at Attie with deadly warning. "I was just telling Miss Atalanta that I shall never be as successful as you because I cannot make everyone like me as you can."

Button frowned. "Oh nonsense. That's not accurate!"

Cabot shrugged. "They think I am cold."

Button sputtered, appalled. "But—but that is untrue! You are never cold!"

I burn for you. Does it show?

Button's gaze flicked away. Cabot allowed him to retreat, as always.

Attie, however, eyed Cabot for a moment. "You aren't cold. I should know. You are ..." Her sharp green eyes narrowed in thought. "You are *private*."

Button turned to Attie, intrigued. "Why do you say that?"

Attie shrugged and gazed indifferently out upon the dance floor. "He's private because he doesn't believe that everything in his thoughts needs to be said out loud. It's no one's business, is it? And he's too honest to be insincere, so he simply says nothing at all."

Button turned to Cabot and gazed at him in surprise. "Yes, that is precisely the right word. You know, I've always wanted the right word for Cabot."

Cabot was not unhappy with the depiction either. He nodded at Attie, who nodded back and then abruptly walked off, dusting her hands as if to say, "there's a job done."

Button watched her go. "I do believe I am truly worried about that child."

Cabot picked up his tankard and drank deeply. If Button felt the need to worry, perhaps it was the rest of the world he should fret about.

GEMMA SHUT THE door on her little bedchamber, leaving the occupants in darkness for she had only the one candle. The Goslings quite frankly didn't care. Jennie, too breathless and exhausted to argue taking over the lady's chamber, was tucked with her three eldest children into Gemma's bed. The littlest had been left at the farmhouse with Jennie's mother-in-law, which was a good thing. Gemma's few remaining usable bedchambers were chockablock with guests.

The First Annual Farby Assembly—also known as the rowdiest and most successful country dance anyone in the village could recall—had wrapped up in the wee hours and Gemma couldn't bear to send her weary, expectant friend any farther in a jostling cart than the manor house.

Shepherd Gosling was bunking in Mr. Bing's room. Mr. Button and Mr. Cabot, along with Mr. Pollux Worthington, had done well enough with the room Lysander had been using, taking up the last of the featherbeds—stuffed with wool, of course, not feathers—to make shift on the floor.

It wasn't until Gemma stood in her own hallway with her lantern in her hand that she realized that she hadn't reserved a bed for herself. Scatterbrain.

It was true that waltzing in the moonlight with a handsome gentleman, and then of course, kissing the aforementioned handsome gentleman until she lost her breath and nearly her reason—well, that would scatter any woman's brains, would it not?

She was fortunate that Mr. Worthington had had the will to resist her own bad nature.

It was bloody disappointing, that's what it was. She'd stalked away in a snit instead of pressing the matter, knowing she was likely sending opportunity on its way, verily giving it the boot in the arse, actually—and to what end? She was no virgin, no cherished and protected maiden. She was a woman, a widow, and as long as she kept her wits and behaved with discretion, there was no reason in the world she couldn't have a lover just bloody once, for pity's sake!

His family had come for him. He would be leaving with them, Gemma had no doubt of it. Atalanta Worthington had not dragged her brother and her friends so far from London in order to leave empty-handed. Gemma knew a ruthlessly tenacious female mind when she encountered one. Even if Lysander wanted to stay—heavens, what a dangerous notion!—Atalanta would club her brother over the head and drag him off leaving a trail of his boot-heels in the Yorkshire Dale soil, likely as not.

That moment, dancing in the waving grass beneath the swollen moon, had been her last chance to take gorgeous, tempting Mr. Lysander Worthington into her arms and into her body the way that they both so assuredly wanted.

I'm going to have to sleep in the stillroom, I suppose.

There were some cushions in the study. She could pile them up in the stillroom. In anticipation of the chill stone floor, she grabbed the last threadbare quilt from the linen press in the upper hall.

Once she closed the cupboard door, she sighed and gave up. Her shoulders slumped wearily as she slowly descended the stairs, one hand leaning heavily on the railing. "Oh, my feet," she whispered to herself. She hadn't danced so much in years.

Or actually, never. Nor enjoyed it so, not really. A swinging Yorkshire country reel was ever so much more fun than a rigidly executed quadrille, no matter how elegant.

Lysander had probably attended a hundred balls in London, yet he'd seemed to actually enjoy skipping madly in circles to Jem's tireless fiddle. He'd taken his sister on several spins about the floor, as had his brother, Mr. Button and Mr. Cabot.

Atalanta had danced with a few village children, girls as well as boys, but none older than ten or eleven. Ah, perhaps Miss Atalanta was more well supervised than she seemed, or even knew. Well, good luck on that one, to all the gentlemen concerned. In a few years, breathtaking Miss Atalanta would make quite an impact on the London social scene and every male within five miles of that young miss was going to feel the ground shift beneath his feet.

"I wonder how Mr. Lysander Worthington is going to bear up under that," she muttered to herself as she entered the library.

"Bear up under what?"

Gemma grabbed the quilt up high to her bosom in surprise, as if to defend herself from a stranger—which seemed doubly ridiculous because in the first place she remained fully dressed, and in the second, she wasn't likely to do much damage to an intruder with a few layers of faded chintz stitched over thinly carded felt.

"Mr. Worthington!"

He rose to his feet, for he'd been crouched by the hearth, poking at the fire. Over his hard-wearing riding breeches, he wore only his shirt, untucked and with the sleeves casually rolled up to reveal his muscled forearms. His boots abided near the hearth, precisely positioned as if a soldier still stood in them. There was something in their regimental placement that made her ache a little inside, but her attention swiftly fastened itself on his bare feet.

She tore her gaze away, forcing herself to look at his face instead. It wasn't that his feet were particular in any way, although they were perfectly handsome feet indeed, and very large. It was the intimacy of seeing them bare, of being alone in the dim room with him in this state of undress, with new parts exposed to her eyes—which her wayward thoughts followed that should he become further undressed, there would be even more fascinating new parts to see.

The placket of his shirt lay open, revealing his throat and a deep vee of his torso, reminding her of his manly amount of chest hair that narrowed over his rippled stomach to a dark vee that pointed farther south.

Fascinating parts indeed.

She had absurd urge to remove some of her own clothing. It was simply the well-conditioned urge for a lady to make her guest feel more comfortable, to feel as if they fitted in.

That was her reason, and by heaven, she'd swear to it to the grave!

Sweet heaven, he was beautiful.

How she had come to cherish this stranger in her life! Because of him, she had talked, and danced, and laughed, and kissed! She'd been so isolated in her manor, and now she was truly part of her village and her dale.

But this was her home, where she belonged. What of his home? What if she went to him now, and then he left her behind?

I think I'd rather know physical love one more time than live the rest of my life without it. It wasn't wise, perhaps, but it was true. She wasn't sure she was strong enough to turn away from the dark longing in his gaze, even if she did believe it was for the best. She ached so.

Oh, to be held, to be touched, to be pleasured!

By him.

That was the crux of it, wasn't it? This man wasn't simply a handsome creature equipped with all the necessary pleasuring apparatus, was he? He was Lysander, reader of poetry, uncomplaining carrier of water and chicken feed, creator of rose bowers and nights of moonlit wonder.

She wanted very badly for what was in his eyes to be real. Yet she didn't know what to believe. Life didn't truly work that way. Handsome, mysterious strangers didn't ride into town and fall in love with exhausted, work-worn widows!

Yet she marveled that he had done such mad, extravagant thing as tonight's assembly for her, simply because of a chance comment she'd made about never having attended a ball. He clearly was not helpless. He was no longer a patient.

He was a man.

Need. Lust. Admiration. Longing. She didn't know what to do with the tumult of emotion she felt when she looked at him, standing there, waiting for her, patiently allowing her time to make up her own mind.

And that was what decided her.

If she turned and left him at this moment, he would not pursue her. She knew that about him, if she knew little else. He would respect her wishes. He would let her go, and have faith it was what she needed to do.

He believed in her.

It was that belief in his shadowed gaze which kept her standing right where she was, despite all common sense and propriety. It had bolstered her when she'd set the little boy's broken leg. It had allowed her to let her guard down for one night, to dance, and laugh, and kiss.

LYSANDER WAITED. GEMMA seemed to be thinking about something, very hard. He did not dare hope it was the same thing he was thinking.

Damn, she was beautiful.

Lysander knew a bit more about women's fashions than most, due to the fact that Elektra would never shut up about it. He knew that Lementeur was a master at bringing out hidden beauty and overlooked virtues. Of course, the gown was stunning.

It didn't matter to him. Gemma would have looked beautiful dressed in a flour sack belted with twine.

Or even better, in nothing at all.

How long had it been since his pulse had pounded so eagerly? How long since his blood had felt afire with want? She was lovely indeed, but she was first and foremost Gemma, his Gemma, the woman who made his soul awaken again, who made his heart long again, who made his body flame again.

Yes, he wanted her. He could not stand there and deny the pulse pounding in his throat, or the bulge in his trousers. He wanted her wrapped in his arms, her bare skin pressed to his. He wanted all of her, her body, her lips, her hair, her touch.

He didn't think he'd live through the night without them. And he wanted to. For the first time in so long, he wanted a tomorrow. He wanted a hundred thousand tomorrows, if he could spend them in Gemma's arms.

He watched her bite her bottom lip. Her eyes were cast down, the faded quilt clutched high. She was thinking so hard he could almost hear the whirring of tiny golden gears from where he waited. What was she thinking? Was it about him? What would she decide?

Finally she looked up and when her scorching gaze met his, the breath left his body.

"Mr. Lysander Worthington, of the London Worthingtons," she said slowly, "Do you think that sofa is wide enough for two?"

WAS THIS MADNESS? Then she was mad and she didn't care.

He was a stranger from the city, a misfit in the Dales. He would leave soon in his fine carriage, with his grand friends, and she must stay.

He was a lost and unsteady soul, quite possibly with only the barest armature of reason bolstering the structure of his mind.

He was also beautiful and alone and he understood her in ways she did not even understand herself.

She dropped the quilt to the floor and never taking her gaze from his dark one, stepped forward into his arms.

Chapter 24

MATTERS PROGRESSED VERY quickly from there. All Gemma's pent-up desire erupted from somewhere just beneath her belly and she couldn't imagine how she'd held it in for so long!

He was tall and strong and so entirely focused on kissing her that the intensity sent shivers through her even as she burned for him. He had both hands around her face, holding her mouth still for his ravishment.

Gemma couldn't strip off the pretty little cap sleeves fast enough. Years of practice doing for herself came in handy as she freed the closure of the gown to the small of her back.

She didn't give a damn about her wrist or the gown or anything but the empty, pulsing ache within her. She needed his hardness deep inside her, filling her, completing her.

She'd been empty for so long.

When he felt the bodice of her gown drop from between them, he pulled away to look down upon her. Gemma held still, letting him see her, letting him decide if he wanted the real woman, without the fancy, uplifting architecture of the dress.

His hot palms slid down, smoothing over her neck and shoulders, tugging the loose, open chemise neckline aside to reveal her breasts. She was not terribly curvaceous, she knew. Hard work kept her too thin for that sort of luxurious plenty.

One large hand slipped around her back, pressing her

upward, while the other bent her back with gentle pressure on her shoulder, arching her body, jutting her breasts forward brazenly while he gazed at her.

Gemma was abruptly sure that despite his reticent social manner, Mr. Lysander Worthington knew his way around a woman's body. And right now he wanted to discover hers. His tinge of dominance excited her. She'd not seen this side of him since he'd played Saint George to the ram's dragon.

The gleam of masculine lust in his gaze melted her knees and made her belly quiver. She'd been cherished and she'd been abandoned. What she'd never been was driven senseless with passion. She was on the brink of something like it, if he could match her step. Was there more such virile authority within him?

Oh, I certainly hope so.

He bent to devour her, kissing her breasts openmouthed and hungry. He moved from one to the other and back again, sucking, nibbling, licking and torturing her nipples with pleasure until she writhed in his hold, willingly helpless under the delicious assault.

His mouth moved back up from her breasts to bite gently down her neck to her shoulder. She shivered at the sting of those small nips. The tiny darts of pain excited her. She was no hothouse flower, fragile and sensitive. What she wanted more than anything at that moment was to *feel*.

He wrapped his big hand around the back of her neck, arching her throat up to his consuming lips while his other hand slid her loosened gown down over her hip. He grasped her bottom through the thin, delicate chemise that she'd been given, the one that she suspected she could quite easily read a printed page though. His hard grasp pulled her lower body into tight connection with his own.

He was hard. She ground her own softness restlessly into him. *Yes, I want you. I want you too.*

He rolled them both to the floor, he onto his back and her above him. He even managed to lose her gown at last in the process. Gemma found herself astride his hard erection, still trapped in his breeches, but her shameless lack of drawers, which Mr. Button has insisted would ruin the line of the gown, was enough to send her keening at the texture of his doeskin breeches against her clitoris.

This was nothing like she'd ever known. The candles were lit! They were on the floor! He bucked beneath her and her head fell back in pleasure. To hell with the candles and God bless the floor!

Her chemise slid to her waist, pinning her elbows to her sides. Gemma shrugged her arms free, too impatient to take care for the costly silk batiste. She heard a tearing sound, her own fault, but it brought a gasping growl from the man she rode.

He reached a large hand and ripped the chemise from her. Gemma gasped at the slight burn left by the wrenched fabric but then moaned as his mouth soothed the pink skin.

At last his mouth returned to her nipples, as she'd wanted so badly. He sucked and tongued them, twirling them in his mouth until she cried out in pleasure. Every sound she made seemed to bring him closer to the brink. He moaned and rolled her beneath him, catching the back of her head in his palm as he stretched her body out before the fire.

"No." She reached for him, she needed him, she ached so!

But he backed away and stood up, looming over her. Gemma realized that she was entirely naked. He was still mostly dressed.

"Well, that won't do," she grumbled and scrambled to her knees. "Take off your shirt!"

A gasp left his lips, somewhere between a groan and a laugh. "Yes, milady."

His deep murmur made her belly shiver, but Gemma had work to do. She'd undone a few buttons in her day and his breeches were no issue for her. The sound of tugging fabric came from above but Gemma was very focused on easing the waist of his breeches down over the fascinating prominence held therein.

His drawers hung loose on his hips and it was no trouble to tug it all down at once. His rigid erection sprang free before her eyes.

Goodness me.

Well, she'd never been one to do things half-heartedly, and she wasn't about to begin now. *It'll be an adventure*, she told herself. A grand, long, thick adventure.

Absently, she pulled the legs of his trousers down and off, never taking her gaze from her latest challenge. Realizing she was staring, she blushed and looked away.

"Touch me," he whispered. It was as much a plea as a command. His need throbbed in his voice and Gemma's apprehension melted away. *Yes. We will care for each other and all will be well.*

AT THE FIRST tentative touch of Gemma's cool fingers on his cock, Lysander curled his fists tightly at his side and stood completely still. Nothing on this earth would make him so much as twitch, for fear of ruining this moment.

Had it truly been a thousand years since he'd been touched? Perhaps he'd never been touched, not really. The other man, Zander, had rolled about in bed with this woman or that, always with friendship and a good-natured sense of adventure. Yet he had never engaged his heart.

Perhaps that earlier Zander had possessed a few walls of his own, after all.

Now, he had no walls where Gemma was concerned. He was naked in every way, exposed and vulnerable. Yet he had never felt more powerful, more linked to the life around him, to the life in her. Powerless without care, vulnerable without fear. He had so much to say to her. He did not think he could express it, that his stumble-tongue would fail him.

Then don't speak. Show her.

All that passed through his mind in the instant before her lips kissed the tip of his cock. Then thought ceased.

GEMMA COULDN'T EXPLAIN the impulse. She'd never done such a thing before. Her tongue flicked out between her lips and caught a salty droplet, then she wrapped one hand around the thick base of him and eased her tongue around him, licking slowly in a circle.

How wonderful to explore. How decadent, and yet at the same time it felt so trusting and giving. She dared a glance upward to see his eyes shut tightly and his jaw clenched. He looked as if he was trying very hard not to reach out to her.

What if she made him do so?

She opened her lips wider and took the blunt head of him into her mouth, still sliding her tongue over and around. His chest rose and fell in sharp rhythm, as if he'd been running, yet still he did not move.

I want you to break past it.

I want you to reach for me first, this time.

She shifted closer on her knees so she could slide a length of him between her lips, and made up for the rest with her hand fisted snugly around him.

The power she felt made a heavy ache between her thighs and she felt herself grow damp when he wasn't even touching her. The way she'd felt watching him pour water over his head, standing in the sun by the rain barrel, gleaming and muscled like the powerful animal he was.

Then, as now, he'd waited on her to call him to her, for her to touch first, for her to kiss first.

He was afraid of the darkness within him. She was not. She'd seen him become chaotic in a state of battle madness. Even when he was lost to himself, his instinct to protect had prevailed over his habituation to violence. She had no fear and she meant to prove his trustworthiness to him.

I want to be taken by you. I want to be claimed.

I want you to race free. I want you to run.

Run to me.

So, being a widow of a reasonable level of experience, she set about breaking down the last wall around Lysander Worthington—the wall of reaching for what he wanted instead of waiting silently for the scraps he thought he deserved.

You will run wild by my hand.

She wrapped her fingers tightly around him and began to move them up and down the base of his shaft.

You will lose all reserve.

She closed her lips around the thickness of him and drew upon him, sucking him deeper and then pulling away slowly, keeping the suction tight, sliding her tongue along the thick vein that ran beneath.

Reach for me!

He withdrew from her mouth and tugged her grip free. Gemma fell back slightly from her perch upon her heels and looked up at him to see the wild, dark heat rise in his eyes, turning them black and unreadable. She shivered slightly and ran her tongue nervously over her lower lip, but she did not break their locked gazes.

He dropped to his knees between her sprawled limbs and took her face into his hands. She'd never known anything like the kiss he gave her, the kiss he took from her. Oh sweet heaven, *the kiss.*

Never. Never had she been kissed like this, never truly kissed before, never knew it could burn so, heal so, ache so.

She closed her eyes and fell freely. She didn't give a

damn if she ever landed at all.

Run free with me.

His secret wolf unleashed, he wrapped his arms about her, sweeping her in a great circle that rolled them both back down upon the carpet.

I cannot breathe. I don't care. If I die beneath him, I will at least have lived.

For all his ferocity, he didn't hurt her. He was all rough passion and violent need, but his touch left her breathless with pleasure, not pain.

One large hand wrapped around the back of her head and the other slid down her neck, over each breast with a masterful squeeze, over her belly and down.

Oh, yes.

Touch me.

Hot fingers, slightly roughened by work and riding. Long, careful, sensitive fingers, playing her slit like a harp, sliding deep into her wet center and slipping out, fingertips circling and tugging, circling and sliding.

And all the while he kissed her. When she arched her body and dug her fingernails into his shoulders and came apart in his arms, he swallowed her moans and cries, never ceasing the pleasure he dealt her.

And when she fell back gasping and shuddering, he rolled upon her even as she shivered and thrust his cock slowly but implacably inside her. She heard herself whimper in surprise, but he swallowed that too.

He was careful and tender, but there was no doubt within her that he would have her and he would have her now.

Gemma moaned into his mouth. Her last conscious thought was, *be careful what you wish for, you just might get it.*

Then began the wild storm that was Lysander unleashed.

Each thrust near to split Gemma in two. Each withdrawal made her gasp with loss. The heat and weight of him upon her, between her thighs, pressing them wide with his big body, the way he cradled her so carefully in his arms with each powerful thrust—

I think I might die.

I think it might be worth it.

She came again, tossed helplessly upon the waves of pleasure, unsure of up or down, uncaring of wrong or right. Lost in him. Lost in the way he made her feel.

Lost, she thought as she floated dizzily down off the crest of her orgasm.

I never want to be found.

LYSANDER LOST HIMSELF in the gift that was Gemma. He forgot his soul wounds at the squeeze of her silken thighs about him. He forgot his life in London when she cried out and he felt her orgasm ripple through her.

He forgot his own name in the urgent passion of her mouth and the languid tangle of her arms as he spent himself within her.

But he remembered hers.

Gemma. The wonder and revolution that was Gemma. She saw pain and it did not frighten her. She'd known violence and battle and horror in the medical tents that he'd never had the nerve to step within. She'd tended the shattered and dying. She had marched through the blood-soaked mud and the memory hadn't stolen her voice, hadn't shut her away in a locked room inside herself, hadn't left her floating a few feet behind her own body like a near-ghost.

I am in my body now. I feel everything.

I feel the warmth, the tenderness, the sweet, aching heat of her, the heart of her.

He turned his face into her neck as if he turned it up to

the sun. He remained over her, within her, around her. He could hear her pulse in her throat. He could feel her sighs on his ear. She slid her hands upward, stroking his back in a blissfully weary way.

He didn't want to lose this moment. He didn't want to open his eyes and find himself unchanged, still broken, still locked in place and twitching with battle instincts.

But most of all, he did not want to look in her eyes and see regret or shame. Or worse yet, pity!

Passion could burn itself out. What if, to her, he was simply a relief from her cold widow's bed? What if he was nothing more than temptation gratified?

Then he must consider it an honor to be the one chosen to warm her chilled, lonely flesh and give her pleasure.

If she regretted giving herself to him, then he would never speak of this moment again. He would respect her wishes, walk out of her life and leave her be. He might die of the loss, in that inevitable way one did, with little shreds of self crumbling away, day after day, until the lungs still breathed but the heart no longer beat. But Gemma would go on, and that was the most important thing.

But if he looked into those beautiful storm-cloud eyes and saw welcome? If she smiled at him and kissed him and said loving things? Then he would spend the rest of his days trying to be the man she believed he could be. He would rebuild himself whole even if he had to pack that damned ram's wool into the empty places until he could grow the wounds closed. For her.

He could feel again. He could hope again. Damn hope anyway, that sweet honey trickling though him once more, telling him that it could be done, he could be healed, he could be someone again. The wounds could become scars and the scars become stories and the stories become lessons in a life well spent.

A life spent with Gemma.

Then she shifted beneath him. His depleted cock slid from her warmth.

"Oh dear," she murmured. "The carpet."

Lysander couldn't help it. He'd been tragically planning his own demise from a broken heart. She'd been pondering much more domestic worries. He laughed.

It was a rusty, rasping sound, but his shoulders shook even as he wrapped her close to him and rolled over with her above him. When he looked up at her, still helplessly making that deep, appalling noise, he saw her eyes.

No pity or regret there. Only a sort of wry delight. She knew he was laughing at her, but she clearly didn't care. Her eyes gleamed with affection and enjoyment.

Lysander's heart began to beat again, not with the pounding gallop of lust and need, but with a steady strong pulse of utter devotion.

I love you, Gemma.

He didn't say it aloud. Not yet. He had no fear of exposing his heart, but only of startling her with too much, too soon. How could he love her? He could almost hear her say it. How could he love someone he barely knew?

I loved you before I kissed you, before I danced with you. I loved you before the pavilion fell.

How could he love someone wholly when he himself was broken?

That was a trickier question. Given time, he meant to work on the answer. He felt certain that she had begun to believe in him. Was it enough?

She grinned down at him. He smiled back, as best he could.

She dropped a kiss upon his chest and flopped wearily next to him, yawning and stretching to press herself to his side. "I never liked this carpet anyway."

Please, let it be enough.

Chapter 25

G EMMA BECAME AWARE of a sharp pain in her shoulder, the one chilled from having the quilt slip down as
she slept.

Poke. A skinny finger dug in deep.

"What?" Poked? In her own bed, in her own house?
Gemma sat up blinking and furious, and not a little bit
alarmed.

I'm not in my bed. I'm on the floor. Furthermore, I'm naked.
She clutched the quilt higher and squinted against the light
of a candle held too near her face. The light drew back and
Gemma saw the bony yet perfect features of Miss Atalanta
Worthington. Gemma drew back, bracing one hand on
something that she suddenly realized was a hard, masculine buttock.

I'm naked on the floor with Lysander.

Oh, hellfire!

She almost took the opportunity to blush deeply and
make vague waffling excuses. Then she remembered the
only reason anyone ever woke her in the middle of the
night.

"Who is ill?"

Atalanta nodded crisply, as if approving Gemma's lack
of prudish driveling about. "It's the pregnant one."

Gemma smiled. "Oh, how wonderful! She's so weary
of—"

"I think it's gone bad."

No more talk. Gemma pulled last night's ball gown over

her head and impatiently turned her back to Atalanta, who did her up at speed. Twisting her hair up out of the way, Gemma grabbed a couple of pins off the floor as she pattered barefoot from the room. "Lysander! Fetch Mr. Bing from his room in the stable!" she barked over her shoulder as she headed down the hall. "You!" She pointed at Atalanta, for she had no time to pronounce that many syllables. "Build up the fire in the kitchen stove and put vast amounts of water on the boil!"

She strode briskly into her bedchamber and pushed a few hovering Gosling offspring aside to move straight to Jennie.

Oh God.

It had indeed gone bad.

LOOKING AT JENNIE, lying sweating and delirious in Gemma's bed, the truth hit Gemma like a rockfall, crushing her with sudden awareness.

Witless. Blasted blind and stupid. It had been right before her eyes the entire time.

She'd dismissed the signs as the normal symptoms of advanced pregnancy, and tragically, they might very well have been. It was only now that she saw the truth. The swelling of Jennie's hands and face was edema. The shortness of breath was the fluids invading her lungs. The headaches, the florid cheeks, those indicated a dangerous rise in her blood pressure. The pain in her abdomen had not been the kicking of the child, but impending liver breakdown. Now, the confusion and panting.

Toxemia.

And when it was this bad, it could be a death sentence for both mother and child. Yet there was no time to hate herself now. She could practice self-loathing at her leisure once she helped her friend.

There was only one thing that could save Jennie and hopefully, her baby as well.

"She'll be alright, I tell ye. Knows what she's about, my Jen."

Shepherd Gosling's words were brave, but in one glance Gemma took in the ashen husband's stark terror.

"I need to work. Take the littles to the kitchen and give them some bread and butter. Have a cup of tea. I'll call you if I need you."

"I'll no' be leavin' my Jen!"

She leaned closer and whispered fiercely. "This is bad and you know it. Jennie wouldn't want them to see. Now go." She gave the giant sheep-herder a firm shove. It barely rocked him, but he swallowed hard, dropped a feather touch of his fingertips to his wife's pallid, sweating brow, and hauled his nervous brood off to the kitchen.

Bing rushed in, bleary-eyed in the dawn light now peeking through the draperies. Lysander lingered in the doorway. Gemma ushered him inside the room with a jerk of her head. Atalanta popped through the door with a pot of steaming water and, bless her wit, a cake of Gemma's lye soap.

"Bing, get some blocks of wood and put them under the head of the bed. I need to raise her upper body. Lysander, my case."

Lysander darted out and Bing lurched away, limping badly. Gemma wasn't worried. Lazy Mr. Bing could move like lightning when he wished. She scrubbed her hands well, ignoring the splashing of soapy water that ruined the delicate silk of the gown she wore.

Lysander returned with the medicine case and took his turn at washing in the painfully hot water without being asked. Gemma gazed at her open case with seeming calm but her mind raced. She selected some willow bark. "For thinning the blood and reducing swelling," she murmured to herself. She swiftly ground it into a runny paste with a few drops of laudanum, because she couldn't bear Jennie's agony. After a moment, she added a very strong red raspberry leaf tincture because she feared the worst was yet to come.

She pried open Jennie's clenched jaw and poured the concoction down her throat. Jennie muttered and shuddered and tossed her head, pulling away from Gemma's touch.

Gemma looked at Lysander. "I need to induce labor. And I can't be delicate about it."

He nodded. "Tell me what to do."

Gemma reached into her bag and pulled out a long iron rod wrapped tightly in waxed linen. It was as slender as a pencil and tapered at one end. She'd prepared it as instructed in *Childbirth and the Practices of Midwifery*, even boiling it twice before sealing it in the impervious linen—and sincerely hoped she wouldn't have to use it. When Attie came back with the next boiling pot, Gemma threw the tool into the steaming water. Better safe than sorry. "I need you two to pin Jennie down. Attie, you hold her head in your lap. Lysander, you must tie her up as well. She's out of her head. Sit on her if you have to. If she moves even a fraction of an inch, I could kill the baby."

Attie climbed to the head of the bed and pulled Jennie's sweat-soaked head onto her lap. Gemma glanced at Lysander. He shrugged. "She's exceedingly strong."

Gemma had no time to protect Lysander's peculiar sister from what she meant to do. When Lysander had used strips of the bed sheet to fasten Jennie tightly to the bedrails, with the primary pressure being exerted just above the mound of her pregnant belly, he lay across the bottom of the bed and pinned Jennie's legs down.

"No, pull her knees up."

Gemma went on one knee at the end of the bed and took a breath. She couldn't falter. She couldn't fail. The only way to save Jennie and the baby was something she'd never done, nor ever seen done. She'd read it in a book. *I might be wrong. I'm not a doctor. What if I'm wrong?*

Firming her jaw against those doubts, she reached uncaring into the blistering water and withdrew the tool. "Hold her. Don't let her move."

She held her breath as she inserted the rod and, mostly by feel and guesswork, got it through the cervix. The tip of the thing was actually rounded into a tiny hook. It shouldn't hurt, the book has assured her. Gemma bit her lip. With a twist of her wrist, she snagged the placenta on the hook and ripped.

The gush of birth waters soaked the bed and Jennie let out an animal wail as the first contraction swept her. Gemma tossed the tool aside.

"Release her now!"

Lysander eased Jennie's legs down and untied the binding sheet. He used it to drape over Jennie's lower body for some privacy. It was a kindly thought, but Jennie was far past caring.

Bing and Lysander got the head of the bed raised to Gemma's satisfaction. It was the last thing she could think of to aid the birth, letting the baby's own weight assist, like with an ewe, who gave birth standing more often than not.

"Atalanta, stay where you are. It's your duty to get as much water down her gullet as you can without drowning her." Water to cleanse Jennie's systems, and fight dehydration.

God, the perspiration alone and now with the placenta open she'll be losing fluids and I don't know if I did the right thing, I don't know—

"Gemma, what comes next?"

Jennie screamed aloud as another contraction gripped her.

Gemma looked up at her platoon of warriors. Mr. Bing's

wrinkled, wonderful face. Lysander's darkly beautiful, trusting, willing eyes. Self-possessed Atalanta, who quite frankly looked intensely interested, but not terribly alarmed by any of it.

I can do this.

I have to.

"First, we birth the baby. Then we save Jennie."

Mr. Bing nodded sagely. "Aye, that's how she'd want it, all right."

"True," Gemma grimaced. "But it's also simply how this works. As long as Jennie remains pregnant, her life is in danger and so is the baby's. Birth will ease the battle going on inside her." And they had to make it happen before Jennie's heart failed. But she kept that part of it to herself, unable even to say the words aloud. That extra bit of truth wouldn't help anyway.

Atalanta tilted her head and regarded Jennie's belly dispassionately, even as she eased another sip of water through Jennie's mumbling lips. "How do you make someone have a baby?"

Gemma swallowed hard. She wasn't looking forward to this part.

"We have to help her push."

All three of her assistants gaped at her.

"Push?" Lysander frowned.

"The baby?" Atalanta tilted her head and narrowed her eyes.

"How?" squeaked Mr. Bing.

Gemma didn't have time to explain. "We must, or I shall be forced to reach in and pull it out," she stated flatly.

That thought spurred them to action. Atalanta began to shift from her position at the head of the bed. Gemma waved her back. "You are still on hydration duty. Lysander, make sure Jennie can't slide down the bed, no matter how she thrashes. Mr. Bing, you and I are going to place her hands just so, and when her contractions start, we shall—"

But Mr. Bing had put his hands behind his back and stood shaking his head.

"What is the difficulty?" There wasn't time for this!

"Lay hands on another man's wife? While she's birthin'?" His head shook faster. "I can't, Missus, I just can't!"

"Very well." Blast it, she'd hoped to spare Jennie's husband but needs must. "Fetch Shepherd Gosling. You," she pointed a finger at Mr. Bing, "go mind the children!"

Childless, confirmed bachelor, Mr. Bing nodded eagerly. "Mind the sprogs. On my way, Missus."

"I'll fetch Poll," Lysander offered. "And Button and Cabot."

Gemma nodded. She didn't care whose hands helped, and although she knew—hoped!—Jennie would later take a snit about being tended by strangers, right now Jennie was in no condition to complain.

Gosling came in and, once allowed through the door, refused to budge again. Gemma compromised by putting him at the head of the bed to keep feeding Jennie sips of water. She sent Atalanta to get more water on the boil.

In the end, the small room was too tight for all the volunteers. Mr. Cabot took over the boiling on the stove when Atalanta curled up on the floor in exhaustion. Poll carried her off to the sofa in the study and Mr. Button begin washing the cleansing cloths in the kitchen and scalding them before running them back to Gemma. Poll went to the well for pail after pail of water.

Lysander never left Gemma's side, not for a moment, not for breath of air. Every single second she felt him near her, following her commands without question or debate. He learned so quickly that eventually she only needed to nod at him, and he would place his hands on either side of Jennie's swollen belly and push the baby carefully but forcefully toward safety. Gemma began to believe it might actually work.

Then Jennie lost consciousness.

Shepard Gosling cried out an alarm. "Jen? Jen!"

Gemma could've wept. It wasn't a good sign, not at all, but there was no time to spare upon it. Without even Jennie's weakened semi conscious pushing, it was up to Gemma to do it all, with Lysander's help.

Up to me? I haven't the foggiest notion of what to do! I only read the bloody book! Childbirth and the Practices of Midwifery *by bloody Dr. Algernon bloody Lumley!*

Still, she'd read it repeatedly. Knowing she would be helping Jennie, Gemma had memorized the book. She could pull the pages up in her memory and read from them when she closed her eyes.

Jennie's body would still continue to work, the contractions would happen with or without Jennie awake. But Jennie was slipping away, she could feel it.

God, there was no time! It'd had already been hours. For the first time Gemma began to doubt she could save either one of them, let alone both!

Dying, they're dying. I'm doing everything the book said, and it isn't working! She'd attended births. She'd seen healthy women bring out child after child.

"Why can't I find the solution?" She pressed hard fingertips to her temples.

Lysander took her hands away from attempting to gouge some missed knowledge from the depths of her memory. He held them in his warm hands until she looked up to meet his dark gaze.

"Can we try harder?"

She shook her head. "I don't know!" Her wail of despair was only whispered. She couldn't bear for Shepherd Gosling to know how tragically she was failing his family. "I've done everything in the book!"

"Why slant the bed?"

She blinked. "To help Jennie bear down. It's easier to push something downhill than over level ground."

"From the book?"

"What?" She shook her head. "No, it was just a notion I had."

"Will higher help more?"

"No. Perhaps. Yes, I think so, a little."

"You'll help her. Trust yourself."

Gemma gulped. "Lysander, I think ... I think they're both going to—"

He shook his head quickly, stopping her next words. "Only dead is dead. Until then, we try."

We. The word bolstered her a drastic fashion. *We.*

Gemma straightened. "When the contractions pass, we must hold the baby in place. We must not let up." She turned to Cabot, who despite being soaked all down the front with water, made Gemma feel abruptly frumpy. She scowled at the poor man. "Fetch four blocks to prop the bed."

"Gemma." Lysander had his hand resting lightly on the upper curve of Jennie's belly. "They're starting again."

Gemma took a breath. "Right. Remember, this time, don't let up between."

THE EFFORT REQUIRED was much more this time, but Lysander made no complaint.

This was a new sort of battlefield, a quieter, grimmer and yet more hopeful battle field. But it was a war nonetheless, and Gemma and Jennie's enemy was the most dreaded of all.

Lysander believed in Gemma the way he'd scarcely ever believed in a commander before. Gemma took the front line, she raised the first sword, she fired the first shot.

She was one of the most valiant warriors Lysander had

ever seen, and as long as Gemma wanted that hill taken, Lysander would strive to take it.

And Jennie—poor Jennie, both victim and last line of defense—Jennie's very body would fight alongside them and they would prevail.

They must prevail. Lysander felt a depth of fear for Gemma that he never felt for himself, not in all the hours of mud and blood and cannon fire.

If Gemma could not save Jennie and her child, Lysander feared that she would lose herself forever in darkness and self-hatred.

The way that he had done.

Without losing any focus on his task of pressing the baby downward-ever-downward, Lysander managed to glance at Gemma's face so near his own.

Her hands were pressed alongside his. She was perspiring and gray with exhaustion. Her hair hung limp with sweat. She had a permanent imprint of tears running periodically down her cheeks, as if her worry and dread were seeping out in a slow leak. Her nose dripped, and he watched her turn her head and dab it hurriedly on the dainty cap sleeve of one of the most expensive gowns in the realm.

"Push!" she shouted at him, her breath hot and none too fragrant on his cheek.

And he loved her.

Chapter 26

J ENNIE GOSLING'S CHILD LIVED.
When Gemma checked to see how near they were to delivery and saw the smooth bulge of the baby's head crowning, her shriek of relief woke Attie from her sprawl of sleep in the next room. Pol, Mr. Cabot and Mr. Button ran in from their duties in the kitchen.

Attie popped up at the end of the bed "Hmm."

Poll made a halfhearted effort to remove Attie from things she might not be ready for.

She brushed him off with a sneer. "You're too late. I saw Aurora born."

Lysander absorbed a weary glance of outrage from his brother and shrugged. "Not my call."

Gemma ignored them all. She plunged her hands into the pail of scalding water and scrubbed quickly with harsh soap.

Attie narrowed her eyes. "What does cleanliness matter? She's already made a mess."

"Cleanliness always matters," Gemma snapped her. "Dr. Oakes taught me that if cleanliness is next to godliness, then soap is at least as important as prayer."

Attie knelt at the steaming pail. "I don't feel like praying."

"Then you'd best wash," Gemma said bluntly as she knelt at the foot of the bed.

Taking the hint, Cabot and Button washed as well. Lysander stayed where he was, keeping up the pressure on

Jennie's belly until her next contraction. Shepherd Gosling bathed his wife's face and kept up a steady stream of encouraging whispers.

It wasn't long. The contractions were coming so close together now, but also seemed to be getting weaker.

Gemma reached for the baby, but the contraction wasn't making much progress. "Push!" She shouted at Lysander.

The fear in her voice drove him to new strength. Then Poll appeared on one side of him and Cabot on the other.

"Its head is out," Attie reported calmly. "It's not as pointy as Aurora's."

Gemma was gently turning and coaxing the baby out. The next contraction began and her gaze flew to meet Lysander's.

"Now," she whispered.

It had to be now, she meant. Now or it would no longer matter.

They threw their strength behind the contraction and Gemma gasped as the long-awaited tiniest Gosling slid into her hands.

Everyone held their breath. There was no sound but the ragged gasps of Shepherd Gosling behind them.

Then the newborn's thin, cat-like wail filled the room. The weight of the last several hours of exhaustion and tension fell from them all like a stone. Gemma looked at Lysander with such naked joy her face that he could not breathe for the tightness in his throat.

Then Gemma unwrapped a small knife from a protective square of linen and used it to cut the cord.

Behind them, however, Shepherd Gosling wheezed. "Oh Jen. Oh, my flower, my pretty Jen." He looked up at them when they turned to him. "I lost my Jen."

At once Gemma handed the naked squalling baby over to Attie. Poll made a stuffed sound of shock, but Attie hefted the little thing to one arm and calmly wrapped it in some swaddling left to warm by the fireplace. She began to walk the room, soothing the baby with a competent touch.

Poll blinked at his little sister. Then he looked at Lysander. "What else have I missed?"

Lysander let out a deep sigh. "Plenty."

Then he turned to confront what no one wanted to face.

At the head of the bed, Gemma had dropped to her knees by Jennie and felt her friend's wrist for a pulse. Then Jennie's neck, as Gemma's hand began shaking. Then Gemma put her ear to Jennie's heart, then held her fingertips to Jennie's parted lips, feeling for her breath.

Lysander had seen death stalk men on the battlefield. He knew that death had now found Jennie Gosling.

Gemma had lost the battle to save the life of her dearest friend. The stillness of one less beating heart in the room muffled even the high-pitched cry from the baby.

Gosling sat where he'd been for hours, his tall bulk curled around his wife's head and shoulders. His shirt was soaked wet with the sweat of them both, trying to bring their child safely into the world. He laid a big calloused hand over his wife's face and gently closed her eyes. Then he looked at Gemma. "Best bring in the children."

Gemma roused from her grief enough to gasp and protest. "The children?"

Gosling nodded. "Go on, clear up the mess if you want, but the bairns deserve a chance to say goodbye."

Cabot left Button's side and swiftly set about ridding the room of the evidence of childbirth. Lysander had a thought and ran to the study to fetch the quilt Gemma had brought down, on what seemed a night a thousand years past.

In the time it took for Poll to run for Bing and the children in the kitchen, the room had been turned from a bloodied battleground-lost to a peaceful bedchamber once more.

"Now then, my own," Mr. Gosling rumbled to his children. "Come kiss your sweet mother goodbye." They did so solemnly with a blankness in their eyes that made Lysander look away. "Now go say hello to your wee—" Gosling stopped and looked at Gemma. She flinched from the depth of pain held there, deeper than any well on earth.

"It's a boy," Attie answered instead. She sat down cross-legged on the rug before the fire and held out the infant like a present to the three eldest Gosling children. The tallest, the same straw-haired girl Lysander had seen clutching her prize piglet, took the baby from Attie with an equal level of practice.

"Another brother," the girl said.

Attie shrugged in commiseration. "I comprehend completely."

Lysander felt an upwelling of love and pride for his outrageous little sister. She was as brave as any soldier.

With a single choked rasp of a sob, Shepherd Gosling kissed his wife on the lips. "My flower," he whispered hoarsely. "My always."

He dropped his forehead to hers and ran work-hardened fingers delicately through her shimmering hair lying upon the pillow.

Lysander's chest hurt at the big man's tenderness.

Then Gosling straightened and laid a last touch to Jennie's pale fingertips before he joined his children by the fire. He took his youngest son into his arms. The baby stopped crying at once.

"So much promise in this wee soul," he said to his children, his voice raspy with grief. "Your mother's last gift to us."

Silence fell upon the room for a moment. The campaign had ended. Lives flickered and shone like night fires on the battlefield.

Another brother. Another spark flared.

Yet another went out.

The dale would remember Jennie Gosling for her kindness, her mother wit, and her fine sturdy children.

The dale would carry on.

It was Gemma whom Lysander worried about now.

GEMMA COULD NOT weep for Jennie. What sort of monster was she to have no tears for the kindest woman she'd ever known?

Without a care for her still-healing wrist, she lifted a heavy crockery jar to her stillroom work table and began to scoop large quantities of dried tansy flowers into a basket. When she filled it, she replaced the tight-fitted lid and put the jar back on the lowest shelf.

Every movement felt slow and careful, yet her thoughts were not at all engaged in her task. She felt as if she floated several feet above herself, watching but not caring.

After picking up the basket of dried blooms, she went up the stairs to the linen press in the hall. After staring at the neatly folded contents of the shelves for a single eternal moment, Gemma reached for a set of finely woven bed linens. The embroidered lengths were from her own trousseau, eagerly worked by her own hands before her wedding to Edmund. They were the best she had.

It was the least she could do.

Down the stairs again, step by methodical step. She heard the baby wail from the kitchen, where Mr. Bing and Shepherd Gosling were hoping to get the little one to take a bit of sheep's milk from the corner of a soaked cloth. The sound halted suddenly, signifying success.

Gemma felt nothing. Her eyes were dry. Her heart felt as cold and still as a stone. *I am unnatural.*

In the room where Jennie lay still and cold, Mr. Cabot and Mr. Button were just finishing bathing her body. When Gemma entered, Mr. Button was combing out Jennie's lovely long hair. It drifted over the pillow like a shimmering fall of sunlight, pooling on the sheet in a lengthy coil.

Gemma stared at Jennie's beautiful hair. She hadn't known Jennie as a young girl, only as a practical farm wife and mother who always pinned her hair properly away. The notion of young girlish Jennie, with her eye on a burly Gosling boy and her entire future before her, facing it with a fearless smile—

An iron spike of agony broke the chill stone of Gemma's shocked heart in half. Inside, it contained such a crushing outpouring of pain and guilt and self-loathing that Gemma felt her knees weakening. At once Lysander was at her side, his supportive arm about her waist. Where had he come from?

Mr. Cabot knelt before them, gathering up the spilled tansy blooms and the wedding linens from the floorboards where Gemma had dropped them. She had no memory of doing so.

"No." She reached for them. "I have to wrap her in the winding sheet. And the flowers must be in the folds. She favored them. I had saved them for dyeing—" The unintentional pun made her breath stop. She gasped, a harsh, desperate grab for air.

"My dear, we shall take ever such great care." Mr. Button stepped forward to take Gemma's cold hand in his warm ones.

Lysander was as solid as one of the stone cairns beside her.

Gemma managed a breath. "You must sew it closed. The children. It mustn't come unwound."

Mister Cabot held the winding sheet and the basket of tansy out of Gemma's reach. "We can sew," he reminded her calmly, although there was a night-sky of sympathy in his silvery eyes. "I know just what to do."

Gemma believed him. This was not the first time the

mysterious Mr. Cabot had prepared a body for burial.

At last, she allowed Lysander to walk her from the room. After one touch of her icy hands, he took a heavy shawl from where it hung draped over the worn chair beside her clothes press.

Thus wrapped against the shivers that had begun to travel through her in waves, she moved shakily with help to the seldom used front door.

She wished she could tell Lysander how grateful she was not to pass through the kitchen where she would be forced to meet the gaze of Jennie's grieving husband. And oh! Those poor children! She flinched from the crushing weight of it all.

The unbearable burden of her guilt.

I did it. I killed Jennie.

THEY SAT ON the front steps of the manor in the last warmth of the setting sun. From dawn until nearly dusk, they had fought for Jennie and her child.

Their last sunset had been such a joyous one. How could so much change so quickly?

Most of Lysander's newfound speech deserted him. A fiercely burning tightness clamped around his throat. The words he'd just recently begun to tame to his hand now took wing, leaving nothing behind upon his tongue.

Sitting beside him, Gemma mourned. She was visibly agonized, every muscle in her body as tight as a harp string. She trembled with it as she stared dry eyed and unseeing at the beautiful day.

"It should be raining," she whispered hoarsely. "Why is the sun shining?"

Lysander knew she wasn't speaking to him. She was lost in the darkest recesses of her mind, pawing for reasons, for explanations, for sense in a nonsensical world.

"You did what you learned from the book." It was a weak comfort and he knew it, yet the notion of speaking actual truth made his breath wheeze in his locked throat.

"Damn the book. Damn it to hell." She did not shout but the repressed rage and self-hatred in her beautiful voice sounded deeply wrong to him.

Straightforward anger would be better. To kick over the rain barrel, take an axe to a tree stump, stand between the stone cairns on the fell and scream at the cruelty of the fates, yes. But that's not where Gemma's rage would come to rest. He could see it happening at that very moment.

"I missed the signs," she whispered. "I looked right past them. All I saw were the words in the book. I missed what was written right on her face."

The vibration became a shiver. She sat so still, her eyes so wide and empty of anything but fury at herself.

"I'm not a doctor. I'm no one. Jennie trusted me, me with my little herb concoctions and my delusional arrogance." She turned to gaze at Lysander for the first time, but he was not sure if she saw him.

"I killed her."

"No. No, Gemma. You didn't." Damn his tangling tongue! He had to speak, he had to reach her through her pain.

"I'm no better than a fraud." She curled against the pain. "Worse, I'm a murderer. I killed her as surely as if I'd poisoned her!"

"No!"

She sneered in his direction, but her hate-filled gaze had turned in upon herself. "No? Is it murder to ignorantly wave a musket about until it goes off? Is it murder to throw boulders blindly into a crowd until someone is struck down? For it certainly was no accident when I used my astute *medical knowledge*," she uttered the words with vile derision, "to allow a woman with her symptoms to dance all night in a hot, crowded room!"

Lysander grabbed her by the shoulders. "Stop. You're not a murderer. You didn't kill your friend!"

She writhed wildly in his grasp and he released her. He had to stop her before those black thoughts and self-flagellating words began to take permanent root in her soul.

"It ... it isn't murder when you try to save someone and they die anyway. That's not ... not the same thing at all!"

She pulled away from him, pressing her back to the post of the doorframe.

"You don't understand!" She cried. "I did kill her! I chose the baby!"

Lysander realized what they'd been sidestepping all along. "You saved the baby. How could that possibly harm Jennie?"

Gemma wrapped her arms about her belly and began to rock to and fro, the pain within her making it impossible for the stillness to continue. "I had a choice. To save Jennie, I needed to get the baby out."

Lysander still didn't quite grasp her meaning. "Yes, you had to deliver the baby. That's what you did. Jennie's body just gave out too soon."

"I chose to deliver the baby *alive*."

Shock rippled through Lysander. He stared at her. "That was an option, to kill the baby?"

She rocked, pale and trembling at the dreadfulness of her own words. "That's what the book said. That it might be for the best, to save the mother, especially if she had other children. I believed I could save them both! Me, an under-qualified nurse with delusions of doctoring! I decided that I could do what real doctors quail before. I'm so *brilliant*. I'm so *special*. After all, I'm the bloody damned *Lady of the Dale*!" She began to strike her fists on her knees, taking her rage out upon herself instead of releasing it into the world.

"I killed Jennie with my arrogance! I did it. I murdered her with my own damned pride!"

Lysander grabbed her hands in his and held them still. This time he did not release her when she struggled in his grasp.

"You did not kill her," he said slowly and firmly, forcing the words to obey and fall from his lips, albeit somewhat haltingly. "Jennie simply died. It's terrible and sad and part of living. But you didn't murder anyone."

"How can you be so sure of that? How can you possibly understand? You've never held someone's life in your hands and had to choose!"

His throat squeezed shut, the words threatened to flutter away again, leaves before the coming storm. And oh, what a storm! He fought the choking silence. He willed the words forth. He forced his stupid, reluctant tongue to speak. For her. Anything to help Gemma.

"I know. Because I ... killed my closest friend." *The words. Find the words, make them come.* "I didn't choose to let him die." The panic nearly overwhelmed him. His throat began to close. He spat the truth out quickly, before his mind could coerce him to silence again. "I murdered him with my own hands."

For the first time Gemma looked at him as if she knew him. But the confusion and tinge of awakening distaste in her eyes was almost worse than her flat, inward stare.

Almost. "It happened during the war."

She pulled her knees to her chest and wrapped her arms around them. "You aren't talking about accidental death on the battlefield, are you? When someone is shot by their own side?"

He could see that she somehow knew it wasn't. He shook his head.

Gemma shivered. "You were confounded? Your mind was overwhelmed?"

He reached a hand out but stopped when she twitched away from it. "Gemma, you cannot absolve me. Please, just listen. Can you listen?"

At her wary nod, he began. At first his words threatened to choke off. His throat tightened. The words took desperate frantic flight—and he knew then that his stumbling tongue and incessant urge to flee was because something inside him had tried to protect him from the truth he must now tell.

Gemma needed to hear him. She needed to understand that her decision to save the littlest Gosling had nothing to do with murder. She needed his story in order to forgive herself for her own actions—even if it meant she could never forgive him for his.

"No one knows my secret. Not the Army. Not my family. No one."

Chapter 27

ONCE UPON A WARTIME, AS THE BRITISH FOUGHT THE FRENCH ON THE BLOODY BATTLEFIELDS OF SPAIN....

O N THE THIRD night of the fourth week of the siege of Burgos Castle, where Napoleon's troops had taken over a strategically valuable point in Wellington's advance, Lysander Worthington dug a shovel into the heavy soil.

As a lieutenant in the Royal Corps of Engineers, Lysander wasn't strictly required to dig the tunnel with his own hands. There was a crew of sappers and miners assigned to the task.

But casualties had been tragically high on the British side. Thousands dead, compared to an estimated few hundred of the French safely ensconced in the castle they'd invaded.

Lysander took his turn, as did his close friend and boyhood partner-in-crime Theo Bankston. Lysander swiped at his sweating muddy face, then grimaced as he heard Theo's hearty laugh.

"You should see yourself, Worthington! You look like you just crawled out of the center of the earth. What would Miss Maisie Sinclair say if she could see you now?"

Lysander laughed and tossed the shovel horizontally to Theo. "She'd say 'Poor Zander, let me bathe you off with my own tiny hands—'" He ducked the shovelful of muck that flew at his head and snickered.

Theo and Zander had been vying for the affections of stunningly beautiful, attractively wealthy and woefully silly Maisie Sinclair for years, each trying to outdo each other with ridiculous expressions of their suit. Lysander had once climbed a trellis and sung a song of heartbreak outside Maisie's window. Which was then revealed to be Mr. Sinclair's bedchamber window instead, thanks to Theo's misdirection.

Theo had laughed himself sick at that, but Lysander had gotten his revenge when Theo had spent every shilling he had to bombard Maisie with her favorite flower—which she was highly allergic to. Lysander, who was the one who'd pried Maisie's preferences from a maidservant, still maintained that it was the maid who'd lied, not him.

It was a good thing that the war had come along to distract their energies or they'd have either killed each other—or worse, one of them would have actually married sweet, vapid Maisie. That was one thing that neither of them would have wanted, not in earnest. It had all been a game. Maisie, who had dozens of suitors on any given afternoon, had likely never noticed they'd gone away.

The Army suited them better. They were fit and restless and too intelligent for their own good. The Army had harnessed that energy and capability, pushing them into the Royal Corps of Engineers and shoving a bit more training down their throats before flinging them out on the battlefield.

For the most part they'd had as good a time as one could in a war. They'd managed to explode a healthy portion of Napoleon's artillery and supplies—done with more naughty glee than with serious patriotic fervor, but the munitions didn't know the difference. Good fun, all in all.

Until this nightmare of a siege. Lord Wellington wanted Burgos Castle taken intact, for it was strategically placed in the supply line for the troops. That meant Lysander and Theo couldn't simply plant charges and run laughing into the night.

Instead, they'd been ordered to tunnel beneath the walls. The first two tunnels had collapsed, losing even more men. Lysander and Theo had tried to explain to their superior that the soil was all wrong. Burgos, built on the convergence of two rivers, had fine waterborne soils, loose and gravelly. However, their immediate commander, Lieutenant Colonel Whitson (a man who had purchased his commission and had likely never touched any tool more common than a fine riding crop) informed them if they knew so much they should take themselves off to the tunnel and supervise the ignorant miners, who were likely doing something wrong, the simpletons.

Down into the tunnel they went. Their commander clearly thought them to be indolent dandies, and that a little dirt would serve them right for arguing his orders. Frustrated but without recourse, Theo and Zander had grabbed shovels and descended.

Theo's had broken on the damp soil and now they shared Lysander's, working side by side with miners, lads sent to the Corps of Engineers for their experience in the mines of Northern England, in Staffordshire and Yorkshire and the like. These stolid fellows were better company than old Witless anyway.

Theo was panting. He tossed the shovel back Zander's way. "I'd swear this soil is getting heavier by the moment!"

Heavier? Zander pressed a palm to the earthen wall of the tunnel. His hand came away wet. He looked at Theo with a frown. "I think it's raining again."

Normally, the officers of the Royal Corps of Engineers would note dangerous weather and pull the men from the tunnel. However, this time two of the three remaining officers were in the tunnel.

Theo swore. "Bastard! What, is it time for his bloody nap?"

Zander wasted no time damning old Witless. He turned and called down the line. "Out! Fast as you can, lads! Run!"

They ran, slipping in the muddy water swiftly accumulating in a widening stream down the tunnel. They weren't fast enough. With a sickening, sliding rumble, the tunnel began to collapse.

WHEN THE TUNNEL began to slump ahead of them, dousing the lanterns strung along the length, Zander stopped where he was. He grabbed Theo's arm to hold his headlong rush. "Wait! We're cut off!" He could only hope the other men had made it out.

"Bloody hell!" Theo shouted furiously at the fallen ceiling ahead.

Zander realized that he still gripped their shared shovel in his hand. He looked up at the dripping tunnel ceiling over his head. It could come down at any moment. Yet what if he could choose when and how it came down?

It might not work. There was a lot he didn't know. How deep were they? How far from the entrance? The entry shaft was the shallowest point. It lay safely behind the British line, but Zander had no idea how close that was.

The icy rivulet on the floor rose to his ankles, chilling him through his boots.

Let's see what happens.

He thrust the shovel straight up, driving it into the dripping earth ceiling just a few inches above his head. He pried out a shovelful of soil and rammed the shovel into the ceiling again. Theo didn't question or debate. He had to know what a ridiculously slim chance they had of survival, but Theo trusted Zander when it came to impossible notions. Worthington always landed on their feet, he'd say.

Theo simply reached up and used his bare hands to claw at the cavity Zander created with the shovel. They dug wildly, scraping the soil down and standing upon the growing pile as they burrowed upward.

Zander ignored the shape of the tunnel, which had once

been admirably cylindrical but now had squashed egg-shaped dimensions.

The gut-wrenching rumble came again from ahead of them. They didn't have long now. Zander pulled off his cravat and knotted one end about his wrist and the other to Theo's. The length of fine linen would keep them no more than a yard apart. "Don't let go!" he shouted as the last lantern shimmied from its peg and disappeared into the oncoming mud. He pulled Theo to stand beneath the cavity they created.

"Remember which way is up!".

And the ceiling fell down upon them even as Zander tried to grab a last lungful of air.

Zander reached and clawed. He kicked upward, swimming laboriously through the slick, choking mud. He could feel the pull on the lashing about his wrist and he knew Theo fought alongside him. The mud was so damned heavy. It tried to pin down his limbs. It tried to push down his chest, to force him to exhale and then drown. It was a monster, that mud, a voracious man-eating monster. Zander and Theo didn't even make a hearty snack.

Zander's chest burned for air. His throat locked tight against the mud that somehow filled his mouth no matter how he clamped his lips tight. He swam up.

And he felt his fingers break through into cold standing water and chill air. The water ran down his arm, easing his way, loosening the suctioning clutch of the monster. It was too late. He wasn't going to make it. He was already starting to black out for lack of air. He began to slip under again. Then he felt a tug on his other arm. *Theo*, he remembered, his thoughts slow and dull.

I have to help Theo.

He gathered his last strength and punched upward again, breaking through the surface. It would've been nice if some comrade had clasped that free arm and dragged them out, but there seem to be a distinct lack of comrades at the moment.

Zander and Theo were on their own. Zander pretended to talk to Theo in his mind.

Remember the time...

He clawed and kicked.

We took Maisie for a stroll...

Claw. Kick.

And the wind took her shawl.

Reach!

We ran after it, right into the deepest puddle...

And then Zander realized that nothing pressed over his face! He spat and gagged, then took a lungful of sweet, cool rainy air.

Theo.

Zander dragged himself out onto firmer soil with one hand, his other hung deep behind him, burdened by the weight of Theo. Once he could brace his knees on solid ground, he pulled and pulled. *Don't let it tear.* And to Theo, *don't let go!*

Then he had him. Theo's head emerged from the slick mud like a mushroom growing in the privy muck. Zander swiped his free hand over Theo's face, scraping away the thickest mud and was rewarded when Theo spat out a wad of sludge and gasped hoarsely for air.

There was some noise and fury going on about them, but it was all Zander could manage to pull Theo free of the hungry mud demon's maw.

The rising relief came out in a choking laugh. He always became unsteady when he got away with something, or beat the odds, or in this case, cheated death.

A huge crack of sound broke the sky. Theo, now crawling up to his hands and knees, looked around them in dismay. "Cannonade!"

Zander snapped out of his relieved stupor and saw that

it was true. They were under bombardment. The nine heavy cannons lined up along the base of the castle palisades were firing as often and as quickly as they were able. The enemy meant to pummel the British army away from their walls.

He scrambled awkwardly to his feet and reached to drag Theo up as well. He pointed to the distant British flag still visible in the growing dusk. "Run!"

They ran for their lives, mud-filled boots sloshing, mud-caked clothing flapping, their mud-slimed hair standing on end. Their situation was deadly serious, for cannonballs fired upward, rising nearly to the castle heights, arced down to hit the ground with an earth-shaking impact and then bounced on at high velocity, rico-cheting off in unpredictable directions. Despite the danger, they laughed like bedlamites as they slipped and sloshed and flapped across the battleground, headed for their own line which stood firm just out of the range of the cannon fire.

They were close, not more than fifty yards away. Theo, always just a hairsbreadth faster, looked back over his shoulder at Zander with a punch-drunk grin.

Zander laughed back at him. Then, inexplicably Theo plunged toward Zander and shoved hard, knocking him right off his feet. Zander fell backward, hands reaching out wide to break his fall. Time seemed to slow as he flew. He saw Theo trying to fling himself aside. He saw the black iron sphere of the cannonball strike Theo in the side and break him like a stick, snapping him double in a way that was never meant to be. Then time sped up again and Theo was flung away into the smoke and rain and disappeared from view.

The battle raged on. Darkness, aided by the heavy cloud cover, fell early on the castle grounds. Still the bombard-ment continued.

Zander crawled through the mud until he found someone. It wasn't Theo. Pale, mud-streaked fingers reached for him, blood flowing in an ever widening pool beneath the fallen form. Zander hesitated, but the outstretched hand fell and the blood stopped spurting.

Poor bastard, Zander thought as he continued his search. It wouldn't be long before he would conclude that the dead man was one of the lucky ones.

Twice cannon fire struck near Zander as he crawled and searched. Both times he fell facedown to the ground with his hands protecting his head, rather like a butterfly trying to fend off hailstones with its wings.

The first impact left him unscathed. The second shattered a wooden munitions cart abandoned near him and the impact showered him with piercing daggers of wood.

Zander ignored his various punctures and crawled onward. He turned around and backtracked twice before he found him. Theo lay in an earthen crater left by a cannonball fired from a great height.

"Oh God. Theo!" When he saw his friend, Zander had to drop his forehead to the ground for a moment, flinching from the sight of his mangled body. Theo was dead.

"Zander? Zander?"

Zander scrambled up on all fours again. "Theo?"

How could Theo be alive when he lay shattered and distorted on the ground? His arms and legs splayed out limply and his body twisted wildly at the pelvis. Zander had never seen anything so broken.

ZANDER SCRAMBLED DOWN into the shallow cavity to his friend. The rain came down hard enough to pound his skin but still the cannons fired.

"Theo?" Zander reached to touch his friend, then stopped. There seem to be nowhere on Theo's body that wasn't scraped, stabbed, or shattered.

At least he could shield Theo from the pounding rain. Zander crouched over him, angling his body to take the worst of the rain on his back and shoulders.

Theo's eyes were shut, his muddy face gray and his lips blue with shock. Zander dug through his pockets. In a deep inner pocket of his coat he found folded sheaf of paper that was still clean within the folds. The tunnel specifications. He drawn them himself two days ago. Zander turned one of the clean inner pages into a towel to wipe Theo's face free of mud and blood.

Theo's eyes opened. "Zander?" Then his eyes widened horribly as his mouth stretched in a rictus of agony. He drew in a harsh gasping breath. Zander could hear broken ribs creaking as he did.

And then the screams began.

There was nothing Zander could do. He had nothing to give his friend, not even the last dregs of his whiskey flask, which now lay buried under tons of Spanish mud.

Theo screamed until he lost consciousness again. Zander had a brief thought that the sound might reveal their presence to the enemy but with the thunder and continuing cannon fire there seemed little point in worrying for his own skin.

It was not fear for himself that made him weep when Theo lost consciousness. It was relief that now his friend had respite from the pain. Zander shielded his friend and swore that he would stay by Theo's side until he died.

But Theo didn't die. He woke up, and the screams began anew. He pawed at Zander with one misshapen hand. The other was a useless dead limb, shattered in so many places that it curled and shimmied in a dreadful boneless manner as Theo's body spasmed in pain.

Zander held Theo in his arms then, for he could hardly hurt him any worse. He sang and spoke nonsense, reciting Shakespeare's bloody *Twelfth Night* when he ran out of words of his own. It was stupid to think Theo could hear him through such hellish agony, but Zander refused to crawl away in the dark and the rain, to flee from the ghastly scene. Theo would never leave him. Zander could not abandon Theo while he yet lived.

Six or seven or a hundred hours later, the cannonade had stopped and the storm had moved on, although a steady rain still fell. Zander left Theo's unconscious side for a moment to look over the crumbling edge of their inadvertent foxhole. He could tell which cook fires were French and which were British by the lantern light up on the ramparts of *Castel Burgos*, as the Spanish called it.

Zander turned away from the enemy and gazed wistfully at the British line. He pondered the wisdom of moving Theo, if he even could. He himself been leaking a bit here and there from his gashes. The struggle against the heavy mud had left him drained.

The ground was wet and slick. Could he put Theo on their combined uniform coats and drag him across it? He realized he could only use his own coat. He was horribly certain that Theo's snug uniform was the only thing holding his torso together in one piece.

The British line was far and the medical tents farther yet. Rumor abounded that after nearly four weeks of siege and high casualties, there was no more morphine, no laudanum, not even a drop of spirits to get a man too blind drunk to feel the amputation of his legs. There was no real succor there for the severely wounded. There were only the blood-spattered blankets on which the men screamed all night and all day until they died.

The entire company had heard the agony coming from those tents, where it was known that the doctors were playing only the safest odds. By necessity, only the men sure to recover were being treated at all. The others were laid out side by side across the tent floor and given water if they could swallow it.

Those doctors would have nothing to give Theo after he went through the torture just to journey across fifty yards. Zander put his face into his cold, water-wrinkled hands and wept for Theo, who wasn't dead.

He heard Theo gasp himself into wakefulness and quickly rejoined his friend, feeling his way in the darkness. He wiped his wet face on his sleeve to conceal his weeping, then realized the foolishness of hiding tears in the rain.

"I'm here, Theo, I'm here." Zander reached to hold his friend as gently as he could to warm him and to provide comfort, even if Theo was too far gone to know it.

This time Theo met Zander's return with words. "Die!" he gasped.

Zander's gut turned to ice. "Yes." He would not lie to Theo. "You are going to die."

Theo's broken hand spasmed toward Zander's. "Die. Now!" Then the screams began to build up beyond Theo's ability to control them, seeping from his broken jaw in a rasping mewling sound that Zander felt all the way to his bones. Theo had no voice left. His screams were naught but long, rasping gasps. It seemed even more obscene that Theo should be robbed of his rightful expression of his agony.

"Now!" Theo insisted before losing his wits to the agony that ripped through him as he screamed himself breathless and then senseless once more.

Zander held him through it all. And now when Zander wept, he gave up tears for them both—for he had never had the will to refuse Theo anything. He pulled Theo's cravat free of his collar and twisted it into a thick cord. Then he waited. For the next quarter of an hour or so, Theo would lie quietly, unconscious from exhaustion before the torment began again.

For this brief time, Zander would hold his oldest and dearest friend in his arms and whisper silly tales about Miss Maisie Sinclair.

For these last short moments, Zander could continue to exist as a man who had not yet murdered his dearest friend.

Chapter 28

LYSANDER LOOKED UP from his hands, which were twisting his own cravat, wrapping and unwrapping around his fists. When had he taken it off?

As the words had come at last, they had begun to flow. His tongue had not faltered much after the beginning. He had relived every moment of that nightmarish day and night as he'd spoken. Never once had he looked at Gemma's face. He didn't want to know. He'd made his confession but he did not feel absolved, for all that his tongue had loosened at last.

He missed Theo, suddenly and fiercely, in a way his frozen emotions had never yet allowed him to. Death had come for Theo. All his lively wit and youthful strength had not been enough to spare him.

Lysander had no reason to expect better from his own life. He yet breathed. He had a family that truly wished to embrace him again. There was a woman whom Lysander loved with the entirety of his patchwork-mended heart, regardless of how she might feel about him.

These were things that Theo would never have. Lysander could not beg Theo's forgiveness and there was no one else with the right to pardon him.

What he wished from Gemma was her own whole heart. Not to give to him, but to have for herself.

No matter how he feared what he might now spy upon her beautiful face, that confession had not been *to* her, it had been *for* her. He must finish this whilst she still listened. "Your choice was to save life, don't you see? My choice was to take it. Those were not the same acts at all."

GEMMA FELT AS if her body was frozen. Even her thoughts felt slushy and cold, spiked with icy crystals of shock.

In a strange way, Mr. Worthington's confession had accomplished its mission. She now understood the difference between a poor medical decision and murder.

She had been arrogant and irresponsible, so sure that her book-fed knowledge made her a better midwife. She'd forgotten that her practical experience was based on battlefield surgery, gunshot wounds and broken bones.

She'd made one decision and Jennie had died. If she'd made another decision, Jennie may have lived but she might never have recovered from the loss of her child. Gemma now understood that for all her flaws of ignorance and arrogance, she was not a killer.

But Mr. Worthington was.

Dr. Edmund Oakes had been militant that a physician should never do harm, never take life, no matter how dire the circumstances. Edmund would abhor a man such as Mr. Worthington.

"Life is sacred to me," she said hoarsely. Her voice sounded rough and strained coming from a throat so frozen with sorrow. "I'm a healer. It is all I believe in."

You believed in it so much that you ignored the danger signs—Jennie's red face, her puffy ankles, her terrible thirst—so that you could dance with this man and play lovers' games on the study carpet.

That was nothing less than undeniable truth. Raw and heartbroken, Gemma absorbed that fact, taking the blow as one well deserved. She hadn't seen Jennie's ailment in time, for she had been too distracted by the hint of spring in her life after so many years of winter.

Yes. Of that I am guilty as well.

"You took the life of your closest friend," she whispered. The hideous irony was not lost on her. So had she. *Oh, Jennie! What I wouldn't do to go back and undo it all! Turn away the stranger, stay focused on my duty—then surely I would have recognized your illness in time!*

Mr. Worthington just kept twisting his cravat in his hands, twisting and tightening it. "Yes."

Then he seemed to comprehend his own horrible gesture and he flung the worn-out length of linen away. Gemma watched it unfurl and float to the grass, to lie there like a flag of surrender on a field of green.

I don't want to know this. I don't want to look at his hands and think of them taking a life, of killing a helpless man. The hands that touched me.

It was all too much. Too much truth. Too much death.

What had she done?

She'd been foolish. Believing that she could toss aside her responsibilities for springtime romp with a handsome stranger? A man she know nothing about?

That was part of the appeal, surely. Not knowing him, she could paint him with the brush of fantasy. She could pick and choose the facets that she wished to see and excuse or ignore the sides of him that didn't fit into her creation.

Then she'd flung herself headlong and foolish into his arms, fleeing her isolation and her burdens.

Deserting her duty and responsibility.

She had been better off living her life alone, assiduously focused on caring for her people. That seemingly dreary life had been calmer. Simpler. Safer. At this moment, she longed to have it back, to return to the way things had been.

It had been a tragic, lethal distraction to want something for herself. All the remorse in the world would not bring Jennie back, not let her raise her children, grow old with the man she loved, someday hold her grandchildren in her arms.

Oh, to have her life back the way it was before!

"You should go." The words came tumbling from her lips, spurred by her fervent wish that she'd never laid eyes upon him in the first place. "Leave with your family and friends. Go back to where you came from and leave me behind you."

LYSANDER DID NOT flinch from the blow. As surely as he knew he loved Gemma, he understood why she could not love him. His darkness was anathema to her light.

He wanted nothing more than to stand fast, to fight for her if he could, to win her heart against any opponent—but who was the enemy, if not he himself and all the troubles he had laid at her door?

There was only one more thing that she deserved to know.

"I love you, Gemma Oaks." He could hear the naked longing in his rusted voice, but he did not spare himself. "I love your strength. I love your healing heart. I comprehend your loneliness. I understand you."

She flinched and stared down at her fisted hands. "What am I supposed to say to that?"

"Nothing." He could not reach out to her, for he knew he had blood on his hands. Now she knew it as well. "I only want you to believe this. Gemma, you can be loved. You are meant to be loved." He stood up, stepping back to allow her some distance. "I want you to be loved, even if it means by someone else—someone more worthy than I."

Then he turned away and headed toward the stable. It was time to hitch up the carriages and take the Worthingtons home to London.

Home.

Lysander felt torn in half, he who had not been whole to begin with. Yet even in his torment over leaving her, he could feel the healing Gemma had begun in him. *I am battered, but I am not broken. Not anymore. She restored me.*

He only wished that he could have given her something a fraction so valuable.

GEMMA HANDED TINY Jasper Gosling up to his eldest sister where she sat beside Shepherd Gosling on the bench seat of the open farm cart.

"I shall come to check in on him tomorrow, to be sure the sheep's milk agrees with him."

Shepherd Gosling nodded at her agreeably enough, although his sorrow hung dark and oppressive about him. All the Goslings were subdued but Gemma had to believe the family would survive. The elder Mrs. Gosling, a spry lady of fifty-six, waited back at the farm with the child who'd been too small to attend the assembly. She would love her grandchildren well. In addition, the community would enclose them all and Gemma would do everything she could. She'd made promises to Jennie that she'd not been able to keep. She owed her friend this.

The farm cart rattled away. The Worthington contingent, who had hung back respectfully, even Miss Atalanta, now stepped forward.

Mr. Button took her hand. "As sorry as I am for the tragic loss of Mrs. Gosling, I am not sorry to have met you, my dear. You shall serve as a mighty inspiration to me. It was an honor to boil water for you." His sincerity made his quirky way of speaking into something charming and insightful. He planted a kiss on her cheek. "Do call on me if ever you are in London."

Mr. Cabot was next. "Mrs. Oakes, thank you for your hospitality. Your dale is very beautiful." His words seem to encompass more than simply the landscape.

Gemma nodded. "Thank you. I think so, too."

Next came Mr. Pollux Worthington. He eyed her carefully, opened his mouth to say something, then shook his
head as if refusing to say it. "Thank you. Thank you for
helping Lysander. You've done wonders for him."

Gemma had not told a soul what Lysander had confessed to her. As difficult as it was to reflect upon what he
had done, she would not betray his confidence. Instead, she
took Pollux's hand. "Tell him that you want to listen. Then
let him choose his words. Just listen." There, that was the
last thing she could do for that particular patient before
sending him home with his loved ones.

Pollux nodded, his brows, very much like Lysander's,
knitting slightly. "Where is Zander?"

"Lysander," said Miss Atalanta in a reminding tone of
voice. "He isn't Zander anymore, remember? And he's
waiting in the lane."

Atalanta stepped up to Gemma. Gemma noticed that
Pollux gave way before his little sister. Were there no adults
in that house? Who was in charge there?

Not my concern, Gemma reminded herself as she looked
expectantly at the fascinating but alarming Miss Atalanta
Worthington.

"Lysander is special," Atalanta said bluntly. "Even for a
Worthington. I don't just love him because he is my brother. I don't want him to stay here. I'm not even sure I like
you. But you should know that Lysander is special."

Gemma look at the girl. Of all the people in the world
who might dispense advice on matters of the heart, a fourteen-year-old girl was the last one Gemma should listen to.
Yet she found herself regarding the girl with great seriousness. "I shall take your opinion under consideration."

Satisfied with that, Atalanta scrambled into the second
carriage like a child. Pollux, who should've known better,

aided her with a shove instead of a gentlemanly hand.

Mr. Lysander Worthington was up on the fine thoroughbred Icarus, standing like a centaur statue out in the lane, waiting for the carriages to roll.

Gemma did not wave to him, nor did he do other than gaze back toward the house with his hat shading his eyes.

There was really nothing more to be said, was there?

IN THE SECOND luxurious carriage that rattled south down the river road, Button mused over Lysander Worthington's decision.

"Mrs. Oakes is such a sincere person, and with such perfect posture! I wish I could dress her again. And those eyes!" He sighed. "I am ever seduced by a gentle gaze." He chewed his lower lip for a moment. "How could he leave such a creature behind?"

Cabot picked nonexistent lint from a perfect cuff. "Lysander left because she asked him to." Then his sharp gaze rose to pin Button back to the velvet seatback cushion with the intensity of it. "Just as I did."

Button drew in a shocked breath. "I never asked you to leave!"

"You never ask for your tea either, but I always know precisely when to bring it to you." Cabot did not back down, nor glance casually away as he usually did when the conversation became a touch too personal. "I know you, Joshua Samuel Button, better than you know yourself."

Button lifted his chin. "No one calls me Joshua. I left him behind when I walked beaten and bloodied from my father's tailor shop." Only Cabot knew that tale, offered up a decade ago to comfort a furious and bewildered young man.

Cabot nodded. "And you created Lementeur, The Liar, master of fashionable artistry and subterfuge. You are a virtuoso, creating a new man, with attentiveness to every last detail. Except for one."

Button opened his mouth to protest but Cabot stayed him with an upraised palm.

"I have something to say and you will hear it, Joshua. That young man's heart could not be made over, for hearts never can be. So you buried it under charming generosity, expending yourself upon every broken spirit, every unfortunate figure, every searching heart. I count the romances you assisted by the hundreds. You are ever driven, my Joshua, my dearest beloved Button, my much admired Lementeur, to give the world the one thing of which you have deprived yourself. Love."

Button couldn't speak. His chest ached and his hands turned to ice.

Relentlessly, Cabot went on. "If Lysander Worthington can batter through his tragic silence to speak of his love, how can I keep hiding my own behind the wall formed of nothing but your illogical resistance?"

He gazed at Button, his cool urbane façade fallen away. In his clever clouded-sky eyes there blazed only his heart, unshielded and unafraid.

Button suddenly, desperately longed for such freedom from fear.

"I love you, Joshua." In the confines of the carriage, Cabot's words were inescapable. "Only you. Ever and always, you. I will not leave. I will not move on to someone else. For me, there is only and ever you."

Button gasped for breath, for words, for a line of reasoning in the whirlpool of fear and hope that choked him.

"But I—I am twice your age—"

Cabot smiled then, a sweet, sunny grin that Button had never seen before. "Not anymore. I am now thirty years to your forty-nine."

"Forty-eight," Button managed, a tiny flare of vanity

piercing his overwhelming turmoil.

"Moreover, I am informed on the highest authority that I was born older than you."

Distracted by the ringing accuracy of that mad logic, Button managed some actual words. "Whoever said that?"

"Everyone's favorite prodigy and speaker of truths, Miss Atalanta Worthington."

"Oh." Attie never lied. "It must be so, then." Button turned away for a moment, his gaze fixed blindly on the grassy slope passing outside.

Silence fell, as if they sat calm and quiet together, as if there was only the trotting of expensive hooves and creaking of expensive woods. As if there was not a tempest within him.

He had been alone for so long.

An eternity ago, fifteen-year-old Joshua had turned to the one person he trusted the most for advice, for answers. Why did he feel the way he did? Why did he think the way he did?

Why was he different?

His father, his teacher, a man so proud of Joshua's skills and finesse, forever boasting of his great future as a tailor, had not answered with words but with a raised fist.

It'd been a long life since then, a good life for the most part. He had achieved so much, for himself and for the people he most admired, and yes, even for his country.

Perhaps he truly did have nothing left to prove.

Resistance and protest floated away, the storm ebbed, leaving behind only clarity and acceptance.

"Cabot," Button said, without looking away from the serenity of the dale, "I think I like it when you call me Joshua."

Chapter 29

I N YEW MANOR, Gemma stood in the precise center of her stillroom until she was certain that the Worthington's fine borrowed carriages were well and gone.

Then she looked down at her aching hands to realize they had been tightly fisted the entire time. Why? She wasn't angry, or frustrated. After all, she'd been the one to ask him to go.

Perhaps to stop yourself from reaching out to stay him?

Gemma spread her whitened fingers wide before her in denial of that wayward thought. She had done the right thing, the responsible thing.

However, she felt stifled by the redolent air of the stillroom. She wanted the grassy breeze upon her face. Turning on one heel, she strode swiftly from the room, through the kitchen and out the door. She needed to breathe.

When she stepped outside, she closed her eyes and pulled in great lungfuls of air.

I just need a bit of quiet.

Yes, the great mob of Worthingtons and friends had quite overwhelmed her. The loss of Jennie, she could not yet bear to touch. She felt raw and restless and as if something was very, very wrong.

Yet all the commotion had passed. Now it was time to go back to her ordinary routines. That would be the most steadying thing. There were herbs to gather and transform into her little store of tinctures and extracts. The chamomile was blooming in the garden already. She was letting the flowers go to waste.

Instead, Gemma pressed her palms to her heated cheeks, her fingers covering her eyes. She felt ripped apart inside, torn by the past days, by the joy and the grief, like a band pulled too far from its original shape, now unable to return to it. She couldn't feel her own place in the world anymore.

She opened her eyes and could not stop her gaze from turning to the road south. The carriage would be well down the dale by now, along the river road.

"Only one road in and one road out."

At that gruff voice, Gemma tore her gaze away from the farthest curve and looked down. Her hands were doing it again. She spread them wide across her midriff, where Mr. Bing would not see. "Don't you have some tasks to attend to?" At that moment, she did not need Mr. Bing's paternal interference.

"The lad and his brother hove to in the stable this morning. Hammered that shoe back onto the Icky horse and did a week's worth o' chores to boot. Not the usual sort of toffs, that lot."

Gemma pointedly ignored him. He huffed. "He worked himself to the bone, that lad. I've never seen anyone so determined to make something right. Except for you."

When she didn't respond, he took her hint and stomped off.

No, the Worthingtons were not the usual sort of anything, were they? Dashing Pollux, with such longing in his eyes. Fierce Atalanta, terrified underneath. Beautiful broken Lysander.

Gemma's knees gave a bit and she sank to sit on the top

step, despite the gritty state of the stone. *I shall have to sweep.* But the thought flowed right through her mind without stopping.

She found she was watching the road again.

Did she truly expect him to come riding back, pounding up the road on Icarus, just to be sent away again? For that was precisely what she would do if he did such a mad thing.

Wouldn't she?

Topknot lurched slowly across the yard. Mr. Bing must've released her from her confinement in the stable. Gemma had been certain the dog would want to follow Lysander, but Topknot was a Yorkshire lass, through and through. London was no place for her.

But it's all right for him?

No. She was quite sure it wasn't. Lysander had been in London for several years, yet it was here in the Yorkshire Dales, in the clean and quiet, where he had found his voice at last.

Thus your prescription for your patient is to immerse himself in grime and noise? To breathe air tinged with soot and try to make himself heard above the city's cacophony?

Excellent advice, Dr. Gemma.

He was not her patient anymore, though, was he? He was something else, something different, something that crossed the line between patient and doctor, something that confused and distracted her.

But you're not a doctor. You're a widow with an herb garden and a pony cart, rattling about the dale with delusions of grandeur.

Gemma did not bow before that critical voice this time. She'd been through the fire yesterday and since then, something had turned to steel within her. She'd loved Jennie and she'd lost her. Yet she now understood something important. There had been a chance to save both Jennie and her child and Gemma had taken it.

Furthermore, she would make the same choice again. She was certain now that Jennie would agree that it had been worth a try.

She lifted her eyes to take in the sweep of the dale before her. *I am only what I am—but I am all they have.*

She mattered here. Lysander had helped her see that.

Topknot stood staring down the road, her nose lifted high. What stories did scent tell dogs? Did Topknot know how reluctantly Lysander had climbed into the carriage? Could she detect the way Atalanta had stared at her wayward brother when he had seated himself across from her?

Atalanta desperately wanted her family to stay together, yet she'd seemed astonished that she'd been able to persuade her brother to leave.

But it was I who convinced him. I broke his heart and stole his words away again.

There. She'd admitted it to herself at last. She, who only wanted to heal, had driven a sword into the heart of someone who had never done her harm.

Why had she done such a thing?

I had to send him away. I don't love him.

She was swept with a sudden memory—his hands, his lips in the dark. The tenderness of his touch that had brought tears to her eyes. The feeling of drifting to sleep with her head on his chest, with his strong arms around her. Stronger for the sharing of themselves, not weakened by it.

And the words she'd heard but not answered because sleep stole her away at just the precise moment.

I love you, he'd whispered into her hair, so nearly silent that she knew she wasn't meant to hear.

She'd been filled with wonder, and then darkness had taken her, but she knew what she would have said if she'd had the chance.

I love you too.

That sweet, sleepy moment had been lost to her until now, swept away by tragedy and grief and guilt, obscured by her own self-hatred and the terrible tale he'd told her.

What Lysander had done in battle was unthinkable, wasn't it?

Or was it? Gemma forcibly set aside Edmund's oft-stated opinions and considered the matter for herself.

Lysander was no physician. He had been a man alone on a field of suffering, injured himself, facing a hell she could not grasp.

Edmund had been a good man, a paragon. But paragons could be uncompromising, like a statue chiseled from stone. When Gemma had assisted her husband in the army medical tents, surrounded by the agonized, dying men who could not be helped, hadn't she sometimes wished he would unbend enough to give those poor doomed soldiers some ease?

Who was she to judge Lysander?

It'd been he alone, abandoned on the storming battlefield, holding desperately to someone he cared about, someone shattered and suffering, someone who pleaded for release from unimaginable pain.

Topknot wandered closer, sniffing at Gemma's hem. Gemma did not reach to pet the dog's silky ears, for she knew Topknot would only flinch from her touch.

She was quite certain she would not be able to bear that

right now.

When she felt the soft weight on her knee, she went entirely still. Surprised, she looked down in wonder at Topknot's black-and-white muzzle resting there.

The dog let out a deep sigh, almost a groan. As Gemma carefully let her hands fall to tentatively caress the patchwork fur, she marveled at how perfectly Topknot's mournful noise reflected her own deepest feelings.

We are all different now. I cannot go back to the life I lived before, or to the woman I was before. She could not make time close over Lysander's presence in her heart, like water closing over a dropped stone.

He had come to the dale and he'd changed it. He had changed everyone he touched: cantankerous Mr. Bing, the angry village, suspicious Shepherd Orren, fearful Topknot, even poor, misunderstood Bad Pony.

Gemma healed people. She kept their bodies well, but Lysander did something else. He saw what they needed in their hearts and he gave it to them.

In his silent, tireless way, he had inspired the village, a pony, a dog, a woman, and even an old curmudgeon like Bing to think beyond mere survival. To hope for more.

I am not who I was before. I am not content with safe routine and tentative medical actions.

I want more. I want to be more.

Her breath left her with the impact of her realization.

I want to be a doctor.

She wanted to study and learn as much as she could to help her dale. This certainty swept over her like a flood, yet she had never felt more grounded and stable.

That is who I am meant to be.

She paid no heed to conservative voices from the past

clamoring to make her stop, to question herself, to doubt.

If Lysander Worthington could claw his way out of a collapsed tunnel choked with heavy mud, then surely she could outlast those faded remonstrations and criticisms?

He had survived everything that had happened to him, and he had come to her dale. Had he ever asked for help? Had he seen her as his remedy, clung to her, sapped her dry with his need?

He had not.

Gemma stroked Topknot's feathery ears and gazed down into the dog's sad brown eyes.

So much healing had followed Lysander Worthington into her dale. So much help had sprung from his tireless hands.

He'd given them all gifts, like a somber Father Christmas, taking the burden of hard labor from Mr. Bing, lifting her own desperate loneliness, adding his strength by her side in her moment of need, even shattering the barrier of his choking silence, offering up his own private sins to convince her that the guilt of losing Jennie was not her burden to carry.

Bad Pony neighed from the stable, calling to his lost friend Icarus.

Lysander Worthington, fallen angel, soldier, mercy killer. And rescuer, healer of creatures, helper of men and women alike. Hadn't Theo's death been a type of rescue as well?

She closed her eyes, remembering Lysander's hands on her. Without the use of his words, touch had been his principal form of communication. Remembering the reverential tenderness of his touch made Gemma realize the true depth of his feelings for her.

I love you, Gemma Oakes.

The unbelievable had happened. A knight in shining armor had ridden right up to her on a fine horse.

Her eyes opened wide. *And I sent him packing.*

Well, not for long!

Gemma grabbed Topknot's fluffy head and bent to kiss her right on her wispy topknot. Grinning madly, the future Dr. Gemma Oakes stood up and shook out her skirts.

"Mr. Bing! Harness Bad Pony at once, if you please!"

POLL SAT WITH Attie facing forward in the carriage while Lysander rode opposite them in the back-facing seat. Poll had induced Lysander to ride with them by implying that Icarus's newly healed leg would fare better without a rider on the journey back. Poll wanted Lysander in sight at all times, and Daedalus would thank him later for granting his prized horse an easy trot home tied behind the carriage.

There was much Poll wanted to know and he could feel a similar tension emanating from Attie. She was bursting with questions as well.

How had Gemma Oakes cured his brother? She was certainly impressive and Poll would never forget the way she had brought that tiny baby into the world. Yet Poll found her cool and rather haughty, despite her physical beauty. He liked strong women, but when they had taken their leave this morning, Mrs. Oakes had seemed resolute and grim, almost hard.

Brave, though, to take on a patient like Lysander. Braver still to take his dark, dangerous brother as a lover.

Poll had found himself alternately alarmed and inspired over the past few days. Yorkshire was hardly the rest cure they had all imagined for Lysander.

And the way Gemma Oakes had so politely but firmly suggested that they should pull their borrowed horses and grooms from her stables, board their carriages and be gone—well, Poll had been thrown out of finer homes than Yew Manor, but never with such chilly efficiency.

Yet, there had been something in her eyes when she had instructed him to *listen*. Poll eyed Lysander across the rocking carriage. His brother seemed as indecipherable as ever, yet there was much less edge on the blade, so to speak.

Had Lysander been happy in Yorkshire?

Did Lysander even remember what happiness felt like?

For that matter, did Poll?

A memory came to the fore, one night of carousing with Castor and Lysander and poor old Theo. How the four of them had laughed, too drunk for good sense, not drunk enough to stay out of trouble. Before Miranda, before the war, before any of them had suspected for a moment that the world as they knew it would soon come to an end.

Poll missed those days. He missed the bond he'd shared with his twin and Zander's easy laughter—Zander the jokester, the prankster! God, the mischief he had dragged them all into. Everyone always blamed Cas and Poll, which just made Zander laugh all the harder.

Poll gazed at the dark facsimile of that brother, who sat across from him now.

Yet at that absurd but amusing assembly dance, Lysander had spoken to him almost as of old. His conversation had been brief, but it had also been calm. As if the lovely Mrs. Oakes had somehow soothed the wild animal that had never quite succeeded in hiding behind Lysander's gaze.

Then it struck Poll. "Oh! You're in love with her!"

Beside him, Attie huffed. "Welcome to the conversation."

Poll flinched. "You knew, Attie?"

"I knew. Button and Cabot knew. I'm fairly certain Icarus knew. So obvious. Really Poll, all that stage face paint has dulled your wits." She looked smug. "Besides, I found them naked in the study."

Poll groaned "Attie, you swore you'd stopped spying!"

"Leave Attie alone, Poll. She wasn't spying on anyone. She came to find Gemma for Jennie Gosling."

Now both Poll and Attie stared at Lysander in shock.

"You really are speaking—"

"—in complete sentences!"

Lysander turned his gaze on them both. "Yes. But I don't want to talk about it."

Attie gazed at Lysander and Poll saw her swallow hard. "She mended you," Attie whispered. "Really mended you, the way that Iris and Archie and all of us could not." Her voice sounded small and somehow shamed and betrayed at the same time.

Poll knew how she felt. They had all struggled so hard. Yet this woman had done what they could not, for all their years of trying.

Attie twisted the end of her braid. "You do love that Gemma person, don't you, Lysander?"

Lysander fixed Poll with his gaze and Poll saw a black and bottomless ache there. "Absolutely and entirely," Lysander said calmly.

Attie bit her lip. "But—"

"She did not find me worthy, Attie," Lysander told her. "And she was quite correct not to."

Listen, Gemma had said. When Attie straightened, ready

to deny Lysander's statement, Poll put a hand on her thin arm. "Just listen," he murmured.

They listened, waiting for Lysander to break his six-year silence, to finally speak of what had happened in the war. The interior of the carriage fell quiet, with only the squeaking and rattling of the wheels penetrating the pregnant hush.

Which was how they were all able to hear the wildly galloping hoof beats on the road behind them.

As one, they all leaned toward the nearest carriage window and thrust their heads out to see what was coming up behind them. There appeared to be a rolling storm of dust coming toward them.

What the hell?

Then from the obscuring dust emerged a severely ugly pony pulling a cart. The pony was catching up fast, his short legs blurring with his speed.

Now they could see the apparition holding the reins of the odd pony. A woman in a dull gray dress, practically standing upright in the cart, her hair a brunette banner flying behind her like Boadicea riding to war.

At that moment, Poll looked back at Lysander. The naked longing and hope Poll saw on his brother's features sent a tremor of certainty through Poll. *Oh, that's what love looks like. I see now.*

Lysander never made a sound. He simply stepped through the carriage door and swung athletically down, leaving the conveyance while it still traveled at a good clip. He landed with both booted feet firmly on the ground.

GEMMA PULLED Bad Pony to a halt just behind the second

carriage, which was just fine with Bad Pony, for his dear friend Icarus was snugly tied there. Gemma became abruptly aware of how ridiculous she must look. Goodness, her hair had lost all its pins!

And then Lysander appeared, his dark coat having blended with the black enameled exterior of the luxurious carriage, making him invisible until he stepped forward. Gemma forgot her hair, she forgot her nerves, she only knew the open depths of his dark-eyed gaze.

It had been just a few hours since she'd seen him, yet she was struck anew by the beauty of him. His tall, lean form vibrated with strength and virility. He strode toward her, his black gaze never leaving hers.

Gemma fought for breath and her heart throbbed. *My heavens, that man is beautiful.* She swallowed hard as he neared. Her throat had gone dry and her thoughts gone blank. It hadn't occurred to her to plan what to say to him. She'd only thought to stop him from leaving her.

He leapt up onto the running board of her pony cart and stayed there, eye to eye with her.

Gemma inhaled and licked her lips nervously. "I ..." She trailed off.

"You." To her astonishment he smiled at her, a sweet, slightly naughty grin that transformed his remote features into something entirely breathtaking and new.

Yet, gazing at him so closely, she could see the shadows had not gone. That was understandable, perhaps a good thing in the end. She would not love a man this much if he could take the life of another and then live lightly with himself.

Oh heavens! She should apologize. That's what she should be saying!

"I'm sorry I reacted badly."

His grin faded but the hopeful light in his eyes did not go out. "I thought your reaction to be entirely appropriate, considering." He looked at her for a long moment.

Gemma could quite honestly admit that she was dazzled. Lysander burdened had been beautiful, dark and lost. This Lysander, who had made some peace with his past, who had at last caught his balance, was another thing entirely. Heavens, what a breathtaking fellow. Gemma wondered if she should look away in order to speak to him sensibly.

"I accept your apology," he said slowly, concern crinkling his brow. "As I hope you accept mine for everything I put you through."

Gemma fought to make her words make sense. Was this how he'd felt? "We both said things." Except he hadn't. He'd said only truth to her and she had scorned that offering, giving back only accusations. "Oh drat. I have so much I wish to take back." Which was an inane thing to say. Harsh words could never be taken back. He'd given her his darkest, most tender self and she'd dashed it to the earth at his feet. *I'm so sorry!*

"Do you want to take back everything?" He drew away slightly.

The look on his face! "Oh no! No, not *that*!" Gemma exclaimed, blushing hotly. No, that night she would treasure until the day she died.

"Really?" The smile began to return and it was like the first warm day of spring after a hard winter. Gemma felt like a flower, turning toward his light.

"Oh yes," she said fervently.

Then Lysander looked back toward the carriages. For

the first time, Gemma became aware of their audience. The four of them, Mr. Button, Mr. Cabot, Miss Atalanta and Mr. Pollux Worthington were perched in a row on top of the rear carriage, where large luggage would rest, looking for all the world like audience members on their private balcony seat. Miss Atalanta was munching an apple.

They're waiting for him. Even as she had that thought, Lysander turned back to her. "I have to go."

Go.

Gemma's mind took a disconcertingly long time to grasp the word. Her heart began to ache. He'd given her so much and in return, she'd given him too little and far too late. Of course, it was no more than she deserved.

"I love you, Lysander Worthington." The words tumbled out, ragged and breathless and hurried. It was a terrible way to say them, on a dirt lane, with her hair in a mess, and an audience, for pity sake! "I love your strength. I love your healing heart. I comprehend your loneliness. I understand you."

Lysander's smile turned a little sad. "Yes, I know."

"You do?"

His eyes flashed possessive pride. "Well, you did just chase me halfway across Yorkshire."

"Yes, I did." Instead of feeling embarrassed, she began to smile back at him. "You are just going home for a visit, aren't you?"

He reached out to tuck a strand of her wild hair behind her ear. "*'For thy sweet love remembered such wealth brings*

That I should scorn to change my state with kings.'"

Sonnet 29, her favorite. Gemma touched his hand and their fingertips caught and held.

This man! This man would stand by her side and fight

for her people and be a worthy partner for the rest of her days. What could she offer him in return?

"If you come back, I'll give you a pony."

At that, her dark handsome stranger threw back his head and laughed aloud.

Up on the top of the carriage, Mr. Button sighed aloud, Mr. Cabot looked very satisfied with himself and Miss Atalanta fed her apple core to Icarus, who stretched his long delicate nose up to her hand.

Mr. Pollux Worthington shook his head. "Damn, I want a beautiful woman to give me a pony."

Atalanta shrugged. "I'd rather have a monkey."

Lysander looked back at them, then met Gemma's happy gaze with a rueful smile. "I come with something of an entourage, you know."

"Seven siblings, you said."

"Yes. And five in-laws. And a niece and another child on the way. And two parents. And Philpott. And Button and Cabot."

"Heavens!" Gemma blew out a long breath. She'd always longed to be part of a family. Yes, she'd specifically wished for "large." *Be careful what you wish for.* "Well, then I suppose it's high time Yew Manor was repaired. We'll need the rooms." Apparently, she was about to become yet another Worthington.

She smiled at Lysander, allowing her full feelings to show in her expression. He blinked, and then his smile grew.

Epilogue

AND SPRING COMES AGAIN, AS IT ALWAYS DOES....

G EMMA?"
"I'm in the stillroom!"
Lysander crossed the kitchen to duck his head under the lintel of the stillroom door. He paused there to smile privately at his beautiful wife. Gemma looked quite business-like in her apron and work-gown and was up to her elbows in something green and slimy and somewhat nasty.

She looked up, eyes wide. "Thank heaven you're here. I need help!"

He stepped closer, concerned.

"Please, scratch my nose!"

Chuckling, he rubbed a fingertip across the bridge of her dainty nose until she sighed in satisfaction. "Anything else, my Lady of the Dale?"

She looked up at him pleadingly. "Help me fill these vials?"

Lysander had no issue with helping in the stillroom. Unlike Bing, he harbored no dark suspicions of unholy doings in Gemma's herb lore.

"I'm sending some samples to the examination board at Cambridge," she said nervously. "This is my third batch. I was worried about getting it right."

With the help of some of Dr. Oakes's old comrades, Gemma had managed to persuade Cambridge University to consider her for admittance. Her battlefield experience had impressed them as well. Now Lysander was sure her herbal remedies would further persuade them.

It would take her a long time to complete her training, for Gemma could not bear to abandon the dale completely and had decided to take her courses in stages.

When the last bottles were capped, Gemma and Lysander washed up only to discover that the concoction had left deep green stains on their hands.

Lysander contemplated his inhuman flesh, then formed his fingers into claws and snarled at Gemma. "*Rowr.*"

Her eyes widened and she backed away. "Don't you dare, Lysander Worthington. I'm a grown woman! I will *not* be tickled!"

She made a dash for freedom but Lysander reached a long arm about her waist and swept her off her feet. "Mine! *Rowr!*" He growled into her silken neck as she slapped at his monster claws amid her helpless giggles.

Then his hands slid higher on her ribs to find her breasts and her laughter turned to sighs. Mostly. Gemma had a hard time stopping her giggles once they started.

Lysander had become very good at working around that. Soon the apron lay crumpled on the floor and Gemma's bodice lay crumpled about her waist. Lysander lifted her to sit on her worktable and slid her skirts up to reveal tempting pale thighs above her stockings and garters.

"Wait." Gemma's hands stilled in the middle of interesting explorations of their own. "Where is Mr. Bing?"

"Mr. Bing took Mr. Bad Pony and Miss Topknot into the village to pick up a delivery. My family sent something from London on the mail coach." He lost himself in her hair, breathing in her herbal Gemma scent.

"Oh good." She wrapped her arms about his neck as he lifted her ankles to wrap them around his back. "Oh *yes.*"

He slid his hands around to grasp her soft, womanly bottom and drove his hard cock into her liquid heat. *Every time*, he thought distantly as he lost himself in the sweet tug of her wet body on his. *Every time is like coming home.*

Murmured words of love and wanting dissolved into hot gasps and yearning moans. Lysander controlled his own need, fulfilling Gemma again and again. His touch danced over her clitoris and his tongue sparred with hers in deep scorching kisses. He drank that in her sighs as she came apart for him. Her throbbing heat tightened around him until at last he could resist no more.

With a roar, he thrust deep inside her. His release was, as always, powerful and profound.

Gemma collapsed against his chest, panting and quivering. They leaned on each other until their breath slowed and their galloping hearts calmed.

When Gemma opened her eyes and gave Lysander that cat-in-the-cream smile, he thrilled once more to the knowledge that he could make Gemma happy. It was a better reward than his own orgasm, to see that smile on her soft, kiss-swollen lips.

Suddenly, her smile disappeared and her eyes widened as she looked over his shoulder. "Lysander, who is that woman?"

Lysander followed her gaze out the stillroom window to see Mr. Bing helping a hearty lady with silver hair step down from the pony cart. The woman was visibly flirting with a dismayed Mr. Bing.

He blinked. "Oh. That's Iris."

Gemma gasped. "Your *mother?* Your mother is *here?*"

With a cry of despair, Gemma slapped at his chest, driving him off her so she could slide down off the table. "I'm a mess! And this is my work gown! And I didn't do any baking because I was busy with the fever treatments! Don't just stand there, button me at once!" She grabbed a cloth from the work table to tend to herself as he did up her gown.

Lysander tried not to grin at the razor-sharp tone of command in Gemma's usually even-tempered voice. "Gemma, if there was ever a woman who wouldn't notice your hair or your gown, it's my mother. She might spout poetry to your roses, however, and she'll excuse herself to a wall if she bumps into it, but she'll absolutely adore you." He finished the buttons and fluffed her bodice, just to be extra helpful.

"But she's your *mother!*" Gemma wailed as she ran for the door, desperately trying to twist her tumbled hair into something sensible. For Iris, yet!

Lysander beat Gemma to the door by a long-legged margin and blocked his mother's view of her when he opened the door wide, trying to grant Gemma a few extra seconds of maddened hair rescue.

"Iris!" He stepped forward to kiss his dear dotty mama. Her cheeks were rosy with health and her eyes sparkled brightly. Lysander breathed a sigh of relief to see her thus. That bout of pneumonia had left her thin and limp with exhaustion the last time he'd seen her.

Gemma had wanted to put off their wedding until all the Worthingtons could make the journey, but Iris had sent her a short note that had immediately changed Gemma's mind.

> *Yet do thy worst, old Time! Despite thy wrong*
> *My love shall in my verse ever live young.*
> Shakespeare's Sonnet 19

So Gemma and Lysander had wed in Yorkshire, with Attie and Daedalus as attendants, with the eldest Gosling girl and the youngest Gosling, sturdy little Jasper, with Jennie's eyes and rolls of plump on his little legs, leading the procession from the church, tossing summer petals before the feet of the newly married couple.

The bride wore Lementeur.

They had stepped into their flower-bedecked cart pulled by Bad Pony, who had eaten his rose wreath as casually as a goat. Even Topknot had sported a voluminous bow.

They had waved goodbye to their Yorkshire community and had driven less than a quarter of an hour to Yew Manor, where they had made love on the study carpet, consumed a luncheon of cold meat and cheese, and whitewashed the kitchen. Lysander smiled at the memory. All fall and winter had been devoted to indoor repairs, while the spring had given them many days of fine weather to mend the roof.

Now the house could actually manage a few guests without anyone sleeping on the floor. And a good thing it was too. "I couldn't wait," Iris was telling him. "I left them all behind at the inn early this morning to ride on the mail coach. But I'm sure they'll catch up."

"Iris?" Lysander took his mother's hand in his. "Who will catch up?"

Iris gazed into his eyes and lifted a hand to stroke her fingers along his temple and cheek. "My beautiful boy. How lovely to see you again." The tears shimmering in her eyes told Lysander that she wasn't speaking simply of a few months separation. Then she smiled brightly. "Oh, everyone! They should be here quite soon!"

Oh hellfire.

In his distraction, Iris slipped past him and pulled Gemma into a prolonged maternal hug.

Everyone? Gemma mouthed at Lysander over Iris's shoulder, her gaze wide with panic. Lysander thought for a moment, that held up ten fingers. Gemma's eyes widened further. Then Lysander held up five more. After another thought, he added in the other thumb. Gemma paled and looked a bit faint, but Lysander wasn't worried. His Gemma had been to war and back. She could handle sixteen Worthingtons any day. Or was it seventeen now?

Iris finally released Gemma and stepped back, beaming at her. "Oh, Attie was right! You do look like Aphrodite!"

She patted Gemma sweetly on the cheek. "Are you having a pleasant afternoon, my dear? Next time, you ought to try making love out-of-doors. Archie finds it most invigorating!"

Oh, yes. Iris was just fine.

All Books by Celeste Bradley

Fallen

The Liar's Club
The Pretender
The Impostor
The Spy
The Charmer
The Rogue
Wedding Knight
(a Liar's Club novella)
A Liar Under The Mistletoe
(a Liar's Club holiday novella)

The Royal Four
To Wed A Scandalous Spy
Surrender To A Wicked Spy
One Night With A Spy
Seducing The Spy

The Heiress Brides
Desperately Seeking A Duke
The Duke Next Door
Duke Most Wanted

The Runaway Brides
Devil In My Bed
Rogue In My Arms
Scoundrel In My Dreams

The Wicked Worthingtons
When She Said I Do
And Then Comes Marriage
With This Ring
I Thee Wed
Wedded Bliss

The Courtesans
(with Susan Donovan)
Unbound
Breathless

The Haven Holiday Novels
Sleepless in Staffordshire

ৱৎ৲৩

For more information about Celeste's books,
visit: celestebradley.com

For updates on upcoming books and events
by Celeste Bradley, you can join
The Voice of Society newsletter
and be the first in the know!
celestebradley.com

About the Author

Photo © Charles M. Fitch 2014

CELESTE BRADLEY is the *New York Times* bestselling author of more than 24 Regency historical romances, including the extremely popular *Liar's Club* spy series and the *Wicked Worthingtons.* She has twice been nominated for the RITA Award by the Romance Writers of America. Before becoming a writer in 1999, Celeste was an artist who specialized in pottery and ceramic sculpture. Although originally from the South, Celeste no resides in New Mexico. "It is one of the last habitats of the Free Range Human." She is fond of food that someone else cooks, animals of all sorts, painting, drawing, reading, and grandbabies.

Printed in Great Britain
by Amazon

36568916R00192